BABIES AT COCONUTS

Book 3

BETH CARTER

SOUL MATE PUBLISHING

New York

BABIES AT COCONUTS

Copyright©2019

BETH CARTER

Cover Design by Wren Taylor

This book is a work of fiction. The names, characters, places, and incidents are the products of the author's imagination or are used fictitiously. Any resemblance to actual events, business establishments, locales, or persons, living or dead, is entirely coincidental.

All rights reserved. No part of this publication may be reproduced, stored in a retrieval system, or transmitted in any form or by any means (electronic, mechanical, photocopying, recording, or otherwise) without the prior written permission of both the copyright owner and the publisher. The only exception is brief quotations in printed reviews.

The scanning, uploading, and distribution of this book via the Internet or via any other means without the permission of the publisher is illegal and punishable by law. Please purchase only authorized electronic editions, and do not participate in or encourage electronic piracy of copyrighted materials.

Your support of the author's rights is appreciated.

Published in the United States of America by
Soul Mate Publishing
P.O. Box 24
Macedon, New York, 14502

ISBN: 978-1-68291-919-4

ISBN: 978-1-68291-885-2

www.SoulMatePublishing.com

The publisher does not have any control over and does not assume any responsibility for author or third-party websites or their content.

I'm dedicating this novel to my incredible,

fun-loving, loyal reader group, Beth's Book Babes.

Your undying support, enthusiasm, reviews,

photos, fan letters, and messages inspire and motivate

me to continually bring you more stories.

Writing is a solitary profession and you,

wonderful readers, are my fabulous,

interactive water cooler.

I am forever grateful, adore you,

and treasure your feedback.

This one's for you, Babes!

Acknowledgments

For moms, dads, and everyone who has had babies (fur babies too) touch their lives in some way, whether as a parent, family member, friend, or caregiver. As you know, babies upend our world (much as it does in my novel) but these wonderful, tiny humans enrich our lives, even during those challenging middle-of-the-night feedings. Here's to sleepy parents.

To every couple embarking on a life-long journey of love, I hope you find your happily ever after. Always remember the joys—and pitfalls—and celebrate your uniqueness. And for those who prefer to be single, that's great too. I was for many years.

To girlfriends. Those true, rare friends who are by our side every step of the way. I cherish my long-time friendships as well as my newfound friends, whether in person or online. My three main characters, Suzy, Alex, and Hope, embody the meaning of friendship. No matter how chaotic their personal or professional lives are, they always make time for one another. And that's how it should be.

Much love to my amazing husband who has accepted my writing quirks, especially writing at the kitchen table, sometimes forcing him to shove my computer aside for his breakfast bowl. Thank you for understanding about deadlines, providing wine at stressful times, and eating out when I'm on a tight schedule.

Much love to our newest, beautiful granddaughter, Grace, who inspired the name of another baby in this novel.

Thank you to Jeanne Schwerkoske who came up with the perfect name for Mama Gia, Fernando's feisty mother!

Thank you to my friends and family who read my work, leave reviews, cheer me on, and attend my book signings. Your love and support will never be forgotten. Here's to you, Mom and Dad. I love you.

Thanks to resourceful readers Amanda Brown, Heather Thompson, and Mary Smith for input, names, and design ideas for my fictional Middle Eastern-themed restaurant.

A smile and thank you to every reader who has given an unknown-to-them author a chance by plucking a book off a bookshelf. And a shout out to book clubs too. I've spoken to three and love interacting with readers.

A special thanks to Beta readers Amanda Brown, Carol Holmes, and Shirley Hales for reading my work before it went out into the world, provided invaluable feedback, another set of eyes, and helped find those pesky typos. I greatly appreciate your time and effort.

Thank you to my wonderful editor, Debby Gilbert, who saw the potential in my Coconuts series, which began with a five-line online pitch. I appreciate your encouragement, professionalism, and incredible organizational skills.

Finally, a big thanks to my cover artist, Wren Taylor, who nailed the cover art for BABIES AT COCONUTS with meaningful colors and elements. It's stunning.

If you enjoy women's fiction, romantic comedy, and contemporary romance and want to join my reader group, please contact me through my website, www.bethcarter.com. I'd love to have you join us for cover reveals, contests, sneak peeks, behind-the-scenes discussions, and much more.

Chapter 1

My son's wedding will be perfect. It has to be perfect. I'm his wedding planner. Oh, God. What was I thinking? Rubbing her throbbing temples, Suzy stared out the kitchen window and noticed the first sign of daffodils sprouting against the half-brown, half-green ground. The perky, yellow flowers usually made her smile.

Taking deep yoga breaths to quell her butterflies, Suzy continually gave herself non-stop, much-needed pep talks prior to the rehearsal dinner.

Tonight's dinner will set the tone. Both families will either enjoy one another's company—or everyone will count the hours until the whole blessed thing is over. I love weddings. That's why I plan them but I never expected this much pressure. I want Jon to be thrilled with the results. Her mind swirled with possible worst-case scenarios.

Filling up her favorite "Best Mom" coffee mug for good luck, she drummed her fingers on the kitchen counter. Happily, the boys—they would always be boys to her even though they were young men—had agreed to pick up Fernando's three brothers and mom at the airport.

She'd only spoken to Fernando's mother once by phone and couldn't get a word in. Not. One. Word. She hoped it was due to wedding jitters and not an everyday diarrhea-of-the-mouth occurrence. Overly chatty people got on her last nerve.

Before they arrived, she decided to check her wedding notes yet again. Suzy placed notes in a file for every bride and groom—or in this case, two grooms. Normally, she drew the wedding theme on the outside of the folder for quick reference since she occasionally had more than one wedding going at once.

Shuffling to the breakfast table where she often worked, she spotted the manila sleeve. Starfish, waves, and palm trees were drawn on the exterior. She smiled when she noticed Izzy had added a heart with *Jon + Fernando* scrawled in the middle. *This is a good sign. Even my surly teen stepdaughter is excited about the wedding.* She shook her head in wonder. *My son's getting married. He's going to be a husband. And a dad. A dad! I can hardly believe both events are happening so close together.*

Her mind skittered to Fernando's family. She had tried to encourage them into flying in a day earlier from Italy, fearing they'd have airplane issues and miss the rehearsal dinner. But Gia Russo had texted from New York City hours earlier saying they were on schedule. Still, timing was tight.

Suzy glanced back at her list. Food. Wine. Engraved champagne flutes. Check. Scanning her notes for the hundredth time, she smiled when she noted a star beside Fernando's favorite color—orange. Suzy had asked the florist to tie orange ribbons on the chairs at the wedding for a pop of color. She chuckled. Her son, Jon, couldn't care less about colors but had requested simple white rose petals to cover the aisle during the ceremony.

Sipping coffee, Suzy's mouth watered as she studied Cheri Van Buren's fabulous rehearsal dinner menu. Her New York caterer friend had come through from afar. The grooms had requested Indian food placing Suzy in unfamiliar territory. Cheri had recommended Indian Summer, the best Indian restaurant in Crystal City, and assured Suzy she had spoken directly with Chef Raj.

We're in good shape. The rehearsal dinner will be an

intimate gathering as Jon requested with Fernando's family; Vanessa, Jon's former high school sweetheart before he came out; my best friends Alex and Hope; husband, Ken; and stepdaughter Izzy. This should be easy. No drama before the big day.

Suzy took another quick peek at her watch. Nothing like cutting it close. *Alex must be rubbing off on me; she was born late.* Rubbing her arms from nervousness, her mind wandered. *I hope there aren't any airline issues. Jon is probably beside himself and pacing the length of the airport about now.*

Izzy was still at school and Ken was at work. Unusually anxious, Suzy wondered if she should drink a glass of wine before the dinner. She picked up her cell to call her husband, but his voicemail indicated he was in a meeting for another thirty minutes. *Why is everyone busy until the last minute? I hope this means the ceremony will be flawless.*

Deciding to take a quick shower, Suzy heard her phone vibrate as she turned off the water. Dripping all over the counter, she reached for her phone full of texts. One was from Alex who was running late. No surprise. Hope wondered if her school attire would be dressy enough. Jon mentioned he was nervous, excited, and leaving the airport. Ken said he would meet her at the restaurant.

I don't have time to reply to all of these messages. Suzy quickly responded to Hope that her clothes would be fine and retreated to her walk-in closet. With a plush, gray towel wrapped around her wet body, she studied her wardrobe.

Originally, she had planned to wear a sundress, but immediately changed her mind and donned a more formal dress. Glancing in the mirror, Suzy frowned. *This doesn't look tropical. They want a luau for a wedding. My clothes should fit the theme.*

Shedding her lacy dress and flinging it on the bed,

Suzy studied her closet. Wearing only a bra and panties, the doorbell rang. She froze when she heard the door creak open.

"Mom, we're here," Jon said. "Er, everyone's here. We're coming in, ready or not."

Chapter 2

Suzy heard several sets of footsteps and chatter, some in English, some in Italian. *Oh, God. I assumed they'd go straight to the hotel.* Suzy threw the dress back over her head and traipsed into the living room.

A short, busty brunette rushed toward Suzy, arms spread wide. "*Ciao.*" The woman giggled. "Do they wear zippers in the front in the States?"

Suzy stared down at her clothes. "Um, no. Whoops." She embraced the Italian woman who kissed both her cheeks. "You must be Fernando's mother. Be right back after taking care of my wardrobe malfunction." Shouting over her shoulder, she said, "Welcome," and retreated to her closet with Jon on her heels.

Staring over his shoulder, Jon locked the bedroom door. "Go ahead and change, Mom, I won't look. I need to talk to you."

Suzy gave him a sideways glance. "What's wrong, hon?"

"Fernando's mother is bossy. She already wants to control everything. She wants to change every detail."

"She's probably just enthusiastic. Besides, everything is in place, son. Fernando's mother can't possibly make changes the day before the wedding."

Switching to a navy jumpsuit covered in giant red hibiscus flowers, she donned gold strappy heels and grabbed a tiny red clutch. Hugging her son, Suzy said, "Don't worry. Everything will be perfect. Now, will you hook the top of my jumpsuit?"

"I hope you're right. You look great, Mom." Jon sighed as he fastened the hook. "You'll see what I mean."

Checking her outfit in the mirror, Suzy hooked her arm through Jon's. "It'll be fine. I promise. Let's go meet Fernando's family."

Raising his eyebrows, he said, "Brace yourself."

Chapter 3

Suzy took a cleansing breath as she closed her bedroom door. Winking at her son, she said, "It's show time."

As they entered the living room, Fernando played "O Sole Mio" on the piano. His mother sang badly and at the top of her lungs. She totally ignored Suzy and Jon who stood in the center of the room until the entire song was over. Three stanzas later, she clapped, then hugged Fernando. "Beautiful, my son. *Bellissimo*."

She splayed her arms and bounded toward Suzy once again. Giving her an appreciative once-over, she said, "Gorgeous outfit." She kissed her cheeks again. "I'm Gia. Everyone calls me Mama Gia."

Mama Gia squeezed a pale Jon and kissed his cheek. "I see where you get your good looks."

In an attempt to steer the conversation, Suzy said, "Welcome to our home, and to the States. Our boys are getting married. Isn't this wonderful?"

Mama Gia nodded but huge tears filled her eyes, spilling onto her cheeks. "My baby is getting married. My ba-by." Suzy noticed she hugged Fernando so hard she nearly strangled him.

Fernando gave a choking sound as he caught his breath. "Mama, it's okay. Calm down. I'm still your baby."

Luigi, who rivaled Mighty Mouse's upside down triangular physique, crossed his muscular arms. "Actually, I'm the youngest."

Mama Gia smacked him. "You're all my babies. I wish you still lived with me."

Three of the brothers chorused, "We do."

Jon snuck a worried glance toward his mother.

Suzy stood stock still. Jon was her only son but even at that she knew he needed wings. He needed to leave the nest. Obviously, Fernando's mother didn't feel the same. Her mind swirled with images of Vanessa, Jon's former high school girlfriend, as she wondered whether Fernando had told his mother the bombshell news. Her heart raced at the thought of Mama Gia's reaction when she learned Vanessa became pregnant with his child after a reckless and drunk prom night. *This could be disastrous.*

Deciding to change the subject, Suzy extended her hand to the three brothers. "As you've figured out, I'm Suzy Jacobs, Jon's mom. Welcome to Crystal City and to our home." Clearing her throat, she added, "My husband, Ken, and stepdaughter, Izzy, will meet us at the restaurant."

"Where are my manners?" Mama Gia said. "Meet my wonderful boys."

One by one, Luigi, Vinny, and Franco, who insisted on being called Frankie, introduced themselves while simultaneously kissing her on both cheeks. Suzy chuckled to herself imagining her best friend, Alex, who would be searching for a wet paper towel to wipe off all of the germs.

Mama Gia wrapped her arms around Suzy's neck. "I'm positive we'll be one, big happy family." She sighed much too loudly. "But I wish the boys could have gotten married in Italy." Her arms waved in the air. "The history. The architecture. The food. It's all so beautiful for a wedding." She shook her head in obvious dismay. "Rome or Florence would have been *perfetto*. Or imagine the backdrop of Venice and a gondola ride for the two grooms. So roman—"

Suzy bristled. "Since I'm the wedding planner and this is my gift to the grooms, it would have been too difficult to plan from afar. Their ceremony will be beautiful, I promise."

Shrugging, Mama Gia said, "If you say so but I could have organized everything in Italy. How hard can it be? You need a priest, a venue, food, and music. What else?" She threw both hands in the air to emphasize her point.

Stiffening, Suzy stole a glance toward Jon who mouthed, "Told you."

Unable to resist, Suzy said, ticking off her fingers, "There's also decorations, invitations, and guests' mementos, to name a few. Jon has always dreamed of a beach wedding, and I think you'll like what I've created at Coconuts."

"What's Coconuts?" Mama Gia asked.

"A restaurant bar my girlfriends and I frequent. It's our weekly oasis."

Mama Gia's mouth fell open. "The wedding is going to be held in a *bar*?"

Jon stepped forward and stood beside his mother. "It's actually in a parking lot beside the bar."

Suzy noticed her son's mouth twitched as he tamped down an obvious urge to grin and needle Fernando's mom. Talking fast before his future mother-in-law could say anything else, he added, "Mom has worked extremely hard on this. It's her gift to us, like she said. She's recreating a beach in landlocked Crystal City. She always pulls off gorgeous weddings. I have full confidence in her." He kissed his mother's cheek and glanced toward his future mother-in-law. "You'll see."

At that moment, Suzy had never loved her son more. She braced herself for Mama Gia's reaction as all eyes turned toward Fernando's mother.

"Whatever you say." The tiny, dark-haired woman shrugged. "Do you have any wine around here?"

"Of course. Great idea." Suzy stepped into the kitchen and placed two bottles of red wine on the counter.

Jon followed her and Fernando set wineglasses on a silver tray. The three worked in unison—and silence.

It was obvious to Suzy that the guys were, in their small way, trying to keep the peace. She placed her arms across the shoulders of the grooms-to-be. "Don't worry, guys. Nothing will go wrong. I've planned weddings a hundred times."

Chapter 4

After compiling an extensive top-twenty priority list for Hannah to accomplish before Show-Me Bank's huge anniversary celebration, Alex hit send and stretched, satisfied the exhaustive assignments would keep her annoying intern out of her hair for a couple of weeks.

Hearing the whir of the printer, the bank vice president smiled. She couldn't wait to hand Hannah a hard copy of her detailed notes. Climbing the stairs to refill her coffee in the employee lounge, Alex returned and waited for her vacationing intern to appear. She didn't have to wait long.

Focused on the lobby as loan assistants, new account employees, and loan officers settled in for the day, often with coffee in hand or talking about their weekend plans, Alex's eyes widened when she spotted her intern cross the room.

Jet-black hair swinging, her assistant waved hello to a string of employees who, Alex noticed, were mostly bug-eyed, with heads turned as Hannah Hooban, her bitchy, know-it-all intern, also known as the daughter of the bank president, Jim Hooban, stepped toward her.

Oblivious to the string of rubberneckers, Hannah strode with renewed confidence toward marketing. Toward Alex.

Biting her tongue to keep her expression blank, Alex's mind raced as she forced herself to stare anywhere but at Hannah's chest. Obviously, Hannah's four-day "vacation" last week wasn't for a quick trip to Gulf Shores, Alabama. Instead, she had clearly gone straight under a plastic surgeon's knife. A giggle threatened to escape. *Oh, God. I can hear Tony now. I don't know how I'll get my blunt cop boyfriend to keep his thoughts to himself.*

As a chuckle bubbled to the surface, Alex pretended to cough and said, "Morning, Hannah. Be right back." Alex rushed to the printer and returned with a newly printed to-do list. Doing her best to concentrate on the bank anniversary and not on Hannah's new look was futile. *Should I broach the subject of her obvious plastic surgery—or pretend everything is the same? I feel like a boy in middle school who is just discovering his hormones. Hell, maybe she wants me to ask about her ginormous boob job.*

Unable to keep from staring, Alex wondered how she could train herself to keep her eyes off Hannah's breasts, which were two, or possibly three, sizes bigger. The young woman looked as though she might topple over.

Obviously proud of her new body, Hannah accentuated her figure by wearing a tight, low-cut, V-neck black tank underneath a red blazer. As if that weren't enough, she had added a bulky, oversized silver arrow necklace which pointed toward her cleavage. *What the hell was she thinking with that necklace? Hey, everyone, look at my new Dolly Parton boobs?*

Hannah sat opposite Alex's desk, plucked an iPad out of her bag, and struggled to position the computer above her bosom and then below it.

Hell, she could set a coffee cup on those. Alex endeavored to keep a straight face as her mind skittered to Hannah's father, the conservative bank president. *I wonder what he thinks* then immediately erased that weird thought.

Acting as if nothing had changed, Hannah said, "Hi, Boss. How's it going?"

"Um, fine. How was your vacation?"

"It was fabulous." Hannah extended her arm to the side. "Look at my tan. I spent most of the weekend on the beach with a cocktail in my hand. I even played a game of beach volleyball. I put my new, red bikini to good use. Want to see my tan lines?"

"Nope." Alex sipped her coffee and locked eyes with her intern. Several seconds passed. "That's all you did on vacation? Went to the beach?"

"Yup. The beach. R & R, you know." Hannah crossed her legs. "What's on the schedule today?"

So that's how we're handling this—as if it never happened. Alrighty then.

Alex produced the freshly printed project list for the bank's upcoming anniversary celebration. Holding it in mid-air, Hannah gawked, keeping her hands in her lap.

Waving the paper, Alex said, "This is your copy. Take it."

"Seriously? We're in the Twenty-First Century now. Can't you email it to me?"

Biting her tongue, Alex persevered. "I know exactly what century it is. This way we can discuss the list together, make notes in the margin, and figure out the timeline."

Hannah cocked her head defiantly. "We can also do that via computers or iPads. Ever heard of track changes? We can make comments and—"

"I'm the boss." Alex scooted the paper across her desk and glared at her intern. "Take it."

Hannah reached for the list and painstakingly and purposefully took forever to find a pen in her purse. Sighing dramatically, she flicked the hard copy in the air with disdain.

Alex glanced at her watch. "I have a rep from *The Crystal City Business Journal* coming in fifteen minutes to discuss some ads. Start reading while I get another cup of coffee."

"Will you get me one too?" Hannah fluttered her eyelashes. "One sugar and one creamer."

As Alex bounded the stairs she muttered to herself, "Those boobs are probably too heavy to take the stairs now. Sure, I'll get your damn coffee."

The bank president appeared at the top of the stairwell. "Morning, Alex."

Alex faced her boss, Hannah's dad, and bit her tongue yet again. She avoided his gaze. "I'm obviously not yet awake, thus the coffee run."

Jim nodded as he passed her in the stairway. "Doesn't Hannah have a nice tan from her beach trip?"

"I hadn't really noticed." She climbed the top stair and shouted over her shoulder, "See you later, Jim. Big day. We're beginning work on Show-Me Bank's anniversary celebration."

"Glad to hear it. I'll look forward to an update soon." Jim retreated down the last step and disappeared.

Alex wondered if he really was that clueless or if he was embarrassed and attempting to deflect the conversation.

She spoke to a few latecomers who punched the clock as she poured two cups of coffee, returned to her office, and grimaced as she plunked one cup in front of Hannah. "Any questions about the priority list?"

Hannah stared at the black coffee. "I asked for sugar and creamer."

"I'm not your gopher. Drink it black or get your own." Alex frowned as she sank into her plush chair. "Let's start over. Do you have any questions about the anniversary plans? We have a lot to do between now and then."

Alex highlighted marketing aspects that needed to be prioritized. "We can't make any mistakes on the invitation list, press releases, giveaways, food, print ads, direct mail pieces, television and radio commercials, traffic flow for the actual event, and—"

Sighing dramatically, Hannah tapped her iPad. "I've got it, Alex. I'm getting my master's degree, remember?"

"How could I forget? You remind me almost daily."

Hannah folded her arms. "Well, it's quite a feat. I'm very proud of myself." She paused. "You don't have a master's, do you?"

Bristling, Alex said, "No, and I haven't needed one. I'm vice president of marketing, remember? My bachelor's degree and vast work experience have served me well."

Crossing her arms, Hannah smirked. "I guess it does help being older."

Ignoring the jab, Alex asked, "Where's the paper I gave you? Why are you working from an iPad?"

"I used your computer to scan it to my device while you were getting coffee." She shrugged. "Easy peasy."

"Where's the document?"

"I shredded it. No need to duplicate everything. We can save some trees." Hannah pointed toward her head with her finger. "Brains. Beauty and brains are an unbeatable combination." Glancing at her online notes, she gasped. "Oh, crap. I accidentally hit *delete*."

"Seriously? Don't they teach you how to save documents in those master's courses?" Alex fished a yellow legal pad from her drawer and thrust it toward Hannah. "Old school but it works perfectly, plus I still have my list if you want another copy. I'm feeling magnanimous today."

Hannah waved it away as though it were a wasp. "I hit 'undo.' I see the document now. Everything's fine." Leaning forward, she said, "One thing they teach us in management courses is to remain calm during stressful corporate situations."

"Whatever. I'm calm. I'm always calm."

Snickering, Hannah said, "You're never calm. You always run late and you—"

"Seriously? Are you scolding me? I'm your boss. Just because you're Daddy's—" Alex stopped herself and shuffled a stack of papers. *The Crystal City Business Journal* rep appeared in the doorway.

Alex stood. "Come in. Hannah, that's all for now. Why don't you work in the employee lounge while we meet?"

Chapter 5

Hope plopped in her squeaky desk chair, checked the time, and stared at her appointment calendar. *Good. I don't have many appointments today.*

Stepping over to the window to watch latecomers race into the school, Hope chuckled. *Alex would be one of the stragglers.* She smiled as her favorite student, Britney, bounded inside. "I need to talk to you, Miss Truman. Is this a good time?"

"It's the perfect time," Hope said.

A smile spread across Britney's freckled face. "I bet you say that to all of your students."

Hope shook her head. "I wish I could say that about all of my students." Putting a finger to her lips, she said, "Shhh. Don't tell. I'm not supposed to have favorites."

Britney plopped into a chair opposite Hope's sparse metal desk. The student's eyes darkened. "I'm not sure I want to go to college, Miss Truman. I don't think I'm smart enough."

"Don't ever think that. You're very smart. Your ACT scores are well above average."

"But my grades aren't great. I miss school because of—"

"I know. Because of your mom. She's out all hours of the night, you don't get fed properly, and you depend on yourself for everything. I get it. I've been there." Hope gazed out the window remembering her former life with her hippie parents, Larry and Montana. Clasping her hands together, she put on her invisible high school counselor hat and locked eyes with Britney. "A college degree is very important. You'll get a better job and make more money."

Britney's brows knitted. "Four years is *forever*, Miss Truman." Staring at her worn tennis shoes, the student said, "I have to tell you something. I never sent in those applications last year." Tears filled her eyes. "I'm really sorry. I just couldn't bring myself to commit to four years."

Reminding herself that teens think a year is a lifetime, Hope quickly offered another alternative. "There are many types of colleges. A community college is a good place to start if you're more comfortable with that timeline. You can get a two-year associate's degree, and after you graduate, either get a job or transfer to a four-year college."

Britney perked up. "I like that idea. I can handle two years. Four sounds dreadful."

"Then let's start there." Hope reached into her drawer and retrieved a bulging file marked 'Community Colleges.' "Are you thinking about a local community college or one in another state?"

"I want to be close to you," Britney said.

"Hon, that's sweet but don't keep from spreading your wings because of me. There's a big, exciting world out there. Your whole life is ahead of you."

Britney's chin quivered. "I want you in my life. You're my favorite person in the world. You're also my role model."

Hope's heart swelled. She had never married, let alone had children. Counseling students was the closest she had ever come to being a parent. Beaming, Hope said, "Thanks, Brit. You're a wonderful student and a lovely young woman. You mean the world to me. Don't ever forget you have a lot to offer this world." Hope sniffed as she thumbed through the bulky file. "Here are some brochures for two local community colleges.

Britney nodded. "Sounds good. Thanks, Miss Truman."

Handing her applications, Hope noted the deadlines, required essay questions, and suggested Britney make a photocopy to practice first. "These won't be much different from the applications you filled out last year and didn't send in."

"Sorry." Britney stood and reached for the paperwork. "You're the best, Miss Truman. I'm gonna make you proud."

"You do every day." Hope grinned. "Now get to class."

Chapter 6

Holding a glass of red wine in the air, Mama Gia, said, "We need a toast. Do you want to go first or should I?"

Smiling, Suzy said, "Guests first."

After a tearful, half-American, half-Italian soliloquy with plenty of "My baby, my bambino remarks," Mama Gia wiped her cheeks with the backs of her hands.

Fernando's three brothers peppered their mother's speech with "Here, Here," "Way to go," or "Cheers," and added a few silly, brotherly jabs of their own.

After a few minutes of torture, Jon gave Suzy the side eye.

In an attempt to put her son out of pain, she said, "Everyone, have a seat." Suzy carried her wine toward the living room.

"Where should I sit?" Mama Gia glanced at the living area. "I wouldn't dare sit on your couch with red wine. The plastic covers are off. I always keep the plastic on." She puffed out her chest. "My thirty-year-old sofa looks like new."

"Yeah, Mama, but the plastic's cold in the winter and hot in the summer," Luigi said.

"And it's noisy," Vinny said. "Ever try to make out with someone on that crinkly thing?"

Frankie cackled and punched his brother. "Only every Saturday night."

Mama Gia shook her head and smacked the three brothers on top of their heads. "Such disrespect. What would your father say?" She crossed herself. "God rest his soul."

Not knowing quite how to respond, Suzy raised her glass. "How about another toast. "Here's to Jon, Fernando, and the entire Russo family. May we have beautiful weather and a perfect wedding tomorrow." She took a quick swallow and observed Mama Gia over the rim of her glass.

Fernando's mother seemed to have calmed down—for now. Suzy checked her watch. "Drink up. It's almost time to go, everyone." Gulping the rest of her wine and craving more, she resisted putting the bottle to her mouth.

Everyone set their glasses in the sink, went to the restroom, and eventually stepped outside.

Fernando's mother and brothers crammed into his SUV while Suzy drove with Jon.

They were barely out of the drive when Jon said, "See what I mean? She's a *lot*."

Suzy lowered the visor as she weighed her words. "It'll be fine. Mama Gia loves Fernando and all her boys. Italians are expressive, that's all."

"We're part-Italian. We're not like that." Jon groaned as he glanced out the window. "She has a funny way of showing her love with all of that head smacking. I have a headache just from watching her thump their heads."

Suzy giggled. "I'm sure it's partly nerves. After you're a parent, you'll understand."

"Oh, God. That's going to come soon." Jon threw his head against the headrest. "I'm not sure how much stress I can take this close together. I mean a wedding is enough stress. But a baby soon after? Both are life changing. Now I'm really nervous."

"Jon, you'll be fine." Placing her hand on his knee, Suzy said, "You and Fernando will be great dads. Vanessa looks up to both of you. I can't tell you how thrilled I am that you two have embraced this surprise—okay, shocker." Eyes filling with tears, she turned toward Jon at a stoplight. "Being one cohesive family and co-parenting, however you three work that out, will be so important in that precious child's life. Just think, the baby will have a mom, and two da—"

"Mom, can we discuss one thing at a time? Let's get through the rehearsal dinner and wedding first." Jon rubbed his belly. "My stomach's churning. I'm not sure I'll be able to eat now."

"You're right, hon. We should focus on tonight's dinner and the wedding tomorrow."

As Suzy drove to the Indian restaurant, her heart pounded. *I don't want to be nervous. I want to soak up this experience. I probably should have hired a wedding planner for the guys so I could enjoy my son's wedding but it's too late now.*

~ ~ ~

"Here we are." Suzy felt immediate relief after spotting her husband's car. Grinning, she said, "Don't worry, Ken will diffuse this situation with Mama Gia."

Jon snorted. "Yeah, maybe even sulky Izzy will be a welcome distraction for once." He unbuckled his seatbelt. "Actually, she's a good kid. Teenagers are difficult. Except me. I'm sure I was a model child."

Suzy turned off the ignition. "You were the best child anyone could ever ask for."

Before Jon could quip and agree, Fernando, Mama Gia, Frankie, Vinny, and Luigi waved frantically from the sidewalk as if it were their first time seeing them.

Suzy managed a smile as she ushered everyone into the restaurant. The spicy aroma of Indian food wafted toward them.

Once inside, Mama Gia wrinkled her nose. "What are we eating? Wet feet?"

Suzy opened her mouth to say something sarcastic, rare for her, but settled on, "Jon and Fernando love curry."

Spinning around to face Fernando, Mama Gia got almost nose to nose with her son. "Since when do you prefer Indian food? You love pasta. You're *Italian*."

Not waiting for an answer, Mama Gia waved both hands in the air. "Where are the meatballs? The fettucine? The ravioli? How about some fish?" Shaking her head, she said, "Suzy, I don't know why you hired a caterer. Fernando's brother, Luigi, is a chef. In fact, he's the best chef in all of Italy."

Luigi placed his hands on his mother's shoulders, likely noticing the hurt look on Jon and Fernando's faces. "Enough, Ma. Cooking out of your kitchen doesn't exactly make me a chef. Besides, we just flew in. There isn't time to prepare food."

Clucking her tongue, Mama Gia persisted. "You're a wonderful chef. I'm sure you wanted to cook for your brother. *I'm* a wonderful cook too, for that matter."

Glancing around the ornately decorated restaurant with a huge mahogany elephant near the entrance, a wooden-etched outline of the historic Taj Mahal along one wall, Mama Gia fixated on the overstuffed purple, orange, and teal pillows strategically placed throughout the restaurant. "Do we have to sit on those? I'll never be able to get up."

Prickling, Suzy counted to ten before answering. "We'll sit on chairs at tables."

Mama Gia turned toward Fernando. "I thought you said your wedding was island themed."

A grin spread across Fernando's face. "Consider this the Island of Curry. Just try it, Mama, you might actually enjoy a change from pasta." He slung his arm across Jon's shoulders as he eyed his mother.

"The Island of Curry?" Mama Gia huffed. "I never." She narrowed her eyes. "What are you serving at the wedding? Hotdogs and hamburgers?"

Normally the most patient person on earth, Suzy felt her blood boil and knew her cheeks were likely bright red.

Obviously anticipating an intervention, Ken stepped across the room and embraced Suzy in a much-needed kiss and hug. He whispered in her ear, "Don't let her get to you."

Standing beside her dad, Izzy glanced up from her cell long enough to give Suzy a quick nod and managed a half-smile for the guests.

The busty, dark-haired Italian bounded toward Ken, arms wide apart, yelling a boisterous, "Kennn." Nearly knocking him over in the process, she kissed both his cheeks. "I'm Gia Russo, Fernando's mother. Everyone calls me Mama Gia. You must be Jon's dad."

"Nice to meet you, Mama Gia." Ken extended his hand. "Actually, I'm Jon's stepfather. You raised a delightful son in Fernando. We love him."

Mama Gia actually batted her eyelashes. "Thank you. Fernando's dad and I, God rest his soul, did our best raising these boys." After staring above and making the cross sign across her chest, she lightened her tone. "Jon is a sweetheart too".

Suzy immediately realized this was a battle of the moms. She could either fight, flight, or be the peacemaker. She was *always* the peacemaker. Alex, on the other hand, would cut this woman to shreds within seconds. Rubbing her throbbing temples, she scolded herself. *Stay calm. This is the most important day of your son's life.*

Chapter 7

Sunlight streamed inside the ornate restaurant as the massive front door opened. Hope rushed to Suzy's side. Beaming, she said, "Look at the stylish mother of the bride. Can you believe the ceremony's finally here?" She whistled as she admired Suzy's attire. "I could never pull off a jumpsuit. I'm too stumpy."

Suzy hugged Hope. "Stop it."

"Where's Alex?" Hope asked.

"She's going to be late. She texted earlier."

"Big surprise." Both women doubled over laughing. "At least she's consistent."

"That she is." Suzy introduced Hope to Mama Gia and her sons. After greetings, she added, "Vanessa should be here any minute."

"Vanessa? Who's Vanessa?" Mama Gia asked.

Opening her mouth to speak, Suzy again wondered if Jon and Fernando had told Mama Gia about Jon's former—and very pregnant—girlfriend, and since she didn't recognize the name, it didn't appear likely. She paused. "Uh, I don't think I have time to explain that before dinner. Maybe I—we can fill you in while we eat or . . . afterward might be better."

Mama Gia's eyebrows shot up. "You have to explain a girl? Sounds mysterious."

Suzy shook her head. "Not mysterious. It's all good. *Very* good in fact."

Mama Gia shrugged. "I guess I'll have to wait." She hugged Suzy again. "We love Jon, by the way. He's so . . .

American." She laughed. "He and Fernando are good for each other, don't you think?"

"They're great together. We love Fernando too. He calms Jon who can be uptight at times. Fernando is so easygoing." Chuckling, Suzy said, "Our household needed a calming influence."

Ken turned as three dark-haired, energetic men appeared from the bar area.

"Meet my boys." Mama Gia pointed to each one in succession. "Luigi is my oldest, then Vinny, and Franco is my baby. Fernando was born between Vinny and Frankie."

"Got it. I think." Ken extended his hand to each of Fernando's brothers. "Welcome to America."

~ ~ ~

Rock music blared as Alex parked in the Indian Summer lot. Her convertible top down, she ran her fingers through her long, blond hair, reapplied red lipstick, and hopped out of her car.

Likely overhearing the music, Hope rushed outside to greet her friend.

"Hey. Sorry I'm late." Alex straightened her dress.

"You're always late. We're used to it." Hope embraced her gorgeous friend. "You look stunning. Why am I always the hick?"

Alex's brows knitted. "Don't ever say that. You're beautiful. Besides, I'm hoping I can steal the show for a while before Miss New York comes back to town." She tugged on Hope's sleeve. "Cute top, girlfriend."

Hope smoothed her new, peach blouse. "Thanks. Where's Tony? Is the cop coming tonight?"

Alex giggled. "He has the wedding flu."

"Wedding flu?" Hope's eyes twinkled as the obvious excuse dawned on her. "But this is the rehearsal dinner. The wedding isn't until tomorrow."

"It's a bad case." Alex's lips curved into a smile as she spotted Suzy talking to Fernando's mother through the window. "Mother of the groom, I take it. I can't wait to meet her."

"Get ready. She's a handful," Hope said.

"Oh, really?" Alex cocked a brow. "You know how I love a challenge." Slinging her yellow Kate Spade bag over her shoulder, she stepped across the gravel in high heels as if she were walking across a smooth hardwood floor.

"How do you do that?" Hope asked.

"What?"

"Make everything appear effortless, perfect, and stylish."

"Shh. I've been dying to eat here. Indian Summer has gotten rave reviews."

Hope chuckled. "Tell that to Mama Gia."

"Who?"

"You'll see."

Alex's phone rang. She groaned. "It's Hannah. I've got to take this." After she instructed Hannah about a contract with Ozarks5 and gave her an idea for several television script drafts, she hung up. "Let's go in. I'm turning my phone off."

Chapter 8

Waiting good-naturedly while Ken talked to Fernando's brothers, Suzy winked at Jon in an effort to calm his nerves. Chewing on her bottom lip, she hoped the venue wasn't a mistake but the boys wanted Indian food, and it was their wedding after all.

Two weeks before, her socialite friend, Cheri Van Buren, had called Suzy completely distraught about multiple conflicts for celebrity events in Manhattan but promised to arrange a capable chef to handle the rehearsal dinner and wedding. Suzy trusted her newest friend. After all, she ran Fifth Avenue Catering in New York City. This would literally and figuratively be cake compared to a high-end celebrity event.

Ken kissed her forehead. "Someone's in deep thought. Stop worrying. Everything will be fine. I'm sure the food will be amazing."

The front door burst open. Several shielded their eyes from the bright sunshine as Hope strode inside with Alex on her heels. "Sorry I'm late."

Chuckling, Suzy said, "You're here just in time. Trust me."

Alex, apparently detecting her friend's uneasiness, sidled up to Suzy, and kissed her cheek. "Happy almost-wedding day."

Hope flanked Suzy's other side.

Alex whispered, "Everything going okay?" She glanced around. "Where's Cheri?"

Suzy blew out her breath. "Unfortunately, she had a conflict in New York."

Alex winced. "Too bad. I know you were counting on her delectable food."

"Cheri should be a magician with her disappearing acts. We aren't used to having friends who live in two different states. Will she be here for the wedding?" Hope asked.

"Not unless her celebrity event falls through." Suzy motioned toward the kitchen with her head. "She recommended this chef, so I assume he's good." Glancing toward Fernando's mother, she narrowed her eyes. "And I'm sure I'll hear about it if he isn't."

Alex followed Suzy's stare and nodded. "Gotcha." She lowered her voice. "Demanding?"

Suzy laughed far too loudly. "You could say that."

Rubbing her hands together, Alex winked. "No problem."

Hope stifled a giggle. "Down, Alex."

"That's no fun." Alex studied the room setup. "Let's get this party started."

As if on cue, Chef Raj, a tall, handsome Middle Eastern Indian appeared with a gleaming tray of glassware. With a flourish, he said, "Welcome to Indian Summer. I'm Chef Raj. Who's the happy couple?"

Suzy pointed toward Jon and Fernando. "They are. Meet Jon and Fernando."

The chef studied the two men and didn't miss a beat. "Congratulations. I hope you'll find my food to your liking." Balancing the tray, he said, "I was instructed to serve wine. Would you prefer red or white?"

In unison, they both said, "Red."

The chef handed them each a glass of cabernet and waited until they smelled the bouquet, swirled the wine in a wineglass, and tasted the alcohol. Nodding, Fernando said, "Delicious."

"Very good." Chef Raj proceeded to ask the other guests if they preferred red or white wine.

Fernando's mother stood frozen as Suzy accepted a wineglass. "What? No limoncello? We always have limoncello at weddings."

Suzy's face fell. "Sorry, I didn't know."

Mama Gia pursed her lips. "This will do." Clearing her throat, she reached for a glass. "I want to make a toast."

"Here, here," Luigi said.

Suzy heard a small groan escape Jon's mouth.

Oblivious, Mama Gia held her glass in mid-air. "Here's to my baby. My sweet, sweet baby." She sniffed. "I can't believe you're getting married and leaving me but—"

"Mom, I'm right here." Fernando's voice rose. "Look at me. I'm a grown man. Please stop calling me 'baby'."

Jon's lips curved into a slight smile. "Remember, you're gaining a son."

Wiping her nose, Mama Gia said, "That I am." She placed her hand on Jon's shoulder. "To my new son."

Luigi held his wineglass in the air. "And to another brother joining our *famiglia*."

"Here, here," the Russos shouted.

Chapter 9

Glancing around the ornate restaurant, Suzy said, "You guys chose a beautiful place." White tablecloths and fan-shaped orange linen napkins adorned two long tables. Turkish glass mosaic orbs and lanterns in shades of amber, ebony, and gold cascaded from the ceiling transporting flickers of warm, welcoming light throughout the room. Sitar music played softly in the background. Soaking up the experience, Suzy felt as though she were being transported to India, if only for the evening.

Finally relaxing, Suzy admired the showy Bird of Paradise centerpieces. Not surprisingly, Marc, from Artistic Blooms, had found flowers that matched the napkins perfectly, not to mention the island flair the spiky orange blossoms and bird-like beak added. Amazingly, the tropical flowers are native to India, meshing with the wedding theme. Marc also promised the arrangements would remain fresh for the wedding—a bonus since Suzy planned to repurpose them on several tables.

Taking Ken's hand, Suzy tapped a glass with a spoon to get everyone's attention. "Take a seat, everyone. Let's get started. Tomorrow is a big day." She grasped her husband's arm. "You've already met my wonderful husband, Ken." Motioning toward her two best friends, she said, "This is Alex and Hope, my two best friends since high school."

Suzy nodded with her head. "And we can't forget my stepdaughter, Izzy." Izzy glanced up from her phone, gave a shy wave, but didn't say a word. Spreading her arms, Suzy said, "Sit wherever you'd like. We thought we'd keep it spontaneous tonight."

Mama Gia dashed toward Fernando who was seated beside Jon. Fernando's three brothers hurried to sit across from them while Suzy, Ken, Izzy, Alex, and Hope took seats at a second table.

Frowning, Mama Gia stood. "This won't work. We need to be together. We're one happy family now, or almost, right?" Placing her hands on Luigi's shoulders, she said, "Boys, make one long table." She glanced at Suzy. "Better, yes?"

Frankie and Vinny jumped up, grabbed a table at each end, and set it down with a thud. One of the gorgeous Bird of Paradise centerpieces crashed to the floor, breaking into pieces.

"Whoa. Slow down, guys. This isn't a race." Ken sighed. "I'll find a broom."

Deciding it would be too difficult to have a conversation from one end of the table to the next, the twins found a third, smaller table and formed a T-shape. After the tables were rearranged, Fernando's mother positioned herself at the head.

Clearly annoyed, Suzy cleared her throat. "The head table is always for the wedding couple."

Mama Gia patted the seat beside her. "They can sit here. By me. It's tradition."

"Mama, who says it's tradition?" Fernando asked as his brothers crammed into position near their mother, using a pecking order from oldest to youngest.

Alex stiffened and glanced at Suzy, likely waiting for the go-ahead to pounce.

Suzy lowered her voice. "This isn't the time."

Chapter 10

A server dressed in all black appeared with a tray of wineglasses filled generously with red and white wines. As he passed by Mama Gia, she grabbed one of the reds.

Suzy motioned for the waiter and plucked a red wine for herself. Glancing out the window, she noticed Vanessa in the parking lot struggling to get the seat belt off her baby bump. She placed her hand on the server's arm. "I'll take another."

The server raised his eyebrows.

"I have a feeling this will be a three-glass night." Holding wine in each hand, Suzy mouthed to Jon, "Vanessa's here." She kept her eye on the door as the young mother-to-be waddled inside.

Fernando was the first person at her side. He put his arm over Vanessa's shoulders.

A hush fell over the room as Vanessa attempted a smile. The minute she smelled the strong aromas, she covered her mouth and sat on the nearest chair along the wall. "Oh, my God. That smell. I think I'm going to be sick."

"It's no wonder," Mama Gia muttered from the table where she held court with her sons.

Izzy, clearly enjoying the antics of Fernando's mother, set her phone on the table to watch the events unfold.

Jon hurried to Vanessa's side and stood beside Fernando.

"Are you okay, little mama?" Fernando asked.

"I'll get a wet paper towel. You look hot," Jon said.

Vanessa fanned herself with her hand. "What is that smell?"

"Curry." Jon shrugged. "Sorry. We love it. It didn't even occur to me that smells might affect you in your . . . state."

"*Everything* affects me." Vanessa held her hand over her mouth and nose. "Maybe I'll get used to it in a minute."

"Be right back." Jon returned with a glass of water and a wet paper towel. He handed Vanessa the water as Fernando wiped her forehead and the back of her neck.

Resting her arm across her expansive belly, Vanessa took a deep breath. "Thanks, guys. I feel better already."

Mama Gia crossed the room in seemingly two steps. She bent down until she was eye to eye with Vanessa. "When are you due? It must be soon."

"Two weeks." The freckle-faced mother-to-be held her hand up. "Go ahead and eat. I think I'll just have a—"

"How about a cracker?" Jon asked. "A cracker or dry toast might help."

She nodded and Jon bounded toward the kitchen.

Suzy leaned over and hugged Vanessa. "I'm glad you're here." She chuckled. "Jon's treating you like you have a hangover or the flu."

Vanessa leaned back. "It's cute," she whispered in Suzy's ear. "I still can't get over the fact that they're willing to be part of this baby's life." Her eyes welled with tears. "Of my life."

Suzy stroked Vanessa's ginger, shoulder-length hair. "I'm thrilled too. If you're sure you're okay, I'm going to eat. We have a huge day tomorrow."

"Yeah, your only child's wedding. No big deal." Vanessa smiled. "Don't worry. I'm fine. The baby is getting so big I sometimes get short-winded." She shooed Suzy and the others away. "Go ahead and eat, everyone. Please."

Fernando stayed by her side.

Vanessa reached for his hand. "You eat too. Sit with Jon. When my stomach settles, I'll take a seat. Don't worry."

Once everyone got seated, Mama Gia asked, "Is Vanessa a family member? Your cousin or something?"

Jon's face turned ashen.

Fernando beamed. "Mama, she's Jon's former high school girlfriend."

Mama Gia spewed red wine all over Jon's white shirt.

"Damn. This shirt is new." Jon must have realized he made a mistake and said, "Sorry. That's probably a shock. I wasn't always gay. I might have experimented once in high school—"

Suzy stood frozen with the two glasses of wine glued to her hands. *So, they didn't tell her.*

Fernando put his hand atop Jon's. "Not only did my fiancé experiment, he and Vanessa got pregnant at their prom—and now she's, well, you can see for yourself." He stopped, apparently in an effort to let the news sink in.

Mama Gia's eyes widened as she stared from Fernando to Jon to Vanessa's big belly. "Wait. You-You're pregnant by my son's fiancé?"

Fernando hooted. "Bingo, Mama. Isn't this exciting? Vanessa's having a—"

Jon put both hands in the air as if he were being arrested. "Why don't we slow this train down? No need to overshare. Give your mom time to process."

"Nonsense." Fernando sipped his wine. "We're all one big happy family—or will be soon. We like to call ourselves the modern Brady Bunch."

Draining her wineglass, Mama Gia stared daggers at her son. "You didn't think your mama would want to know about this before your wedding?"

Chapter 11

Suzy interjected, "Maybe the guys should have told you but I assume they wanted to tell you in person. That's how we all found out, even Jon and Fernando. It seemed easier seeing the burden of proof, so to speak." She moved closer to Vanessa and beamed. "I'm going to be a grandma." She paused. "So are you, Mama Gia. How do you like the sound of that?"

Mama Gia stared at Vanessa for several long seconds before she got back up, embraced her, buried her face in the young woman's neck, and sobbed. Loudly. Stroking the young girl's auburn hair, she spoke in Italian saying, "*Bambino*," "*Amore*," and "*Nonna*." Glancing at Suzy, she said, "*Nonna* means Grandma." She reached for Vanessa's belly. "It's okay if I touch you?"

Vanessa nodded while Mama Gia rubbed her belly. "A baby. A wedding *and* a baby." She glanced upward, mumbled, and finally said, "I can't believe this."

Mama Gia called her sons over. "Boys, come here. I want you to meet someone. First, I make a speech." Clanging on her wineglass, she said, "We've gathered here to celebrate Fernando and Jon. This is a momentous occasion. Not only is Fernando my first son to marry but he has chosen a fine man to join our family. Welcome to the Russo family, Jon." She sniffled. "And there's more big news. Sons, meet Jon's former girlfriend, Vanessa."

The room fell silent.

"Girlfriend?" Luigi said. "Ma, I think you've had too much wine."

Vinny grinned. "Our mama gets confused."

Mama Gia shushed her sons and likely would have thumped their heads if they had been standing closer. "I'm not confused. Vanessa was Jon's girlfriend in high school. Now she's pregnant with his baby."

"What?" Frankie said.

Luigi's mouth fell open.

"Now *I'm* confused," Vinny said.

A red-faced Vanessa attempted to scoot her chair back. Eventually shuffling into a standing position, she leaned on the table, nearly toppling over her water in the process.

Jon's eyes grew wide. "What are you doing?"

Clearing her throat, Vanessa said, "I know this is difficult to understand. Almost impossible." Her voice broke. "I sprang this on everyone. Jon and Fernando have been wonderful about the unexpected baby news." Her voice cracked. "I hope you'll accept it too." She took a breath. "As Fernando mentioned, Jon and I dated in high school. For two years, actually. He told me he was gay our senior year. I didn't care. I thought I was in love with him. When the prom came, I was sick of being a virgin and made sure he was drunk. Very drunk and—"

The blood drained from Jon's face. "They don't want to know every detail."

"Yes we do," Luigi said.

"I'm all ears," Frankie said.

"Yo, continue," Vinny said.

"Boys." Mama Gia frowned at her sons before saying, "Go on."

Vanessa glanced toward Jon as if asking for his input. He shook his head and shrugged, giving mixed signals. Blowing out her breath, she said, "Basically, I was afraid I'd lose Jon forever once he went to Europe after graduation. I knew he'd probably meet someone . . ." She winked at Fernando. "And he did. At the prom, peer pressure got to me and I wanted to have sex with my boyfriend. It's as simple—and as complicated—as that." Rubbing her belly, she said, "Now we're going to have a baby." She stared from face to face. "All of us."

Fernando blurted, "We're having a girl!"

As everyone cheered, clapped, and clanked wineglasses, Jon helped Vanessa back into her chair and kissed her on the cheek. Fernando kissed the other cheek.

Mama Gia burst into tears, muttering a string of Italian phrases.

"English, Mama," Fernando said.

Puffing her enormous chest out, Mama Gia said, "I'm going to be a Nonna."

One by one, Vinny, Frankie, and Luigi stood and made boisterous toasts razzing their brother and warning Jon.

"Yo, Jon. Call me if you need help with Fernando," Vinny said.

Frankie held his glass in the air. "It's all good. Don't worry 'bout it."

"I'll help with anything besides babies." The Mighty Mouse-shaped Luigi laughed. "That's not my territory."

Suzy noticed Izzy texting so fast she was surprised her phone didn't catch on fire. *She's probably telling her friends about her unorthodox, crazy family.*

Alex studied Izzy and whispered to Hope. "I thought I was addicted to my phone. Izzy never puts that damn thing down."

"Are we ever going to eat?" Ken said, getting everyone back on track. "I'm starving."

"Cheers to that," Luigi said.

Chef Raj had been standing near the food, appearing amused by the announcements. He spread his arms. "Welcome to Indian Summer. On this happy occasion, I've made for you quinoa soup, chick pea curry, butter chicken, Indian shrimp curry, lentils, basmati rice, and Naan.

Mama Gia wrinkled her nose. "I don't have any idea what any of that is. No minestrone soup?"

Frowning, the chef peered at Suzy, who shrugged and glanced at her guests for moral support.

The chef shuffled from foot to foot, obviously weighing the quandary of the guests who apparently weren't familiar with Indian cuisine. He simply said, "Enjoy," and motioned toward the food.

Ken tapped on a glass with a knife. "Everyone, let's get started before the food gets cold. We have a wedding tomorrow."

Happy her husband was attempting order, Suzy stepped near her friends.

Alex fell in line and leaned over. "How do you think the baby news went over?"

"I'd say pretty well considering she didn't know a thing about it." Suzy ran her fingers through her hair. "This may be a wild wedding."

Chapter 12

After a heated argument with her sous chef, Cheri reassured the staff, double and triple-checked the catering menu including many allergy-related food requests, and finally found time to glance at her phone. An urgent text from Alex about Fernando's mother and her wedding food intrusion caught her attention. She reread the message and made a face. Peering at the clock, she knew the rehearsal dinner had already begun. It was too late to try and change the menu.

What a day. I wish I were there to help. I miss my new friends, plus Suzy needs me. Cheri set her phone on the counter. It immediately vibrated. Glancing at the screen, she saw a message from her limo driver, Gage.

I, uh, might be in the Times *tomorrow.*

Cheri texted back: *Good or bad?*

Not great. Sorry, boss.

Tired of texting, she dialed his number. "Gage, what happened?"

"Bottom line, I drove a famous pop singer to an event last night. After I parked and opened her door, she jumped my bones—literally wrapped her legs around my waist—and laid a wet one on me. The photographers went wild."

Cheri suppressed a giggle. "Doesn't every single guy want a famous pop singer to jump his bones?"

Gage groaned. "I wasn't finished."

Cheri switched ears. "Go on."

"Apparently, this singer's boyfriend is a boxer-slash-photographer on the side. I think she wanted to make him jealous."

"And?"

"It worked. He punched me. Almost knocked me back inside my limo. That's the photo that'll likely be in the *Times*."

Cheri swallowed. "I hope you're okay."

"I'm fine. A little sore and a lot embarrassed," Gage said.

Sighing, Cheri said, "Sorry that happened but I have to ask. Did you mention the Van Buren name?" Since her jet-setting parents were still in Europe, she tried hard to stay under the radar. Cheri hated the paparazzi and often wore wigs, hats, and sunglasses so she could do normal things in Manhattan. Being a wealthy socialite appeared to be rainbows and unicorns, but high society had its disadvantages. When her limo driver didn't answer right away, she continued. "Well, Gage? Did you mention us?"

He paused. "Yeah, the *Times* reporter asked about my employer. It was a messy blur but I also heard someone mention they were with TMZ. Sorry."

"Dammit." Cheri blew out her breath. "It's not your fault. Don't worry about it and take care of yourself. I'll think of something. I don't want to bother Mom and Dad with this. Hopefully, they're too busy in Europe to read newspapers and magazines." As she chewed on a pen, her mind raced. "I want you to take a month off. Go somewhere else. Visit your family or friends. Don't worry. I'll keep you on the payroll."

Gage brightened. "Go somewhere like Crystal City and Coconuts?"

"No, definitely not there. I enjoy my privacy in Crystal City. Besides, as you know, I don't need a driver there. No one except my three girlfriends are aware of my persona, and I work hard to keep it that way. I can't risk having paparazzi chase me there too. Let's give it a few weeks and reassess."

"Shit." Gage's voice fell. "I had hoped to see Alex again."

"Oh, really? You miss Alex, do you?" She couldn't help razzing her favorite employee who was more like a friend. "Sorry, bud. You'll just have to wait." Cheri stepped into her modern kitchen and poured herself a Diet Coke. "And Gage?"

"What?"

"You might want to be more selective about your freelance gigs." Wiping up soda which overflowed onto her gray and black granite counter, she couldn't resist teasing him. "Seriously, after you get settled somewhere, send me your address so I can forward your paycheck."

"Will do. Anything else?" he asked.

Cheri heard the disappointment in his voice. "Don't worry. Alex isn't going to marry that cop anytime soon. Not from what I can tell anyway."

Gage's tone brightened. "I hope you're right. I'll text you the names of some other drivers."

"I want a female or an older male until this blows over. See you in a month or so. Bye, Gage, and stay safe." Cheri hung up and reached for a bag of almonds. *Mom and Dad won't be pleased if they hear about this. I can't wait to get to Crystal City where there's no paparazzi.*

Chapter 13

After everyone filled their plates and sat down, Suzy watched as Fernando's mother scooted food around her plate, taking miniscule bites. She overheard Mama Gia say, "We should have had spaghetti and meatballs. You make the best meatballs, Luigi." She motioned toward her plate. "This needs more garlic."

Fernando shushed her. "Mama, everyone can hear you. It's delicious. Eat."

Suzy ate quickly, hoping the evening would end soon. She couldn't wait to get home and clear her head before the wedding. When the commotion finally died down, the outer door creaked open filling the room with sunshine.

Everyone turned toward the light as Bill, Suzy's ex-husband and Jon's father, sauntered inside.

Suzy glanced at Jon and mouthed, "Who invited him?"

"Me. He's my dad." Jon glanced at his watch and crossed the room. "Hey, Dad, you're two hours late but glad you could make it. You know Fernando and Mom. Have you met Ken and Izzy?"

Bill reached across the table. "Don't believe I have." He shook Ken's hand so hard his knuckles turned white. He gave Izzy a fist bump and said, "Suzy, lookin' good as ever." Bill's voice boomed as he hugged her a little too long. "Long time no see."

Still holding her orange napkin, Suzy said, "Thanks, Bill. Remember Alex and Hope?"

Suzy's macho ex grinned. "You ladies are more beautiful than I remember. How many years has it been?"

"We don't discuss years." Alex winked. "Good to see you, Bill."

Bill flashed a devilish smile toward Fernando's family. "As you might have guessed, I'm Jon's Dad and Suzy's ex." He turned toward Suzy. "Did you forget to invite me, Suze?"

"Um, I thought you moved out of state." Still standing near the table, she drained her wine.

Bill shoved his hands in his pockets. "I did, but as they say, 'I'm baaack.'" He hugged Fernando and slapped him on the back. "Be good to my son." He embraced Jon. "And you be good to Fernando."

Suzy sat down, almost afraid to make eye contact with Ken, imagining how uncomfortable he must feel. She noticed Izzy was speed texting again. *No one can say this was a boring rehearsal dinner.*

Bill extended his hand to Mama Gia who absentmindedly fluffed her hair before flinging herself against Suzy's very handsome ex-husband.

After a too-long first hug, she said, "These are my other boys—Luigi, Vinny, and Frankie."

Bill greeted the brothers and stood behind Jon and Fernando, placing his hands on each of their shoulders. "I never thought I'd say this but how's the happy couple?"

Fernando's mother visibly stiffened. "What is that supposed to mean?"

"Doesn't mean a thing, ma'am." Continuing in his baritone voice, he said, "Fernando's a fine young man. I think the world of him. I may even teach him to hunt someday. Jon never showed any interest, so maybe I'll have a son to hunt with."

Mama Gia fluffed her hair again. "Why, thank you. Jon's a good boy too."

Bill took a seat beside Alex as the chef brought out dessert platters featuring petite, creamy filled cups and white powdered balls.

Mama Gia stared at the dessert with dismay. "What? No gelato or tiramisu?" She threw both hands in the air. "*Mama Mia.*"

"*Ma.*" Fernando gave his mother a stern glance and shot an apologetic glance toward Suzy.

Ignoring Mama Gia's outbursts and feeling sorry for the crestfallen chef, Suzy forced a smile. "Chef, tell us about your desserts."

With a flourish, Chef Raj motioned toward the tiny cups containing Kulfi. "This is our Middle Eastern version of ice cream." He addressed Jon and Fernando. "I made mango to go with your beach theme." Pointing toward the tray of tiny white balls, the chef said, "These are Coconut Ladoo, which are delicate, sweetened coconut balls."

"Perfect." Suzy winked at her girlfriends. "We love anything named 'coconuts,' don't we?"

"Yes, ma'am." Alex suppressed a giggle. "And we're in fierce need of that place, stat."

"I'm all over coconut anything. Pass one of those coconut balls over here." Hope patted her belly. "And don't forget the ice cream. I'm not on a diet." She paused. "To clarify, I'm never on a diet."

Between bites, Alex said, "Tony's going to be really sorry he missed this eventful evening."

"I thought you were taking a break from the cop," Suzy said.

Alex shrugged. "He's good in bed."

Obviously listening, food flew out of Luigi's mouth. "I like these friends of yours, Jon."

Winking, Bill said, "I like them too."

Vinny grinned. "Americans."

Everyone ate for several minutes in blissful silence until Mama Gia wiped her mouth and set her fork on the plate. "What's the baby's name?"

Vanessa's mouth curved into a smile. "We're still deciding. We might not know until we see her little face."

Mama Gia pressed. "Want some suggestions?"

"No, Mama. We get that honor."

Frowning, Mama Gia said, "But I have several ideas. Good family names. Good *Italian* names."

Fernando shifted in his chair. "Thanks, Mama, but if any family names are used, I think it should come from Vanessa or Jon's family, don't you?"

"Speaking of—" Mama Gia fixed her stare on Vanessa. "Where are your parents?"

The young woman's eyes welled with tears. "They're, uh, they're—"

"They're not here," Jon said.

Mama Gia crossed her arms. "Why not?"

Suzy noticed everyone's forks were poised in mid-air as they studied a woeful Vanessa. Deciding to interject, she said, "Vanessa's parents aren't willing participants right now. Let's leave it at that."

Oblivious to Vanessa's family dynamics, Mama Gia pressed. "Why not? Why aren't they involved?"

"Anyone want more coffee or wine?" Suzy asked.

"I do." Ken gave his wife a sideways glance. "I'll get the chef."

Suzy did her best to distract Mama Gia. "Decaf for me, hon, and maybe another half pour on the wine."

Ken nodded knowing full well why his wife needed more wine. "Be right back."

"But what about her parents?" Mama Gia asked.

Fernando made a face. "*Mom*. Enough."

Chapter 14

Two servers broke the awkward conversation as they cleared the uneaten food, dirty dishes, and brought fresh coffee.

In order to keep Mama Gia at bay, Ken stood and made a beautiful toast to the two grooms-to-be, discussing how Fernando was a welcome addition to the family.

Glancing at a now semi-relaxed Jon, Suzy noticed he and Fernando were both having seconds of the Kulfi and had already polished off their Coconut Ladoo. From where she sat, she could see specks of powdered sugar on her son's bottom lip and resisted the urge to tell him. She assumed Fernando's mother would have wiped the white substance off if it were on his mouth and was determined not to be an overbearing mother.

"My turn." Already tearing up, Suzy stood and tapped her wineglass. "I'd like to toast my son and son-in-law-to-be." Her voice cracked. Locking eyes with Jon, she said, "I hope I can get through this. You've truly been the best son a mother could have. You're wise beyond your years—stubborn at times—but definitely one of the good guys. The best, actually. You excelled in school, but more importantly, you always did—and continue to do—the right thing. You're kind, sweet, smart, and generous." Her voice broke. Taking a sip of wine for fortitude, she continued. "You've chosen a wonderful life partner in Fernando. I couldn't be more proud to be your mother." She glanced at Fernando and added, "And I'll be equally proud to be your mother-in-law. I love you both." Wiping her nose with a napkin, Suzy said, "And

Vanessa, having Jon's baby with Fernando fully embracing the little bundle is icing on the—"

"Baby? What baby?" All heads swiveled toward Bill.

Suzy heard Jon mutter, "Shit. Here we go again."

Turning toward Vanessa, Bill said, "I can see you're pregnant. What's this baby news?"

Suzy rubbed her forehead, sorry Vanessa had to endure the conversation yet again. "I'll fill you in later, Bill."

A vivacious, always spirited Fernando piped up. "Why wait? I'll fill you in now. Vanessa's having Jon's baby. She got pregnant at their high school prom. We're going to be one big happy family so get ready, Grandpa #2."

Alex burst into laughter. "I wish I could give a succinct recap like that at one of my bank board meetings. Congratulations, Grandpa #2."

"Sorry, Dad. I meant to tell you. We've been so busy with the wedding and—"

Bill set his coffee cup down. "No problem, son, but just so we're clear, I want a sexier name than Grandpa."

Alex snorted. "I don't blame you."

Bill winked at Vanessa. "Congratulations, darlin', and same to you, boys." Rubbing his hands together, he said, "So I'm not late again, what time is the wedding tomorrow?"

"It's at five o'clock but feel free to help us set up at two," Suzy said.

Ken's jaw tightened. "Thanks anyway, Bill. No need. I've got everything covered."

Suzy noticed Izzy worked both thumbs again. She reached for her husband's hand. "Honey, I think we can use all the help we can get. Remember we're transforming a huge section of the Coconuts parking lot into a beach."

"Whatever," Ken muttered.

Bill glanced at his ex-wife. "I'll be there early tomorrow."

Ken lowered his voice. "As if we don't already have enough friction with—" He nodded toward Mama Gia.

"Do you want to lug one hundred chairs?" Suzy asked.

Rolling his eyes, Ken said, "All right."

Suzy noticed Vanessa and Izzy were deep in conversation.

The teen perked up, placed her phone on the table, and laid her hand on Vanessa's belly. Izzy squealed. "The baby kicked. That's so dope."

Vanessa grinned. "It is dope. You can play with her any time."

Suzy couldn't believe her eyes. Izzy finally seemed interested in something other than her cellphone.

Straining to hear a conversation between her husband and her ex, Suzy heard Bill enthralling Ken with his latest elk hunting adventure and mentioned going to Canada for a boys' hunting trip. *He hasn't changed a bit.*

"Ooh." Vanessa lurched and rubbed her belly. "That was a big kick. Baby is super active tonight."

Jon's eyebrows shot up. "She just needs to hold on another week until we get back from our honeymoon."

Bill chimed back in. "So it's a girl. I guess I'll have to get the news piecemeal."

Alex crossed her legs. "Fernando announced the sex earlier but you were even later to the party than me."

"Dad, enough with the questions, okay?" Jon made his way toward Vanessa. "I think we need to get her home."

Nodding, Vanessa yawned. "It has been a long day. I'm really tired all of a sudden."

Fernando pulled out Vanessa's chair. "We don't want to wear you out. You'll need your strength for—"

"Don't say it." Jon held his arms out to the side. "Don't jinx anything."

"Right." Fernando helped Vanessa up.

Luigi set his wineglass down. "Can you put a plug in that thing until after the wedding?"

"*Luigi.*" Mama Gia smacked him on the head.

"What's the matter? What do I know about baby stuff?" His brothers playfully punched him on both sides as Jon and Fernando ushered Vanessa outside and helped her into her car.

Suzy glanced at Ken. "Let's call it a night. We have a big day tomorrow." She asked Mama Gia if she needed directions to her hotel.

Holding her phone in the air, Mama Gia said she had it under control and mentioned they had a couple of stops to make before checking in.

Suzy wondered what in the world she'd need the night before the wedding but decided it was probably something mundane like a toothbrush or shower cap.

After a server attempted to refill her coffee, Mama Gia shooed him away. "Jetlag just hit me. I've got to get some rest before the wedding. Let's go, boys. We have errands to run."

"Jon, do you want to join us for a nightcap at the hotel? I'm sure my mother has some wine in her suitcase."

Jon shook his head. "Thanks, but I'm exhausted. I'll walk out with you."

Suzy and Ken paid the chef and thanked everyone for attending. Soon, the room was empty sans dirty dessert dishes.

In the parking lot, Luigi grabbed Fernando around the neck then raked his knuckles back and forth across his scalp.

"Ow. Stop it," Fernando said.

"My little bro's getting married. You deserve a noogie for that." After a throaty laugh, Luigi raked his knuckles across Fernando's head a few more times for good measure.

Vinny and Frankie circled them chanting, "Fernando's getting married. Fernando's getting married."

Fernando grimaced. "I see some of us haven't grown up."

Obviously not sure what to do, Jon muffled a stilted laugh. "I'm glad I'm an only child."

"What?" Luigi released Fernando's neck slightly. "And miss all of this brotherly fun? You're next."

Chapter 15

Alex rolled her eyes at Fernando's playful brothers in the parking lot and watched Bill saunter toward his Ram truck. "I wonder when Suzy's ex turned into a dark-haired Sam Elliot?"

Hope snorted. "Bill has held up well. I don't remember his being so handsome."

Alex fished inside her purse. "He's cute but that would be weird. Besides, I'm taken." Retrieving her phone, she said, "I'm going to text Cheri. Suzy needs help with this-this meddling woman. She's worked far too hard on Jon and Fernando's wedding for"—she made air quotes—"Mama Gia to mess everything up."

Hope nodded in agreement as Alex scrolled through her phone. "Aha. Here's Cheri's number." She quickly typed a text.

Hey, Cheri. It's Alex. Is there any way you can come to the wedding tomorrow? Charter a private plane or something? Suzy has her hands full with Fernando's mom, if you know what I mean. I don't mean to intrude but Jon's former girlfriend looks like she's about to pop with the baby, and I don't know how much Suzy can take. We need all hands on deck. If you can leave New York, please do. Thanks, Alex.

She hit *send*. "Fingers crossed." Transfixed on her screen, Alex said, "Want to go to Coconuts?"

"Is that even a question? See you in ten." Hope crossed the gravel lot toward her gray Honda.

Meanwhile, Alex climbed into her white Mustang and raised the convertible top. She felt her phone vibrate but concentrated on the road.

Chapter 16

After thanking the chef profusely in an attempt to make up for all of Mama Gia's cracks about his Indian cuisine, Suzy and Ken headed toward their respective cars. As she climbed in beside her son who was already buckled in, she said, "I think Fernando's right. We're going to be one big, multi-cultural Brady Bunch."

Jon stared ahead, non-communicative.

After several seconds, Suzy asked, "You okay?"

"It's a lot to get my head around. That's all."

Placing her hand on his arm, she said, "You aren't doing this alone, remember. You have a loving partner, your soon-to-be husband, plus me."

Jon leaned back against the headrest. "Thanks, Mom. Keep reminding me."

"Will do." Suzy glanced toward Vanessa who slowly put her car in reverse and turned the steering wheel. She noticed the young woman's belly nearly touched the steering wheel and considered flagging her down to ask her to scoot her seat back allowing more room for the precious bundle inside but knew she had to stop being such a mom, especially after seeing Fernando's mother in action.

When she finally backed out, Vanessa blew Suzy and Jon a kiss, which warmed Suzy's heart. Their lives—all of their lives—were about to change drastically. She knew Jon was still on edge about being a new father, but secretly, she couldn't wait to be a grandmother.

After she drove onto the street, Suzy followed Ken and Izzy.

Voice flat, Jon said, "She's a piece of work, isn't she?"

"You're not used to an overbearing mother." Suzy didn't make eye contact knowing Jon would see right through her. "She loves her son, that's all."

Picking lint off his slacks and rubbing his wine-stained shirt, Jon said, "I suppose."

Suzy faced Jon at the stoplight. "She's only here for a few days. You can put up with anything, or anyone, for that long."

"You're right." Jon ran his fingers through his hair. "I'm being a dick."

"No, you aren't. You have the wedding jitters. It's natural. Almost every bride—" Suzy cursed herself.

"It's okay, Mom. As accepted as gay marriages are, I know it's hard not to immediately think of a traditional couple in your mind." He grinned. "You, Dad, and Ken have been great. Let's leave it at that."

"You know I love Fernando. I'm accustomed to saying brides, that's all. I'm exhausted and my brain isn't working. Now I feel like a jerk."

"Enough said. Drop it." His voice softened. "Thanks for arranging the rehearsal dinner. It was delicious. Fernando and I devoured every bite, even though his mother couldn't stop complaining about the lack of meatballs."

Suzy shook her head. "There's definitely no gray area with Mama Gia."

"I know I told you to surprise us with the wedding meal. Now I'm almost afraid to ask. Any meatballs on the menu?"

Suzy gave her son the side eye. "It's a beach-themed wedding. Does that sound like it should have meatballs to you? Think fish, a lobster-stuffed ravioli, and one vegetarian entrée."

"Perfect. She should like that."

Suzy cleared her throat. "As you mentioned earlier, we're part Italian. My dad—your grandfather—is half-Italian, so

I'm one-fourth and you're whatever that lesser fraction is."

Laughing, she said, "One-eighth. I always hated math."

"Actually, that's a great point. I always think of grandpa as grandpa, not an ethnicity. I guess you understand all of the Italian phrases they throw around."

"Not at all, but Izzy translated a few."

Jon raised his eyebrows. "She did?"

"Yep. I'm sure she Googled them. She kept texting me during dinner. I'm glad you didn't notice me checking my phone."

Jon's mouth twitched. "That's hilarious."

As she rounded a corner toward home, Suzy said, "Who would have imagined Izzy and I would bond over Italian curse words."

"Something had to bring you two together. Might as well be foreign cursing." Jon leaned against the headrest. "I'm worried about Vanessa. Do you think all of this activity is too much for her? I don't know anything about pregnancy but I doubt that stress is helpful."

After Suzy parked, she said, "It's a worry. But her due date is in two weeks. We're cutting it close." She paused. "I'll keep an eye on her tomorrow."

Chapter 17

As soon as Alex and Hope were seated at their favorite high-top at Coconuts, Gus appeared. "The usual, ladies?"

"Yes, but we're just having one nightcap and maybe coffee after that." Alex didn't bother looking at their favorite server. Instead, she frowned while reading Cheri's text.

"What did she say?"

Alex frowned. "In a word, 'no'."

"Well? Spill." Hope accepted a margarita and a bowl of peanuts from Gus.

Alex took a sizable gulp of chardonnay. "I'll read it."

Hi! I'm sorry to miss the wedding but I have two huge catering events here in New York City. One is a major celebrity. I'm under contract to keep it quiet but it's a famous musician. I simply cannot leave. This has to go off without a hitch. How was the rehearsal dinner? Did they enjoy the cuisine? Chef Raj is fab. Miss you girls. ~Cheri

Hope rolled her eyes. "I love Cheri but damn." She held her hands out to the side, palms up, as if she were Lady Justice. "Let's see. Cheri's life or mine. I choose hers."

"Silly." Alex peered over her wineglass. "Who wants to be a wealthy socialite in New York City entertaining a famous musician? We'd much rather be spending time with a mouthy Italian broad, wouldn't we?"

Almost choking on a peanut, Hope said, "You're right. We have our own show right here. Poor Suzy."

Scanning the Coconuts crowd, Alex motioned with her head. "I wonder when Mr. Cigar Chomper is going to choke on that damn thing."

Hope giggled. "He's a mainstay. I think I'd miss his unlit cigars. I'm glad none of the teachers from Hilltop have discovered this place. They'd love the beachy feel of it. Maybe I should tell them."

"Don't you dare tell them about our oasis. It's getting hard enough to get our regular table." Scanning the room, Alex said, "I see a new batch of 'Hello, My Name Is' conference goers are here." Glancing toward the suit-wearing crew, Alex did a double take. "Look at Miss Commando in the short, red skirt at the bar." She covered her eyes. "Oh, God. Wear some freaking underwear. I can't unsee that."

"Thanks for the warning." Hope swiveled her chair away from the bar. "The wedding's tomorrow. Maybe we should leave early. I've had enough to drink."

"Me too. Let's go." Alex left half her chardonnay and hopped off her stool avoiding the direction of the red skirt-wearing offender. She left a twenty on the table for their two drinks. "Suzy will need us at full speed tomorrow. See you then."

Chapter 18

After reading Alex's text, Cheri paced in her striking, nearly all-white, Manhattan penthouse apartment. Staring at the Empire State Building, she wondered if she had forgotten anything for her mega event.

She had held pre-event meetings with her sous chef, head server, and manager multiple times. Her staff at Fifth Avenue Catering had been given a pep talk with promises of bonuses if the famous musician's party went off without a hitch. Annie Leibovitz, famed photographer, had been retained, as well as Manhattan's best florist. Tables were already decorated to perfection. A sextet from the New York Symphony would entertain guests during the pre-party, and the entertainer's musician friends had several surprises in store, including a group birthday song that would be videotaped live.

They were ready. This event would put Fifth Avenue Catering on the celebrity circuit, so why was Cheri unhappy. *Naturally, I land the catering gig of the year for Elton John's birthday and miss the son's wedding of one of the few, true friends I have.*

Her trilling phone jarred her into the present. She glanced at the screen. "Hi, Mom."

"Darling. It feels like ages since we've talked," her wealthy, jet-setting mother, Victoria Van Buren, said.

Glad her mother didn't have her on Skype, Cheri rolled her eyes. "Yes, it's been all of a week."

"Do you know how long that is in dog years?"

Losing her patience, Cheri asked, "What's up, Mom? I'm crazy busy."

Victoria paused. "Nothing's up. Can't I just call my daughter?"

"Of course. Sorry." Cheri stepped into the kitchen and reached for the glass handle to the mini-fridge. She grabbed a chilled Diet Coke and popped the tab.

"What's that noise?"

"Just a soda."

"Oh."

Cheri sipped her drink. "How's Europe? Sick of traveling?"

Her mother laughed for far too long. "Never. I, we, love to travel."

"How's Daddy?" Cheri paused. "By the way, I can tell you're smoking again. I hear you exhaling."

"One little cigarette never hurt anyone. And . . . Daddy's fine. He's working out like crazy."

"Really? That's new." Cheri rummaged in her fridge for some pepper jack cheese and grapes. "Does he have a personal trainer?"

"Honestly, I don't know. He goes to the gym almost daily. He's getting really buff."

"That's good, I suppose. Nice to stay fit." Cheri bit into a grape. "Do you go with him?"

Victoria cackled. "And interrupt my shopping? Not in a million years."

Cheri wondered where her mother put all of the stuff she bought on her thrice-weekly shopping excursions. "Mom, I have a mega event tomorrow. I can't talk long."

"Anyone I know?"

"It's someone everyone knows." Cheri waited for the typical response.

"And?"

Chuckling, Cheri said, "I can't say. I knew you'd ask but I'm under contract."

"Dammit. I hate it when you do that. I think you get that secrecy gene from your dad."

"If I could tell you, I would. I really don't want to get sued. This guy has more money than us. A lot more."

Her mother gasped. "Indeed. So . . . it's a male celebrity."

"See how you are? I'll tell you afterward. I promise." Cheri drained her soda. "I need to run. Love you."

Her mother hung up before saying good-bye which wasn't unusual. Cheri mentally checked her to-do list one last time before getting ready for bed. *I've got to remember to text Suzy tomorrow and congratulate her.*

She studied her massive closet that would be the envy of any upscale boutique but still couldn't decide what to wear to Sir Elton John's party. Unlocking her jewelry armoire, she sifted through diamonds, pearls, emeralds, and rubies. A tiny, signature blue Tiffany box in the back corner was like a punch in the gut, but she ignored it, pushing the unwanted memory far into the recesses of her mind.

Locking the jewelry armoire, Cheri focused on her clothes and decided on a silky black jumpsuit, Chanel belt, gold, strappy heels, and a gold clutch. After charging her phone, she crawled underneath her gray, plush comforter. *Now maybe I can sleep.*

Chapter 19

Suzy's stomach churned. As a wedding planner, she was normally a pro and effortlessly calmed her brides. But this was different. Today's wedding was for her son.

Ken shuffled into the kitchen and kissed her as he reached for the coffee pot. "Big day."

"I'd say." She refilled her pink and black *Weddings by Suzanne* mug for luck. "What did you think of Fernando's mother?"

Before Ken answered, Izzy appeared. "She's bossy."

"Guess she makes me look good," Suzy said.

Izzy actually smiled. "Did you get my texts last night? I learned some new swear words. I translated her Italian for you."

"Is that what you were doing?" Ken asked. "I figured you were chatting with friends."

Suzy retrieved her phone from her purse and showed Ken fifteen texts from Izzy. She turned toward her stepdaughter. "Thank you, Iz. That was helpful." Pausing, she said, "Maybe I should learn Italian."

"Unless you want her talking about you." Izzy reached for a box of Raisin Bran while Ken set the milk on the table.

"Eat up, you two. We'll need our energy today." Suzy placed a blueberry English muffin in the toaster and poured orange juice into three glasses.

~ ~ ~

After breakfast, Suzy rushed to the Crystal City Salon where the stylist fashioned her red hair into a messy side bun. Racing home to change, Suzy noticed Ken had already donned a navy and white tropical shirt and khaki pants to fit the luau wedding theme. "You look great, hon."

"What about me?" Izzy appeared in the hallway wearing a green and white striped one-shouldered sundress adorned with colorful parrots.

"That's a cute dress, Iz. Love the parrots."

Ken handed his wife a cup of coffee and gave her a light kiss. "This is decaf. Relax. Everything will be fine."

"How did you know I was nervous?" Suzy accepted the java and disappeared into her closet. Tears filled her eyes as she searched for her mother-of-the-bride dress. *I want today to be perfect for Jon and Fernando.*

She donned a gold and white strapless dress with a huge, striking jewel-accented orange blossom at the cinched waist. *The orange clashes with my red hair but Fernando loves orange so . . .* Deciding to wear white flip-flops to be comfortable while she set up the venue and grabbing a change of casual clothes, Suzy added a pair of gold, strappy heels and a beaded, orange clutch. Adding tasteful pearl earrings as the final touch, she twirled in the mirror.

Ken whistled when Suzy stepped into the living room. "Thanks, hon. We've got to go." Ken and Izzy piled into Suzy's Suburban and drove mostly in silence to Coconuts. After parking, Suzy groaned. "Look at her."

"Her who?" Ken asked.

Izzy chuckled. "Mama Gia already looks pissed off."

"Izzy. No cursing," Ken said.

"She does look pissed." Suzy unlatched her door.

Izzy hopped out with her phone practically glued to her hand. "I'll translate."

Ken glanced around the lot. "I don't see Bill anywhere. Guess I beat him here." Grinning, he said, "I'll get the Russo boys to help me set up the chairs when they arrive."

"Thanks, babe. Leave space for an aisle down the middle." He gave an okay sign and motioned to Izzy. Suzy knew beating Bill to the punch was a small victory in Ken's eyes but her ex was the least of her worries. As she crossed the crunchy parking lot, Suzy waved to Mama Gia who stood with her hands on her hips, scowling.

With obvious trepidation, Fernando's mother followed Suzy inside Coconuts. After stepping inside the darkened bar, she watched half amused as Fernando's mother surveyed the room.

Mama Gia's lips were pursed. "Where is my boy getting married?"

"Right here." Suzy held both arms out to her side.

"In a bar?"

"I had a lot of wine last night, but I'm sure we discussed this." Suzy reached for Mama Gia's hand. "Follow me back outside." They both squinted as they strode into the bright sunshine in the lot beside Coconuts. "Actually, to be specific, they're getting married here."

Mouth agape, Mama Gia swiveled her head from side to side. She studied Suzy as if she were a unicorn. "In a parking lot? My boy's getting married in a gravel parking lot?" Her voice rose a notch. "I don't think so."

Chapter 20

Suzy could barely contain her glee. "Just wait. It'll be perfect in an hour or two."

"*Cazzo*." Fernando's mother threw both arms in the air. "I can't believe this. My son is getting married in a parking lot when we have the beautiful country of Italy. This is absurd." A string of heated Italian words peppered the air followed again by the term, *Cazzo*.

As they stepped across the lot, Suzy wished Izzy were by her side to translate and made a mental note to remember the word. Feeling a slight stress headache coming on, Suzy hoped she'd made the right decision but there wasn't any backing out now. On top of the venue issues, Jon and Fernando had insisted Vanessa participate in the wedding and had even bought her a white maternity dress. With the pregnancy, Vanessa's doctor wouldn't approve a flight at this late date, so their choices were limited. Jon had always wanted a beach wedding and Suzy had lined up every vendor she knew to bring the beach to him.

The *beeep beeep beep* of a large dump truck broke the inquisition. The driver backed up and hit his air brakes. Poking his bald head out the window, he waved a piece of paper in the air. "Are either of you with Weddings by Suzanne?"

Suzy cupped her hands around her mouth to shout above the noise. "Yes, I'm Suzy. That's my wedding company. Glad you're here."

He nodded. "Where do you want all of this sand?"

She pointed a few feet away. "Right there. Dump it."

Mama Gia's eyebrows knitted. "What a mess."

Ignoring her, Suzy yelled, "You have a spreader, right?"

He gave her a thumbs-up. Soon the gravel lot was covered in thick, powdery sand. Suzy kicked off her shoes and motioned for Mama Gia to do the same. "See, it feels like we're on the beach. Try it."

Fernando's mother hesitated but stepped out of her heels. The woman always wore heels. She set them underneath a table. "Okay, we have sand. Now what?"

Suzy grinned. "Get ready for a transformation." As if on cue, two enormous rental trucks arrived with eight fake, albeit realistic, towering palm trees, box after box of white twinkling lights, an archway covered in silky white orchids, one hundred white folding chairs, and several rectangular tables for food and gifts.

Mama Gia grabbed her phone and began dialing. "Vinny, tell Luigi and Frankie to come to Coconuts right now." She added, "The rental car is already packed." Pausing, she said, "It doesn't matter how I got here. While you sleepyheads were sprawled on the floor, if you must know, I took a cab. Now, hurry. We're gonna have a beach wedding for your brother and need help setting up." She hung up without bothering to say good-bye.

Suzy grinned to herself. *Mama Gia might be coming around.* Scanning the area, she decided to leave the chair setup to the guys and asked Mama Gia to help drape white linens over the tables that Ken and Gus had placed next to the building.

Smoothing the cloth and straightening a corner, Suzy said, "We need to get the tables ready before the food arrives. I've ordered all of Jon's favorites—"

Mama Gia waved her hands. "I've got the food covered. I know exactly what Fernando likes."

Suzy bristled. "The food order was placed with a caterer months ago." She glanced at her watch. "In fact, it should be here within the hour."

"I know food." Mama Gia spewed several angry-sounding Italian phrases in rapid succession.

"In English, if you don't mind." Suzy realized she had her hands on her hips and lowered her tone. "Please."

"Caterer?" Mama Gia shouted. "We don't need a silly caterer. Look at me. I'm an Italian mama. Leave the food to me. Besides . . . it's already cooking."

Chapter 21

"What? How?" Suzy's mouth fell open. "You just landed yesterday and we had the rehearsal dinner last night."

"You don't know much about Italians, do you? We're resourceful."

Suzy stared at her flip-flops. "Actually, my dad is half-Italian."

"He's living? Why isn't he here?"

Shame covered Suzy like a thick fog. "It's a long story. A *very* long story. I love my dad—and my mom—but they didn't support me after my sister slept with . . . Never mind. I don't want to discuss this on Jon and Fernando's happy day. Suffice to say, my parents aren't aware of the wedding. I think they live in Banff, Canada, now anyway."

Mama Gia shook her head and tsk tsked. "Family is the most important thing. Oy vey. Nothing's more important." She placed her hands on Suzy's shoulders. "Your parents should be here for this momentous occasion."

Tears filled Suzy's eyes. She knew she had made a mistake in not inviting her parents but it was too late now. They could never get here in time from another country. While dealing with her still-new marriage, mostly bratty stepdaughter, and the wedding, she had refused to add to the stress by inviting her parents since they weren't exactly on speaking terms.

Suzy felt Mama Gia's dark eyes pierce her but pushed through her guilt and shame. This woman is not going to ruin my only child's wedding. In an attempt to brighten the situation, Suzy said, "Let's get back to the wedding and food situation. I found the cutest oversized scallop clam shells to hold the food. The white containers will look adorable and go with the beachy theme."

"Spaghetti and meatballs might look odd in a clam shell but whatever." Mia Gia shrugged as she glanced around the parking lot. "Where are my boys?"

Tense, Suzy rubbed her shoulders. *I know she wants to be involved in her son's wedding. I've got to make this work. Spaghetti and meatballs will look ridiculous for the island theme but maybe no one will care. Hell, I care. Alex would stand up to Mama Gia but what's the point?* Suzy draped white, pristine tablecloths over several more tables and muttered to herself every step of the way. *Alex would tell Mama Gia to back off and in no uncertain terms let the woman know exactly who the wedding planner was. But I'm not Alex.*

Suzy kept working while Mama Gia punched numbers into her cell. She hollered, "Where are you, boys? Hurry up. Mama's not gonna tell you again."

Before she put her phone away, brakes screeched and sand flew everywhere. Suzy rubbed her eyes from the dust as Mama Gia ran to the car.

Swinging the car door open, Mama Gia poked her head inside. "It's about time you got here. Do I have to do everything?" When Frankie stepped out she thumped him on the head.

"Ow." Frankie covered his head with his hands.

Vinny climbed out of the back seat and tried to avoid his mom. She ran around the car and thumped him too.

"*Ma.*"

"You boys need to help your mama. Your brother's getting married today."

Luigi took his sweet time getting out of the car. Mama Gia glared at him. Luigi simply strode toward his mother, bent down, and offered the top of his head. She smacked it and then embraced her sons in a group hug. Kissing each of them, she said, "I love you boys."

"We love you too, Mama."

"What can we do?" Frankie asked.

Mama Gia pointed. "Start by setting up those white chairs. Theater-style, right, Suzy?"

Suzy nodded, glad to have the help so Ken wouldn't have to do it alone since Bill still hadn't shown up. "Please leave a four-foot aisle down the middle. Thanks, guys."

Vinny grabbed four chairs at a time, two under each arm. "Done."

Suzy turned toward the seafood bowls she had purchased, placing some on clear risers and leaving a few at table height. Reaching for a cooler Artistic Blooms had provided, she clutched already-arranged tropical Bird of Paradise bouquets in orange glass vases and placed them on the food, cake, and gift tables. Marc, the owner of Artistic Blooms, had an emergency water leak at the shop but had worked through the night to provide massive orange bows for the backs of each chair end.

Wondering what food Mama Gia and her boys had brought, Suzy ignored her worst suspicions as she placed colorful beachy hibiscus flowers around each serving bowl.

Suzy waved Izzy over. "Will you put the umbrella drink holders near those empty silver ice buckets?"

The teen shrugged. "Okay. Want me to go inside and get ice?"

"It's too soon." Suzy peered up at the bright, glaring sun. "It's surprisingly hot for a spring day. The ice will melt but if you'll do that later or ask Gus to help when I give you the signal that would be great."

Izzy nodded, put her cell in her purse, and took a handful of tiny drink umbrellas.

Suzy pointed toward Izzy's purse. "Keep your cell handy. I might need more translations." She winked at her stepdaughter and stepped over to the sandy, makeshift dance area. Cupping her mouth with her hands, Suzy shouted, "Will two of you guys come over here and smooth out the dance floor? When the DJ arrives, remind him to start playing the Jimmy Buffet and Kenny Chesney songs we selected to set the beach tone."

"No problem," Luigi answered.

Suzy's heart raced as she considered the seafood buffet she had planned. She had ordered Jon's favorite lobster-stuffed ravioli, blackened grouper, wild grain rice, roasted asparagus with almonds, and salads with tomatoes and artichokes. Counting the number of clam shell containers, her eyes widened as Mama Gia waddled toward her with a gigantic stock pot. *Oh, my God. I've got to know how Mama Gia made this food—and when and where she cooked it.*

Chapter 22

While Vinny and Ken set up chairs, Frankie and Luigi opened the trunk. Soon they carried platter after platter of steaming food covered in aluminum foil.

Luigi's muscles bulged and his feet nearly disappeared in the sand from holding two stacked coolers. "Where do you want these, Ma?"

Mama Gia pointed toward the white linen food tables. "Over there. Underneath the tables."

Holding a giant pan of lasagna, Frankie said, "This is hot, Mama." He grimaced. "Where do you want the lasagna?"

"Where else, son? On top of the food table. Move dishes around. Find space. Use your head."

Suzy prickled as her carefully planned meal turned into bedlam. She knew Jon would be miserable at his what-was-supposed-to-be-a private, intimate ceremony. The entire event reminded her of the movie *My Big Fat Greek Wedding*, only Italian-style.

Pulling Ken and Izzy to the side, Suzy said, "I don't know what the hell is going on. Mama Gia made food. *Food.* Don't ask me how or where but I can't watch. I've lost control. I'm going inside to talk to the caterer and servers." Taking a deep breath, she handed her husband and stepdaughter armfuls of green plastic grass.

"What's this?" Izzy asked.

Suzy fanned herself with her hand. "Grass skirts for the food, cake, and gift tables."

Ken chuckled. "Kind of like a hula girl without the girl."

"Exactly." Suzy winked. "Will you use two-sided tape and clips to attach the grass skirts? If you run out, I've got more supplies in my car."

Ken kissed his wife's cheek. "Iz and I are on it. And don't worry about the food. Everyone loves food. The wedding will be perfect. What could go wrong?"

Suzy rolled her eyes as she stepped inside Coconuts. Glancing around the darkened room, she found Gus and discussed the champagne toast yet again. The server assured her he had the alcohol under control.

She studied her song list for the first dance and took a phone call form Marc at Artistic Blooms who said he'd already made another Bird of Paradise centerpiece to replace yesterday's disaster, adding a driver was on his way.

"Wonderful. I owe you, Marc." Stomach summersaulting, Suzy considered downing a glass of merlot to calm her nerves but decided against it. She wanted to be clearheaded. Stepping toward the restroom to freshen up, she wished her friends would arrive early, then laughed. *Alex arriving early might give everyone a heart attack.* As she pushed the restroom door open, she wondered what Fernando's mother was doing outside. *Food is food, right?* She placed her face in her hands. *Who am I kidding?*

~ ~ ~

An empty table proved irresistible to Fernando's brothers and mother who took full advantage of the space. Bruschetta, two huge pans of lasagna, and two enormous platters of spaghetti and meatballs now adorned the crowded food table.

Mama Gia crossed her arms, stood back, and admired the feast. Pointing, she said, "Those two. Switch those platters. Will look better."

In a rush to adjust the hot, heaping dishes, Luigi slopped nearly half of the spaghetti onto the white tablecloth. "*Cazzo.*

Fuck. Fuck. Fuck." Grabbing a handful of hibiscus flowers, he threw them in a clump over the glaring, red sauce.

Smacking him on top of his head, Mama Gia said, "What's wrong with you? Your brother's getting married. Everything must be perfect."

"Ow, Ma," Luigi said, as he rubbed his head.

Frankie spit on his hand and wiped at the red sauce, which created a bigger smear. "Shit."

"Now look what you've done." Mama Gia thumped him on the head for good measure.

Vinny crossed his arms and planted his feet. "I ain't touchin' notin'."

Izzy's eyes bulged as she observed the chaos. "I'm glad I didn't do that." She grinned and texted someone. "I learned a new curse word."

Ken noticed the commotion, fished in his pocket, found antibacterial gel, squirted it on the stain, and rubbed it with the heel of his palm. But the spot wouldn't budge. "I don't suppose anyone has an extra tablecloth."

Suzy came back outside and crossed the sand. "It's looking very beach-like and—" She stopped short. "You brought so much food. Where's the actual planned wedding food going to go?"

Luigi stood in front of the stain. With one hand, he scooted another platter to the side. "No worries. We'll make room." More red sauce slopped onto the tablecloth. "Dammit."

Mama Gia thumped him again.

"Ma, stop it. I've got a headache now."

Suzy ran toward the table. "Oh, my God. There's red sauce everywhere." She picked up several sticky, dripping Hibiscus flowers and leis splattered with marinara sauce. Her shoulders drooped. "The leis are for the guests. They're supposed to be at the guestbook."

Her voice rose to a fever pitch. "You've ruined the table. You've ruined the menu. You're ruining everything. Who do you think you—"

Mama Gia crossed her arms. "I'm the groom's mother."

"So am I. *Plus,* I'm the wedding planner. That means I plan weddings—by myself. I've done this for years."

Mama Gia glared at her. "Wedding guests need food. Lots of food." She gestured wildly with her hands. "I don't see any food here except mine. It's a good thing we stayed up half the night cooking."

Suzy's eyebrows shot up. "How did you manage—"

Mama Gia spewed several Italian phrases, Izzy reached for her phone, and Ken and the boys stood stock still.

In an attempt to calm the situation before Jon and Fernando arrived, Suzy asked again, more calmly. "Please tell me—in English—how you managed to cook this food since we were all at the rehearsal dinner last night."

"Simple. We cooked in our room. We have a suite. Plenty of room. All I needed was a sink and a microwave. I talked the breakfast manager into letting me use their oven. Vinny and Frankie made two runs to the supermarket while Luigi and I cooked non-stop for three hours." Pleased with her cooking prowess, she dusted her hands. "*Finito*. Done."

Suzy's mouth flew open. "You cooked *all* of this in your hotel room?"

Mama Gia threw her hands in the air. "Of course. What's so difficult about that?" Her eyes challenged Suzy's.

Incredulous, Suzy suddenly felt like laughing. "Nothing, I suppose. Nothing at all." Part of her wanted to be angry but now the entire episode made her giggle. She felt like she was in a sitcom. "Our wedding guests certainly won't go hungry."

"I wanted to contribute. Fernando's my son, you know."

Suzy's tone softened. "You're right. Thank you. I guess we should have worked this out beforehand, but it's done.

Finito, as you said." She grinned. "Very impressively, I might add." Weighing her options, Suzy knew battling Jon's future mother-in-law would not be in his best interests. Turning toward the men, she said, "Will you bring another table out and see if Gus has a fresh tablecloth we can use. If it's a different color, we'll use it for the gift table." Winking, she added, "I'm learning to be flexible."

Chapter 23

After the soiled tablecloth was switched, Suzy eyed the makeshift beach. The sand had been smoothed, the white chairs were set up, the food tables were overflowing, and Izzy had rinsed off the leis in a bathroom sink inside Coconuts.

Fernando's brothers were busy stringing hundreds of glittering tiny white lights on the towering fake palm trees. Suzy stepped back to admire the makeshift luau.

It worked. The Coconuts parking lot is actually transforming into a beautiful beach. The food issue was a bump on the sand.

Suzy, Izzy, and Mama Gia worked in unison as they set out the guests' mementos and multi-colored leis on a table beside the guestbook. Jon and Fernando had chosen sand ornaments with a light dusting of glitter as wedding keepsakes. Guests could choose from hearts, palm trees, or flipflops. Each ornament had an orange ribbon at the top.

Suzy studied the parking lot. "I wonder where the hell Bill is."

"Bill?" Mama Gia asked. "I'm getting all of the names mixed up."

"My ex. Never mind." Suzy took a calming breath as the two women worked. "I wonder what Jon is doing right now."

"I was thinking the same thing about my Fernando." Mama Gia chuckled. "Knowing him, he's probably doing the salsa around the house. He's such a happy guy."

"I love that about him. He's a joy to be around." Suzy placed her arm around Mama Gia's shoulders. "You raised good boys."

Actually blushing through her smooth olive skin, Mama Gia said, "I know you wanted everything just so, but I cook when I'm nervous. Thank you for letting me contribute to the menu."

Suzy held up her hand. "No need to say any more. Your food looks and smells delicious."

After the DJ arrived, Suzy indicated where he should set up and was pleased he remembered to dress in a tropical yellow and white shirt. He wore frayed jeans and kicked off his shoes.

"Gotta get in the mood. The sand feels good. Nice touch, man, I mean, Suzy."

"Testing, testing." When the DJ was satisfied with his sound equipment, he played "Margaritaville" by Jimmy Buffet. "Let's get this party started."

Mama Gia grabbed Suzy's hand and they danced on the sand.

When the song ended, Suzy said, "We need a pre-wedding cocktail. I'll get Gus to bring us some wine. I hired him to serve. He's the best." She poked her head inside Coconuts and saw Gus behind the bar cleaning glassware. "Think we could get a couple of glasses of merlot, Gus?"

He grinned. "Wedding jitters?"

"Something like that."

Soon Gus appeared outside and handed them both a glass of wine. The mothers clanked their glasses together. Suzy said, "To our boys." Mama Gia repeated the phrase then they took a sip and hugged.

After drinking half her wine, Suzy set her glass near the floral arch and adjusted a couple of orchids. Once the sun set, she knew the lights on the palm trees would twinkle and checked to make sure each strand worked.

"When The Sun Goes Down" by Kenny Chesney blared from the speakers. Suzy grinned when she spotted Mama Gia and Gus dancing. After the song ended, she clapped and heard Gus mention his serving duties before he escaped inside Coconuts.

Suzy reached for Mama Gia's hand. "Let's make sure the altar is secure." After the women eyed the setup, Suzy asked, "What do you think?"

Mama Gia touched her chest and shook her head. "*Bellissimo*. It's breathtaking. I shouldn't have doubted you. This really does look like the beach." She chuckled. "Except for the ocean, of course."

Winking, Suzy said, "I'm not that good."

Ticking off a mental to-do list, Suzy remembered something she had forgotten. "Come with me."

"Where're we going?"

Pointing, Suzy said, "Near the altar. We need to find a big stick."

"A stick?" Mama Gia's brows furrowed. "For what?"

"You'll see." They scoured the area beneath a large maple at the edge of the parking lot until they found a thin branch. Suzy stepped toward the archway, poised the stick above the sand, and drew half a heart. She handed the stick to Mama Gia. "You draw the other half."

Mama Gia nodded. "Ah, I see what you're doing." Fernando's mother completed the heart and both women wrote the initials of their respective sons."

Mama Gia beamed. "Nice touch, Suzy. You think of everything."

"Thank you. I try." As they crossed the sand, Suzy stopped mid-step and stood transfixed.

Mama Gia halted her stride as she followed Suzy's gaze. "What's wrong?"

Chapter 24

Suzy's mouth went dry as she studied the couple whose eyes met hers. Everyone stood in place in what felt like a slow-motion film. Eventually, she found words. "I can't believe they came."

Mama Gia peered at the sixty-something couple. "Are those your parents?"

Suzy nodded, unable to speak. Her dad's dark, curly hair was now edged in gray. Her mother appeared thinner and possibly shorter. Swallowing, she whispered, "Jon must have told them."

Mama Gia patted her behind. "Go to your parents. Weddings are about family."

Suzy pushed her disastrous almost-wedding, her sister's involvement with her then-fiancé, and her mother's ridiculous reaction out of her mind. It was in the past. The *distant* past. Now she had Ken, Izzy, Jon, Fernando, and a baby granddaughter on the way. Her life was happy and full. It was past time to forgive.

Breaking into a near-gallop, Suzy spread her arms wide, kicking up sand, and nearly stampeding her parents. Her father ran toward her and embraced her in a tight bear hug. Burying her face between his shoulder and neck, she sobbed. "I'm so glad you're here, Dad. I should have called you long ago. I've missed you so much."

Gianni, Suzy's handsome father, smoothed her hair. "Shhh. It doesn't matter who called us. We're here now. We wouldn't have missed it."

Her mother, Ellie, flung her arms around her neck. "We've missed you, Suzy. I'm sorry about how I reacted at your wedding. It was, you know, messy with your sister and—"

Wiping away tears, Suzy put her finger to her mother's lips. "It's over. Let's don't talk about this ever again. I'm happily married now. Everything worked out."

She wrapped her arms around both parents. Between sobs, she said, "I've missed you so much. You haven't even met my new husband, Ken, or my stepdaughter, Izzy."

"You have a stepdaughter? Now you'll see the complications of a mother-daughter relationship." Ellie stared at her tan sandals. "Sorry. I shouldn't have gone there."

Suzy let the remark go. "Trust me, I've already endured several upheavals with Izzy. We're working on our relationship. But today is Jon's day." Pausing, she said, "By the way, I assume your grandson called to invite you." Feeling her cheeks flush, she added, "I'm ashamed I didn't call first."

"Let's don't discuss that either." Her parents exchanged glances and broke into wide smiles. "Jon *did* call us, but your new husband actually beat him to the punch."

Gianni chuckled. "Ken told us over the phone that you two were married. He apologized for not asking my permission but said you had a whirlwind wedding at your high school class reunion."

Suzy put both hands on her cheeks. "I can't believe this."

Her mother added, "We both remembered Ken from your high school days. You always pined for that boy. We're glad you're happy."

Gianni kept his arm around Suzy's shoulders. "We had a long chat with Ken. He's a good man. In fact, he insisted on paying for our flights to Crystal City. He wanted to surprise you."

Suzy stood, stunned. When she found words, she said, "I definitely married the right man."

Setting her tote bag on the sand, Ellie beamed. "And the very next day, Jon and Fernando called to tell us about their wedding and made the same offer."

Her father winked. "It appears everyone wanted to make sure we were here."

Suzy clapped a hand over her mouth. "My husband *and* my son called you. That makes me unbelievably happy." She squeezed her parents' hands. "Follow me, I want to introduce you to Fernando's family."

After handshakes, hugs, and many exchanges in Italian between the Russo clan and Suzy's half-Italian father, Suzy cajoled herself for never learning the beautiful language.

Clearly in her element, Mama Gia continued speaking in Italian, much to Suzy's dismay. Unfortunately, her translator Izzy had disappeared.

After a long exchange with Mama Gia, her father turned toward her. "Jon told us he has a big surprise—even bigger than the wedding. How is that possible? I hope he isn't moving to Europe."

Mama Gia's face fell. "I hope they *do* move to Europe someday, but probably not for a while with the—"

Suzy shot her a look. "I don't think it's our place to tell."

"Do you know what the surprise is?" Suzy's mother asked. "We're dying to know."

"Yes, Mom. Of course I know." Suzy's mind raced. Her parents were in for a shock. A *huge* shock. "I haven't yet seen Jon and Fernando. I'm sure they'll be happy to tell you everything. I'm sure you won't have to wait much longer."

Her parents glanced at one another. "So many secrets," Ellie said. "But we can wait."

Recognizing the loud muffler on Vanessa's car, Suzy watched as Vanessa parked across the street. "Hold that thought. I'll be right back."

Chapter 25

Rushing across the road to assist Vanessa, she watched as the freckle-faced beauty unbuckled her seatbelt, which was loosened to the max over her pregnant belly. After she finally disengaged herself, she gingerly stepped out of the car. "Hi, Suzy. Big day."

Suzy still couldn't believe how well the baby news had gone over. At first, Jon was mad at himself—and the entire world—since he had finally come out. But after he came to his senses and told Fernando the revelation, his partner embraced the astonishing news as if he were being told they had to move across town.

Vanessa leaned against her car. "Are you okay? You seem like you're in another world."

"I should be asking you that. I'm fine. Let me hold your purse." Suzy rubbed Vanessa's back. "You look beautiful, by the way."

"Thanks. Fernando and Jon chose this gorgeous dress for me. I'm glad they found one with a pink sash for the baby." Vanessa wiped sweat off her nose. "I'm hot and my feet are swollen." She flinched. "Ow. That was a big kick."

Suzy's eyebrows furrowed. "Are you sure you're up to this, hon?"

Bobbing her head, Vanessa said, "I'm sure. I wouldn't miss it."

"The ceremony won't last long, and we'll get you into the air conditioning soon."

Nodding, Vanessa plucked a miniature fan out of her purse. "Don't worry about me." She waddled a few steps and slipped her arm through Suzy's. "I get so out of breath these days." She rubbed her baby bump. "It won't be long now. I'm ready."

Suzy gulped. "I'm sure you are. By the way, Jon's grandparents—my parents—are here all the way from Canada."

"Really? I can't wait to meet them."

Suzy noticed her father never took his eyes off them as they crossed the street and wondered if her dad had guessed the momentous news.

After they crossed the street, Gianni extended his hand. "*Bambino*." He grinned. "That means baby."

Suzy's mother, Ellie, reached over and patted Vanessa's belly. "Sorry. I know you don't know me but I couldn't resist."

Vanessa laughed. "Don't worry. Strangers do that in the grocery store. I've gotten used to it." She turned toward Gianni. "Yes, I'm having a baby. In fact, this might be a jolt but I'm having your—"

Suzy tugged on Vanessa's arm. "We don't have time for the whole story." She glanced from Vanessa to her parents. "We'll fill you in after the wedding, Mom and Dad. It's time to get everyone in line for the procession. Dad, will you follow me? I'd love for you to escort me down the aisle." Her voice wobbled. "Since you didn't get to . . . before."

Her father beamed. "I'd be honored, Suzy Q. Just tell me when you're ready." He reached for his wife's hand. "Let's go sign the guestbook before the crowd arrives."

~ ~ ~

After straightening a few chairs, Suzy dusted sand off her hands and checked the time. Glancing at Mama Gia, she said, "I'm glad I brought a change of clothes. My wedding dress would have been sweaty and sandy by now." She peered down at her denim shorts and tee. "I'd better go freshen up before the guests arrive."

She studied a few early cocktail-drinking wedding guests and chuckled. "Guess I'm too late."

"I'll guard the beach." Mama Gia laughed. "Don't worry. I won't let my boys devour the food."

"Be right back." Suzy nodded and disappeared inside Coconuts.

Suzy rushed into the restroom, wiped sand off her feet with wet paper towels, opened the garment bag with her dress and shoes, changed, and reapplied lipstick at warp speed. Sticking a loose tendril back in her messy bun, she stepped into the bar area where she spotted the caterer and two servers carrying platters of seafood and vegetables for the food table. She gave them a thumbs-up. *Good luck finding a space. I'm tired of dealing with food.*

Chapter 26

Peeking out a side window, Suzy noticed guests had lined up to sign the guestbook. Smiling, she noticed Izzy had remembered to place leis around their necks and appeared to be enjoying herself and off her phone for once. Suzy marveled that the men remembered to wear Hawaiian floral shirts while most of the women wore tropical sundresses. *I guess some people read wedding invitations after all.*

She grinned as many guests kicked off their shoes and placed them in large baskets strategically placed near the guestbook. Many sported hats or sunglasses and chatted while holding little umbrella drinks: piña colada, rumrunner, and strawberry daiquiri cocktails, which Gus had pre-made, and placed in rows on a grass-covered bar.

Checking her watch, Suzy wondered where Ken was, why Bill still hadn't appeared, and jumped when she heard a familiar voice.

"How's the mother of the groom?" Alex hugged her from behind.

Suzy swiveled. "Impressive. You're here sort of early."

"You can thank Hope for that." Alex twirled in her knee length red, strapless sundress adorned with white sequined tropical flowers. A white gardenia was tucked behind her ear. "Approve?"

Whistling, Suzy said, "Definitely, as will all of the guys." Suzy glanced at Alex's shoes. "You look gorgeous but those red heels will sink in the sand."

Hope cleared her throat. "Hey, I'm here too. What about me?"

Both friends swiveled toward Hope who wore tan Capri pants, a pink blouse accented with dark green palm fronds, and silver sequined ballet flats.

"You look adorable, girlfriend, but you need this." Alex removed her flower and tucked it in Hope's mass of brown curls. "There. Perfect."

Hope touched the delicate floral. "Are you sure?"

"Positive." Alex fished in her purse. "Besides, I have another one." She plucked a silk purple hibiscus and pushed it over her ear.

"Do you have a rabbit in there, too, because I might need a magician today," Suzy said.

"Uh-oh. Trouble already?" Alex scanned the sparse crowd. "Where's Fernando's mother?"

Suzy glanced over her shoulder. "I just saw Mama Gia go into the restroom. From the red stain on her bosom, it looks as though she splashed a little marinara sauce on her dress."

"Marinara sauce?" Hope asked. "Did you change the menu? I thought you were serving seafood for the luau?"

Suzy lowered her voice and waved as a guest walked by. "*She* changed the menu. Apparently, she and her sons cooked all night so we'd have Italian food too."

Alex cocked an eyebrow. "She cooked at your house?"

"No. Somehow, they cooked a feast in her hotel room."

"Wow. That's impressive." Alex grinned. "It'll be eclectic."

Hope rubbed Suzy's arm. "I'm surprised you're handling this so well after all the planning you've done for Jon's wedding." She hugged Suzy. "Surprised—and proud of you."

Shrugging, Suzy said, "I'll be honest. My blood boiled at first but the more she discussed wanting to contribute and how much they love pasta, I realized it's her son's wedding too. I'm forcing myself to go with the flow."

"Aren't you mature?" Alex readjusted the flower in her hair. "Too bad I don't have that gene."

Leaning forward, Suzy whispered, "My parents are here."

Hope gasped. "What? After the falling out from your—"

"Almost-wedding." Alex finished her sentence. "How did your parents know about Jon and Fernando's wedding?"

Filled with emotion, Suzy's voice wobbled. "Both Ken and Jon invited them. They said Ken paid for their plane tickets from Canada."

"I'm glad. Family feuds are horrible." Hope teared up. "I know that all too well. Having them here will make the day complete."

"Ditto." Alex put her hands on her hips. "We need some wine to celebrate. Where's Gus?"

As if on cue, Mama Gia toddled over with a wet spot above her breast and a tray of small shot glasses containing a yellow liquid. "Suzy, I hope you don't mind but I had a little chat with the bartender earlier and made sure he had limoncello. Let's have a celebratory drink before the wedding. It's a must at every Italian wedding."

Suzy reached for a tiny shot glass. "I'm glad you remembered."

Mama Gia nodded and smiled. "Drink yours first."

"No." Alex reached for the tray. "I'll hold this, so the two moms can enjoy the first two shots."

Hope whispered, "I think you have a maturity gene after all."

"Haha. Not really." While Suzy and Mama Gia clanked their miniature glasses together, Alex added, "I simply don't like limoncello, but I'll force it for this happy occasion."

"Cheers." Hope clanked her glass against theirs as one by one all four women drank a shot and gave quick toasts to Jon and Fernando.

"To our boys. Where are they?" Mama Gia asked.

Suzy reached for her hand. "They must be outside by now. Let's go find them."

Alex took Hope's arm. "I think that's our cue to take a seat."

~ ~ ~

After Alex and Hope signed the guestbook, were donned with multi-colored leis by Izzy, they trudged through the thick sand.

Hope glanced from side to side. "Suzy outdid herself. I actually feel like I'm at the beach. I've never walked on sand before." Kicking off her ballet flats, she said, "It's easier to walk barefoot. The sand feels great. Try it."

Alex peered at her friend sideways as her heels dug into the sand with each step. "Don't you remember who you're talking to? I don't do bare feet on sand—or anything."

"Oh, yeah, Miss OCD." Hope shrugged. "Never mind."

Hope and Alex made their way to the fourth row opposite Vinny, Frankie, and Luigi, who waved and winked, obviously recognizing them from the previous night. The men were dressed in khaki slacks and matching floral shirts, one green, one red, and one blue.

Waving back, Alex whispered to Hope, "I can't imagine raising four boys."

Hope's mouth flew open. "I've never heard you utter anything about kids except for Tony's son, I mean nephew, Joey."

Adjusting her dark, oversized sunglasses, Alex said, "That's because I don't plan to have any."

"That's what they all say," Hope said.

Alex raised her chin defiantly. "You're one to talk. You don't have any kids."

"How did we get on this? My students at school are kids enough for me. Besides, that would require a husband—or at the very least a boyfriend."

"Not really with modern science, but let's change this dicey subject." Alex glanced at the mingling wedding guests as she scanned the beachy venue. "I feel more relaxed already. Maybe I can ship some sand into my office. Dump some on top of Hannah."

Giggling, Hope said, "That's terrible but understandable." Pushing her toes under the sand, she dabbed sweat off her forehead with a tissue. "I hope they start soon. It's remarkably hot for this time of year."

Chapter 27

After not finding the grooms-to-be outside, Suzy and Mama Gia glanced around the darkened bar for Jon and Fernando.

Suzy's stomach lurched as Jon's impulsiveness gnawed at her. *Surely, he wouldn't chicken out. Maybe they're hiding out in the men's room.*

While Mama Gia downed another limoncello, Suzy gave last-minute instructions to Vanessa and her dad and made sure her mother was already seated on the second row. While peeking at her watch for the hundredth time, Jon came from behind and kissed her cheek.

"Hi, Mom. I can't believe the big day's finally here."

Fernando kissed her other cheek as Mama Gia bustled over and gave them all a group hug. "*Sono felice.*" He grinned. "That means, 'I'm happy'."

"I'm happy too." Suzy hugged them both, took a deep breath, and clapped her hands together, clearly in wedding planning mode. "We need to start the procession. Everyone's waiting in the hot sun." She turned toward the grooms. "The priest is already standing at the arched platform. Have you two decided whether you'll walk down last or would you prefer to go out the side door and stand at the front before the procession begins?"

The men exchanged glances and simultaneously said, "We're walking down last."

Fernando grinned. "We might as well make a grand entrance, don't you think? I'm all about grand entrances. I wanted to salsa down the aisle but Jon wouldn't go for it."

Jon reached for Fernando's hand. "I think we're going to shock everyone enough with Vanessa and the baby. Why don't we walk as normally as possible and hold hands like the typical couple we are?"

"Ah, yes. We're definitely typical, well, except for the baby thing." Fernando smiled at Vanessa. "It might be unorthodox to some, but not to me."

"Hey, who said we're unorthodox?" Vanessa playfully punched him.

Fernando kissed her freckled cheek. "You know I love you."

She beamed. "Ditto."

Gianni's face was a combination of excitement and puzzlement. "I might be discovering your surprise but I'm confused."

Suzy patted his arm. "Later, Dad. We've got to begin."

"Enough chatter, everyone." Mama Gia wiped her hands on the sides of her dress and glanced at the wet spot which was thankfully almost dry. "Tell us what to do, Suzy."

"On it." Suzy put her hands on everyone's shoulders and lined them up near the outer door. She placed Mama Gia at the front to be escorted by her son, Vinny. Her three sons had fought over who would get to accompany their mom. After a few bombastic arguments, they ended up arm wrestling for the honor. Suzy shook her head at how different Fernando was from his rough and tumble brothers.

Suzy positioned her father behind Mama Gia to hold her spot. Vanessa would proceed after the moms and didn't want an escort, saying baby made two. Jon and Fernando lined up to go last. Once everyone was in place, Suzy asked, "Ready, everyone?"

They proceeded to the side door as a sweaty Vinny appeared and propped it open. Suzy noticed Vinny's dark hair had begun to curl around the edges. She winked at Jon and Fernando, and kissed her dad's cheek. "I'm so glad you're here."

Gianni squeezed his daughter. "Likewise, honey."

Everyone squinted as bright sunlight filled Coconuts. A few patrons were at the bar but Gus had told the regulars about the wedding and most had steered clear of the venue.

Heart racing from both nerves and excitement, Suzy attempted to will herself to relax. *The boys' luau beach wedding came together. My parents are here, Fernando's family made it over from Europe, the grooms are ecstatic, and Vanessa still hasn't had her baby. Even Izzy is being pleasant. All is finally going according to plan.*

Chapter 28

Alex peered over her shoulder. "I wonder if Vanessa will be in the procession." As if directed, she saw the young, pregnant woman toddle past the door. Wincing, Alex said, "Poor thing looks miserable. When is she due again?"

"In two weeks, I think. I don't know the exact date." Hope held her frizzy hair off her neck and fanned herself. "Can you imagine how this baby is going to change Suzy's life?"

Alex shook her head. "Our best friend is going to be a grandmother."

Hope grinned. "I can't wait to babysit."

"Have fun. I'm afraid of babies." Alex adjusted her dress. "They make me feel old."

"Don't be silly. We're young at heart and always will be."

Alex watched as Izzy placed leis around the necks of a few last-minute stragglers. Soon, everyone settled onto a chair facing the floral archway. The priest smiled as beads of sweat formed on his forehead. Guests snapped photos, fanned themselves, and chatted.

"Isn't that sweet?" Hope pointed toward a huge heart drawn in the sand near the altar. Jon and Fernando's initials were carved in the middle.

"Nice touch," Alex said. "Suzy thinks of every detail but I'm nervous for Suzy and Jon."

"I'm nervous, period," Hope said.

Another guest shushed them as Mama Gia and Suzy were escorted down the aisle. Leaning over, Alex said, "Suzy's dress is stunning."

"It's gorgeous." Hope touched the flower in her hair. "I see Suzy added a Bird of Paradise bloom beside her chignon. We all have flowers in our hair."

Mama Gia posed for the cameras as Vinny held his head high, likely trying to appear taller since he was the shortest brother—and since he had won the honor of escorting his mother.

~ ~ ~

Suzy squeezed her father's arm. "Ready, Dad?" Her eyes glistened with happy tears.

Gianni kissed Suzy's cheek. "You look beautiful, honey."

"Thanks, Dad. It's our turn." They took a step toward the door leading toward the sandy ceremony.

Gianni whispered as they stepped onto the sand. "I wish your sister could have come. Tara wanted to surprise you but couldn't get off work."

"I understand." Suzy turned back toward Jon one last time and blew him a kiss. She smiled at the photographer and well-wishers as they made their way down the white rose petal-filled aisle. Perfectly shaped orange ribbons hung from the back of the chairs at the end of every row.

Dressed in a maxi-length green dress with sequins, Mama Gia waved so much her Bird of Paradise wrist corsage nearly fell off. Vinny puffed out his chest and made a cocky face as he passed his brothers.

Both mothers took their seats on the front row on opposite sides of the aisle.

"Suzy looks gorgeous," Hope said.

"She's already crying. Look." Alex pointed. "She's dabbing her eyes."

"You would be too," Hope said.

"I don't cry."

Another guest hushed them as Vanessa ambled down the aisle. Wearing white sequined flip-flops and a floor-length white gown with a pink ribbon at the empire waist, the red-faced young woman adjusted the sash above her baby bump.

Hope whispered, "She looks miserable."

"She's as big as my Mustang."

Hope frowned. "*Alex*."

Shrugging, Alex said, "Well, she is."

Once she made it down the petal-covered aisle, Vanessa unceremoniously plunked down in a chair on the second row near Jon's grandparents.

As the traditional wedding march began—seemingly the only thing traditional about this day—everyone rose and stared toward a beaming Jon and Fernando. Holding hands, the two men were dressed in matching white linen pants, white button-down shirts, and sported Bird of Paradise boutonnieres. Both were barefoot and couldn't stop smiling.

A photographer snapped photo after photo as the grooms made their way down the aisle while enjoying raucous cheers, thumbs-up, and a few happy tears. Once they stood before the priest, the photographer crouched nearby.

Luigi, Vinny, and Frankie hooted and whistled.

"Yo, Fernando."

"Yeah, baby."

"He's all yours, Jon."

Alex studied the grooms. "Aren't they handsome? I love their matching white outfits." She chuckled. "I think someone went to a tanning salon first."

"Shhh. Let's watch," Hope said. "This is dreamy."

As the priest welcomed everyone, Bill slid in beside Alex who jumped.

Grinning, he said, "Sorry to startle you. Scoot over."

Alex whispered, "Glad you could make it. You're making me look good. I'm usually the late one."

Suzy's ex grimaced. "Not only am I tardy, I promised to help set up today."

"What happened?" Alex asked.

"I was researching a hunting site in Chama. I got excited, called my buddies, and lost track of time. Simple as that." He ran his fingers through his hair. "Suzy will kill me. She always hated how my hunting got in the way of our marriage." Bill sighed. "Guess she was right."

Another guest quieted them. Alex glared at the woman, saying, "Relax." She turned toward Bill. "Yep, she's going to kill you."

Hope stared at the two grooms as if she were watching her favorite movie. Elbowing Alex, she said, "This almost makes me want to get married."

"Not me," Alex said.

Chapter 29

In a dream-like state, Suzy reached for Ken's hand and whispered, "I can't believe it's finally here. We did it."

"*You* did it." Ken kissed his wife's cheek. "I hope you're finally able to relax and enjoy every moment."

Suzy nodded as she listened to the priest. Her heart swelled as Jon and Fernando locked eyes. She could tell Jon was nervous by the twitching vein in his forehead but he masked it with a wide smile.

The priest read a short passage, then asked Jon and Fernando to exchange their carefully written vows.

Jon cleared his throat. Voice wobbling, he said, "Never in my life did I think I would find someone who would com—"

Blinking back tears and dabbing her eyes with a tissue, Suzy strained to hear over a rustling commotion behind her.

An animalistic moan filled the air followed by a second groan and a long wail. "Oh, my God! My water just broke."

Suzy's eyes bulged. "No way." She glanced back at Vanessa and knew what was about to unfold. Her heart thrashed when she saw a pool of water underneath Vanessa's folding chair creeping toward her own feet. Yelling in the direction of the priest, she bellowed, "Hurry up. We're having a baby." Scrambling out of her chair, she rushed toward Vanessa. "Someone call 9-1-1."

As if choreographed, Jon and Fernando snapped their heads around at exactly the same time. They stared at Vanessa, mouths agape, then winced as she writhed and attempted to pull her wet dress off her crotch.

"Holy shit." Jon clapped his hand over his mouth and glanced back at the priest. "Sorry. But holy shit."

The crowd gave a collective gasp.

Vanessa endeavored to stand but Suzy eased her back down and waved frantically toward Fernando's three brothers. "Help, please. Two of you get on either side of her. Pronto."

Murmuring, guests shifted in their seats, some horrified, others excited. Hope ran inside Coconuts and returned with a clean, white tablecloth. She laid it on the ground. "Steer Vanessa over here."

Alex and Bill ran over and held one end of the tablecloth.

Face glistening with sweat, Vanessa's auburn hair stuck to her forehead. She moaned like a wild animal. "The baby's coming. I don't think we can wait for the ambulance."

"Oh, my God." Suzy stood and cupped both hands around her mouth. "Is there a doctor or nurse here?" She and Ken helped ease the young woman atop the tablecloth as a woman jumped up saying she was an orthopedic surgeon.

Suzy waved her over. "Hurry." Managing a smile, "I'm sure you can help, even though this isn't your usual territory."

The surgeon reached for Vanessa's wrist, checked her pulse, and told her to take even, calming breaths.

Wide-eyed, Suzy glanced at Ken. "We may have to deliver a baby at Coconuts."

He stared at a writhing Vanessa. "Let's hope not."

A siren filled the air. Red and blue lights swirled and brakes screeched. "Thank God they were fast." Suzy raked her fingers through her hair and glanced toward Jon, whose face was ashen and twisted, obviously torn between standing beside his groom and tending to his former girlfriend.

Suzy bellowed again. "Hurry up, Father. Marry them. Jon and Fernando need to witness this birth."

Fernando addressed the Father. "Get to the bottom line, please." He glanced toward Vanessa. "Hurry."

Even more sweat formed on the priest's face. "Do you, Jon, take Fernando to be your wedded husband and do you, Fernando, take Jon to be your wedded husband?"

Both men said "Yes" and plucked matching, engraved silver bands from their pockets. Without being told, they shoved them onto each other's ring fingers.

"I now pronounce you married. You may kiss each other."

Suzy's eyes glistened as she heard murmurs of the familiar, extremely rushed vows, followed by "I do" from both men. Standing, so she could watch her son get married, Suzy witnessed the two men thrust rings on each other's fingers. Jon and Fernando embraced, kissed, and the crowd roared as Vanessa punctuated the ceremony with moans following each contraction.

In the background, the minister said, "Congratulations to Mr. and Mr. Jon Jacobs and Fernando Russo."

The second after their quick kiss, the grooms bounded toward Vanessa. Wide-eyed guests exchanged banter and nervous laughter as they remained seated and gawked in the direction of the howling pregnant woman. The ambulance sirens didn't quite mask her wails.

"Is she okay?" Fernando bent down and stared at a distraught Vanessa. He reached for her hand. "Are you okay? You sound miserable."

Vanessa curled on the sheet and twisted her face. Through clenched teeth, she hissed, "I'm fine."

Alex grimaced as the young mom writhed. "Remind me to never have a baby."

"I can't believe this." Jon gulped as he caressed Vanessa's cheek. "We're here for you. We're going to the hospital with you."

Fernando chimed in. "Absolutely. We wouldn't miss this."

Vanessa said a faint, sorrowful, "I've ruined your wedding."

Jon reached for her hand. "No, you didn't." He managed a chuckle. "You just sped it up a bit."

Fernando smoothed her hair. "You didn't ruin anything. In fact, you added an extra special bonus."

Paramedics exited the ambulance and ordered everyone out of the way. After they slid her onto a gurney, Vanessa raised her head. "If you come to the hospital, what about your reception and all that food?"

Fernando tsk tsked. "Honey, a baby trumps a reception. We can have always have a party later."

Heart full, Suzy beamed, overcome with happiness and joy. All of the waiting for this momentous occasion, and now, the men were handling it, well, like men. She couldn't be more proud.

Fernando held Vanessa's hand as Jon crouched on the other side. "Let's go have a baby."

Suzy overheard one guest say, "I'll never forget this wedding." An arm around her husband, she sighed with relief as the paramedics worked.

"*Bambino*." Mama Gia dabbed her eyes and stood in the healthcare workers' path.

"Ma'am, step back. We need to get her to the hospital unless you want to have a baby right here in the parking lot."

Kissing her cross necklace, Mama Gia handed a rosary to Vanessa whose hands were clenched into fists.

"Mama, I'll take it. She has other things on her mind right now." Fernando slid the rosary into his pocket.

Vanessa wailed and writhed as two paramedics lifted her inside the ambulance. The female driver got behind the wheel, rolled her window down, and shouted in Suzy's direction, "See you at the Crystal City Hospital."

Chapter 30

Breasts bouncing, Mama Gia corralled her sons. Between breaths, she asked, "Where's the hospital? We're going too."

Suzy's heart raced thinking about all of the commotion but knew the Russos had as much right to be there as the rest of the family. "Crystal City Hospital's on Sunshine and National. Meet you there. Come on, Jon and Fernando." Sprinting toward her car, Suzy stopped midway as she remembered Izzy. "Wait. I almost forgot my stepdaughter."

"What's new?" Izzy said.

Ken actually frowned at his daughter. "Izzy, this is Jon and Fernando's big day. We had a talk about this. There's going to be a new addition to the family. Hurry up and get in the car."

As Suzy backed out, she glanced toward the wedding venue. The crowd had gathered around the food and drinks. The DJ flooded the air with beachy songs. *The show must go on—with or without the wedding party.*

Happy the guests stayed, she drove away, but frowned. *The cake. Their beautiful tropical cake complete with palm trees, a colorful parrot on the side, and topped with two miniature grooms.* Suzy let out a small groan. "Jon and Fernando didn't get to cut and eat their gorgeous cake. It doesn't matter. The baby matters."

"I hope we get to the hospital in time," Izzy said from the backseat.

Rubbing her temples, Suzy didn't respond. Instead, she pushed harder on the gas pedal. Running a yellow light and then a red one, she put her flashers on. "I hope she doesn't have the baby in the ambulance."

A white-faced Fernando nodded. "Me too."

"Mom, hurry." Jon tightened his seatbelt. "Don't lose the ambulance."

"I'm on it." Suzy glanced in the rearview mirror and noticed Jon and Fernando were holding hands so tightly that both of their knuckles had turned white.

Ken reached over and rubbed Suzy's leg. Eyes twinkling, he said, "Hi, Grandma."

"Not yet. I'm not a grandma yet, anyway. I'd much prefer she have the baby in a sterile delivery room." Gasping, Suzy said, "My parents. I forgot my parents."

"Under control. I asked Alex and Hope to bring them." Ken wrinkled his nose. "I think I saw Bill cramming into Alex's car too."

Suzy shrugged. "I guess we really are one huge, extended family now."

The next ten blocks felt like fifty. Suzy pressed on the gas, passed Mama Gia, and rolled down the window, motioning for her to follow.

Another siren wailed. Suzy glanced in the rearview mirror. "You've got to be kidding me." Her shoulders slumped as a patrol car with swirling lights got behind her. Peering in the mirror again, Suzy said, "That cop looks like Tony. I'm not stopping."

Ken stiffened. "You might get arrested."

"And I might not. I think there are surely exceptions to the rule. Like a baby."

Ken's eyebrows shot up. "I hope so."

Izzy peered back at the officer. "This is lit. I feel like I'm on a cop TV show. This has been the best wedding ever."

Ken turned to face his daughter in the backseat. "Don't get any ideas, Iz. Suzy would normally never speed."

"Right. A baby delivery is an exception, Izzy." When Suzy caught the next red light, she stopped and checked her rearview mirror. The cop jumped out of his car. It wasn't Tony.

Sauntering toward her vehicle much too slowly, a short police officer with a buzz cut said, "Do you realize you were speeding, ma'am? Pull over to the shoulder after this light turns green."

"I can't. Baby." The light turned green and Suzy stepped on the gas.

The cop jumped back in his car and followed her all the way to the hospital, siren blaring.

Undaunted, Suzy parked near the emergency room entrance in time to see the paramedics take Vanessa out of the ambulance and rush inside. "Thank goodness she hasn't had the baby."

Jon and Fernando hopped out of her vehicle like they were kangaroos.

As Suzy threw her purse over her shoulder, the uniformed officer approached her again. He wasn't smiling.

"License and registration, please." He put one hand on his hip. "You're going to get a ticket, lady. Maybe two."

Suzy felt her face flush. "My, my . . . Vanessa is having a baby."

The officer raised his eyebrows. "Your daughter?"

"No, she's my—"

Fernando's voice rose. "The baby's going to be my daughter." He pointed toward Jon. "Our daughter. My new husband's daughter." Motioning with his head toward Suzy, he added, "Her granddaughter."

The cop narrowed his eyes. "Sounds complicated." He followed their eyes as the doors closed behind the paramedics.

"Complicated isn't the half of it." Suzy sighed. "If you must give me a ticket, will you please do it inside? My son got married a few minutes ago. Now he's about to become a father. We don't want to miss the birth."

The officer regarded Jon, Fernando, Suzy, Ken, Izzy, and the bustling scene as the Russos ran over and filled the air with Italian phrases. An almost-smile crossed his lips. He closed his ticket book. "Go on." He added, "But don't run any more red lights." The cop paused. "And congratulations."

They sprinted toward the hospital. Suzy shouted, "Thank you" over her shoulder.

As everyone bolted toward the enormous revolving doors, they nearly toppled an elderly man and woman over in the process. Many "sorrys" later, they shot past the couple explaining "baby." The older couple nodded and waved.

Chapter 31

Suzy approached a stern-looking nurse whose black hair was pulled into a too-tight bun. Speaking fast, she said, "I'm Suzy Jacobs. A pregnant woman was just brought in through the ER. Her name is Vanessa Nelson. What room is she in?"

"I can't give out any information." The employee turned toward her computer. "HPPA regulations, you know."

Between the rushed wedding, the cop, and the early birth, Suzy had had enough. "You must be kidding."

Standing at the counter, Jon's voice rose to a crescendo after the clerk continually asked whether they were family. "We don't want to miss the birth."

Staring at her computer screen, the strict nurse said dully, "We keep the doors locked for security. I repeat. Are you family?"

Suzy decided to let Jon take the lead.

He shifted from foot to foot. "Not exactly."

Fernando's voice rose. "Yes, we are."

Over her half glasses, the clerk peered from one man to the other. Jon and Fernando were still dressed in matching white linen outfits wearing flip-flops that read "Groom."

Mama Gia stepped toward the counter, waved her arms, and said a string of sentences in Italian, including *Bambino*.

Suzy leaned across the counter, getting nearly nose to nose with the clerk. She pointed toward Jon and hissed, "He's the dad. Let us in."

The clerk studied Jon and Fernando. "It looks like you two just got married, so, I'm sorry, but this doesn't compute. We have to be very careful, you know." Lowering her voice, she added, "We had an attempted baby kidnapping last month." Staring behind them at the growing line of patients and family members waiting to check in, she waved them aside. "Next."

Easygoing Fernando stepped up to the counter, pointed toward Jon, and said a little too loudly, "My husband knocked up his former girlfriend at their high school prom, okay? That's his baby. Will you let us in now?"

The woman's mouth fell open as she simultaneously hit the buzzer. "Why didn't you say so?" The wide steel doors magically opened. Everyone rushed inside the gleaming, antiseptic hallways. The clerk ran after them. "Wait. With all of the commotion I almost forgot. You need these." She handed a fistful of hospital badges toward Suzy. "You have an interesting family."

Like in a cartoon, everyone crowded into the hallway and nearly got stuck in the waiting room doorway. The usual-sulky Izzy burst into giggles. "Two at a time, everyone, just like the Ark."

As soon as they took over the waiting area and plopped on worn, gray chairs, Ken, Izzy, Jon, and Fernando said they were going in search of coffee. Each returned with two fistfuls of coffee cups.

Ken sipped his coffee and handed a cup to Suzy. "We pretty much cleaned out the break room."

"I'm too jittery to drink caffeine. You can have mine." Suzy rubbed her arms. "It's freezing in here. Why are hospitals always so cold?"

Pacing, Jon asked, "What's taking so long?" He walked in the same spot so many times, Suzy feared he'd wear a hole in the carpet.

"I'm sure everything's fine. First babies generally take longer," Suzy said.

"But her water brokc," Jon said.

Suzy crossed her legs. "So did mine with you but it still

took another three hours before—"

Jon put his hands over his ears. "La. La. La. Honestly, Mom. No one wants to hear that, especially me."

"Or me," Izzy slouched in a corner chair beneath a television.

"Add me to that list too." Alex and Hope practically galloped inside with Bill and Suzy's parents on their heels. "Who's the Nazi at the front counter?" Alex asked. "What a witch. I thought I'd have to call our bank attorney before she'd let us come back here."

Suzy giggled. "I'm surprised she let you inside the family area. We were barely allowed admittance."

"You know Alex. She's persistent," Hope said.

"Easy peasy." Alex blew on her knuckles with satisfaction. "I told her we're the aunties, grandparents, and great-grandparents."

Hope hugged Suzy. "Any news?"

The door to the waiting room flew open as a woman dressed in green scrubs with a white mask dangling below her chin rushed inside. "Who's the family of Vanessa Nelson?"

"We are," every single person said in unison.

The doctor grinned. "Big family. Vanessa and baby are doing fine."

Jon and Fernando whooped and hugged. Suzy cried, and Mama Gia murmured prayers and kissed the cross on her necklace.

Alex and Hope embraced Suzy. "Congratulations, Grandma."

Jon turned to the doctor. "When can we see the baby and Vanessa?"

"Soon. Vanessa's getting breastfeeding instructions now. Baby and mother will both be in the same birthing room.

Fernando's face lit up as he reached for Jon's hand. "We're dads."

Jon stroked his chin and grinned. "Yep. We sure are."

Chapter 32

A too-long twenty minutes later, the doctor returned and asked if the father was present. Jon and Fernando exchanged glances.

Fernando gave Jon a nudge. "You are. Go ahead."

The doctor observed the interplay but only said, "Follow me."

Hesitating, Jon said, "Actually, we're co-parenting." He pointed toward Fernando. "We're both dads. Can he come too?"

The weary doctor said, "One at a time, please. Vanessa's extremely tired."

"It's okay." Fernando forced a grin. "I'll be fine."

Alex whispered to Suzy, "Fernando's crestfallen. Look at his sad face. This isn't right. He's going to be the dad too."

"I know but what can we do? I'd love for them both to see the baby at the same time but hospitals have policies."

"I don't like it." Alex jutted her chin out and paced. "I'll think of something."

Fernando's brothers played a card game in the corner. Bill and Ken alternately read magazines or watched television. Izzy stared at her phone, and Suzy's parents cuddled in the corner, content and excited after Suzy had filled them in on the momentous backstory. Hope held hands with Suzy while casting worried glances in Alex's direction.

Alex chewed on a nail, then brightened. "I've got it." Reaching for Fernando's hand, she said, "Come with me. You should be with them." She studied the group. "Am I right?"

Everyone nodded or murmured "Yes" as Alex tugged on Fernando's hand. "Trust me. I'll get you in the room."

Fernando's forehead creased. "How?"

"Watch and learn, baby." Alex took a deep breath, winked at Hope, and pushed the heavy door open.

Fernando took a tentative step behind Alex, obviously nervous about whatever stunt she had in mind. As the antiseptic smell filled his nostrils, he started as Alex took a few steps, tripped on something, and yelled out in pain.

Splayed on the shiny floor, Alex adjusted her position, rubbed her ankle, and moaned. "Ow. Help! Help!" She glanced around the empty hall, half sat, and spoke louder. "Hey. Does this hospital have any nurses or doctors?"

Frozen in place and clearly unsure as to whether he should retreat to the waiting area or continue with the charade, Fernando shoved his hands in his pockets, crouched down, and whispered. "Are you really hurt?"

"Shhh." Still dressed in a red strapless sundress, heels, and a purple Hibiscus flower behind her ear, Alex knew most men would find her irresistible.

Fernando tried to relax when he spotted two male nurses glance up from their computers, notice the gorgeous "patient" on the floor, and leap from behind the nursing station. He contained his amusement as they bounded toward Alex.

Both dressed in scrubs, the nurse with a mass of curly black hair bent down first and pressed on her leg. "Did you fall?"

Alex winced. "Uh-huh."

He gingerly touched her ankle. "Does this hurt?"

"Ow. Yes. My knee hurts too. I think I might need an x-ray." She snuck a glance toward Fernando and pointed with her head toward the patient rooms while the unknowing nurse continued to examine her ankle.

Fernando took the hint and disappeared down the hallway.

Alex waited until he was out of sight before assuring the nurses she didn't need a gurney. Smiling her biggest toothpaste-commercial smile, she said, "You guys are so good. I think your being here made me better." For good measure, she rotated her foot. "See? Nothing's broken. I'm fine."

The tall, balding nurse wasn't having it. "Let's get you to x-ray. I'll find a wheelchair."

"Wheelchair? What am I? Ninety?"

"Procedure, ma'am." The tall nurse persisted. "We take every precaution at CCH. In fact, I'll need to write up an incident report."

Alex groaned. "You're kidding, right? People trip all of the time. We don't need to make a federal case out of this." Suddenly regretting her decision, she decided to flirt with the curly headed nurse, turning all of her attention toward him. "How long have you worked here? I bet all of the female patients request you."

She watched as his eyes crinkled and had a feeling he knew she was up to something. "I love your curly hair. Do you take after your mom or dad?"

The nurse gave her an 'aw shucks' look. "Neither. I'm the only one with curly hair. Lucky me."

"You *are* lucky. Do you know how many people would kill for a head of hair like that?" She cocked her head, turning on her best charm as she adjusted her dress.

The tall nurse smacked his lips and stood. "Why don't you fill out the incident report, *Curly*? I've got my own paperwork to do for several, um, actual patients."

"Yeah, man. I've got this." Curly felt her ankle again. "Are you sure you don't want this x-rayed? I can get you to the Radiology Department in two minutes. Of course, they may be backed up and you'll sit in the hall for two hours but—"

Alex held up a hand. "I'm positive. I don't need an x-ray and I won't sue the hospital. You won't get into trouble unless your friend spills the beans. I'm perfectly fine. Besides, my friend is having a baby, er, his girlfriend is. Anyway, I don't want to miss the happy news. You wouldn't want that to happen, would you, Curly?"

The nurse grinned. "Guess not. I'm all about new beginnings and life."

Alex extended her arm. "Good. Thanks. Help me up." She paused. "If you ever need to open a checking account or take out a loan, hit me up. I work at Show-Me Bank."

His eyes twinkled. "I might just do that. What's your name? I'm Alec."

She bowled over laughing. "You won't believe this but I'm Alex. Alexandra, actually, but everyone calls me Alex."

"Alec and Alex. Interesting." He pulled her to her feet. "I'll ask one more time if you want a doctor to look at this."

"Nada, Alec." She winked. "You can take that to the bank."

"To Show-Me Bank. Cheesy but whatever." He took a step and turned back. "Wait. Weren't you with a guy earlier?"

Gulping, Alex said, "Not *with* him exactly. He's a friend of a friend. Actually, this is his wedding day. He married my best friend's son. It's complicated." Wanting to get the nurse off track, she said, "Remind me where the coffee is again."

"Follow me."

The nice nurse assisted Alex with finding the coffee area and even helped her carry a few cups into the waiting area. She cursed herself for the ploy because he truly was a kind man. But with Tony's antics and Gabe in New York, the last thing she needed was a third guy in the mix. Cheerfully, she pushed the door open with her hip while holding three cups of coffee. The nurse followed her inside with another three cups. "Thanks, Alec. You're one of the good guys."

A slight flush crept up his neck. "You're welcome. Watch where you're walking, okay?" He set the cups on the coffee table and exited, his eyes glued to Alex the entire time.

Hope sighed. "I peeked out the window. Only you could fake an accident and end up with a cute guy." She put her hands on her hips. "Wait. You rear-ended a cop two years ago, and now he's your boyfriend. Why don't these things ever happen to me?"

Alex shrugged. "Dumb luck, I guess. Who wants more coffee?"

Suzy sat next to her husband, Izzy scrolled Facebook, and Bill read a newspaper. Mama Gia held court with her sons, and Suzy's mother was sound asleep on her father's shoulder.

"It doesn't look like I missed anything." Alex sipped her coffee and complained about the cold java as Fernando burst through the door.

Chapter 33

Waving frantically, Fernando said, "Come. Come see our beautiful baby."

Everyone scrambled for the door, and again, nearly got stuck.

Hope giggled. "What is this? A fifties comedy routine?"

Sighing, Alex held out her arms, umpire style. "I say the grandparents and great-grandparents go first. Suzy, Ken, and Mama Gia, you three go ahead. Gianni and Ellie are next." Eager faces stared back at her as if she were an elementary school principal. After everyone lined up as she suggested, she said, "The rest of us will follow in an orderly fashion."

Giggling, Hope said, "Listen to Alex. She's our boss—or thinks she is."

Once they made it down the pristine hallway to the birthing room, Suzy burst into tears the moment she saw her scrub-wearing son holding the newborn. *His* baby girl. *Her* granddaughter.

As she cherished the touching scene, she noticed Fernando had also donned green scrubs and was glad Alex had diverted the healthcare professionals long enough for him to be part of this once-in-a-lifetime occasion.

Patting Vanessa's arm, Suzy asked the new mom if she felt okay, told her she loved her, and made a beeline for the baby. She stroked the baby's wet, red hair and kissed her plump, pink cheeks. "Looks like we have three generations of redheads."

Ellie fluffed her own red hair and beamed at Gianni. "That makes me happy. She's beautiful."

"Congratulations, everyone. She's a wonderful addition to our family." Gianni chuckled and glanced at Fernando. "Our second wonderful addition in a day."

Suzy beamed. "You're great-grandparents, Mom and Dad."

Vanessa propped herself up on two pillows, never taking her eyes off Jon and the baby. Fernando stood close by, pulled the white mask over his mouth and nose, and extended his arms. Glancing at Suzy and Mama Gia, he paused. "Unless you two want to hold her."

Mama Gia took a step but Suzy said, "Dads first. We'll get plenty of baby time." She stood by Vanessa's bedside and stroked her cheek. "I bet you're exhausted." The young mom's sweaty hair was pushed off her forehead and auburn ringlets framed her face.

"I'm good." She watched Jon and Fernando with her baby—their baby." I'm really good. In fact, this is my most perfect day ever."

Hovering, Mama Gia asked, "Where are your parents, Vanessa? Are they on their way?"

An uncomfortable silence filled the room. With the busy rehearsal dinner, wedding preparation, and wedding itself, Suzy hadn't had time to fill Mama Gia in. She couldn't even remember if she had told Alex and Hope how Vanessa's parents had basically abandoned her once they heard she was an unwed mother.

Suzy noticed Vanessa's eyes filled with tears. The last thing they needed on this celebratory day was a black cloud. "They won't be here."

"Why?" Mama Gia persisted.

"Because they're, uh, busy." Suzy pursed her lips and lowered her voice. "We don't need to discuss this now. I'll fill you in later."

Thankfully Mama Gia didn't press and lumbered over to Fernando who held the baby girl in the crook of his arms while Jon caressed her tiny pink arm. She leaned forward. "Beautiful *bambino. Amore Tesoro.*"

Jon frowned. "English, please." He stared at Fernando. "You're gonna have to give me a crash course in Italian. Grandpa never taught me. He always spoke English."

"I haven't forgotten." Gianni spewed a string of Italian phrases to prove his point.

Everyone laughed and Mama Gia joined in. Fernando translated. "Mama said, 'Beautiful baby. Sweet love'."

"Oh." Jon beamed at his new mother-in-law. Thanks. I, we, think so too."

Swaddled in a soft fleece blanket, the men placed the sleeping baby on Vanessa's chest. Vanessa pulled the blanket away and rubbed her wrinkled back. "Isn't she beautiful?"

Fernando's voice cracked. "She's perfect."

The young mother turned toward Jon and Fernando. "Sorry I messed up your wedding."

"Don't ever think that." Jon leaned over the bedrail. "Have you named her?"

Vanessa shook her head. "I was waiting for you and Fernando. There are way too many choices online and in baby books. It's overwhelming." Vanessa peered at both men. "Let's decide together."

Fernando snapped his fingers. "Let's call her Princess."

Suzy laughed, then her eyes moistened. In her wildest dreams, she still couldn't believe how this awkward predicament had already brought such joy and closeness among all of them.

Mama Gia never took her eyes off the baby. "She's a beautiful *bambino.*"

Fernando and Jon stood on either side of Vanessa's bed. "Take a picture, Mom."

"On it." Suzy angled her cell phone and took a gazillion photos.

Alex grabbed the cell from her. "Get over there, Grandma and Grandpa. You should be in the photo too."

After seemingly a hundred pictures were taken for every family and generation, and some posted immediately on Suzy's Weddings By Suzanne Facebook page, Fernando and Jon stared at the swaddled bundle.

"When will she open her eyes?" Fernando asked.

As if on cue, the baby's eyes fluttered open.

Jon leaned closer. "Her eyes are stunning. They're grayish blue. No, wait. They're bluish purple, almost violet."

Fernando clapped his hands together. "And . . . I believe we have a name: Violet."

"I love it. Vanessa and Violet. We'll be V-squared." She kissed her baby. "Hello, Violet. Your mother loves you."

"What a perfect, beautiful name," Jon said.

Fernando stroked the baby's cheek. "Princess Violet, welcome to your crazy, modern family." He sniffled. "I love you already."

Hope embraced Suzy. "That's a beautiful name and a darling baby. Congrats."

Alex slipped her arm through Suzy's. "Another Hallmark movie moment. I can't take much more of this sweetness." She kissed Suzy's cheek. "I'm thrilled for you, Suzy Q."

Cradling the newborn, Vanessa pulled a soft knit pink cap over the baby's head and kissed both her cheeks. "Hello, Violet."

Mama Gia nodded. "Lovely. And her middle name?"

Vanessa laid Violet on her chest and reached for Jon and Fernando while Jon kept his other hand on Violet's tiny back. "I've thought of a middle name. Since Jon and Fernando took the baby news so graciously, I want her middle name to be Grace." Vanessa wiped a tear trailing down her cheek as her voice caught. "Everyone, meet Violet Grace."

The room crupted with claps and cheers.

"What a gorgeous name," Alex said. "Violet Grace. She sounds like a movie star."

"Or a romance novelist," Hope added.

Tears streamed down Suzy's cheeks. "I love the name. I love her. Welcome to our family, Violet Grace."

Ken hugged his wife. Izzy smiled, adding, "Lit name," before retreating to the sanctity of her phone.

Jon scanned the room. "Where's Dad?"

"He said it was our moment since we're no longer married and left. I'm sure he'll catch up with you later, hon."

Jon's face fell. "He should have stayed, but okay."

The curly haired nurse, Alec, burst through the door. "Time for everyone to leave. The patient"—he glanced at the white board on the wall—"Vanessa must be tired. We don't want to wear her out, plus she needs to nurse." As he glanced around the room and spotted Alex, his lips curved into a smile. Giving an I-know-what-you-did nod, he said, "You were trying to distract me earlier, weren't you?" He waved his hand in the air. "Never mind. Don't answer. Everyone, say your good-byes." He glanced at Jon and Fernando. "The dads can stay if they wish."

Alex gathered her purse and elbowed Hope. "Let's go to Coconuts. We have a baby to celebrate." As she passed the male nurse she nudged him with her elbow. "Thanks for being cool."

Mama Gia clapped her hands. "Chop, chop, boys. You heard the man. Let's go. Besides, I need help warming the food. We never got to eat earlier."

Jon and Fernando exchanged glances.

Fernando grabbed the bed rail in a vise grip. "We're staying."

"Go ahead, Mom. Enjoy the food. We'd rather be here."

Suzy couldn't have been more proud of Jon and her new son-in-law. Glancing at Mama Gia, she said, "Let's save the food for tomorrow. Everyone come over to our house. We have a lot to celebrate." Giving both dads a group hug, she said, "You have your priorities in order, guys. I love you both."

Chapter 34

Cheri's heart hammered at the thought of seeing her friends, having cocktails at Coconuts, and staying in her late grandmother's, now her, home in Branson.

After a flawless event for Elton John who gave her a huge bonus and booked her for next year, Cheri proofed an exhaustive email to her staff at Fifth Avenue Catering. She outlined over a month's worth of celebrity events and menus, so she could enjoy her time in Missouri. Stretching, she shut off her computer.

As owner of Fifth Avenue Catering, she had worked hard to build her business and garner new clients such as Radio City Music Hall and a variety of Broadway and off-Broadway afterglow parties. A wildly successful romance author had hired Fifth Avenue Catering to provide champagne, wine, caviar, chocolate-dipped strawberries, cupcakes featuring edible mini-book covers, and expensive cheeses to celebrate her twenty-fifth book signing.

Several celebrities had retained her company's catering services for kids' graduations, anniversaries, and surprise parties for film crews after movie production ended. Cheri always showed up at those events because even though she was a celebrity chef she was still star struck by major movie stars. Happily, her client list had grown fast.

Unloading her dishwasher, Cheri chuckled to herself. Much to her mother's dismay, she had told her maid-slash-nanny, Pearl, to take a paid leave of absence—at least until her parents returned from Europe. At first, Pearl had been taken aback and said she wouldn't know what to do with herself. But after Cheri surprised Pearl and her daughters with an all-expense paid trip to Disney World, her maid happily and tearfully accepted.

Cheri grinned as she remembered the conversation with her mother, Victoria Van Buren, whose voice had risen two notches when she told her about sending Pearl and her family on an extended vacation. After a spirited discussion, Cheri had informed her mom she was capable of loading her own damn dishwasher. *My friends do it. So can I. I even know how to run a vacuum. Horrors.*

After she put the last glass away, her mind raced. *I know many people want to be like me but they don't realize I'd rather be like them. My jet-setting mother will never understand. She doesn't crave normalcy like I do.* Saying aloud to the walls, Cheri said, "I can't wait to see my new girlfriends and drink Angry Balls. What's wrong with me? I'm talking to myself—out loud. I must be lonelier than I thought."

Crossing her mostly white, modern penthouse apartment, Cheri peered out the window. She could see millions of twinkling lights on a multitude of Manhattan skyscrapers. Tourists lined the streets and horns blared non-stop. *I love this city.*

Escaping into her gigantic closet, Cheri rolled up her sleeves as she prepared to pack. Plucking massive amounts of casual and dressy clothes off hangers, she laid them neatly on the bed. Choosing skirts, jeans, shorts, yoga pants, tops, dresses, sweaters, and light jackets, she turned her attention to shoes and boots, placing rows of flats, heels, sneakers, and boots beside the bed. Satisfied she had enough attire to clothe a female army, Cheri opened her jewelry armoire.

Reaching for a string of pearls, gold and silver statement necklaces, turquoise and coral necklaces, gemstones, and several chunky bracelets, Cheri added her favorite elongated animal print necklace, a black turtleneck, dark jeans, and leopard print pumps for the next day's flight. She breathed a sigh of relief. *Done.*

Curious about the wedding, Cheri tossed and turned in bed. She checked the clock. *It's an hour earlier in Crystal City. I'm going to call Suzy.*

Chapter 35

After leaving the hospital, Ken hugged his wife and drove Izzy home. An exhausted-but-still-ready-to-celebrate Suzy rode to Coconuts with Alex. Hope drove behind them. In the hospital parking lot, Mama Gia and her boys mentioned jetlag and agreed to eat leftovers at Suzy's house the following day. More than happy to be alone with her girlfriends, Suzy told them good-bye.

Within minutes they arrived at the still-sandy wedding locale. Suzy was thrilled Coconuts had agreed to keep the truckloads of sand, saying they wanted to install a volleyball court. She noticed the rental company had already picked up the palm trees, white chairs, and tables. The food had been moved and some wonderful soul had lined up the flowers and gifts along a wall inside Coconuts. *Thank goodness. I don't have an ounce of energy left.*

Arms around her friends, Suzy dragged herself onto a stool and put her head on Alex's shoulder.

Squeezing Suzy, Alex said, "Look at us. We fit right in with the Coconuts theme in our tropical wedding clothes."

Hope strutted in her chair. "For once, I'm a fashionista."

Suzy giggled but groaned as her phone rang. "Now what?" Glancing at the caller ID, she noticed the person on the other end was Cheri Van Buren. "Hi, stranger. We missed you today."

"I'm absolutely sick about missing your son's wedding. After my event, I considered chartering a flight but had an emergency at Fifth Avenue Catering. In fact I've been putting out fires all day."

Suzy gasped. "Oh, no."

"Not real fires. I had to deal with a drunk sous chef and a couple of client issues. It's under control now." She paused. "This is your big day. Tell me all about the wedding."

Suzy cackled manically as tears of joy, relief, and exhaustion streamed down her cheeks. "The wedding is so *yesterday*."

"What?" Cheri switched ears. "I thought it was today."

"It *was* today, among other eventful happenings. Cheri, I'm too exhausted to talk. I'll let Alex explain. Thanks for calling. I hope to see you soon."

Suzy put her phone on speaker and handed it to Alex. "Will you bring Cheri up to speed?"

Snorting, Alex said, "Hello, Miss New York. We've missed you. Now, about the wedding . . . where should I begin?"

"I don't understand. Why is this wedding so funny? Last I heard you were having issues with the food at the rehearsal dinner."

Alex motioned to Gus for some wine. "Let me bottom line it for you. The wedding luau was gorgeous. Suzy outdid herself, as usual. Fernando's Italian family flew in—his mom, Mama Gia, and his three crazy brothers, Vinny, Frankie, and Luigi. The scene in the Coconuts lot could have been a movie set for *Jaws,* without the man-eating shark. Everyone wore tropical attire, had little umbrella drinks, and oh, I almost forgot. Suzy's estranged parents surprised her from Canada."

Gus appeared with their drinks. Alex took a sip of wine. "Hold on for the best part—"

Cheri's voice rose. "There's more?"

"Way more." Alex winked at Suzy, clearly enjoying being the wedding news reporter. "Did you ever meet Vanessa, Jon's former sweetheart, who he knocked up in high school before he came out?" Alex waved her hand in the air, even though Cheri couldn't see her. "It doesn't matter. Jon and Fernando magnanimously insisted Vanessa be in their wedding, and the bitch stole the show by having a baby on their wedding day."

Hope and Suzy simultaneously said, "*Alex*."

"Okay, I'm joking about the bitch part. She's a sweet, freckle-faced kid." Alex set the phone on the table and blew on her knuckles. "How's that for a recap?"

"I'm trying hard to keep up. Vanessa had her baby during the guys' wedding?"

Chortling, Alex said, "She was at least considerate enough to let the boys have a rushed ceremony after her water broke."

"I can't believe I missed this. What did she have?"

Grinning, Alex said, "A bouncing baby girl. Her name is Violet Grace. Now you're all caught up. In other news, how's Gage, and when are you two coming back?"

Cheri whistled into the phone. "Let me absorb this." She giggled. "And I thought living in New York City was exciting. As to your question, my flight leaves tomorrow. But Gage is another matter. He had a little incident, plus I don't really need his services in Branson. I love driving."

Alex's face fell. "Incident? Is he okay?"

"Yes, it's one of the rag magazines that follows me around. One of the paparazzi punched him after his pop singer girlfriend jumped Gage's bones after he drove her around. Gage is fine but my family doesn't need bad publicity. I told him to take a month or two off."

"What a raw deal. I had hoped he'd join you." Alex shifted in her chair. "Tell Gage hi when you talk to him. Listen, we're all ready to collapse. Give us a call when you're back in town."

"I will and congratulations on . . . everything. *Ciao*."

"Bye." Alex handed the phone back to Suzy. "I miss Cheri."

"Me too," Hope and Suzy both said.

Hope shook her head. "This was an incredible day. I mean, a wedding and a baby hours apart. It's unbelievable." She fluffed her frizzy hair. "My life has gotten much more interesting all of a sudden." Grinning, she added, "I'm an auntie."

"That you are, and so am I." Alex shifted in her chair. "I feel kind of old now. I love the baby's name. It's unique."

Hope nodded. "I agree. The baby's name is beautiful and significant at the same time." She pushed the lime down in her margarita. "We're real rule breakers today. First, you fake fell inside the hospital—cute nurse, by the way—which leads me to wonder about Tony. You haven't discussed your cop boyfriend much lately."

Alex smoothed her dress. "He's been super busy on some case." Sighing, she said, "Little Joey is apparently still having a rough time after the divorce, is moody toward Tony, and his nasty, witchy ex doesn't want me anywhere near her precious son." She sipped her chardonnay and frowned. "I hate all of his baggage."

"Maybe he's not worth it. Remember that pep talk Suzy and I gave you about Tony?"

Alex held up a hand. "Save it. I'm in no mood. Besides, we've had enough drama today."

"Here, here, but what an unbelievable day." Suzy drained her wine.

"That's one adjective for it," Alex said.

After finishing their second drink, Suzy invited them over the following day for leftovers and wedding cake.

"I've got to work," Hope said.

"Ditto," Alex said.

"Come over afterward if you want. Now, who's going to drive me home? Ken took my car and I'm spent."

Chapter 36

The morning after the wedding and birth, Vanessa awoke to Violet Grace's cries. Soothing her newborn, she cuddled her, kissed both cheeks and belly, and nursed the baby while Jon and Fernando slept on the couch and recliner.

"Good morning," a hair-net-wearing cafeteria worker bellowed. Carrying a tray of breakfast food, she said, "With all of the hubbub yesterday, you didn't get to fill out menu options. I brought you oatmeal, wheat toast, and orange juice. Hope that's okay."

"It's perfect." Vanessa propped the baby in the crook of her arm as she simultaneously raised the bed.

Obviously awakened by the worker and still dressed in green scrubs, Jon yawned while Fernando stretched.

Vanessa glanced at the men. "I bet you're hungry too. Can they get a tray? They're the dads."

"Dads as in plural?" The employee shifted her feet as she studied both men. "Let me see what I can do. Be right back."

Jon and Fernando yelled "Thanks" to the employee's back and concurrently reached for Violet Grace. Laughing, both said, "You go first."

"You two are definitely in sync." Vanessa giggled. "Don't worry. There's enough of Violet Grace to go around. I'm going to need plenty of backup."

"No problem there but I've got to pee. Go ahead, Fernando." Jon escaped into the restroom. When he returned, Fernando bounced Violet Grace, two more breakfast trays had appeared, and a lab worker was drawing blood from Vanessa's arm.

Jon grimaced. "Do you really have to do that while we eat?" He put his hand in front of his face. "I can't watch."

"My husband gets queasy around needles. Me? You could take my blood while I eat my bacon."

"I won't be long." After the lab worker drew two vials of blood, she asked Vanessa to verify her name and date of birth, slipped the labeled vials in her pocket, and nearly ran into a volunteer carrying a huge bouquet of pink carnations. A pink balloon attached read, IT'S A GIRL!

Jon and Fernando's mouths fell open. Fernando spoke first. "When did you find the time? I feel like a jerk."

Shaking his head, Jon said, "I wish I could take credit but they're not from me. Maybe Mom sent them."

The elderly pink-smocked volunteer placed the flowers on a nightstand. "Congratulations." She handed Vanessa the card.

Vanessa turned the envelope in her hands.

"Don't keep us in suspense," Fernando said.

As she tore the envelope open and read the card, Vanessa's face became red and splotchy. Silent tears spilled down her cheeks.

Jon took a wild guess. "Your parents?"

Bobbing her head, she wiped her nose with the back of her hand while rereading the card written in her mother's familiar scrawl.

"I hate how they upset you," Jon said, as he reached for the baby.

Vanessa's voice broke. "It's actually good—no, wonderful—news."

"Then tell us." Fernando paused. "If you want to."

Sniffling, Vanessa said, "I'll read the card."

Dear Vanessa,

Your father and I cannot tell you how sorry we are for how we've reacted to your pregnancy. We were wrong, so very wrong, and hope you can find it in your heart to forgive us. We love you more than anything and can't wait to see you and meet our new granddaughter. Please call or text if you're willing. We want to see both of you as soon as possible.

Love, Mom & Dad

Crossing his arms, Jon said, "About time they came around. After all, your dad's a preacher. I never could understand why they were so judgmental—"

"Jon, be nice. This is good news. Very good. Vanessa, I think you should give them Suzy's address. She invited us over to enjoy our wedding food today. After you're discharged, of course. What do you think?"

Reaching for her phone, Vanessa's voice broke. "I agree. I-I want them to meet Violet Grace today. If I hear their voice, I'll probably blubber the entire time. I'll text them now."

~ ~ ~

After Vanessa and Violet were discharged, Jon gathered her belongings, Fernando carried the flowers, and Vanessa held Violet Grace in a wheelchair. Before they got through the revolving door, the sky darkened and sheets of rain pelted the windows.

"What timing. I hope Mom has an umbrella in her car. She should be here any minute." As if on cue, Suzy pulled up to the front entrance.

Drenched, Jon helped Vanessa into the car. Fernando held an umbrella over the baby while Jon struggled to secure the infant car seat. "I guess we should have practiced." After fumbling with the seatbelt, facing it forward in the wrong direction, he turned the seat around. "Car seats are no joke."

Fernando stifled a chuckle. "I've got faith in you, Jon." Rain dripped off Fernando's umbrella as Vanessa hopped back out of the car. "Let me help. I learned how to do this in a pre-natal class." Within seconds, she placed the baby in the seat as if she had done it all her life.

When he heard the latch of the safety belt to secure the car seat, Fernando rushed around to the other side, stepped in a huge puddle, swore, and jumped inside.

Once everyone was in the car, Suzy twisted to admire the baby, patted Vanessa's leg, and turned the wipers on full speed. "Morning, everyone. Pretty flowers. I wish I had remembered to send some."

"You've been a little busy." Vanessa rubbed her belly, obviously from habit. "Guess who they're from."

"Who?" Suzy asked.

"My parents."

Suzy gasped. "They came around. That's wonderful. I'm so glad. I hope you invited them to my house."

"I did. Thanks for . . . everything."

"Violet has plenty of grandparents." Smiling, Suzy said, "You can never have too many. And we have tons of food leftover from the wedding." As she rounded the corner to her house, Suzy said, "I have a surprise. Before the wedding, I ordered a bassinet and diapers for the homecoming. They arrived early this morning."

"You think of everything, Mom. Fernando and I have a lot to learn." Jon rubbed the fog off the glass window. "Man, this rain won't let up."

As they parked, Fernando's family appeared. His three brothers jumped out of their rental car and ran for the house, hopping over mud puddles. Mama Gia put her giant purse over her head and nearly slipped on the wet grass, swearing in Italian.

Suzy grinned. "The gang's all here. Well, except for my girlfriends and Ken, who are working. Izzy's at school."

Jon rubbed his hands together. "More food for us."

Once inside, Mama Gia insisted on holding the baby while Vinny, Frankie, and Luigi fought for the remote.

Vanessa sat in a rocking chair beside the white wicker bassinet while Jon, Fernando, and Suzy placed mounds of food on the counter.

Jon rubbed his belly. "My stomach's growling."

Fernando clucked his tongue. "We just had breakfast."

"Hospital food doesn't count. What can I do, Mom?" Jon flipped a switch to brew the coffee and made a pitcher of tea.

"You're doing it. How about some lemonade too?"

Mama Gia pressed her nose to Violet's cheek. "I love the way babies smell." Reluctantly, she handed her back to Vanessa. "Dibs on holding her later."

Vanessa grinned. "Right after my parents get to hold her."

Mama Gia's eyebrows shot up. "Your parents? I never heard the story with all of the fuss yesterday."

Suzy winked at Vanessa. "Nothing to tell. In fact, they're on their way here, right? Did you give them my address?"

Nodding, Vanessa cuddled her baby and rocked. "I imagine they'll be here any minute."

"Good." Suzy tied her apron. "Now, who's hungry?"

Frankie, Luigi, and Vinny hustled toward the kitchen with a chorus of "Me."

Fernando and Jon fell into line but the brothers insisted the newlyweds go first.

Mama Gia smiled. "That's my boys. Let's use paper plates, Suzy. We might as well make it easy on ourselves."

Suzy reached for plates and napkins and handed them to Mama Gia to place on the end of the counter. Grabbing forks, spoons, and knives, she said, "Eat," then hesitated. "Vanessa, would you rather we wait until your parents get here?"

"No, go ahead. They're used to free-for-all potluck church suppers." She glanced at her watch. "They'll be here soon. According to Mom's text, they left twenty minutes ago."

Chapter 37

Hope studied the stiff back of Hilltop's star golf student as he exited her office. She knew he wasn't happy about her decision, but hopefully, she had gotten through to him.

Jeremy had complained to Hope about his crappy, worn golf clubs and asked if the school could buy more expensive ones. Slumping in his chair, he said, "It affects my game. I could be so much better if—"

"You do realize you're our star golfer, don't you?" Splaying her hands across her desk, the counselor leaned forward and explained about tight budgetary constraints. She bit her tongue to keep from mentioning how far down the line golf clubs would be.

Jeremy shrugged. "I know the school has other needs besides my golf game, but still." He picked at his jeans, obviously hoping for a better outcome.

"I'm sure you've talked to your coach about this. I wish I could help." She brightened. "Have you practiced at the public country club?"

The student golfer's face fell. "Their clubs are worn out too." In an obvious attempt to change her mind, Jeremy said, "I really want to improve my game to try and get a college golf scholarship."

"Let me see what I can do. I have some contacts who may be able to get you in at one of the private clubs in Crystal City."

"That would be awesome." Jeremy stood. "Thank you, Miss Truman."

"Remember, I said I'll *try*. No promises. I don't belong to a country club—never could on my salary—but I know some people who do. In the meantime, keep working on your stellar game." She grinned. "Now get to class."

After Jeremy left, Hope shuffled papers on her messy desk and glanced at the clock. Stomach growling, she reached for her purse to get in the cafeteria line. Hearing the familiar jangle of Willow's excessive bracelets, she grinned as Willow entered her office. "How's the best art teacher at Hilltop?"

Waving her arms dramatically, Willow said, "I've made a major decision."

"Really? What?" Hope asked.

"I've decided on my art students' senior project. I think they'll love it."

"It'll be fabulous, I'm sure." Hope motioned to one of the drab, gray chairs across from her desk. "Have a seat."

Bracelets clanging, which distracted Hope to no end but obviously didn't faze Willow, the art teacher sat down. Her prematurely gray hair hung in a thick side braid. As usual, she wore layers of clothes, making it difficult to determine her actual body shape.

Hope crossed her arms. "Well, don't keep me in suspense."

"It's good. Really good." As usual, Willow spoke with dramatic flair. "Actually, the art project was Mac's idea. He's very creative, you know."

Keeping up with both of his names—Mac or Larry—continually confounded Hope, plus she had never considered her former hippie dad as the least bit inspired nor creative. In fact, all her life, he had been mostly stoned and a deadbeat. Obviously, the right side of his brain had kicked in after his horrific train accident. Keeping his identity to herself was a daily strain. Hope persevered. "Are you going to tell me or keep me in suspense all day?"

Willow leaned forward. "The students are going to paint Buttercup."

"Buttercup?"

"You know, my VW Microbus. I love her beautiful, buttery yellow color, but I've decided she needs some pizazz. It'll be a fun project for my students. Mac suggested I let the students paint whatever symbols or words they want—with any color they want. What do you think?"

Nodding, Hope said, "That'll be unique and fun. How and where do you plan to accomplish this?"

"Easy. We'll meet in the Hilltop parking lot on a weekend to be determined. I'll supply the paint, brushes, and Buttercup. The kids will do the rest. Afterward, Mac said he'd order pizzas."

Hope was almost jealous. Her dad, Larry, now known as Mac to everyone else, had never done anything like that for her when she was a kid. Not even close. In fact, he expected her to take care of him. This was an unbelievable new side to the man who had raised her. At least she was 99 percent sure he was the same man, sans his memory issues and an anchor tattoo on his arm.

Chapter 38

Feeling downright gleeful as the Uber driver drove her from the airport to her Branson home, Cheri's heart swelled once he rounded the corner to her familiar, wooded neighborhood. Spotting the welcoming, red front door of her beloved late Nana's home, she relaxed.

After paying the driver, she dragged her leopard print luggage up the sidewalk, unlocked the door, and flipped on nearly every light. Opening several windows, she inhaled the fresh, unpolluted air. Her favorite room in the house was the kitchen with a floor-to-ceiling view of Crystal Lake.

Opening her French doors, Cheri never tired of the serenity of the lush, green Ozark Mountains above the tranquil lake dotted with boats.

As she unpacked her bags, she smiled as she pictured Suzy as a grandmother. *I can't believe they had a wedding and a baby on the same day. I've missed so much.*

Glad she had asked the driver to stop by the grocery store before coming to her house, she put the cold items away and restocked her pantry with essentials—coffee, Diet Coke, and wine.

Re-familiarizing herself with the kitchen, Cheri found sauce pans and made a light dinner of smoked salmon and steamed broccoli. As the food cooked, she imagined her parents' luxurious European bungalow, being waited on hand and foot, complete with champagne chilling. She missed them terribly but didn't want their lifestyle.

Thomas and Victoria Van Buren had literally built their multi-millionaire real estate empire from the ground up by putting their savings into inexpensive homes they later renovated and sold. Cheri always said her parents flipped homes before flipping was in style.

Cheri enjoyed luxury but building her own growing empire at Fifth Avenue Catering was more than enough adventure for her—at least for now. She surprised herself by actually enjoying the slower pace of the Midwest. Having Gage around to drive their limo was nice but she preferred driving her grandmother's red Mercedes.

Lost in her thoughts, she squeezed lemon on the broccoli and salmon and sat at her granite bar with a full view of the outdoors. *This place is so different from New York City. It's the perfect escape.* She took three big bites. *I can't wait to see my friends.*

Chapter 39

After everyone stuffed themselves with the eclectic wedding food, the guys retreated to chairs or the sofa while Suzy and Mama Gia cleaned up the kitchen.

When the food was put away, Mama Gia yawned and asked if she could nap in the guest room. "Sure." Suzy was secretly thrilled to rock the baby as they waited for Vanessa's parents. She and Jon exchanged several glances mouthing, "Where are they?"

Vanessa sat in the living room beside a window with a view of the street. Suzy placed Violet Grace in her arms. "I think she's hungry, hon. I just changed her diaper."

Swaddled in a pink and white polka dot baby blanket, Vanessa stroked her baby's red hair as she nursed, while constantly checking the clock and glancing out the window.

"Will music bother you or the baby?" Jon asked.

"No, she has to get used to noise sometime. I can't walk around my house like a church mouse." Her face fell. "Speaking of church, I can't imagine what's taking them so long."

Suzy glanced out the window. "Maybe they're running late, ran out of gas, or had a flat. Who knows?"

Vanessa's eyes reddened. "I hope they didn't change their mind."

"Why would they after sending you flowers and that nice note." Suzy placed her hand on Vanessa's shoulder. "You need to eat and keep up your strength. Want me to fix you a plate?"

Shaking her head, Vanessa said, "I'd rather wait for them."

~ ~ ~

Two hours later, Jon attempted to tamp down his anger at Vanessa's AWOL parents. Pacing, he turned on the news as he picked at more leftovers. Half eating and half watching TV, he stopped with his fork in mid-air. "Fernando, come here."

"I'm heating some lasagna in the microwave. Be right there." When Fernando stepped into the den, he noticed the TV was paused. Jon stared at the screen robotically. "What's wrong?"

Jon peeked around the wall and waited until Vanessa put the baby in the bassinet before asking, "What kind of car does your parents drive?"

"Last I knew it was a Chevy truck."

Jon shot a glance toward Fernando whose face was blank. Jon persisted. "What color is their truck?"

"Black. Why?" Vanessa scooted the rocking chair beside the baby.

"Nothing." Jon reached for Fernando. "Follow me."

In the kitchen, he told his husband about the news report. Speaking fast and voice lowered, Jon said, "A couple in a black Chevy pickup was killed an hour ago in an automobile accident. Apparently, the truck hit black ice and went airborne. A reporter announced the passengers were killed instantly."

Cupping his mouth with his hand, Fernando's face drained of color. "You don't suppose—"

"It would explain why they're late." Jon paced. "But I don't want to worry her until we know for sure."

Fernando peeked at a serene, unknowing Vanessa and returned to the kitchen. "No, we can't say anything until we know for certain. Oh, my God. What if? Do you think the police will tell us their names?"

Running his fingers through his hair while fixated on the television, Jon swallowed hard. "I'm going to tell Mom. She knows someone who dates a cop."

Chapter 40

Suzy stepped into the kitchen. Hands on hips, she asked, "What's going on? Why are you transfixed on the television and whispering to Fernando? I can tell something's up. Tell me."

Jon tugged on his mother's sleeve. "Follow me." Once they got into the laundry room, he closed the door, and told Suzy about the automobile fatality. Glumly, Jon said, "I bet it's Vanessa's parents. She said they drive a black truck and they're now three hours late."

"Oh, no. Where's my phone? I'm calling Alex." Suzy raced toward the kitchen, found her cell, and disappeared into her bedroom. After filling her in, she asked Alex to call Tony immediately.

Suzy stepped back in the laundry room where Jon and Fernando were in a worried huddle. "This is one time I wish I smoked."

"Want a glass of wine?" Fernando asked.

"No, I, we need to be clearheaded. Don't say a word to Vanessa until we know for sure."

Rolling his eyes, Jon said, "Duh."

Within minutes, Alex called back and relayed Tony's off-the-record account. He said they still hadn't identified the victims and would only say it was a man and woman.

Suzy groaned. "Please call the minute you know."

"I will."

~ ~ ~

Thirty minutes later, Vanessa sobbed as she picked at the food Suzy insisted she eat. "I don't know why my parents sent flowers and didn't come to see my baby."

Rubbing her back, Suzy said, "I'm sorry, sweetie. Try not to wor—" The doorbell interrupted her.

Jon, Fernando, and Suzy rushed to the front door where Lt. Tony Montgomery stood in uniform.

Removing his hat, Lt. Montgomery said, "Bad news, I'm afraid. Is their daughter still here?"

Suzy led a wide-eyed Vanessa to the door. Jon took Violet out of her arms as Fernando slung his arm around the young mom's waist and held her tightly.

"Are you Vanessa Nelson?" the officer asked.

"Am I in some kind of trouble?"

"No, ma'am." Lt. Montgomery blew out his breath. "I hate days like this. I'm sorry to inform you but your parents, Reverend and Mrs. Nelson, were involved in an automobile accident earlier today."

Gasping, Vanessa fell back a step but Fernando caught her. Her voice cracked. "That's why they're late, isn't it? Are they in the hospital, Officer?"

Lt. Montgomery shook his head and swallowed. "No, ma'am. I'm sorry." He stared at his feet. "The accident was fatal. It was instant. They didn't suffer."

Wailing, Vanessa fell to her knees. "Noooo. They never saw my baby. They just now forgave me. They just accepted me. Noooo."

Jon handed the baby to Fernando then sat on the floor beside Vanessa and held her close as she sobbed. Fernando bounced the now-crying baby while Suzy stared at Tony, unable to find any words.

Mama Gia, Fernando's brothers, and Izzy raced toward the door after hearing the commotion and cries. All of them stopped short at the sight of the policeman.

Lt. Montgomery put his hat back on. "I'm very sorry for your loss, Miss Nelson. If you have any questions about the accident, call the CCPD or me. Suzy knows how to reach me."

Sobbing so hard her chest heaved, Vanessa pounded her fists on the carpet. "This can't be true. I don't believe you."

Shock, disbelief, and silence filled the room. No one spoke. No one *could* speak. Mostly silent tears streamed down speechless faces as they watched the officer get back into his patrol car and drive away.

"Please tell me I'm dreaming," Vanessa wailed, making the baby cry even louder. Mama Gia and her sons poured wine and handed a glass to every adult. No one spoke except for someone who simply said, "Jesus. Why?"

Chapter 41

Hope entered the teachers' lounge, grabbed some wretched, mostly cold coffee, and sat next to Willow. The art teacher's head was down as she sifted through a huge pile of her students' latest work.

Likely hearing Hope's footsteps, Willow glanced up and greeted Hope with a smile. Tugging on her gray braid, she said, "Morning. Guess what? My students are thrilled about their senior art project."

"I knew they would be." Hope sat down. "You amaze me with your creativity."

"It was Mac's idea, remember?" Willow set the paperwork aside and clasped her hands together.

"Will they paint the entire van?" Hope asked as she sipped her coffee.

"Yup." Willow patted the stack of drawings. "Here are their submissions." She fanned them out for Hope to admire.

Hope thumbed through pictures of lions, sunglasses, peace signs, daisies, and guitars. "How fun and unique. This will be cool."

"I'll be able to drive their art around town." Willow extended both arms. "What better way to spread joy around Crystal City."

Hope shook her head in amazement. "Will they be graded?"

"If I can work it into my curriculum, you bet."

Grinning, Hope said, "And they'll all get an A, right?"

Willow shrugged. "Unless they don't show up, paint a solid blob, or stare at their phones the entire time, probably so."

Hope got another refill of the hideous coffee. As she poured the black tar-like java, she chuckled. "Who makes this nasty stuff? Congrats on the creative project. It's too bad Britney isn't a senior. I've seen her doodles. She's very good, to my untrained eye at least."

Waving a theatrical hand in the air, Willow said, "I'm easygoing. If Britney wants to join in the fun, she's welcome. But she won't get graded since I'm not her teacher."

Hugging her colleague so hard Hope almost sloshed coffee down Willow's pink and orange paisley blouse. "Oops. I almost drenched you. Thank you. Britney needs something to look forward to. Her home life is terrible."

"Then by all means, tell her about the project. I'll let you know the date soon." Willow gathered her students' paintings, grabbed a cup of coffee with the other hand, and strode down the hall. Her baggy clothes swished as she walked.

Hope could barely contain her excitement and couldn't wait to tell Britney about the van painting class. *I wonder what she'll paint.*

Chapter 42

Alex raced up the stairs, greeted a few employees, and returned to her office. Lately, she had managed to get to work not exactly early—that would be a miracle—but not exactly late either. She had learned the hard way that she needed downtime before her busybody intern arrived.

Hannah entered the office behind her breasts. "Hi, boss. What's on tap today?"

Scowling at Hannah's unrestrained cleavage, Alex stared at the piles on her desk as she attempted to avoid gazing at her intern's puffy mounds of flesh. *Why the hell is she wearing lower cut tops every damn day? To torture me? To show off?*

Forcing herself to focus, Alex met Hannah's eyes. "What's not on tap? I'm snowed." She held up her fingers and ticked off several items. "We could work on television scripts, update the bank website, prepare for the next trade show, or focus on the bank anniversary party, which is what we're doing. It's our top priority." Alex paused. "Actually, it's what *you're* going to do."

Hannah reached into a purple leather tote and retrieved her iPad. After making a few notes, she tucked it back inside.

"Don't put that away. We're not finished. I don't want any hiccups or Jim will have my head—and yours."

Hannah eyed Alex. "Daddy would never have my head. I'm his little girl."

"Not so little in certain areas," Alex muttered.

Hannah's voice rose a notch. "What did you say?"

"Never mind. The guest list is in a file on my computer under 'Bank Anniversary'."

"Clever name." Hannah dared Alex with her eyes.

Alex wasn't taking the bait. "Thanks. I thought so." Her mind raced, wondering if she should leave this important task in the hands of Hannah. *I don't have any choice. I've got to finish my damn budget and presentation to the board. I'm already a week behind.*

"Make sure you get the invitations out by the end of the week. The printer will work with you and rush the job since we give them so much business." Alex noticed Hannah had stopped taking notes. "You do know who our printer is, right? It's Liberty Press on College Street."

"Got it, but there are a gazillion printers online." Hannah adjusted her belt. "Honestly, Alex, with my higher education I can figure all of this out. Stop worrying."

"It's part of my job. Stress and deadlines. Get used to it." Alex considered opening the file to show Hannah but someone with her education could find a simple file. "You'll need to order 500 invitations, no, 600. We'll want a few extras for bulletin boards, the New Account desks, teller windows, and for employees."

Hannah studied a chipped silver nail. "Anything else?"

"I have a friend who owns a catering company, so I'll handle the food. As soon as you get the invitations proofed—and carefully—get them in the mail pronto. Send out press releases to the media—television, radio, print, and Internet. And we need a nice direct mail piece to send to neighboring businesses and residents in the zip code surrounding the bank. Proof those too. If there are typos, Jim goes nuts."

Already apparently totally bored with the bank anniversary planning conversation, Hannah stepped toward the window and took a photo of a redbird perched on a tree branch. "No worries. I don't make mistakes."

Alex ignored her intern's posturing. "Glad to hear it. I hate mistakes. The bank president hates them even more." Scanning her to-do list, she said, "After you do all of this, draft several thirty-second radio spots to announce the bank's anniversary. Maybe television too. I'm still working on the contracts." Alex paused. "You can get creative with the scripts. I, uh, trust you."

After Hannah left with a long to-do list, Alex checked her phone. She had ten messages from Tony saying 'Urgent.' Closing her door, she called him. After he relayed the tragic news, all she could manage was, "Poor Vanessa. Poor Suzy. Oh, my God. They go from one extreme to the other. A wedding, a baby, and now-shit. This is—"

"Tragic," he said and hung up.

Alex's eyes filled with tears. *I didn't even know them and am heartsick about this.* Glancing at her phone, she wondered whether she should call Suzy but decided to leave her alone until she heard more.

Chapter 43

After the longest, saddest, most somber night of their lives on top of their happiest day, Fernando's family expressed their love and support and flew back to Italy. After tearful goodbyes, Ken drove Suzy's parents to the airport for their return to Canada. Except for happy moments with the baby, everyone's mood was morose, and that was a good day.

Since hearing the tragic news, Suzy had insisted Vanessa sleep in Izzy's room and sent Izzy to stay with a friend for a few days. Jon and Fernando slept on the living room floor atop a pallet of blankets. The newlyweds postponed their honeymoon indefinitely and focused on taking care of the baby and getting Vanessa to eat.

Alternating shifts every few hours, no one slept well, but it didn't matter. They were together.

Alex and Hope sent pizza, salad, and a chocolate cake to the house but gave the family a wide berth to deal with their grief. Coconuts was out of the question. No one was in the mood for joy. Their elation and celebrations had turned into the gloomiest days, seemingly overnight.

Normally a coordinator of happy events, Suzy knew she had to plan the heart-wrenching funeral. At Vanessa's request, she assured the young mom she'd take care of everything. All Vanessa had to do was take care of herself and Violet Grace. And by taking care, Suzy insisted Vanessa only handle the minimum—eat, bathe, and sleep. She tried to make Vanessa laugh by telling her bathing could go by the wayside if she preferred.

In a zombie-like state, Suzy watched as Vanessa nursed Violet Grace, changed her diaper, if Jon and Fernando hadn't beaten her to it, and picked at her food. Barely sleeping, the young mom had dark circles under her eyes and cried constantly.

Numb herself, Suzy couldn't wait until they got past this shroud of misery. Throwing herself into planning mode, she contacted Rev. Nelson's church members, a funeral home, and the cemetery. She knew an attorney would be in order and added a reminder to schedule a meeting.

~ ~ ~

Two days later, a simple graveside burial was held on a surreal—virtually cosmic—rainy day. The weather coincidence was almost too much. As if they weren't depressed enough, the reminder of the slick streets, which had caused the death of Vanessa's parents, was nearly too much to endure.

Sitting under a morbid black tent, Jon and Fernando flanked Vanessa who clutched her sleeping baby. Sniffling, both men held her—one draped his arm across her shoulders and the other held her hand. It didn't matter which. At this point, the young parents were in total solidarity. Suzy, Ken, and Izzy sat behind them. Alex and Hope stood underneath Show-Me Bank umbrellas as rain pelted unforgivingly.

"Damn rain," Alex said.

"Shhh." Hope narrowed her eyes. "You shouldn't swear at a funeral."

"Sorry, but it's depressing."

Throngs of friends and churchgoers filled the chairs or stood underneath umbrellas as the muddy cemetery soon filled to capacity. Several people sobbed; others were stony faced. Someone said, "Tears from heaven" while it poured.

After many heartfelt songs, prayers, and several profound memories of Rev. and Mrs. Nelson, church members paid their condolences to Vanessa, revered the baby, and made their way toward the casket. An exceedingly long line, all dressed in black, formed to pay their respects.

After the preacher concluded the memorial, Vanessa struggled to rise, switched Violet to her other arm, and laid a handful of pink and blue roses on the casket. Standing silent for several minutes, she wiped tears off her face with her free hand.

"Goodbye, Mom and Dad. I love you. Thank you for sending the flowers—and for everything. I want you to meet your precious granddaughter, Violet Grace." Sniffling, she added, "I'll miss you and will make sure Violet knows who you are." Leaning over, she kissed the top of their casket.

There wasn't a dry eye on the grounds.

After the last person paid their respects, funeral goers stepped across mud puddles to their cars.

Even Alex wiped away a tear. "I can't take this rollercoaster of emotions."

"Me neither." Hope shook the rain off her umbrella. "I know what you mean. I'm ready for normalcy." Hope hugged her friend. "I'll be glad when we can take Suzy to Coconuts."

Nodding, Alex said, "She needs it more than we do."

Chapter 44

The day after the funeral, Alex couldn't wait to go to work and enjoy life, even if that meant dealing with Hannah.

After a much-needed cup of coffee and chatting with employees in the lobby, she interviewed the bank's handsome new lender for a press release. Hannah hovered, giving the loan officer full view of her new cleavage.

Barely containing her disgust, Alex asked, "Would you like to photograph him?" Not waiting for her intern to answer, she said, "He's all yours." It was obvious the new employee had already caught Hannah's eye, and based on the way he was glued to her new breasts, the feeling was mutual.

Good. Anything to keep daddy's girl out of my hair. Alex traipsed across the lobby, shook hands with a few customers, and made her way to her office. She checked her appointment calendar which was empty that afternoon and emailed a note to Hannah asking her to send a press release to every media outlet, along with the loan officer's photo. After checking the clock on her computer, she remembered Tony mentioned Joey had started playing Little League baseball.

After the wedding, a surprise baby, and horrific tragedy, a baseball game sounds like the perfect diversion. I think I'll leave early and surprise Joey—and Tony—at the ballpark.

After saving and closing files on her computer, Alex reached underneath her desk and grabbed a tote containing a casual change of clothes and white tennis shoes. Taking the steps two at a time, she changed in the upstairs employee bathroom. Pulling her shoulder-length blond hair into a high ponytail, she donned denim shorts, a hot pink tee, spritzed herself with perfume, and freshened her lipstick.

As she drove to the Crystal City Park, Alex turned down Battlefield toward Lone Pine. After circling the lot twice, she finally secured a parking space. Stepping across the dusty, graveled lot, she noticed a crowd had already gathered on the bleachers. Covering her eyes from the blinding sun, she scanned the grounds for Tony.

Excited parents, grandparents, and kids filled the bleachers, but there was no sight of her cop boyfriend. Alex sat on one of the filthy top bleachers—after wiping it off with every single tissue in her purse. After putting the nasty wipes inside her last clean tissue, she folded it into a tight ball so nothing could escape, stuffed the wadded mess inside her purse and shuddered, imagining the germs—and other unmentionables—the little gremlins left on the seats.

Have fun, Alex. Just relax and have fun for once. Crossing her arms, she noticed red and black team colors for one team and orange and blue for the other. Suddenly realizing she wasn't sure what Joey's team colors were, not to mention his team's name, Alex frowned. *I need to pay more attention when Tony talks about his son-turned-nephew, thanks to his cheating ex, brother, and a DNA test.* Pushing the complicated family dynamics out of her head, she tried to focus on the ballgame. A lot had happened the past several days. Watching a kid's game sounded like an ideal escape.

Numerous moms sat together, as well as a few couples. Young teens were huddled at the top corner of the bleachers, likely siblings, who were too cool to sit with their parents but wanted to cheer on their little brothers. Alex squinted from the sun's glare and fished black and gold leopard print sunglasses from her purse.

A booming voice cut through the chatter, making her jump. "Hey, blondie. Haven't I seen you before?" A uniformed cop bellowed from the bottom bleacher where all could hear. As everyone turned in her direction, he cocked his head and tapped his watch. "I remember now. You're the one who's always late. It looks like you found your watch."

Alex grimaced. *Sean.* Tony's nasty brother. She had managed to elude him for nearly a year, especially since his wicked wife, Nikki, AKA Tony's ex, had stalked her and tried to run her over in a parking lot. And since Sean and Tony were estranged rivals who dodged one another like two wary alley cats, it had been easy to avoid Tony's jerk brother—until now.

Alex gave Sean a half wave and turned her head, hoping he'd get the message to sit elsewhere. But the thundering steps on the bleachers indicated otherwise. *Dammit.*

Without so much of a hello, Sean plopped down beside Alex. His heavy cologne turned her stomach on this sweltering day. Not bothering with niceties, he barked, "Exactly why are you at my boy's baseball game?"

Staring straight ahead, Alex attempted to will Tony to the ballpark as she ignored his arrogant brother's question.

Sean obviously didn't appreciate being discounted. In police mode, his voice rose. "I asked you a question."

"I'm at a ballgame. Last I heard, it's a free society. I haven't done anything wrong, so watch your tone and back off." She paused. "*Officer.*" Alex shifted her position and scooted away from him.

"Well, well. Aren't you the feisty one? No wonder Tony likes you." Sean lit a cigarette. "Mind if I smoke?"

Alex glared at him. "Actually, I *do* mind."

"Too bad." He cocked his head. "Free society, like you said."

She huffed. "Honestly."

"I'm always honest."

"Yeah, I bet." Alex glared at him. "Joey's the proof of your honesty."

"You're a real pushy broad, aren't you?" Sean blew smoke in her face. "Don't mention my son's name."

"You're an asshole. No wonder Tony can't stand you."

He took another drag. "Feeling's mutual."

Alex crossed her arms. "Listen, I was here first. Why don't you and your cancer stick move over there?" She pointed with her finger. "I'm not into second-hand smoke."

Sean tossed his lighter up and down as if it were a toy ball. "Nada. I like this seat."

Waving dramatically to clear the air, Alex blew the smoke back in Sean's direction. "Nice, isn't it?"

"It don't bother me none."

She grimaced as the teams ran onto the field, somewhat breaking the tense mood. Onlookers stood, clapped, and cheered for their little ones. Alex weighed her options while Sean stood and clapped with a cigarette dangling precariously from his lips. *If that damn thing falls on me and burns my new Skechers, he's buying me a new pair. Where the hell is Tony?*

No sooner were the thoughts in her head, Tony appeared, still in uniform. Alex broke into a wide smile, stood, and waved. Just as quickly, her face fell. "What the hell?"

Sean grunted. "Yeah, what the fresh hell? Why is *my* wife coming here with *your* boyfriend?"

Chapter 45

Fuming from the toxic combination of Sean's cologne and cigarette smoke, not to mention Tony and Nikki's joint appearance, Alex cursed herself for trying to surprise her boyfriend at Joey's game. But just as quickly, she decided she was glad she had come because maybe, just maybe, she had caught Tony in the act with his ex. Perhaps this was what she needed to move on from this freaking nightmare of a relationship. "Fuck."

Sean lit another cigarette. Grimacing, Alex waved her hand to clear the air. "I'm leaving. Enjoy the game and those cancer sticks. Don't bother telling Tony I was here." She threw her bag over her shoulder, pressed her sunglasses harder on her sweaty nose, and bounded down the bleachers on the opposite side.

Before she got to her car, Alex felt a hand on her shoulder. She froze, wondering who the hell was touching her.

"What are you doing here?" Tony asked as he leaned forward to kiss her.

Alex pulled away. "Get away from me. Go enjoy the game."

"What crawled up your ass?"

Alex held up two fingers. "Two things: Your bitchy ex-wife and your disgusting brother."

Tony reached for her. "Come on. Nikki just happened to park at the same time as me, and yes, my brother's a dick." He tugged on her hand. "Joey will be thrilled you're here. *I'm* thrilled you're here. It feels like I haven't seen you in forever."

Firmly planted on the gravel, Alex didn't budge. "I'm out of the mood for a ballgame."

"I'll buy you a hotdog."

"Gee. That's hard to resist." In spite of herself, Alex felt herself softening. She couldn't understand why this cop undid her but he did. "Do hotdogs come with wine?"

"Later at your place." He wiggled his eyebrows. "If I'm lucky."

Alex felt herself waver. "I don't know. It's hot, dusty, and now I'm covered in Sean's filthy smoke. I can smell it in my hair. I need to shower."

"That can be arranged." Tony moved closer and kissed her on the mouth. Once, then twice. "Let's start over, babe. We can sit wherever you want—far away from Sean and Nikki."

"Don't become a nice guy on me." Alex managed a half smile. "You'll ruin your reputation."

Tony obviously picked up on her weakening condition and slipped his arm around her waist. "Please. For Joey. We'll have fun."

Against her better judgment, Alex let Tony lead her back to the ballpark near a shaded corner bleacher. She peeked inside her purse. "I don't have any more tissues."

"Huh? Do you have a cold?"

Alex pointed toward the dusty bleachers. "Those seats are filthy."

Tony wiped them down with his hand. "There."

She laughed. "Don't touch me with that hand."

He shook his head. "You and your OCD."

Cocking a brow, she said, "Take my OCD or leave it."

He slung his arm across her shoulder. "If it's attached to you, I'll take it."

Starting to relax, Alex studied the teams. "Which one is Joey's?"

"Orange and blue."

"Does the team have a name?"

"Orange Rockets." He shrugged. "Don't ask. Coach McArthy let the kids name the team. Coach is a great guy." Tony pointed toward the short, ballcap-wearing coach. "He's always got a smile for everyone and is multi-talented. You wouldn't believe his nature photography."

"That's cool. I bet he'd take the team pics for free."

Tony nodded as he studied Joey at first base. "I don't know how he catches anything with that small ball glove but he rarely misses grounders. He's good with pop ups too. I know I'm bragging about my little man but I can't help myself." Tony adjusted his dark sunglasses without taking his eyes off Joey. "The field is his strong suit. He isn't that great at batting, though. He gets nervous."

"Maybe we can take him to the batting cages or hit balls to him. There's a big field across from my house, you know."

Leaning over, Tony kissed Alex for far too long in a public setting. Afterward, he said, "That makes me happy. I'd love for you to get more involved in Joey's life."

A raspy, cigarette-fueled voice cut through their sweet moment. "What the hell do you think you're doing here, husband stealer?"

Nikki. Nikki and Sean in the same park didn't exactly spell a good time. Alex stiffened. "I'm watching Joey's ballgame, same as you."

Nikki lit a cigarette and waved the glowing ember toward both of them. "Are you two going to screw right here on the bleachers? Really, Tony? You think it's a good idea to stick your tongue down her throat in front of my boy?"

Rolling his eyes, Tony said, "He's my boy too—my nephew now—but still my boy."

Ignoring Tony's claim, Nikki narrowed her dark eyes and glared at Alex. "I don't know who the hell invited you to Joey's game but you're not welcome. Why don't you leave?"

She crossed her arms and took another drag. "Now would be a good time."

Usually the strong one among her friends, Alex felt herself falter under this cunning woman's wrath. "I-I just came to watch Joey's game." She felt the stares of several parents who likely believed she was a husband stealer. She wished she could magically disappear.

"Don't look like you're watchin' no game to me." Nikki hissed. "Looks more like you're swallowing my husband's tongue."

Alex felt her cheeks redden. "He's your *ex*-husband. Isn't your real husband here? Remember Sean, the one you cheated on Tony with? The one who is actually Joey's fa—"

"You bitch." Nikki climbed over the bleacher like a goat and got nose to nose with Alex.

Tony placed a protective arm in front of his girlfriend but took Nikki's side. "Maybe you should go, Alex. You can come another time." He lowered his voice. "Everyone's watching and listening. I don't want to embarrass Joey."

Alex's eyebrows shot up. "But- . . . Whatever." She stood and slung her purse over her shoulder. "Just so you know, I'm never coming back. Enjoy the game and your dysfunctional family." She stormed off and glanced over her shoulder but Tony didn't follow. As she stumbled across the gravel, she muttered to herself. *I'm so sick of this bullshit.*

Chapter 46

Alex blasted the air conditioning and turned up the radio to drown out the noise in her brain. Someone knocked on her car window. Turning, she recognized Tony's dirty, dusty knuckles and lowered the window an inch.

His voice was husky. "Let me in."

She kept her hands on the steering wheel and shook her head. "No. You made it perfectly clear where your priorities lie. I'm going home. Alone." She paused. "Besides, you need a shower."

A laugh escaped Tony. "We can take one together, like I said earlier. I'll scrub your back. We can use that perfume-y stuff you like." Tony's arctic blue eyes bored into her. "I'll even light candles. It'll be romantic. What do you say?"

After hateful, tough-talking Sean and his bitch ex-wife, she wasn't in any mood for more antics from the Montgomerys. "Nope. I'm beat. I have an early morning meeting tomorrow at the bank."

He snorted. "What's new?"

"Gotta make a living."

After spitting on the gravel, Tony said, "Come on, Alex. I know it was rough out there. Let me make it up to you."

Why is this my life? Alex knew she had to win Joey over in order to even be considered a miniscule part of this-this unorthodox family. Still not positive whether she wanted Tony long term, the more roadblocks thrown in her way, continued to push them further and further apart. She brightened. "I have a better idea."

Tony raised his eyebrows. "Better than a hot shower together?"

"Hear me out. The only way to make our relationship get off of first base, to use a baseball analogy, is to involve Joey, right?" She waited a half second before continuing. "Why don't you find out if we can take him out for a celebratory pizza tonight?"

"Two reasons." Tony ticked off his fingers. "Number one they may not win so there won't be much to celebrate, and number two, it's a school night. He goes to bed right after the game."

"Oh." Alex sighed. "Got any better ideas?"

"A shower—together."

"You never give up." A half-smile spread across her face.

"Nope. Never." Tony thumped the top of her car. "See you in a few." He crossed the parking lot toward his vehicle before she could say yay or nay.

"Dammit. I could use a hot shower. Why does this guy have to be so good in bed? It would be much easier to break it off if he weren't." She put her Mustang in gear and headed home.

As Alex rounded the final corner toward her house, she tensed when she spotted a purple Jeep in her driveway. *Nikki.* Slamming her fist on the steering wheel, she muttered aloud, "What did I do to deserve this?"

The moment Nikki noticed Alex she jumped out of her car.

Slamming her car door, Alex yelled, "Get off of my driveway. This is private property."

Crossing her arms, Nikki said, "You broke that rule tonight, darlin'." She lit a cigarette and blew smoke in Alex's face.

Alex took several steps toward Tony's vile ex while waving her hands in front of her face to dissipate the smoke. "A ballgame is public domain. My residence is private or didn't they teach that in middle school? I assume that was your last grade of educa—"

Nikki's face reddened. She charged Alex while yelling, "You smartass, man-stealin' banker bitch . . ." Raising her hand, she attempted to slap Alex who ducked.

Tony arrived and raced out of his car, not bothering to close the door. "Calm down. Both of you." Voice booming, he said, "God, I hate it when two women fight. What are you? Hoodlums?"

Alex crossed her arms, eyeing Nikki's every move. "She's a hood, a thug, and a bully. I'm not." Alex kept her steely gaze on Tony's ex. "For the life of me, I don't know what you ever saw in this piece of white trash, Tony."

Nikki charged Alex again. Tony jumped between them. "That's enough, both of you. Nikki's the mother of my son and you know it, Alex."

Putting her hands on her hips, Alex narrowed her eyes. "I think you're confused, Lieutenant. You *thought* she was the mother of your child but Joey's your brother's son."

Seeing a throbbing, blue vein form in Tony's temple, Alex knew she had gone too far. "Sorry."

Nikki took another step toward Alex and spit on the ground. "And I don't know what you see in this slut unless you're into fancy clothes, a show-off job, and a splashy car. Big fuckin' deal. I thought you had better taste, Tony. You know you ain't no high-society guy." A cigarette dangled from her lips as her words hung in the air.

Alex waited for Tony to defend her but he stood silent for ten seconds too long. She stomped across the grass. "I'm going inside. You two can jump into bed for all I care. I've had it with this nonsense. Life is too short. Hope and Suzy were right."

Tony glared at her. "Your friends don't approve of me? Of us? When were you planning to tell me?"

Unlocking the front door, Alex didn't bother turning around. "I'm not answering that. The two of you had better be off my driveway in ten minutes or I'm calling the police."

A raspy laugh filled the air. "He is the police, sugar."

"Don't call me 'sugar.' Get off my fucking driveway and get out of my life. Both of you." Alex slammed the door so hard her windows shook.

Opening the fridge, she took out a bottle of chardonnay, uncorked it, and drank it right out of the bottle. Tears filled her eyes as she angrily swiped one that spilled down her cheek. She slammed the bottle on the counter. *This is bullshit.*

Alex paced like a caged lion. Checking the time, she knew it was still early enough for a friendapy session at Coconuts. She texted Hope and Suzy and later copied Cheri after receiving a group text that the New Yorker was back in town. *Emergency meeting at Coconuts in one hour, ladies.* Alex added a postscript. *If you're up to it, Suzy. No problem if you can't make it.*

Chapter 47

Alex settled into their favorite table at Coconuts. Suzy and Hope arrived within minutes of each other. After a group hug and a quick conversation about the baby, Vanessa, and the funeral, Alex said, "Suzy, I know your family needs you more than ever. Are you sure you're up to this?"

Waving her hand in the air, Suzy said, "This is exactly what I need, trust me." Her eyes reddened. "It's been unbelievable but I don't want to talk about my problems." She paused and grinned. "I'd rather hear about yours, Alex."

Alex balled up a napkin and threw it at her. "Suzy Q, that's not nice, but considering everything, you're forgiven."

At that moment, Cheri ran inside, attempting to throw her arms around all three women. "I've missed you girls."

After the group hug, Alex said, "I'm so glad you're back."

"We've missed you, Cheri." Hope waved Gus over.

When Gus appeared, Cheri said, "Angry Balls all around. It's on me." She hung her leopard print purse on the back of her chair. "I insist."

Laughing almost maniacally, Alex said, "Angry Balls is the perfect drink right now."

"Let me guess," Hope said. "This is about the cop."

Alex studied her nails. "My problems feel trivial after what you've been through, Suzy. I hate to even bring them up, but still—" She waited on the drink. "I need reinforcement first."

"That means it's definitely the cop. Am I right?" Hope asked.

Alex nodded. Tears threatened but she forced them away.

Once the amber drinks containing two maraschino cherries arrived, Cheri held hers in the air. "To girlfriends and nice guys."

"Here, here," everyone added.

Hope sipped the cocktail. "I know your relationship is complex."

Alex laughed like a hyena as she ran her fingers through her hair. "Complex. Yeah, that's a nice term for it but our relationship falls more into a catastrophic realm. That isn't even a strong enough word."

"What happened?" Suzy sipped her cocktail. "It must be pretty bad to call an emergency meeting."

Cheri studied Alex. "I'm glad I don't have a boyfriend."

Hope clinked her glass with the New Yorker's. "Cheers to that. Go ahead, Alex."

Alex took a deep breath. "Who knew that Tony would have the ex from hell and brother from whatever's worse than hell." She threw both hands in the air. "I'm ready to give up."

Suzy reached for the truffle-flavored popcorn Gus had slipped in front of them. "So tell us already."

Alex splayed her hands on the table. "For a change of pace, I had the *brilliant* idea to surprise Joey and Tony by showing some interest in the little guy."

"That's a good thing." Hope studied her friend. "And . . . what did you do exactly?"

"I went to Joey's Little League ballgame."

Hope's eyebrows knitted. "Someone had a problem with that?"

"It seems *everyone* had a problem with it." Alex ticked off her fingers. "Tony's brother, Sean, a total jerk, sat beside me, and blew smoke in my face. His ex, Nikki, nearly accosted me when she spotted Tony kissing me. She told me to leave the ballpark. The worst? Tony concurred."

Cheri's mouth fell open. "He didn't stand up for you?"

Shaking her head, Alex said, "Nothing comes between Tony and Joey. Nothing and no one. Meanwhile, our relationship continues to deteriorate."

Hope patted her arm. "You know Suzy and I told you nearly a year ago to date around."

Alex held up her hands. "I know, I know. Trust me, I've thought about it." She glanced at Cheri. "Maybe I should try some of those online dating sites you used."

Suzy chimed in. "Because those freak shows worked out so well." She turned to the socialite. "Sorry, Cheri, but—"

"You're right." Cheri shrugged. "They never worked out."

Hope popped a handful of popcorn into her mouth. "Too bad Gage isn't around. You two had definite chemistry."

Alex studied a crack in the table a little too intently. "I miss Gage. Too bad that stupid pop singer jumped his bones and kept me from seeing him again."

Suzy giggled. "Somehow, I bet he misses you too." Her phone rang but she ignored it. "This is our much-needed girls' night. I'm ignoring my phone."

"Good, because I want to change the subject." Hope reached into her bulging, brown tote bag. "I have something for you, Cheri."

The socialite's eyebrows shot up. "For me?"

Hope plunked a thick envelope on top of the table. "Yes, for you. The Hilltop neighbors still talk about your generous donation for furnishings and appliances after last year's tornado. Since they don't know your name, they gave the letters to me to pass along." Shoving the weighty parcel toward Cheri, she continued. "There are letters from parents, grandparents, and even sweet, scrawled thank-you notes from Hilltop students' younger siblings written in crayon."

Cheri blushed as she held the thick envelope against her chest. "You're going to make me cry. I'm glad I had the resources to help. And thank you for keeping my name anonymous." After setting the students' notes on the table, she patted the hefty stack. "This means the world. I'll read every single note."

Hope beamed. "I'm thrilled they took the time to write. It's hard in the days of email and texts to get kids to actually go old school."

Reaching for her cocktail, Hope grinned at the New Yorker. "You did an amazing thing. I'll never forget it and neither will they."

"Enough about me." Cheri reached for Hope's hand. "That's a cool ring." She studied the oval orb. "It has changed colors since you first got here. What is it?"

Hope glanced at the antique filigreed silver ring. A solitary tear rolled down her cheek. "It's called a mood ring. This is one of the few things I have from my late mother. Officially, she's my adopted mother. It's confusing, I know, but I'm so thankful she left her ring beside my kitchen sink, likely after washing the dishes—right before I threw my parents out of my house. That was the last time I saw them." Her voice broke. "After our horrific fight, they were killed in that wretched train accident—at least she was."

Cheri shifted in her seat. "Sorry to be dense but I'm obviously behind on your family saga, Hope. I remember hearing something about the accident from Suzy or Alex. I wish I had been here to help you through that ordeal."

"I'm okay. Really." Hope sniffled. "It's been a while now, although the memories still haunt me." She brightened. "It seems my adopted dad somehow lived. Remarkably, he's working as a janitor at my school. It's unbelievable even to me. At first, Alex and Suzy didn't believe me, but after seeing the tornado recognition ceremony including Larry, the janitor, on television, they agree it's him."

"Does your adopted dad remember anything about the accident?" Cheri asked.

Hope shook her head. "Nope, he doesn't remember me, the accident, his wife, nor anything about his past. I haven't pressed him and keep hoping his memory will return organically."

Sighing, she said, "He calls himself Mac, but I know he's Larry. In my head, I call him both names. Sometimes I call him Mac in front of the kids so they don't ask questions. But I occasionally slip and refer to him as Larry. It's baffling, plus he's dating a colleague."

Cheri swirled the cherries in her cocktail. "That must be uncomfortable."

Hope's head bobbed. "It is, and we were becoming fast friends. Willow—that's her name—is an art teacher at Hilltop High. She's really cool and a hippie like my dad. I'm sure that's why they connected—"

Interrupting their conversation, Alex returned from the restroom. She glanced from friend to friend. "Why the somber mood. Did someone die?"

No one said a word.

After the uncomfortable silence, Alex said, "Foot in mouth, I see." Alex screeched a barstool across the floor and lowered her voice. "Who is it this time?"

"You already know. Larry. Mac. My adopted dad." Hope shrugged. "I was bringing Cheri up to speed."

"Oh, that man's definitely Larry. Remember we saw him on television last year? He's a dead ringer—" Alex blew out her breath. "Dammit. Sorry, Hope." She patted her friend's arm. "I thought we already told Cheri about this."

Cheri interjected. "If you did, I was so absorbed in losing my grandmother and adjusting to non-New York City living that it didn't sink in."

Hope waved both hands in the air. "Let's don't ruin our night out. It was tragic and horrible and the worst thing that has ever happened in my life. But I have all of you and my students. I'm good."

Cheri tapped Hope's finger. "I'm still curious about how that gorgeous ring changes colors."

Hope glanced at her hand. Her ring had turned from black to yellow.

"What do the colors mean?" Cheri asked.

Staring at the orb, Hope said, "Apparently black means depressed, fear or overworked."

"Oh, God." Alex chuckled. "Mine would always be black."

Hope studied the ring. "I think yellow indicates either caution or mellow."

"Remember the song, 'Mellow Yellow'?" Suzy leaned forward to get a closer look. "This is interesting, Hope. Maybe I should get a mood ring for my next anxious bride."

"Now, 'Mellow Yellow's' stuck in my head." She studied her ring finger. "I noticed it was orange when I drove here, which normally means stressed or nervous, but now the orb is blue, so maybe this thing actually works."

Crossing her toned legs, Cheri asked, "What does blue indicate?"

Hope fluffed her unruly hair. "Calm and peaceful."

Alex practically snorted her drink. "Mine would never turn blue. Ever."

Gus came by, asked if they wanted refills, and peered at Hope's hand. "What's so interesting over here?"

Flexing her fingers, Hope said, "Me for a change. I'm the interesting one. Actually, it's my mood ring."

"Weren't those popular in the sixties or seventies?" Gus leaned forward as he balanced a tray of foamy beers.

"Yep. My parents were hippies. Maybe you never knew that."

"Cool. I'll be right back with refills, ladies. I'd better deliver these beers before those ball players want to tussle."

Suzy patted Hope's hand. "Your ring is still blue. You're still at peace. Maybe your hippie mom is sending you a sign."

Hope smiled. "I hope you're right."

Suzy glanced at her half-ringing, half-vibrating phone. "It's Ken. I've got to go. I promised to make dinner tonight since we have the evening to ourselves. Jon and Fernando went to dinner with Vanessa and the baby to try and get her mind on something else. Izzy's with a friend." She paused. "We're trying to find our new normal. He's sending me a gentle reminder with promises of an extended massage afterward."

"Lucky," Hope and Alex said in unison.

Alex waved her hand as if she were shooing a fly. "Go. Enjoy your healthy relationship. God knows I wish I had one." She drained her drink. "Thanks for coming tonight, Suzy Q. I know your life has been turned upside down recently."

Suzy scooted her chair back. "Yes, it has, but we'll make it. See you soon, ladies." She turned to Cheri. "Thanks for the drink. I'm really happy you're back."

Alex turned to Cheri. "How's everything in New York?"

Grinning from ear to ear, Cheri said, "Our catering event for Elton John couldn't have gone better. He was thrilled with the gala, gave me a huge bonus, and already hired Fifth Avenue Catering for his birthday next year."

Hope couldn't stop laughing. "Yeah, that about sums up my life. Hanging with Elton John. I'm sure I'll see Mariah Carey tomorrow."

Giggling, Alex said, "She's right. What the hell do you see in us?"

"This." Cheri spread her arms. "All of this. I love you girls."

Chapter 48

After Suzy arrived home, she parked in the garage and stepped into the kitchen. "Hi, hon. Hungry?" Without waiting for an answer, she retrieved a cutting board from beneath the sink.

"I'm famished. Can I help, babe?" Ken turned away from the television.

"Nah, it'll feel good to cook again. Normalcy, you know?" Suzy leaned around the counter. "I'll take a glass of wine, though."

Ken headed to the kitchen and patted his wife on the rear. "I'm glad you're home. We never have the house to ourselves anymore."

Wrapping both arms around her husband's neck, Suzy nuzzled him. "I've missed you. I've missed us."

"You can say that again." Stroking Suzy's hair, he kissed her softly at first, and then probed. "You taste good. I've missed us too."

Giggling, Suzy said, "I guess you like the taste of Angry Balls."

"Huh?"

"It's a drink. Cheri Van Buren introduced us to the cocktail."

"So the New Yorker's back?"

"She sure is. Alex brought her up to speed about . . . everything."

Frowning, Ken made a scotch for himself and poured a glass of merlot for Suzy. "We've definitely had our share of extremes."

As she rinsed the asparagus, Ken reached for a knife. "I want to help."

"Knock yourself out." Suzy sipped her merlot as she busied herself with the blackened seasoning. She rubbed it on the salmon and placed it in the oven, handing a lemon to Ken. "Will you slice this for later?"

"You know I'm the best sous chef there is." After he sliced the asparagus, she sprinkled parmesan cheese on the vegetable and drizzled balsamic dressing into a serving dish. "Want any bread?"

"Nah." Ken shook his head as he carried plates to the table. "I'm cutting back."

"Right." Suzy winked as she pulled the salmon out of the oven and let it rest while Ken refilled their drinks.

Dining at their breakfast table, the couple ate ravenously. After several moments of silence, Suzy said, "I almost miss the commotion, do you?"

Holding a piece of salmon in mid-air, Ken said, "I don't know. I'm enjoying the peace and quiet, but I think we should discuss Vanessa's parents' house. Do you know any attorneys? I'm sure we'll have to handle this for her. She has her hands full with the baby."

Staring at the ceiling, Suzy groaned. "We jump from one huge project to another." Pausing, she said, "Hope's dad is an attorney. I think his name is Paul. I can call him but do we really need to get on this right now? Can't we take a little breather?"

Ken headed toward their makeshift bar near the kitchen and poured a second scotch. After he polished off his food, he said, "We need to find out if their house belonged to them or to the church. Also, whether they had a will. I don't think Vanessa is in any shape to handle this, do you?"

"Definitely not." Suzy chewed thoughtfully and stared out the darkened window. The sun had long set on what was her first non-hectic day. The last thing she wanted was to embark on this endeavor but knew she had to help. She owed it to Vanessa and Violet Grace.

After placing his plate in the dishwasher, Ken waited for Suzy to finish and gestured toward the couch. "Let's get comfortable. I'll clean the rest of the dishes up later—or better yet—in the morning."

Suzy settled on the sofa with her barely touched wine in hand. Ken rubbed her stiff shoulders. "Someone needs a massage."

She grinned. "I'd kill for a massage about now."

"Later." He winked. "Do you think we should mention this to Vanessa or contact an attorney first?"

Folding her legs beneath her, Suzy leaned against her husband. "I'm not sure. She's fragile right now. Why don't we do some checking on our end before we drag her through what could be a dead end." Wrinkling her nose, she said, "Bad choice of words. I mean if they don't have a will, there's no need to get her hopes up or make her think about anything but herself and baby Violet right now."

"Agreed."

"Like I said, Hope's biological dad is an attorney. I'll get his name and number from her tomorrow." Her phone beeped indicating a text from Jon. She glanced at the screen, saw a photo of Violet Grace, and smiled. *Jon always seems to know when I need him.*

After showing the photo to Ken, Suzy said, "Now, about that massage."

Chapter 49

The next day, Suzy texted Hope and explained the situation. After getting the number for Paul Taylor, Attorney at Law, she called, gave him the name of Vanessa's parents, the link to their obituary, and the late reverend's church name.

The attorney listened to her elongated story without interrupting. After Suzy finished, Paul Taylor said, "I see. This is an intricate situation. Let me check some records. I'll call you back this afternoon. You said you're Hope's friend?"

"Yes. We went to high school together. Hope, Alex, and I go to Coconuts nearly every week, or as needed, which is sometimes often."

Chuckling the attorney said, "Of course, now I remember. She has mentioned you both many times. I didn't recognize your last name at first. I'll be happy to do some research and will call you back this afternoon."

Within two hours, Suzy learned from the attorney that Vanessa's parents, in fact, did have a will. They also owned their house. It was not retained by the church. Paul Taylor offered to represent Vanessa at the office of her parents' attorney later that week.

Suzy breathed a sigh of relief. "Thank you very much. I'll call Vanessa and coordinate a time for the meeting." She hung up and started dialing.

~ ~ ~

A day later, Suzy, Jon, Fernando, and Vanessa went to the attorney's office. Ken stayed home to babysit baby Violet.

The drive over was somber without much conversation. Suzy could only imagine what was going through Vanessa's mind. After she parked in front of Williams & Williams, a short, friendly Paul Taylor met them on the sidewalk. Suzy noticed he shared Hope's big, brown eyes.

After introductions, Paul escorted them inside a small office with a stark, nondescript boardroom. Mr. Williams, Attorney at Law, shook hands with everyone but focused on Vanessa. "I'm sorry about your parents. What a tragedy."

Already sniffling, Vanessa nodded as a tear trailed down her cheek. Both Jon and Fernando flanked her and offered tissues.

The attorney opened a manila file. "The good news is your parents left their house to you, Vanessa. You're the sole beneficiary. You can either keep the house or sell—"

"They did?" The young mom's eyebrows shot up. "Dad always said he'd leave it to the church."

Mr. Williams flipped a page. With his index finger, he scrolled the document with his finger. "Ah, here it is. They revised their will six months ago. I made a note in the margin about a newborn." He stared over his glasses at Vanessa. "Did you have a baby? Their grandbaby?"

Fernando leaned forward. "She did. Actually, we all sort of had the baby. It was on our wedding day." He clamped his hand over his mouth. "Sorry. Vanessa can answer for herself." Reaching for his phone, he asked, "Want to see a picture?"

Both attorneys smiled.

Fernando's excitement made Vanessa relax. "He's right. *We* had a baby. Violet Grace is the granddaughter of Suzy"— she pointed to Jon's Mom—"and also of my parents." She swallowed. "My late parents."

"I'd love to see a photo," the attorney said.

Fernando thrust his phone in Mr. William's face and

started scrolling. Jon reached for Fernando's arm. "He probably doesn't want to see all five hundred photos."

The happy baby news made everyone at ease. Reaching into a drawer, the attorney retrieved a small envelope. Vanessa's name was on the front. "This contains their house keys. They had a duplicate set made for you, just in case."

Vanessa's voice cracked. "I can't believe this. I thought they hated me."

Paul Taylor spoke up. "Why in the world would you think that?"

"Because my dad is . . . *was* a preacher. I had Violet out of wedlock. He feared he'd lose his job at the church, so I laid low." She wiped her eyes. "I wanted to protect them. I didn't want to embar—"

"Damn shame," Jon muttered. He reached for Vanessa's hand. "Looks like they made it up to you, though."

"I'd rather have my parents, but I guess you're right." Vanessa reached for the envelope.

Mr. Williams studied the young mom. "Any questions?"

"Can I go there any time?" Vanessa peered from Mr. Williams to Paul Taylor. Both men nodded.

"It's your house now. Do whatever you want with it." Standing, Mr. Williams said, "Feel free to use the conference room. I've got another client unless you have more questions."

Vanessa's voice rose. "Can I sell it if I want?"

"Certainly." The attorney smiled. "It's yours. In many cases like this an auctioneer is called to handle the estate sale of the house and contents, but that's up to you."

Nodding, Vanessa said, "This is a big decision. I'll consider all of the options." Clutching the envelope, she crossed the room and wrapped her arms around the surprised attorney's face. "Thank you."

He teared up. "I'm glad there's somewhat of a happy ending here. It seems odd to give you my condolences and congratulations in the same sentence, but there it is." Mr. Williams, her parents' attorney, picked up the legal file, shook hands with everyone, and left them alone in the conference room.

Vanessa placed her hand over her chest. "I wondered how I was going to pay my rent, car payment, and afford diapers. She glanced toward the sky. "Thank you, Mom and Dad."

Chapter 50

Three days after Vanessa had moved out of Suzy's house and back to her duplex, she called Jon and Fernando saying she was desperate for sleep and pleaded with them to take a night with the baby.

Jon agreed with more confidence than he felt. After they arrived, he reassured her he and Fernando could handle the baby. They were dads, after all.

Hair askew with dark circles under her eyes, a sleepy Vanessa thrust bottles of breast milk in their hands. "I've pumped all I have. This should last throughout the night. The baby's over—" She forced a giggled. "Just follow the screams."

"We've got this. Go to bed," Fernando said.

Jon and Fernando exchanged glances, checked the baby's diaper, grabbed a change of clothes and baby blanket, and eventually managed to get Violet strapped into her car seat.

They drove across town, luckily catching every green light. Once they parked, Fernando wrapped a soft blanket tight around her to swaddle the baby as Vanessa had shown them. Racing inside their apartment, both men stared wide-eyed at one another as her screams got louder and louder.

"Christ. Someone might call the police." Jon peered into Violet's red face. "Shhh, baby girl. It's okay." The baby screamed louder. He whispered to Fernando in a panicked tone. "We've got to get her calmed down before she wakes up the entire apartment complex."

In a soothing tone, Fernando said, "Don't act nervous. Violet Grace will pick up on it."

Jon's eyes widened. "What do you suggest?"

Both men alternately bounced, rocked, paced, and sang lullabies to no avail. After several minutes, which seemed like hours, the men loaded Violet back into Jon's car. "Let's go to Mom's."

A wild-eyed Fernando peered into the backseat. "Maybe the longer car ride will put her to sleep."

"We can only hope." Jon winced as his half-sleeping, half-tortured baby howled. He stared ahead and focused on the curvy road. "Let's hope Mom didn't change the locks."

Once they gained entry, the dads, already worn out, breathed a sigh of relief after stepping into the kitchen. Jon put a finger to his lips. "I'll let them know we're here." He tiptoed into Suzy and Ken's bedroom and tapped on the door.

Ken called out, "Izzy, is that you?"

Jon heard his mom turn over in the bed and cleared his throat. "Sorry to wake you guys. We can't get Violet to sleep and told Vanessa to get some shuteye. He glanced at his still-sleeping Mom and whispered, "Let her sleep. I'll close the door. Fernando has an idea."

Ken half sat up, mumbling, "Okay. Good luck." He crawled back under the covers and rolled over.

Trudging past Izzy's room, Jon assumed if she were like most teens she'd sleep through a hurricane. Her door was shut and what Fernando had in mind was at the opposite end of the house.

Jon watched his new husband bounce a red-faced, bawling Violet. "Doing okay?"

A perspiring Fernando said, "For now."

"Looks like a long night. I'll make some coffee." Jon forced a smile but his heart thudded. "Surely we can handle a newborn. We're grown men."

Fernando stared at him. "I hope you're right. She's got a set of lungs on her."

"I'll hurry." Jon made his way to the kitchen. As the coffee brewed, his thoughts jumbled. *What if we aren't cut out for this? What if we can't handle a baby? Vanessa's baby. My baby. Fernando's baby.* Soon he poured two giant mugs full of black, stout coffee and returned to the sounds of squalling.

After Jon set the coffee down, Fernando thrust baby Violet into his hands. "Watch and learn."

"Go for it. Good luck." Jon set his coffee mug on an end table as he cuddled a distressed Violet.

Pulling back the wooden piano cover to reveal well-worn ivory keys, Fernando flexed his fingers and rotated his shoulders.

"Will you hurry up? This isn't the symphony." Jon smoothed Violet's sweaty hair. "It's a good thing we didn't name her Patience." A chuckle escaped. "We'd definitely have to rename her."

Fernando snorted as he played a soft rendition of "Scarborough Fair." Within seconds, Violet's waterworks stopped. Her body visibly relaxed as she appeared to listen to the soothing melody.

As Fernando continued with the second verse, Jon rubbed her back. "I think she just cooed."

Smiling, Fernando asked, "Is she old enough to coo?"

Jon shrugged. "Who knows but she loves the music. Keep playing." Balancing the baby while he sipped coffee, he added, "Thank goodness Mom has a piano."

"And thank goodness I know how to play." Fernando played the song three times until Violet fell asleep in Jon's arms.

Suzy stumbled into the room. "What's going on?"

Both men shushed her and pointed toward the sleeping baby.

Nodding, Suzy retreated to the den where she kept a bassinet for drop-in baby visits. She easily picked up the lightweight baby bed and moved it toward the piano.

After Jon eased the baby into the bassinet, they all peered at Violet as though she were something in Ripley's Believe It Or Not Museum. Convinced the baby was fast asleep, Suzy motioned toward the kitchen.

Tiptoeing into the next room, Suzy embraced both men. "I'm so proud of you two. You're great dads, both of you. I'm also thrilled the piano's finally being used. By the way, you play beautifully, Fernando."

He gave her an *ah shucks* look. "I'm happy it worked."

Laughing, Suzy said, "You may need to keep sleeping bags here if this becomes routine."

"Let's hope not," Jon said. "This middle of the night routine wrecks me."

Suzy winked. "Welcome to parenthood. Want some scrambled eggs?"

"Now you're talking," Jon said.

"Did my mother rub off on you?" Fernando laughed. "She's all about food, you know."

"Really? I hadn't noticed." Suzy winked as she rattled around the kitchen retrieving a frying pan, spatula, and eggs. After the guys gobbled their eggs and toast, Suzy yawned.

"Aren't you going to eat, Mom?"

"Nah, I'm actually meeting my friends for breakfast in a couple of hours."

"That's new and different." Jon rinsed the plates and loaded the dishwasher. "Thanks for letting us barge in and take over your house."

"Any time, guys. You know you're always welcome."

Fernando reached for Jon's hand. "Before we leave, I want to discuss something important about the baby."

Suzy took a step. "I'll give you some privacy."

"No, Mom. We're all one, big happy family. Let's hear him out. What's up?"

"You know I don't mind driving here in the middle of the night to play the piano. I'd do anything for Violet Grace. But I was thinking about Vanessa's parents' house . . ."

"What about it?" Jon and Suzy both asked.

Picking at a toast crumb, Fernando said, "Vanessa's an only child. Remember she said she might consider auctioning the house. She told me it has four bedrooms and a basement. That's huge. Plenty of room for privacy." Fernando chewed on his bottom lip. "I don't want to overstep my bounds—"

"What are you getting at?" Jon's brows furrowed. "And you're not overstepping any bounds. Tell me." He glanced at his mom. "Tell us."

As usual Fernando wasn't one to mince words. "I think we should move in together. You, me, Vanessa and baby Violet. We can be the contemporary family we've told everyone we are. What do you think?"

Jon grinned. "I think we had better call Vanessa."

Suzy poured another cup of coffee. "This sounds like a wonderful idea to me. Let me know how it goes." She yawned.

"Bye, Mom. Thanks for letting us barge in."

As she watched Jon and Fernando head outside with the still-sleeping baby, Suzy wondered how her life had gotten so full so fast.

Chapter 51

Alex arranged a breakfast get-together at the Crystal City Diner. After the mountain of monumental, life-changing events in their lives, she texted her friends the night before saying they needed to change up their routine.

For once, she arrived first. Suzy and Hope strolled in together and scooted around a cushioned corner booth. After ordering coffee, Alex grabbed the first cup the server placed on the table and downed half of it.

"What a night. I'm exhausted." Alex glugged her java as Suzy and Hope added cream and sugar to theirs.

"I had a heck of an evening too." Suzy blew on her hot coffee.

Grinning, Hope said, "I slept like a baby."

"Haha. If *only* babies slept all night. I was up for hours with Fernando, Jon, and baby Violet. In fact, I cooked breakfast for them earlier."

"Babies and zero sleep. Not interested." Alex took another swallow, stared inside her cup, and screeched, "Oh, my God."

Alarmed, Suzy reached across the table. "What is it?"

Hope stiffened. "Don't tell me there's a bug."

"Worse." Alex held her coffee cup sideways. "There's a ring around the inside of the cup as dark as Hope's eyebrows."

Hope leaned over to examine the contents and wrinkled her nose. "Uh-oh. Looks like someone else drank out of that before you—"

"I *know.*" Alex scrubbed her lips with her napkin. "I

think I might be sick." She waved the server over as Suzy stifled a giggle.

"It couldn't have happened to a worse person." Suzy and Hope exchanged amused glances.

A waitress appeared and plucked a pencil from behind her ear. "Ready to order?"

"No, we are not ready." Alex pointed toward the vile coffee cup. "Someone else drank out of this. It's dirty. Probably some old man or woman who had the plague, drooled, or worse, had a cold sore. If I get sick—"

"I'm sorry. I'll get you a fresh cup right away." The waitress scampered off.

"I'm going to the restroom to wash my lips." Alex continued to wipe them with her dry napkin. "There's no telling what kind of dreadful disease I'll get."

Suzy bit her lip to keep from laughing. "You'll probably just build up your immune system from all of that antibacterial gel you use."

"Suzy's right. Imagine the germs I get at school. Kids constantly sneeze and cough on me. Don't worry." Hope covered her mouth in an obvious attempt to hide her smile. "But go wash your mouth out if it makes you feel better."

"Whatever. Laugh all you want. It's gross." Alex scurried to the bathroom, splashed water inside her mouth, gargled a few times, and added soap to a paper towel. She cleaned her lips three times, got another paper towel for the door handle, and returned to her friends who were already on their second cup of coffee and staring at menus.

"Why does this always happen to me?" Alex asked.

Suzy shrugged. "Likely because you have OCD. With everything that's gone on, I probably wouldn't have noticed."

Alex rolled her eyes. "Surely, a ring inside a coffee mug would bother you two."

"I wouldn't like it but I also wouldn't go ballistic."

"I didn't go ballistic," Alex said.

Hope shrugged and rubbed her belly. "It's over. I'm starving. Let's order."

Alex inspected the new cup the server had plunked on the table, wiping the area twice where her mouth goes. Satisfied, she picked up a menu. "If I weren't starving, I'd leave. I'm disgusted."

"Try to put it out of your mind." Suzy flipped the menu over. "The food smells delicious. I think I'll order multigrain pancakes and crispy bacon."

Pointing to the number 3 option on the menu, Hope said, "Eggs, hash browns, and sausage for me." Her face fell. "I shouldn't but I'd also love biscuits and gravy."

"Get some," Suzy said.

Hope groaned. "I'd rather have a nice body like you two. I've gained thirty pounds—at least."

"Stop it. You're beautiful." Alex scanned the plastic menu. "I'll get oatmeal and rye toast. Surely, they can't mess that up."

"Unless someone ate out of your bowl earlier," Suzy teased.

"Or licked your spoon." Hope winked.

Alex made a face. "I thought you two were my best friends."

"We're trying to help you relax. Let's change the subject," Suzy said. "I'm glad Cheri's back. We should have invited her. What do you think of our socialite friend?"

"She's gorgeous, sexy, and rich. I hate her." Alex stared into her shocked friends' faces. "Relax. I'm teasing. Actually, I like her a lot, designer shoes and all."

"Me too." Hope shrugged. "Maybe in another life I'll get good genes or have money, but I won't hold my breath."

Suzy stared at Hope over her coffee cup. "You're a doll."

"Suzy's right. Stop putting yourself down or I'm sending you to a self-esteem class."

"Old habits." Hope shrugged. "Social media doesn't help. It appears that everyone has a perfect life."

"Seriously? Everyone lies. Don't believe half the shit they post." Alex stared into her new coffee cup again before taking another tentative sip.

"I love you, Alex, but just so you know, everything I post is true." Suzy leaned back as the server plunked down steaming, heaping platters.

After several minutes of silently devouring food, Alex said, "We need to go back to Coconuts with Cheri again soon. Angry Balls are in order before she disappears to New York again."

"Speak of the devil." Suzy glanced at her beeping phone. "Cheri just sent a text. She wants us to meet her at Coconuts tonight."

"I'm in," Hope and Alex both said.

Chapter 52

Cheri heard her phone chirp and recognized the Skype call from Victoria Van Buren, her wealthy, gorgeous, *absent* mom. As the fuzzy image cleared, Cheri squinted and frowned.

"Mom, I thought we talked about plastic surgery months ago. You promised you wouldn't go over—"

"Hello to you too." Victoria rolled her eyes. "Geeze. Between you and your dad, I feel like I'm alone. He's always . . ." After a long pause, she muttered, "Oh, never mind."

Cheri scowled into the phone. "He's always what? I hate it when you do that, Mom."

Victoria shrugged. "I don't know. It's probably my overactive imagination."

Feeling a sinking feeling, Cheri pressed. "What? Tell me."

Waving a manicured hand in the air, Cheri noticed her mother's ring fingers were painted a glittery silver while her other nails were burgundy red.

Sighing, Victoria said, "Your dad is still working out. A *lot*." Lighting a cigarette, she blew smoke into the screen. "Between the gym, his meetings, and business dinners, I rarely see him these days."

"I hate it when you smoke." Dread overcame Cheri. She drummed her fingers on the table. Her parents had always been the perfect couple. Her mind worked fast as she attempted to find a positive solution. "Working out is good, right? He probably wants to stay fit and healthy, simple as that." After hesitating, Cheri offered, "Maybe you should join him at the gym."

Sipping a martini while alternately taking a long drag, Victoria said dryly, "He told me in no uncertain terms he wants to work out a-l-o-n-e."

"Oh." Cheri studied the two-inch-long ashes perilously dangling above her mother's elegant white pants. She felt herself holding her breath as she stared fixated on the glowing embers.

Just in time, Victoria tapped her cigarette and the ashes fell into a crystal Tiffany's bowl.

Cheri blinked. "That was close."

"What, darling?"

"Nothing." Glancing at a huge clock on the wall, Cheri knew she had to broach the difficult subject and took a relaxing tone. "Mom, I know there's a six-hour time difference between the Midwest and Europe, but isn't it a little early to drink?"

Defiantly, her mother took a big gulp. "It's never too early, darling."

"Okay, fine." Cheri's mind raced as she considered her mother's frozen forehead. She decided to let any plastic surgery lectures go, for now. Brightening, she asked, "Why don't you travel? Maybe you could plan a surprise trip for Daddy. Don't you have an anniversary coming up? Or a birthday? There has to be some event to celebrate. Sorry, you know I'm horrible with dates."

Victoria smiled mid-sip. Setting her martini glass down, she licked her lips and said, "That's not a bad idea. I'd have to catch him between business dealings but surely he could manage seven or ten days away."

"Do it. Plan something really cool that he can't resist. Something other than Europe. I know you love it there but this needs to be out of the box to get Dad's attention. Want me to send you some ideas? I can research destinations or ask my friend who is a wedding planner. I'm sure she knows of several romantic des—"

Victoria peered over her cocktail and batted her false eyelashes. "No need, darling. I have an idea. In fact, it's a place I've dreamed about since I was a teen—somewhere that's been on my bucket list for eons." She giggled. "Not that I'm *that* old."

Wriggling in her chair, Cheri fought the urge to check the time again. "Don't keep me in suspense, Mom. Where are you thinking?"

Crossing her toned legs, Victoria said, "I want to surprise you. Hopefully, I can tear your dad away. Don't worry. We'll send photos if I can pull this off. Thank you for the pep talk, darling. Gotta run. I want to get right on this. *Ciao.*"

The call ended before Cheri had a chance to say goodbye, as usual. *Bye, Mom, and good luck with your secret vacation.*

She texted her new girlfriends and asked Alex, Suzy, and Hope to meet her at Coconuts, writing:

Hi, ladies. Coconuts at 6 tonight? Parental trouble. Maybe. Angry Balls on me.

After everyone responded affirmatively, Cheri changed into a denim shirt dress, leopard print ankle wrap sandals, and braided her hair into a side braid. Climbing into her grandmother's red Mercedes, she drove to Coconuts with her parents' relationship on her mind.

Turning up the volume on the radio to drown out her worries, she eased north onto Highway 65. Finally having real girlfriends for truly the first time meant getting valuable feedback on all aspects of her life. She pushed on the gas pedal. *I can't get to Coconuts fast enough.*

Chapter 53

After a grueling day at Show-Me Bank, Alex couldn't wait for Happy Hour with her friends. She and Cheri arrived at the same time and saddled up to their familiar high-top table.

Alex said, "Let's order."

Cheri placed her designer bag on a hook beneath the table. "Doesn't anyone bother with greetings anymore?" Hugging her friend, she said, "You sound like my mom earlier."

Alex scrunched her nose. "Ouch."

Cheri patted the barstool beside her. "We Skyped earlier. She didn't say hello either, nor goodbye, for that matter."

"Oh, then, hi." Alex straightened the lapel on her turquoise blouse.

"It's okay. My nerves are on edge."

"Join the club." Alex waved Gus over to the table and both women ordered wine. "Let's ease into the Angry Balls later."

Soon Hope and Suzy ran inside, plopped on barstools, shared a big group hug, and everyone talked animatedly at the same time.

After giggles and drink orders, Alex turned to Cheri. "So spill. What's going on with your parents?"

Cheri explained how her mother had begun smoking again, was drinking earlier and earlier in the day, and getting one too many cosmetic surgery procedures."

Suzy interrupted. "Isn't that the life of the rich and

famous?" After no one said a word, she winced. "Sorry, that was rude."

"A little tacky." Alex nudged Suzy. "You've been hanging around me for too long."

Suzy shrugged. "Want my diagnosis?"

Cheri nodded.

"As odd as it sounds, your mom may be bored with her life."

Hope sipped her margarita, licking off some salt. "I'd love to be bored with world travel and too much money."

Taking a healthy swallow of her cocktail, Alex said, "I'll take some tedious shopping trips off your mom's hands. I have a feeling there's more, though. You've got the floor, Cheri. You can tell us anything."

"And it'll stay here," Hope said.

The New Yorker sighed. "It's probably nothing."

"Try us," Alex probed.

Cheri took a deep breath, leaned forward, and lowered her voice. "According to Mom, Dad stays in his office all day, has even more business meetings and dinners than usual, and now has a newfound obsession with working out."

After a few nods, frowns, and shared glances, Alex spoke first. "He's probably having an affair."

"Oh, my God. That didn't enter my mind." Cheri's eyes widened. "Why would you think that?"

Alex shrugged. "Men who suddenly have the urge to work out like fiends are usually trying to impress a woman." She paused, "Unless, of course, he's had a health scare. That's a possibility, I suppose."

Cheri's face fell. "I hate both options." Her eyes filled with tears. "Gee, I'm so glad I asked you guys—"

Alex sipped her chard. "I should have kept my mouth shut. I'm still in a bitchy mood because of Tony and Nikki. My ridiculous intern is almost a peach compared to my boyfriend's nasty ex." Waving Gus over, she said, "Angry Balls all around, Gus. Put the tab on my ticket."

Cheri raised her hand to obviously object. "I promised to buy."

"There'll be another time," Alex said.

Reaching for the bowl of peanuts, Hope said, "I'm glad men aren't on my radar. They'd be way too much trouble for my simple life. I have zero interest in—"

Gus interrupted Hope by placing a tray of amber-filled drinks on the table, containing two maraschino cherries in each.

"I'm so glad you introduced us to this crazy drink, Cheri." Alex raised her glass in the air. "Here's to girlfriends." She paused. "And to hell with men."

After chuckles, they clanked glasses and Suzy set hers down. "I have to defend some of the men. My husband and son are wonderful—as is my new son-in-law."

Alex poised her cocktail in the air and refined her toast. "Okay, how's this? Here's to non-husbands and non-gay men, the bastards."

The women nearly doubled over laughing as they sipped their drinks.

"I love you, Alex," Hope said.

"Ditto," chimed the other women.

"Thanks, ladies," Alex said. "Cheri, how did you leave it with your mom?"

Splaying her cherry red nails on the table, Cheri said, "I suggested she surprise Dad with a vacation, and she loved the idea."

"Good plan. A romantic destination, I hope," Suzy said.

Hope ate another handful of peanuts. "Someday my vacation will be something other than Coconuts with you guys."

Alex elbowed Hope. "Hey, what's wrong with us?"

"Not a thing. I don't know what I'd do without you."

Suzy patted Hope's arm. "Same here. Change of subject. How's the janitor, Hope? Any news?"

Her brown eyes dulled. "Nope. He still doesn't remember me."

Alex studied her friend as she waited for three rowdy Greek tee-shirt-wearing college frat students to pass their table. Once the unruly guys settled in the back, she spoke. "Now that I can hear myself think, that's got to be surreal. I hope his memory returns but it has been a while."

"No kidding." Hope rubbed a drip on her glass. "Sometimes I wish I could shake his memory into him."

Peering at Hope over her cocktail, Alex said, "I can only imagine. I'd be the same way, only worse. Are Larry and the hippie art teacher still tight?"

Hope nodded. "Yep. In fact, he and Willow go camping most weekends. I'm not sure if they take a tent or sleep in her VW Microbus. I don't ask and don't really want to know any details." She shivered. "It's weird."

Suzy reached for Hope's hand. "Even though you have Larry, it must be surreal."

"Surreal. That's one way to put it." Hope shook her head. "He's still going by Mac instead of Larry. I try to play along so the students aren't confused but often mess up." Hope held up her hand. "Let's change the subject. Surely one of us has happy news."

"Now that you mention it." Suzy held her phone in the air. "These photos of Violet Grace will put a smile on anyone's face." She showed the women photo after photo of the baby. In one, she was surrounded by a filmy pink blanket, in others the baby wore violet clothes after Suzy said Fernando insisted they add an abundance of lavender to her wardrobe to match her name. Several pictures included Jon and Fernando and many with a beaming Vanessa holding her baby. "Ken and I love being grandparents." Suzy scrolled through her photo gallery. "Here's another cute one. Oh, and look at—"

After what felt like the hundredth photo, Alex turned to her best friend and said, "Suzy, you're really into this baby thing. I think that's enough photos for one night. Sorry if that hurts your feelings. You know I'm not much of a baby person—or a kid person, for that matter."

Suzy chuckled. "You'll change your mind after you have your own."

"No, I won't." Alex focused on Cheri. "Back to your parents. Any idea where your mom will choose for a vacation spot?"

"Your guess is as good as mine. Mom was cryptic but mentioned it's someplace she has dreamed of since she was a kid."

"Hmmm," Hope said. "Where would you ladies choose if you could go anywhere?"

"Italy," Suzy answered.

"Tahiti," Alex said. "How about you, Hope?"

She tapped her fingers. "I'm not crazy about airplanes—not that I've been on one—but the thought of it scares me. So, I'd probably have to choose a drivable destination." She brightened. "Maybe Orlando to see Mickey and Minnie Mouse."

Alex rolled her eyes. "Lame."

"No, it's not." Hope's brows knitted as she obviously searched for another destination. "Or . . . maybe a national park like Yellowstone or I could drive to a beach in Florida, Alabama, or California." She paused. "New Orleans or Nashville might be fun."

"Much better," Alex said. "The Mall of America would be a hoot."

"We aren't all avid shoppers like you, Alex." Hope studied Cheri. "What's your guess for your parents' trip?"

Shrugging, Cheri said, "Maybe Australia, Africa, or New Zealand. Possibly Thailand or China or somewhere even more exotic. Who knows? My mom always surprises me." She glanced at her gold Rolex. "I should be at home testing new recipes. I hope to land another celebrity event."

Alex straightened in her chair. "That reminds me. Show-Me Bank will celebrate its anniversary soon. Think I can hire Fifth Avenue Catering to cater it?"

Cheri brightened. "Sure. Who will attend?"

"A few of our best customers, employees, prominent business leaders, and our board members."

Cheri extracted her phone from her enormous leopard print bag. "What's the date and how many people do you expect?"

Alex gave Cheri the information and they shook hands to confirm the catering arrangement. Glancing at her watch, she said, "Gotta run, ladies. I have another early bank meeting tomorrow." She took another sip but left her half-filled glass.

Hope reached for her purse. "I need to go too. School's always early."

Alex glanced over her shoulder. "Wish me luck with Hannah the Horrible. We're working together way too often on the bank anniversary. I can't wait until it's over. That bitch Daddy's girl gets on my last nerve."

Chapter 54

After the eye-opening meeting with the attorney, Jon and Fernando discussed several what-if scenarios. They knew Vanessa was likely in over her head and decided to invite her over for dinner to test her reaction about living together.

As Fernando picked up his cell to dial, Vanessa's name appeared on the screen.

Yawning into the phone, Vanessa opened with, "That meeting overwhelmed me. I don't know what to do. Maybe I should call an auctioneer." She sniffled. "I'm not sure I can live in my parents' house. It might be too difficult."

"Let us help you consider your choices. Load Violet up and drive over here." Fernando glanced at Jon who nodded. "You have our address, right?"

"Yes, I know where you live." Another yawn. "I napped with the baby. Big decisions like this wear me out. I'd love some help."

"Good. Dinner's already started." Fernando opened a cabinet and reached for the oregano while Jon sliced garlic. "Come hungry, sweetie."

While they waited for Vanessa, Fernando added parsley and more tomatoes to his spaghetti sauce.

Within minutes, the buzzer rang. Jon pushed a button to open the outer gated door, ran downstairs, and met Vanessa and baby at the door. Reaching for Violet, he kissed her pink cheek. "I've missed you."

Once inside their pristine apartment, Vanessa set her purse on the floor and crossed the taupe and silver living room into the kitchen. "Something smells delicious."

Fernando pointed toward the huge pot with a flourish. "Thanks. It's my mom's special marinara sauce."

Vanessa stepped toward the big pot and peered inside.

Fernando dipped a spoon in the sauce, blew to cool it, and held the heaping spoonful in mid-air. "Want a taste?"

She took a tentative sip of the hot sauce and licked her lips. "That's incredible. Thanks for inviting me over." Glancing around the gleaming kitchen, Vanessa added, "Your apartment is, well, very nice—and clean—but not exactly baby friendly." She shook her head. "You must think my shabby place is country cluttered."

Jon handed the baby to Fernando as he took over stirring duties. "Your duplex is great but that's a nice segue for what we wanted to discuss tonight." He elbowed his husband. "Right?"

Fernando asked, "So I get the honors? Let's sit down first." He led Vanessa to a small retro table for two and added a third chair from a tiny corner desk. As he waited for Vanessa to take a seat, he said, "You know I'm not one to bloviate, so basically, here's the bottom line. We've tried living apart, and as you know, we've had a few middle-of-the-night, uh, driving around town incidents to calm Violet, so Jon and I thought—"

Jon blew out his breath and jumped into the conversation. "I know you mentioned possibly calling an auctioneer and selling the house, but we wondered how you'd feel about all four of us living together in your parents' home." He studied Vanessa's freckled face for a reaction. "There it is. I suppose Fernando's bluntness is wearing off on me."

Vanessa sat stunned as she studied both men. "I . . . don't . . . know what to say. I'm not sure if I can handle being there. I'm afraid it would make me sad." Her face became splotchy as tears trailed down her cheeks. "I mean I'd love to have you nearby to help me raise Violet. I-I'm just not sure." She stared at the floor. "I'm sorry to disappoint you, especially after how wonderful you've both-"

"Shh." Jon wiped her tears with his thumb and reached for Vanessa's hand. "Think of it this way, maybe it would make you feel closer to your mom and dad. You could see what you've missed while you've been estranged." He paused. "But it's up to you."

"Of course it's up to her." Fernando spritzed the bottom of a casserole dish with olive oil. "It's your call, sweetie. We'll be supportive and involved no matter what you decide." He began layering the baked spaghetti with noodles, sauce, and mozzarella cheese and placed it in the oven. Crossing the tiny kitchen in three steps, he sat beside Vanessa and stroked her ginger hair. "It's entirely your decision." He added, "But we're exhausted, honey. You must be too."

Chuckling, Jon said, "Sleep is definitely not overrated. This parenting thing is harder than it looks. We'd ask you to move in with us but our bachelor pad isn't exactly conducive to babies."

"Plus, Columns IV doesn't allow babies." Fernando kissed Violet's pudgy, pink arm. "The owners don't know what they're missing."

"Sleep. They're missing sleep," Jon said. After Vanessa shot him a look, he added, "But Violet's totally worth it."

Vanessa glanced upward as if channeling her parents. After several seconds, she said, "I-I simply don't know. There are so many decisions. I'm not old enough to make all of these life-changing choices." Her face crumpled. "You've both been beyond supportive." Her eyes reddened around the edges. "I feel terrible about disappointing you."

"No worries." Fernando kissed Vanessa's cheek. "We knew it was a long shot."

Vanessa sniffed. "Thank you for understanding."

Fernando took a green salad out of the refrigerator and

reached for a white ceramic pitcher. "Who wants peach tea?" Everyone murmured affirmatively.

"Or red wine," Jon said.

"That too. Jon, will you wrap the garlic bread in foil and put it in the oven."

"On it." Jon hovered in the kitchen near Fernando. Glancing over his shoulder, he said, "Vanessa, don't give it another thought. We respect your wishes. Besides, I'm starving. Let's eat."

"Let me help." Vanessa held the baby in one arm, fumbled in a drawer for silverware and napkins and set the table in the men's minimalistic black and white kitchen.

Baby Violet wailed just as the oven timer went off. All three adults groaned. Fernando shrugged. "Nobody said parenthood was easy."

Chapter 55

Excited about a fun-filled Saturday, Hope jumped out of bed and dressed in jeans and a Hilltop football jersey for the special van-painting day.

She sliced a banana on top of her Cheerios and poured a large glass of orange juice. Staring out the window above her kitchen sink, she smiled when the neighbor's dog recognized her and barked. Her mind shifted to the art project as she attempted to imagine the outcome of Willow's artsy VW Microbus. Wondering if Britney would show or become intimated by the seniors, Hope ate quickly and brushed her teeth. Grinning into the mirror, she could hardly wait to get to the Hilltop High parking lot.

Eager to leave, Hope poured coffee in a thermos and drove across town. Luckily, she had gotten all green lights. After she arrived, she spotted several opened cans of paint—red, green, blue, black, white, purple, orange, and yellow.

Larry-Mac, the janitor, was helpful, as always. Stooped over, he busily pried each lid open with a now-paint-splattered screwdriver. With a roll of paper towels tucked underneath his arm, he bent down, whistled, and placed two towels beneath each lid, obviously to protect the parking lot from paint drips.

Hope noticed Willow struggling with a blue tarp. After her third attempt, she hollered, "Will someone help me spread this thing? It's attacking me like fly paper."

Several students, Hope, and Larry-Mac came to her aid. Eventually, they managed to stretch three tarps on either side of the van, placing one in front, and a beach towel in the back.

Unwrapping a package of paper plates, Willow placed various sizes of paintbrushes on top of the disposable plates. "Choose colors and brushes well, kids. You can deviate from the drawings you submitted if your muse takes you elsewhere, but remember this drivable mural will boast your name, plus it's my vehicle—so nothing obscene, please. This will be a great way to provide movable art around Crystal City. Remember, you'll be graded on your work. Ready? Go."

Hope wished she could draw more than a stick figure and participate but knew she'd ruin the mural if she attempted more than a stencil of her hand. Laughing at herself, she scanned the parking lot for Britney while senior art students scrambled for paintbrushes and dipped them inside the paint color of their choice.

Within minutes, Britney arrived, hopped out of her run-down car, and ran toward Hope. "Hi, Miss Truman. Thanks for inviting me." She glanced at the seniors, took a step, hesitated, and retreated toward her counselor. "I'm probably not good enough. I'll just watch."

Placing her hands on Britney's shoulders, Hope gave her favorite student a nudge. "You're most definitely good enough. I've seen your doodles. You're really good."

"They're cartoonish." Britney never took her eyes off the other students who had already begun painting.

"Do you know how much cartoon and animation artists make?" Hope tugged on Britney's arm. "Come on. I'll walk over with you."

Britney's eyes widened as one student painted an electric guitar, another an enormous eye, while yet another added a gigantic pair of black sunglasses near the front headlights. There was the beginning of an extravagant orange, pink, and yellow sunset along one side, musical notes, a huge tie-dye peace sign on one door, a cup of fancy latte, and an enormous bouquet of daisies.

"See, everyone is painting a variety of things. There's no right or wrong." Hope stared at Britney. "What are your favorite things to paint?"

Hesitating, the young student said, "I don't know. Maybe a rainbow because they're happy but that's too basic." She kicked a pebble. "I've never tried to paint a peacock but I love their feathers."

Hope steered her toward the green, blue, and yellow paint cans. "Go for it. I'll order pizza for everyone soon."

Britney brightened. "You will?"

"Only if you paint a peacock." Hope grinned and turned on her heel. She wanted Britney to come out of her shell and not be dependent on her.

Making her way over to Willow, Hope asked about ordering pizza. "Great idea. I'm sure the kids will appreciate it. The paint can dry while they eat. Want some cash?"

The janitor obviously overhead and plucked a worn wallet from his back pocket. "Here's a ten from me."

Willow handed Hope an additional twenty dollars away from Larry-Mac's eyes, in an obvious attempt not to outdo him. Hope said she'd add twenty dollars and started dialing.

Larry-Mac disappeared into the van. "I brought some tunes." He returned with a black boom box. Emptying his pockets, cassettes spilled onto the sidewalk. Fiddling with the player, the janitor inserted a cassette.

A few students ran over and picked up the small, rectangular cases. "What are these?"

Hope laughed. "Old school. I love it."

"It's how we listened to music besides the radio or cell phone, kids." Holding a tiny cassette in the air, he said, "The sixties and seventies was when music was good. I have some eight-tracks too. The janitor pushed the *play* button and bopped his head to the beat of "Move It On Over" by George Thorogood.

Kids, swayed, snapped their fingers, and a couple of students danced as they made their way back to the van. Echoes of appreciation filled the air.

"Cool, man."

"That music's lit."

"Thanks for bringing the rad songs."

"You're the coolest janitor ever."

As "Edge of Seventeen" by Stevie Nicks blared from the boom box, Willow said, "Keep working, kids. Remember, this is my beloved Buttercup and *your* senior project."

While they waited for the pizza, Hope admired the students' work.

Willow folded her arms. "They're good, aren't they?"

"Very." Nervous for Britney, Hope's heart thudded as Britney finally got up the nerve to select a brush and dip it in paint. *You can do this, Brit. Build some confidence.* Hope watched as Britney—who had chosen a spot on the back away from the other students—made wide black strokes in a big arch. The younger student's art covered almost the entire backend which surprised Hope. *I guess she's all in now.* She bit her lip from nerves. *I can't watch.*

Chapter 56

Cuddling on the couch in the middle of the afternoon, Ken and Suzy watched the movie *Four Christmases* for the gazillionth time, even though it wasn't the holiday season. Ken always made Suzy giggle when he requested the flick because he could never remember how many Christmases were in the title. He'd say, "Let's watch *Five Christmases*." Suzy would cock her head and smile.

He'd try again. *"Six?"*

"Ken, they each have two sets of parents who divorced and remarried, so that makes four. It's 'Four Christmases'." Suzy shook her head. "It's not that difficult, hon."

He shrugged and pulled her tighter. "Whatever." Pointing toward the screen, Ken said, "We should role play like Vince Vaughn and Reese Witherspoon in the beginning of the movie. It's pretty hot." He wiggled his eyebrows. "What do you think?"

"I think you're a nut. A crazy nut who I love." Suzy reached into a bowl of popcorn she had sprinkled with steak seasoning.

Ken popped a handful in his mouth. "What's on this?"

"Steak seasoning."

"Because everyone puts that on popcorn. Now, who's the nut?" Ken reached for another handful.

With her mouth full, Suzy mumbled, "I like it."

After he swallowed, Ken said, "It's surprisingly good." He nuzzled his wife. "We have a good life. I know Izzy is a challenge but do you realize she'll be looking at colleges soon?" Squeezing her, he said, "You're a good mom, stepmom, grandma, and wife. I'm a lucky man."

"I'm lucky." Suzy stroked her husband's arm, then laughed.

"What's so funny?"

"Alex would gag over our sugary sweet conversation. She isn't into sweet nothings whispered in her ear."

"Who cares?" Ken tipped his wife's chin up and kissed her. "Do you realize we'll be empty nesters in a few years? Jon and Fernando are married. Izzy's in high school. Soon, it'll just be us."

Suzy paused the movie and turned to stare at Ken. "I guess I hadn't thought about it. Our short marriage together has been such a whirlwind. I can't imagine an empty house. What will we do with ourselves?"

"I can think of a few things." Ken stroked her cheek. "We only waited twenty years to reconnect. It's finally going to be our turn. Just you and me."

"I love the sound of that." Suzy ran her finger along his lips. "Honestly, I can't wait until it's just us. But I do plan to babysit our granddaughter often."

"That goes without saying." Ken reached for another handful of popcorn and kissed Suzy. "I love you."

"I love you too, popcorn breath." She grabbed the remote. "Are we ever going to finish this movie?" Winking, she added, "You know you're at risk of my putting the holiday decorations up early every time I see this film."

Chapter 57

Cheri sat at her desk to review emails from her Fifth Avenue Catering staff. She had hired a manager before leaving for Crystal City who expertly handled multiple events at Rockefeller Center, a famous mystery author's novel launch party at the 92nd Street Y—after receiving a glowing reference from the romance author—and two more bar mitzvahs. There was always a bat or bar mitzvah, which was great for business. Cheri always marveled at the thousands some high-society parents spent on extravagant entertainment and food when their kids likely would have been just as happy going to the zoo, bowling, or having a pizza party. Then again, her parents did the same for her.

After considering special requests for each event, Cheri typed an email with a list of menus for each occasion, even including the napkin colors and edible centerpieces. Before hitting *send*, she decided to authorize her manager to hire more staff, adding, *When I'm away, I want Fifth Avenue Catering to be fully staffed. I trust you to handle these events in my absence but call if you have any questions or issues.* Satisfied her catering company was in good hands, she scrolled through her personal emails and stopped reading when she spotted an email from her parents. As she read it, her forehead creased.

Darling,
Daddy and I will be in Europe a bit longer than expected. The downturn in the market has our finances in a bit of a shambles, I'm afraid. No worries, though. You know how

hard Daddy works. It'll all get straightened out soon. We hope your catering business is doing well and are so proud of you. Much love.
Ciao,
Mommy & Daddy xo
P.S. You should see Daddy. He's getting so buff!

Cheri reread the email and frowned. *Their stocks must have really taken a hit. My parents have never had financial difficulties except when they first built their business. I hope they don't suffer too much of a loss.* Then a selfish thought crossed her mind. *I wonder if my trust fund has been affected.* Her mind shifted to the conversation at Coconuts. *I hope Alex's guesses aren't right about Daddy's exercise. Maybe it's to relieve stress.*

After turning the computer off, Cheri padded to the kitchen and reached for a bag of almonds. Eating over her sink, she giggled. *I'm a celebrity chef who's eating nuts over the sink. I'm glad my clients can't see me.*

Pouring Diet Coke over ice, she added a freshly squeezed lime and stepped into her bedroom where row after row of designer clothes beckoned but the earlier email from her mother nagged at her. *My parents and financial problems don't compute. I suppose if their bottom line affects mine I could sell my clothes online or to an upscale resale boutique. Clothes are just things. Hope's family tragedy pointed that out in billboard-sized letters.*

Deciding on yoga pants and a simple tee, Cheri put on her favorite Skechers and took a long walk through her wooded neighborhood to clear her head. She waved to neighbors, petted several dogs, and decided to sweep off her front porch, something she realized she had never done. Being super wealthy, she never had to do mundane chores but found them strangely enjoyable and relaxing.

After using the broom to remove an elaborate cobweb, she straightened a floral swag on the front door and decided to check her email one more time. Being far from New York and her business was challenging. As the owner, she was constantly worried there would be a kitchen fire at her company, food poisoning for a client, a food allergy at an event, or vital employees would quit leaving her shorthanded. Not seeing anything that needed her attention, she scrolled and deleted junk mail but stopped cold when one email caught her attention.

Her eyes widened when she read the subject line: *Bridal Bonanza and Celebrity Bake-Off.*

After scrolling the lengthy message inviting her to attend an upcoming bridal show featuring caterers, wedding planners, brides-to-be, florists, bakers, photographers, DJ's, bridal dress shops, entertainers, jewelry store owners, and food vendors, her pulse raced. *This is exciting. It looks like a major event.*

Cheri scanned the rest of the email. Each business was encouraged to rent vendor booths for the event which was touted as the premiere trade show for brides and weddings. The email mentioned the entertainment would consist of models wearing bridal gowns, a champagne taste testing, plus a celebrity bake-off. *A bake-off? I've got to get involved in that.*

I wonder if Suzy knows about the Bridal Bonanza. Reading further, to her surprise, there was an entry form for a wedding cake decorating contest. *This will give Fifth Avenue Catering the name recognition it needs here in the Ozarks.* She checked the date of the event and the requirements which mentioned three chefs would be chosen to compete. The competition would be timed and judged by the audience. She clapped her hands together. *I hope they choose me as one of the three chefs. I've got to practice.*

Wasting no time, she filled out the online form to enter the competition and listed Fifth Avenue Catering rather than her own name, always guarding her privacy. One question asked why she wanted to participate. Cheri typed that she was new to the area and hoped to open a second Fifth Avenue Catering shop in Crystal City. She scratched her head and decided to stretch the truth to increase her chances, mentioning she worked with local wedding planner Suzanne Jacobs with Weddings By Suzanne. Cheri knew Suzy wouldn't mind. Besides, she had meant to ask Suzy if they could team up on some of her weddings, so it was mostly true.

Cheri reread the entire email so she wouldn't miss a single word, especially the details describing how the three participating chefs would be asked to decorate a wedding cake in twenty minutes or less. The cakes were to be baked beforehand, brought in "naked" and transformed entirely at the show. The cakes and chefs would be judged by participants on the best time, appearance, and uniqueness.

Cheri groaned. She was more of a savory cook than a pastry chef but decided she could practice at home prior to the event. She loved cooking competitions and had won several in culinary school, albeit none involving a wedding cake. Quickly scanning the information, she noted the date, contact person, and phone number and couldn't wait to ask Suzy if *Weddings by Suzanne* had secured a booth. Cheri printed out the email and tucked it in her purse to show her friend.

I've got to practice. I can make my mark in Crystal City with this. The exposure for Fifth Avenue Catering will be invaluable. Stepping into her kitchen, she made a cup of coffee for fortitude. *I've got to research wedding cakes.* After the coffee brewed, Cheri reviewed Pinterest boards and Googled a plethora of wedding cake designs. Perched on a bar stool at her kitchen counter, her back ached from sitting in the same position. Cheri glanced at the clock and realized she had spent hours poring over cake photos. Her right hand was now in the form of an eagle's claw after moving the mouse around for hours.

The variety of cakes was endless—traditional, modern, seasonal, quirky, spooky, vintage, themed, you name it. She studied the photos, mentally deciding which would be the fastest to make, yet unique enough for the Bridal Bonanza competition.

Stepping outside for fresh air, Cheri stared at the sky to clear her head since the cake designs were blurring together. After she wrapped her head around a cake-baking plan, she couldn't wait to begin experimenting.

Chapter 58

Hope watched as one meticulous student painted a Picasso-like face on the hood using bright colors, graphic patterns, one eye, a lopsided nose, and a crooked mouth. "That's really cool."

Nodding in agreement, Willow gave the student a thumbs-up.

Larry-Mac nodded. "Modern art."

"I love Picasso's work." Willow folded her arms. "In fact, this gives me an idea."

Now nervous about Britney's traditional peacock, Hope paced. *I hope I didn't steer her wrong. She'll be so embarrassed if everyone's art is modern.*

The pizza driver's muffler filled the air, stifling Hope's concerns. He opened his door, grinned, and stacked four large pizzas and three two liters of Coke.

"I hope he doesn't drop those." Hope ran over to help and paid the driver as Willow crawled into the one dry door of her van where she retrieved paper plates, napkins, and plastic cups.

Clapping her hands to get the students' attention, Willow said, "Clean your brushes and place them on a paper towel. It's break time, everyone."

Hope placed the pizzas on the hood of her Honda. "They won't hurt this old thing." Opening the lids, the smell of garlic, pepperoni, and sausage filled the air, making her mouth water.

Students hungrily grabbed several slices each. Sitting in a row on the curb or sidewalk facing the VW van, likely to admire their work, students held a paper plate in one hand and a soda in the other.

The janitor pushed a button on his retro boom box and "Peace Train" by Cat Stevens filled the air.

Hope noticed several students swayed to the music while pointing toward the van and chatted excitedly about their artwork.

Glancing from side to side for Britney, Hope wondered why she hadn't yet joined the group. Crossing the parking lot with a slice of pepperoni, Hope made her way toward the back of the van.

Britney shooed her away. "Don't look yet, Miss Truman. I'm still working." The young student reached around the back of the van with one hand. "I'll take the pizza, though. Thanks."

"You're welcome." Hope pointed toward her car. "There's more pizza and soda over there."

Britney nodded. "This is enough. I'm too busy and excited to eat any more." She disappeared behind the van, waving Hope away.

Helping herself to a slice of sausage and green pepper, Hope motioned toward the vehicle and studied the half-painted masterpieces. "It's going to be incredible. I can't tell you how impressed I am with your idea, Willow."

"It was Mac's idea." Willow brushed against him and beamed. "It'll be a work of art."

"We're gonna have to rename her," the janitor said. "She don't look like Buttercup no more."

Willow nodded. "Great minds." She patted Larry-Mac's leg as the threesome sat on the curb balancing pizza and soda. "I already thought of that." Whispering, she said, "I've got non-alcoholic champagne, also called white grape juice, chilling with plastic flutes I found at a party store." Winking, she added, "And the real stuff for the grownups." She put her finger to her lips. "But shhh. We're being rule breakers today." She elbowed Hope. "That's what hippies do, right? We'll tell the kids we're all having grape juice."

"Brilliant," Hope said. "That will really top off this day." After switching to pepperoni and polishing off her third slice, she wiped her hands. "That hit the spot. I think I have a trash bag in my car." She retrieved a bag and gathered up trash as students went back to painting. The janitor helped her toss trash in the bag. When the lot was clean, Hope suggested Willow take photos to post on Hilltop's Facebook page.

"Why didn't I think of that?" The art teacher clicked several pictures from different angles. When she reached the back of the van, she stopped, eyes wide.

Hope's mouth went dry, already nervous that Britney had taken the entire back side for her canvas. After all, she wasn't a senior, and Hope didn't know if Britney really could pull off a peacock. *I hope it wasn't a mistake asking her to participate. Britney will be crushed if Willow paints over her work.*

After Willow gawked for several seconds, Hope sat in agony, unable to swallow or even blink. Eventually, Willow snapped photos of the back and whispered something in Britney's ear.

Practically strutting across the parking lot, Willow said, "That student of yours should be in senior art class, Hope. Britney has a great eye."

Letting out the breath she didn't realize she was holding, Hope relaxed. "Thank goodness. She wouldn't let me see her work until she was finished. I assumed she'd take a tiny space on the van—not the entire backside. That's so not her nature."

Grinning, Willow said, "I'm glad she did. Her painting is gorgeous. She's adding tiny details now and told me she has only painted once before. Apparently, she usually sketches or doodles with pencil or markers." The art teacher shook her head appreciatively. "She's a natural."

Staring toward the van, Hope said, "I can't wait to see it. Maybe this will help Britney get art scholarships."

An hour later, the students added their final brushstrokes, stood in the parking lot, cheered, and high fived one other.

Hope couldn't wait a second longer. She ran over to where Britney had painted and gasped. "Brit, this is stunning." Rubbing her arms, she said, "I've got goosebumps. Look at the gorgeous blue and green colors. Look at the intricate details. Look at *you.*"

A beaming Britney stood back to take in her creation. Splattered paint covered her jeans. As her eyes lit up, a wide grin spread across her face. "I guess it's pretty good."

"Pretty good? Sign it, Brit. Put your whole name. People will be photographing this and sharing it on Facebook and Instagram just like they did your tornado jewelry last spring. You're a gifted, multi-talented artist, young lady."

"Who knew? Thank you, Miss Truman. You always make me feel special." Face flushed, Britney picked up a skinny brush, dipped it in black paint, and carefully signed her name.

After each student signed their masterpieces, Willow, Larry-Mac, and Hope filled plastic flutes with champagne for themselves and gave the students white grape juice.

Standing in the Hilltop High School parking lot near Buttercup, Willow held her flute in the air. Everyone followed suit. "Students, your work is nothing short of stupendous. You have gone above and beyond for your senior art project. I couldn't be more proud of each and every one of you. I could go on all day, but I've decided we'll have a celebratory renaming ceremony." Raising her glass higher like a torch, her many bangle braces clanked as they slid toward her elbow. "I hereby rename you Buttercup, and dub you Picasso."

"Here, here," the janitor and Hope said.

"Picasso," one student repeated.

"Dope," said another student.

Britney beamed and said, "Lit."

Everyone cheered and clapped. After the commotion died down, Willow said, "Before you clean up and leave, I want to take group photos for our school Facebook page and for the Hilltop High Times." Motioning with her hand, she said, "Stand beside Picasso but don't block your artwork."

As the kids scattered and decided who would stand in front—usually the shortest students—Hope noticed Britney hung back. She pointed toward the younger student to alert Willow.

Willow flung a long, gray braid over her shoulder. "Britney, get in the picture. You're part of this endeavor too."

Running over, Britney shyly stood in the back but was so short you couldn't see her.

"Move to the front, Brit," Hope said.

Willow took several photos of the students and Picasso. When she finished, she waved her arms. "By the way, you're all getting an A." There were more cheers as students closed paint cans, washed brushes, and threw away more trash.

Hope nudged Britney. "You need to take photos of your peacock and any other artwork you create for your college applications."

Britney stared at her work. "I'm as shocked as anyone that mine's any good." With renewed confidence, she cleaned a few more brushes and actually made small talk with some of the senior girls.

After removing the last of the stray pizza plates and soda cups, Hope stuffed the trash bags in her trunk, stepped across the lot where Willow was embroiled in conversation, and gave the art teacher a big hug. "This was an inspiring project and a delightful Saturday. Thanks for letting me join you."

Chapter 59

The following week, Vanessa called Jon and Fernando. After clearing her throat twice, she blurted out, "I've been thinking about what you said. I'm ready to see my parents' house. I'd love it if you guys went with me." Her voice wobbled. "I don't think I can do this on my own."

"I've got you on speaker," Jon said. "Of course we'll go." Fernando nodded.

"She can't see you through the phone, silly." Fernando leaned closer to Jon's cell. "We're on our way to get you."

Within minutes, Jon parked in front of Vanessa's duplex. Fernando was already halfway across the lawn when she opened the front door holding Violet with one arm and hugging the men with the other. "Thanks. You're the best."

After they strapped the baby into her car seat, which again took nearly all three adults, Vanessa climbed in beside Violet and gave Jon directions to her parents' house. She pointed out familiar landmarks while growing up including their favorite Dairy Queen hang out, her elementary school, a park where they had picnics, and a now-dilapidated Piggly Wiggly grocery store.

Leaning out the window, she said, "Just two more right turns."

After they parked in the shady driveway, unfastened the baby, and climbed out, Fernando whistled. "Your family home is charming. It's much bigger than I expected. I'm not sure why I pictured a one-level house in my mind." He gawked. "It's really nice."

"I remember it now," Jon said. "I always loved your parents' home."

"It's older but—" A sob escaped. "Our house used to be filled with so much love." Vanessa wiped away tears. "I promise I won't cry all day. Stress isn't good for Violet or me."

Jon put his arm around Vanessa. "I can only imagine what you're going through. Your parents were nice people."

"Until I got pregnant." Her face hardened. "That's old news. They're not here to defend themselves. I shouldn't bring it up." She steepled her fingers against her nose and sniffled. "I know what they did seemed right to them at the time and they did come around. But—" Her voice cracked again.

Fernando and Jon exchanged glances. Clearly, this wasn't going to be an easy transition. Fernando kissed her cheek. "Let's try not to dwell on those memories. Think positive things because I bet you're right about babies and stress, but what do I know?"

The three stood on the sidewalk and stared at the older Carthage stone house, mostly in silence, as Vanessa held her sleeping baby.

As they studied the home and expansive yard filled with mature trees, Fernando's eyes widened. "That big screened-in porch is wonderful. We'll be able to sit out here with Violet and not worry about pesky bugs."

Still sniffling, Vanessa nodded. "I have a lot of fond memories drinking lemonade and playing board games with my mom on that porch."

"We'll create even more memories," Jon said.

Vanessa perked up. "If the boards haven't rotted, there's a deck out back."

Fernando puffed out his chest. "I can barbecue. We'll have the best dinner parties."

Laughing, Jon said, "Since when do you know how to barbecue?"

"Hey, I've cooked on a George Foreman indoor grill. How much harder can this be?" Fernando nudged Jon. "Trust me."

"You know I do."

Vanessa turned to Jon and Fernando. "I know I said I wasn't sure about living here—about the flood of memories it would bring—but if you two join us on this new family adventure, I think we can make it a loving home again."

She handed baby Violet to Jon who cradled her in one arm. Reaching for the men's hands, tears threatened Vanessa's eyes but she blinked them away. "I feel like I should get down on one knee. Will you, Jon and Fernando, live with Violet Grace and me?" Pausing, the young mom quickly added, "Please say yes."

Whooping, Fernando said, "How can I resist those freckles?" He twirled Vanessa on the sidewalk. "My answer is yes." He glanced at his husband. "If you agree, Jon."

Jon paused for several seconds. He and Fernando had had several lengthy discussions about this possibility. He knew Fernando was ready but he was still a bit unsure. His idea of a new marriage didn't involve his former high school girlfriend, but he was the baby's father. And Fernando had wholeheartedly embraced their new family. As both Fernando and Vanessa stared at him, Vanessa broke the silence.

"It's okay, Jon. It was a stupid idea. Forget I said it."

"I was going to say yes." Jon bounced Violet in his arms. "Whatever Fernando wants, I want. It'll be an adventure."

"A grand adventure." Fernando's usual chirpy tone took a serious note as he addressed Vanessa. "Hon, I know you loved my husband at one time but he loves me now and I love him. And we'll both love you in a different way. I wouldn't agree to this arrangement if I didn't think it would work. Besides, I'm not insecure-"

Vanessa laid a hand on Fernando's arm. "If this makes you uncomfortable at any time, let me know. You two have been beyond supportive. As long as you're involved in Violet's life, I can handle-"

"Shhh. No need to say any more. I don't have any doubts." Fernando brightened and danced a sidewalk salsa. "We'll decorate the nursery for you too, right, Jon?"

Jon playfully shoved his husband. "Are you ever in a bad mood?"

"Not anymore." Fernando turned toward Vanessa. "We should go inside." Realizing how emotional it would be to see the interior, he added, "If you're ready, of course. There's no rush."

Vanessa straightened her shoulders. "I'm as ready as I'll ever be. I don't think it'll get any easier." She kissed her baby's back and wrinkled her nose. "I think Violet has a number two. We should go inside so I can change her—unless you want to, Jon."

Jon scrunched his face. "Been there, done that the past few days. You can have the honors."

Fernando reached for Violet. "Honestly, you two. It's a normal bodily function. Give her to me."

Vanessa's smile spread across her face. "Living with you guys is going to be a hoot."

Jangling the house key and crossing the lawn, she said, "Let's go inside. I'm ready."

Chapter 60

Cheri barely slept all weekend after reading the Bridal Bonanza email. On Monday, she raced to her computer, coffee cup in hand. Scrolling past work and junk emails, she spotted a new email from Bridal Bonanza. Hovering over the incoming message, her stomach lurched, almost afraid to read the email. Finally, she forced herself to open the message and squealed.

They want me to be one of the three chefs in the cake competition. Dancing around the room doing fist pumps, Cheri refilled her coffee and made out an exhaustive grocery list.

Driving to her favorite grocery store in Branson, she bought a cart full of baking items. Once home, Cheri plunked bags of food on her counter, then rummaged through her pantry and fridge.

Face glistening with sweat, she set out several mixing bowls, measuring utensils, flour, sugar, oil, applesauce, sour cream, various nuts, fruits, edible flowers, pastry bags, and decorating tips.

Placing three large stainless steel mixing bowls on her brown and tan speckled granite counter, she scurried to the panty to gather armloads of ingredients. She put powdered sugar, white and brown sugar, vanilla, dark and semi-sweet chocolate chips, almond bark, caramel chips, pecans, and more on the countertop. Grabbing a long wooden spoon, Cheri shoved her hair out of her eyes, set the oven timer yet again, and ferociously mixed the batter.

In her rush, icing overflowed, dripped down the bowl, and onto the floor. The sticky bowls stuck to her hands. Cheri glanced at the clock as she licked her fingers. *To hell with salmonella. I've never gotten sick from raw eggs before.*

Stirring and scraping the sides with the wooden spoon, Cheri rushed to get the correct consistency as the buzzer went off. *I feel like I'm on "Chopped."* According to her oversized stainless steel kitchen clock featuring a fork and spoon for hands, she had been working for forty minutes. Frustrated, she sighed and poured a glass of water. *I haven't even decorated the cakes. I've got to improve my time by fifty percent.*

With her finger, she tasted the three frostings she had prepared—vanilla buttercream, lemon, and chocolate ganache. The sink overflowed with pans, bowls, and utensils. The mixer handle was covered with dried chocolate batter, and edible flowers were strewn across the counter.

Setting the timer once again, Cheri plunged in and began baking and decorating even more cakes. Savory treats were her specialty but her pride wouldn't allow her to consult with her Fifth Avenue Catering pastry chef. She knew not doing so could prove to be a disastrous error, but since she owned the business, she hated for employees to see any weaknesses, plus she wanted to prove this to herself.

All weekend, she had researched cake photos on Google and Pinterest. Her favorites were printed out, spread across the counter, and dotted with icing from the spray of the mixer. After an hour, her kitchen looked like a sack of flour had exploded. Sticky batter dripped everywhere, but she couldn't take the time to clean it up. Instead she simply straddled the mess.

Glancing back at the clock, she forgot what time she began and reset the timer on the microwave while the bare cakes cooled on racks. Wiping her brow with the back of her hand, she stirred more batter in one of the few clean bowls she could find. The kitchen felt like a sauna but Cheri was too busy decorating to take the time to turn the air conditioning down.

I'm glad Nana can't see this mess. She'd think I destroyed her gorgeous kitchen.

After three hours, Cheri assessed her progress. The chocolate ganache cake took one hour. The lemon cake layers took forty-five minutes, and she crossed the thirty-minute mark with the banana cake. However, the decorations looked sloppy and so did she. *Maybe I can donate these to my neighbors or the Crystal City Senior Citizen Center.*

Wiping her hands on her apron, she sighed as she blew stray hair out of her eyes. *I've got to improve my speed if I have any chance of winning.*

After the buzzer went off, Cheri pulled three more cakes out of the oven and touched the golden tops. Her imprint sprang back indicating they were done. She placed them on cooling racks and broke into a full-body sweat. The room was unbearably hot. Wiping perspiration from her brow with her sleeve, she poured her hot coffee down the sink.

Glancing at her many cake photos as if for an answer, she couldn't decide which would be best for the competition—a modern black and white cake with dark chocolate and vanilla baked in square tiers, or a sweet, romantic raspberry lemon cake with round tiers. Or maybe a middle-of-the-road banana cake with fresh strawberries. She knew some brides preferred modern while many enjoyed traditional weddings.

I've got to go outside and clear my head. After a quick stroll around her neighborhood, Cheri had an epiphany and ran back inside. After washing a mixing bowl and finding the right ingredients, she created a glamorous all-white cake with rolled fondant pearls and a draped, pooled bottom, resembling an exaggerated train of a wedding dress.

Surprising herself, Cheri stood back to admire her creation. If the cake hadn't been slightly off kilter and slanted, it would have been stunning—and perfect for the Bridal Bonanza. She sighed. It had taken far too long to decorate. Exasperated and exhausted, she said to no one, "I hope I'm up to this."

Chapter 61

As they strolled through Vanessa's late parents' house almost afraid to touch anything, Jon spotted a corner filled with billowy pink. Vanessa had taken the baby into the kitchen. He heard drawers open and doors creak and knew she was opening cabinets, unaware of their findings. Elbowing Fernando, he pointed toward his find.

Beside a dark green recliner, a basket overflowed with balls of pink yarn, knitting needles, and an instruction guide for baby items. Obviously, Vanessa's mother had been knitting for the baby.

Fernando clapped a hand over his mouth as he pointed toward a pink baby hat, booties, and a mostly made afghan.

Eyes rimmed with tears, Jon said, "I can't wait until she sees these. Her mother did care. She wasn't heartless like we thought."

"Thank goodness for small miracles." Fernando held the tiny booties in the air, placing one on his finger. "These are adorable."

Nodding, Jon said, "They'll be a keepsake for Violet Grace and her children someday." As he turned the knitted bonnet over in his hand, he shouted, "Vanessa, come here. You've got to see this."

As the young mom entered the room, both men held the miniature, hand-made items in the air, saying simultaneously, "Look."

Vanessa's brows furrowed. "What-What is . . .?"

Fernando's grin spread across his face. "Sweetie, your mom obviously made these for your baby—for baby Violet."

Jon laughed. "One that isn't communal. I hope you plan to crank up that barbecue grill."

Fernando glanced toward the tiled patio area. "Count on it. I can't wait to have everyone over."

Jon reached for his new husband. "I know this isn't exactly how we envisioned starting our new lives together. You've been incredibly accepting of my high school shenanigans." His eyes reddened. "I can't tell you how thankful I am that you're my husband. I could never have chosen a more loving—"

"Thank you but never refer to this in that way again, okay?" Fernando's tone was harsher than usual.

"I'm trying to say thank you."

Fernando shook his head. "No thanks necessary. We're family. This is what family does. They stick together." Peering over his shoulder, he said, "And, please, never use the word shenanigans again. I never *ever* want Violet to hear anything like that. She only needs to know she was brought into this world with love."

"You're incredible, and you're right." Jon embraced Fernando. The two men held one another for several seconds before a wailing Violet filled the air.

"Sorry to interrupt," Vanessa said. "We can go back inside."

"Don't be silly. Give her to me." Fernando held out his arms. "It has been a full thirty minutes since I held Violet."

"I'm next." Jon glanced at the orange and yellow streaked sky. "Take a look at that sunset."

Everyone turned toward the magnificent sky.

"I've always loved this view." Vanessa pointed. "If you squint, you can see the Crystal City Hospital where Violet was born."

"I love this place already. Maybe we should head back. We need to get some empty boxes," Fernando said between kissing the baby's cheeks.

As they drove away from the house, everyone talked at once.

Vanessa leaned between the seats. "Shh. She's asleep."

Both men whispered about the best place to find boxes, newspapers for packing, and contacting U-Haul.

"I can't imagine packing up my house with a baby." Vanessa frowned. "How will this work?"

"Don't worry. We'll take care of everything," Fernando said.

Jon nodded. "Honestly, I'm much better at packing and hauling boxes than middle-of-the night feedings."

Vanessa giggled. "I've got that covered."

After driving across town, unbuckling a miraculously still-sleeping Violet, the men escorted Vanessa to her front door.

Jon fidgeted. "We should give notice at Columns IV." He eyed Vanessa. "If you're absolutely positive you want us all to live together?"

Holding Violet Grace to her chest, she said, "I've never been surer of anything in my life."

Jon extended his hand. "Let's do this."

Fernando stepped in front of Jon's outreached palm. "Pashaw. No handshakes. We're family. Give me a hug— both of you— but don't squish the baby."

Chapter 62

I hate Mondays. Since the bank car was in use, Alex drove her Mustang to the print shop. At a light, she scribbled down her mileage on the back of the vendor's business card.

It was a warm, sunshine-filled day which always made her drive a little too fast. Observing the road in front and checking the rearview mirror for potential police officers, she sped up and reached over to turn on some music. Scrolling through local radio stations, she heard the Show-Me Bank jingle followed by ear-shattering rap music. She bristled.

Oh, my God. I can't believe this. Hannah never told me she finalized the radio spots. Now, they're on the freaking airwaves.

Trying to calm her nerves, Alex turned the air conditioning up to full blast, found a station playing a bluesy song, and cranked the volume. Just as her blood pressure began to normalize, another head banging bank radio ad played yet again. Her stomach churned. Before the thirty-second spot ended, Alex picked up the phone and dialed her office's direct line.

"Marketing," Hannah chirped. "This is Hannah."

"What the hell were you thinking using that shitty music?"

"What shitty music?"

Alex pictured her intern's feet on her desk. Blood boiling, she said, "You know exactly what I mean. Don't play dumb. That shitty rap crap background music you used for our freaking bank anniversary ads."

Hannah huffed. "What's wrong with rap? Show-Me Bank needs to engage younger customers."

"I'm on my way to the office. Don't leave." Alex hung up, drummed her fingers on the steering wheel, and raced to work. Within minutes, she punched in the back door code and rushed to her office.

"Get out of my chair."

"Well, well." Hannah moved like a turtle to a seat across from Alex's desk.

In an attempt to maintain her composure since her office walls were glass, Alex took a deep breath and lowered her voice. "Hannah, do they discuss targeted marketing in college?"

"Of course."

Alex folded her arms. "And it means?"

Hannah froze. "I know what it means. You aren't my professor."

Alex leaned back. "Go ahead. Tell me what targeted marketing means."

Hannah typed a few keys into her iPad.

"Are you Googling the answer? Stop. Hell, I'll just tell you. The bottom line of targeted marketing is finding the appropriate audience for your goods or service. We provide a service. We're a financial institution."

Hannah pouted. "I know what a bank is. My daddy's the—"

"President. Yes, I know. Tell me. Who is our target market?"

Glaring, Hannah said, "Apparently you have all of the answers so why don't you stop playing games."

Alex motioned with her index finger. "Follow me."

"What?"

"Follow me into the lobby." Alex stepped toward the customer area and glanced back at Hannah. "Come on. This will only take a minute."

Begrudgingly, the young intern stomped behind Alex as she greeted long-time customers, stopped to shake their hands, introduced Hannah, showed a few to new accounts, and others to tellers or the appropriate loan officer. She got a cup of coffee for one customer and held a door for a woman with a walker.

When they eventually made their way back to Alex's office, she asked, "What did you learn?"

Hannah slumped in her seat. "Stop with the pop quiz and tell me already."

Alex did her best not to smirk. "Our target audience skews older. We don't cater to millennials—not that we don't want their business—it's just that most of them bank online or use debit cards. Our long-time customers and board members, for that matter, are in the fifty-plus age group. Older Baby Boomers. In fact, most are over sixty-five and many aren't exactly tech-savvy, so we still need to market using many different methods, not just online. Didn't they teach you about targeted marketing in your master's classes?"

Hannah huffed. "Whatever. I'm just trying to drag you into the Twenty-first Century."

"Always consider the customer. I'm all for higher education, but step out of the classroom and look away from the textbooks to get a feel for your customer base." Alex grinned. "Class is now over." Feeling victorious, she texted her friends and asked if they could meet at Coconuts. All but Cheri said they'd be there within the hour.

Chapter 63

As the cakes cooled, Cheri's stomach growled. Realizing she had missed lunch, she made a cucumber, tomato, and hummus sandwich. Deciding the heaping sink full of dishes could wait, she tore several pieces of fresh mint into a glass pitcher and added cold water. To escape the heat of the kitchen, she stepped onto the deck and kicked off her shoes. A cool breeze blew her hair across her face. Leaning against an orange and brown striped lounge chair while devouring her sandwich, she sipped the fresh, minty water and stared longingly at Crystal Lake. As usual, it was filled with jet skis, pontoon boats, sport yachts, and fishing boats. Also as usual, she never seemed to have lake time, nor downtime, for that matter.

Setting her plate on the table, she studied a man and his son who sat in a bass boat. They were fishing near her unused dock. The little boy cast a line into the water as his father struggled with a large fish wriggling on the end. The weight made his fishing pole arch. The idyllic sight was so stark from anything in New York City that she couldn't look away. Making a mental note to either get a boat or learn to fish, Cheri giggled. *Who am I kidding? I'm just getting used to driving a car.*

After watching the father and son for several minutes, Cheri crossed her wooden deck and stuck her finger inside her clay pots overflowing with red geraniums. The flowers had begun to shrivel and the dirt was dry and hard. Uncoiling the garden hose, she filled the pots, bringing the geraniums back to life. Impulsively, she leaned over and sipped water out of the hose. H2O dripped down her chin and the front of her shirt. She stared at her spa-like mint water in the pitcher and smiled. *Sorry, fancy mint water. I prefer refreshing, cold water out of the hose.*

She could only imagine how horrified her rich mom would be if she saw her grown daughter drinking out of a lowly garden hose. After all, who knows what must have crawled inside? Almost in spite of her upbringing, she took another protracted sip, held her arms out to the side, and twirled like a kid. *I almost feel like the child I was never allowed to be.*

Being a Van Buren in New York City didn't exactly bode well for playing outdoors. There was Central Park, but the paparazzi nearly always ruined the handful of outings she had attempted with her parents.

After one more sip, she sprayed cold water on her feet, sat down, and propped them on the railing to dry.

After her break, she stepped back inside and glanced at the clock. *I need to improve my decorating speed.*

Cheri cleaned several mixing bowls to make batter for more cakes. Deciding she needed mood music, she found a jazz station. The instrumental saxophone calmed her. She studied her favorite Pinterest photos for inspiration, glanced at her already-decorated cakes on the counter, and planned a strategy.

After a few epic fails, Cheri created another wedding dress-shaped cake by cutting wedge-shaped indentions in the sides. This cake resembled a voluptuous, Marilyn-Monroe-like lacy wedding dress. It stood more upright than the first cake with the pooled hem, but like the first, took too long.

She studied the cake from all sides. *Maybe it needs a pop of color. It definitely needs to be simplified.* She photographed the cake, front and back, to show Suzy. At the very least, one of her brides might request it in the future when timing wasn't an issue.

Resetting the buzzer, Cheri mixed and poured more batter into pans. Once the cakes cooled, she iced the yellow tiers with lemon buttercream frosting, then piped edible green ivy along the top and sides. She finished her creation with rolled fondant purple clematis, trailing from top to bottom. Standing back, Cheri examined the striking color combination and stopped the timer. *Nineteen minutes. That's my best time yet.*

One more. I've got to make one more. After searching Pinterest again, she turned her iPad off, determined to create her own design. She was a chef. A caterer. Besides, her head was already too full of other people's creations.

After opening cupboards and drawers, she chose square baking pans to try the modern cake, deciding it could also be considered retro. Fishing through the cabinets, she found her last clean bowl. Quickly adding the ingredients to make more chocolate ganache, she alternated the chocolate and buttercream icing on the square cake layers. Working fast, she decorated the tiers with geometric shapes. The end result reminded her of a sixties go-go dancer wearing white go-go boots and "walking" up the side. Wet with sweat but excited, she checked the clock. Eighteen minutes. *I'm ready.*

All I have to do is improve my time by a minute or two. I've got this. Wiping her hands on her apron, Cheri untied it and crumpled it on the counter.

Kicking off her shoes, she flopped onto a kitchen chair, and checked her phone. She noticed a text from Alex about meeting at Coconuts. *I'm too tired to drive to Crystal City.* She replied that she was practicing for the Bridal Bonanza cake competition and reminded them to add the event to their calendar. Suzy responded, saying she had a booth reserved and would be there with wedding bells on. Alex and Hope both replied they'd be in the audience to cheer her on and would have a drink on her behalf at Coconuts tonight.

I'm so happy I finally have girlfriends. They won't care whether I win or lose this competition. But I care . . .

Chapter 64

After Suzy, Alex, and Hope ordered drinks and chatted about their day, Alex scanned the crowd at Coconuts. As usual, the bar was filled with the loudmouth unlit cigar chomper who hoped for an audience—any audience—a sixty-something woman clinging to her teens with too-young attire, couples who only had eyes for each other, eager backpack-wearing college students, and bustling suit-wearing businesspeople. After all these years, she still didn't know most of their names but recognized nearly every face.

As Alex waved to Gus on the other side of the room, her eyes bulged. Gasping, she said, "Oh, my God. That's her."

"Who?" Suzy asked.

Hope swiveled to match Alex's view.

Alex clenched her teeth and seethed. "That, my friends, is Hannah the Horrible, my bank marketing intern."

Suzy turned to get a better view. "She's cute."

"In a big boobs kind of way." Hope's eyebrows shot up. "Um, impressive, I suppose."

Alex blew out her breath as Gus brought their favorite cocktails. "Apparently I forgot to tell you guys about Hannah's transformation." She crossed her arms. "A while back, my intern asked for a few days off to go to the 'beach' and returned as Dolly Parton."

Suzy and Hope both covered their mouths and giggled, likely more from watching Alex squirm, than from the comment or transformation.

Brows knitted and a worry line forming, Alex said, "Coconuts is sacred to us. I never should have told her about this place. *Dammit*." Hunkering down in her seat, she said, "I don't want her to see me."

Hope eyed the newcomer. "Uh-oh. Looks like she has company."

Suzy rubbernecked around one of the regulars. "You're right." She lowered her voice. "A tall, handsome guy with a super-short haircut just joined her."

Alex groaned as she took a healthy sip of chardonnay. "I hope it isn't anyone from work. Shit. It's probably the cute, new loan officer. Now everyone from the bank will start coming here. That would ruin this place for me." She rubbed her temples. "I feel a stress headache coming on. I'm afraid to see who it is."

Gus blocked her vision with a tray full of foamy beers for a group of boisterous golfers. After he chatted the men up for far too long, Alex waved her hand frantically sideways in an effort to get him to move out of the way. Apparently, the server thought she needed service and approached their table, blocking her view yet again. "Another round already, ladies?"

Alex pointed to her half-full wineglass. "No. I wanted you to move." She motioned with her head and lowered her voice. "Do you know who Hannah is with?"

The server balanced his tray with one hand. "Who's Hannah?"

Alex rolled her eyes. "Right. The one with the huge breasts."

Gus cocked an eyebrow. "Oh, Brick House?"

"Huh?" Hope asked.

"The woman's built like a brick house." Gus chuckled. "Surely you've heard the song."

Alex crossed her arms. "Not you too. Okay, I'll take another glass of wine now. Bye, Gus."

After the server scampered behind the bar, Alex peered

over Suzy's shoulder to study the man with Hannah. When he turned to the side, she gasped.

"What's wrong?" Suzy asked.

"I think I know him."

"And . . .?" Hope asked.

Squinting in the dark bar, Alex swiveled to study the couple. When she faced her friends, she said, "I'm not sure and I've got to be sure before I say. I'll go to the restroom to get a closer look." When she returned, fresh drinks were on their table.

Suzy winked at Alex. "You're going to love this."

Alex narrowed her eyes. "What?"

Hope chirped, "Gus said the drinks are compliments of Hannah and her friend."

"Shit. She saw me."

"Oh, well, free is free." Hope raised her margarita in the air. "Did you get a better look at the guy she's with?"

"Not really. Those two bar flies who always come here crossed in front of Hannah's table at exactly the wrong time." Alex poured the remainder of her chardonnay into her new glass. "I'll be patient."

Suzy suppressed a grin. "You? Patient?"

Alex balled up a cocktail napkin and threw it at her. "Yes, me. I can learn new tricks."

Within minutes, Hannah and her date stood. Alex clamped her hand over her mouth. "Oh, crap. It's him."

"Will you stop being so melodramatic and tell us already?" Hope asked.

"The man with Hannah is . . ." Alex gawked. "I can't believe this." She studied their backsides as the couple swung open the front door, flooded the darkened room with sunshine, and left.

"Who is he?" Suzy and Hope shouted.

Alex leaned back and crossed her arms. "I think it's Sean, Tony's asshole cop brother."

Suzy glanced out the front but the door had closed. "Quite a coincidence. I can see why that upsets you." She shrugged.

"Right. Sean's married to Nikki, Tony's bitchy ex, or at least I think they got married. Remember all of the drama about Sean being Joey's biological father?" Alex shook her head. "I'm speechless."

"That would be a strange coincidence. I guess you'll have to ask Hannah or see if they come in again." Hope rubbed her belly. "I'm hungry. Can we eat?"

After ordering hummus, veggies, and salads, the women ate quickly and decided to leave early. As they strode outside, Alex said, "I can't wait until this damn bank anniversary event is over. I let Hannah handle a large portion of the details. I'm not the greatest at delegating but I'm trying to change my ways." A laugh escaped. "She reminds me daily of her higher education degree, so I'm sure it'll go off without a hitch. Well, except for the stupid radio commercials."

"What happened?" Hope asked.

"She used shitty rap music."

"Oh," Suzy said.

"Some of rap is cool," Hope offered.

"Sure, but our customer base skews sixty-five-plus. I don't think that's on their playlist. Oh, well. We have other media going. Maybe it'll be fine."

Both Hope and Suzy said, "It will be."

Suzy shouted over her shoulder, "The Bridal Bonanza will be here soon. Don't forget."

Chapter 65

After work, Ken came home to a darkened house where he found Suzy resting on the couch. Placing a hand on her forehead, he asked, "Feeling okay?"

"Not great. Not terrible," Suzy said. "I've been a little woozy lately."

He brightened. "You need some of my world famous Campbell's Chicken Noodle Soup." Ken crossed the room and rattled around in the kitchen cupboards until he found a pan, lid, and can opener. While the soup heated, he handed Suzy a glass of water and placed a burnt orange chenille throw over her legs.

Suzy didn't have the heart to tell him she hated chicken noodle soup and had already eaten with her girlfriends. "Thanks, hon."

Much too soon, it was ready, and Suzy moved to the table. The smell made her queasier but she forced a few tiny bites.

"Taste good?" Ken asked.

"Uh-huh." Suzy told the white lie as she forced half the hot liquid down. Afterward, she pushed the bowl across the table. "That's all I can manage. Thanks, babe."

"Want me to save it for your lunch tomorrow?"

The thought made Suzy's stomach churn. She shook her head as Ken dumped the contents down the sink. "Want anything else?"

Chewing on a saltine cracker, Suzy said, "I think I'll go to bed early."

Ken frowned. "This isn't like you. Should I call the doctor? Make an appointment?"

Suzy shook her head. "No. It's probably a slight case of flu or maybe food poisoning. I had grocery store sushi for lunch."

Ken wrinkled his nose. "I don't know how you eat that stuff."

Winking, Suzy said, "You don't know what you're missing." She refilled her water and crossed the room. "The bed's calling me."

"Wait for me. I'm tucking you in."

~ ~ ~

The next morning, the smell of morning coffee made Suzy's stomach recoil. *What's wrong with me?* She drank ice cold water from the fridge, leaned against the kitchen counter, and ate a piece of dry toast. Ken had already left for work, so she turned on *The Today Show*. A commercial caught her attention and her stomach lurched. She immediately put the ridiculous thought out of her mind and brightened when she received a call from Jon who asked if they could come by with Violet Grace. He explained Vanessa had errands to run and he and Fernando were babysitting.

"She's fussy. Fernando's piano playing always calms her."

Suzy smiled into the phone. "Sure, come by. I'm not feeling well, so as hard as it'll be, I'm not going to hold Violet in case I'm contagious. I'll observe from across the room, but hearing Fernando play the piano would be lovely."

Soon the men arrived with a bundle of pink in Jon's arms.

Fernando put his finger to his lips and mouthed, "She's asleep."

Suzy situated the bassinet nearby and Jon placed the baby inside. Standing a safe distance away where she could still see Violet Grace, she marveled at her soft, pink skin and perfectly pouty lips. She whispered, "I wish I could kiss that sweet baby but I don't dare in case I'm contagious."

Jon put both arms out straight. "Don't come near me either, Mom, I don't have time to be sick. We're still packing and painting Vanessa's parents' house."

Fernando embraced Suzy. "I'm not afraid of germs. Can I make you some hot tea, Mama Suzy?"

"That sounds delicious." Suzy was thrilled Fernando had added the moniker, 'Mama' in front of her name.

After Fernando added water to the teakettle, he rummaged around until he found a bag of green tea. As he danced around the kitchen, a cup crashed onto the floor. Violet wailed.

"Darn it. That's my fault." Fernando raced to the piano and played "Twinkle, Twinkle Little Star." Like magic, Violet fell back asleep.

Jon beamed. "My man has the touch."

"I'd say." Suzy accepted a cup of hot green tea and felt her stomach settle. "I feel better already. Thanks, guys. You're just what I needed."

Chapter 66

At work the next day, Alex pounced on Hannah before her intern had a chance to set her purse down. "Why were you at Coconuts last night?"

Shrugging, Hannah said, "Why not? It's a fun bar. I like the tropical-theme."

"It's *my* hangout." Alex's voice rose a notch.

"Yours? Do you own it?" Hannah dared Alex with her eyes.

Exasperated, Alex said, "Of course I don't own it. I work *here*, remember? But I've gone to Coconuts for years with my girlfriends. It's *our* oasis. Our happy place. Not yours."

Hannah adjusted her bra strap. Alex had to bite her tongue to keep from telling a boob joke but didn't want to get into trouble with Human Resources. Besides she was beginning to wonder if she was a tiny bit jealous of Hannah's voluptuous figure. Her C-cups looked like a budding teenager compared to her intern.

Crossing her arms, Hannah pouted. "Why can't it be my oasis too?"

"Find your own damn bar. I'm sure there are a hundred in Crystal City." Alex brightened. "I hear there are some cool, new bars downtown. Try one of those. They probably play that rap music you like."

"I can go to Coconuts if I want. Last I heard, it's a free country." Hannah plopped in a chair across from Alex's desk. "What's on tap today, *boss*?"

Alex fumed at the thought of Hannah's ruining her weekly girlfriend outing. "What's on tap is still the bank anniversary celebration, but not so fast. Who was with you last night?" Alex watched as Hannah's face grew pale.

"No one special." She shrugged. "A friend." Retrieving her iPad in an obvious attempt to avoid Alex's inquisition, she asked, "What's up first on the anniversary planning?"

Alex decided to let it go—this time. She was ninety percent sure Hannah was with Sean but never got a clear frontal view of him, plus Coconuts has a dark interior. *My life is complicated enough with Tony and his hateful ex. I certainly don't need Hannah and Sean throwing a wrench into the absurd mess.*

Straightening her orange and ivory striped blouse, Alex said, "I need coffee. Since you're interning for college credit, why don't *you* tell *me* the top ten order for the celebration? Think of it as a class assignment."

Within minutes, Alex returned with two cups of coffee—both for herself—which she sorely needed after seeing her nemesis invade her favorite hangout. She placed both cups beside her computer and glanced at her busy calendar.

Hannah glanced up from her iPad. "Is one of those for me?"

"Nope."

Both women started as the bank president leaned inside Alex's office. "Morning, ladies. How's everything in marketing?"

Hannah beamed. "Daddy, Alex put me in charge of the bank's anniversary celebration. Isn't that wonderful?"

"I knew she'd see your value. Hannah is indispensable isn't she, Alex?" Jim patted the doorframe. "I'm thrilled you two get along so well."

Hannah shot Alex a daring expression that her dad couldn't see. Alex bit her tongue. Again.

After Jim left, Alex powered up her computer, hating the fact that she had to put up with an intern from hell, and worse, had to share a damn office with Daddy's darling.

"Well? Let's get back on the anniversary plans. What have you got for me?"

Clearing her throat for noticeable added emphasis, Hannah ran down a list of social media suggestions to announce the anniversary date, online apps and giveaways, and bank website updates. After she went through her technical spiel, she set her iPad on Alex's desk.

"What do you think? Pretty good, right?" She dusted her hands in a satisfied motion. "I'm pretty quick on my feet." She pointed to her head. "Beauty and brains. Can't beat 'em."

Alex silently counted to ten before responding, trying hard not to laugh. *Oh, how I'm going to enjoy this. Putting Hannah in her place is becoming almost as important as my morning coffee.*

Sighing for emphasis, Alex said, "Remember our discussion about targeted marketing and how our customers skew older? It's fine to have both an online presence, apps, and the like, but be sure you combine them with what you call 'old school' marketing like radio, television, billboards, and print. We need to have a marketing mix for many age ranges."

Obviously bored with Alex's lecture, Hannah leaned forward giving Alex full view of her twin summits. "Is that it? I have an appointment for a massage."

Alex thought about how much she could use a massage. "That's it. Update what we discussed and make it happen."

Striking a perfect model pose with one hand on her hip, Hannah said, "No worries. I've got this."

Chapter 67

All week, Jon and Fernando had gathered what seemed like a thousand boxes, gave their landlord notice, and packed up their apartment, as well as Vanessa's duplex. After days of fast food carry-out including pizza, sub sandwiches, Indian food, and Chinese, a persistent knock on the door followed by a shrill doorbell forced the men to freeze in place.

Fernando groaned. "Who could that be? You get the door. I have a hot date with bubble wrap."

With newspaper stuck to his shoe, Jon flung the door open. "Mom? What's this?"

Beaming, Suzy said, "I know how hard you've been working and thought you could use a home-cooked meal."

"I smell heaven." Fernando jumped up and cleared a path, throwing boxes into a corner. "Mama Suzy to the rescue. Please come in at your own risk." Chuckling, he said, "It's like Roller Derby in here. Seriously, don't trip." He kissed her on both cheeks as he reached for a still-warm casserole dish. "I'll try to find a countertop. There's got to be a bare square inch somewhere."

After hugging her, Jon said, "Thanks, Mom. You're a lifesaver. We're sick of takeout."

Ken appeared with another covered dish. "Hi, guys. We thought you could use some help."

Whistling, Jon said, "You've got that right."

Suzy balanced a salad bowl in one hand while placing her purse on the floor.

"This smells amazing." Jon rubbed his belly. "What did you bring?"

"Your favorites—artichoke chicken, roasted asparagus with cherry tomatoes, and a Caesar salad. Let me wash my hands. I need to warm them up." Suzy's eyebrows shot up at the sight of the men's usually tidy kitchen. "You're right about finding a square inch of workspace. I bet this mess is driving you batty." She laughed. "But it'll all be worth it."

"What can we do to help?" Fernando asked.

Jon had already moved boxes off the round dining table and began setting out plates.

"I've got this." Suzy took foil off a casserole dish. "You guys take a break."

Ken stepped back outside, retrieved a bottle of wine from the backseat, and thrust it in Fernando's hands. "Where can I find a wine opener and glasses?"

Jon unearthed the wine opener and pointed toward a cabinet with glasses. "I'll text Vanessa so she can join us. She's running errands nearby."

Before the wineglasses were filled, Vanessa knocked and stepped inside. Suzy reached for the baby. "Eat with the boys. I'll watch Violet. I've been having baby withdrawal. Ken and I can wait to eat. There isn't room for all of us at the table."

"We have to wait?" Ken's mouth fell open. "I'm star—"

Suzy shot her husband a look.

"Uh, sure. Go ahead." Ken reached for a plate. "I'll eat later in the living room with Suzy and the baby."

After they ate among much *oohing* and *ahhing*, Vanessa cleaned the kitchen while Violet napped.

"Are any boxes ready to load?" Ken asked. "I see you've rented a U-Haul. Smart move."

Fernando pointed. "Every box on that side of the room is packed."

"And labeled," Jon offered.

In a procession, Jon, Fernando, Ken, and Suzy carried

box after box outside. Soon the covered trailer was bulging with boxes, rugs, lamps, wall hangings, and furniture.

When they finished, a sweaty Jon and Fernando ran inside.

Fernando twirled Vanessa in the kitchen. "Tomorrow's the big day."

"Yep. Moving day." Jon peered at the sleeping baby. "Living full time with a baby will be interesting."

Vanessa's face fell. "If it's going to be too much-"

"No. I meant a *good* interesting." Jon winked at her. "Actually, I'm excited about living together."

Fernando hugged Vanessa. "I can't wait."

She beamed as she placed her arms around both men. "Me neither."

Chapter 68

Alex loved casual Fridays since she wore stuffy, albeit sleek, bank suits all week. Wearing a turquoise embroidered Show-Me Bank logoed sweater, black slacks, and black heels, she settled behind her desk and glanced at her packed calendar.

She had barely set her bag down when Hannah traipsed inside wearing a form-fitting, low-cut red sweater.

Staring at Hannah's attire, Alex frowned. "Knee-length shorts aren't allowed."

"Why?" Hannah glanced at her clothes. "And good morning to you too."

"Bank dress code. It's conservative around here, if you hadn't noticed." Alex paused. "Per your dad's rules, of course."

Putting her hands on her hips, Hannah said, challenging her, "It's Friday, which means it's also casual dress day."

Already tired of her intern's bluster, Alex turned toward her computer. "Check the policy manual. Shorts aren't allowed."

Hannah pouted. "But they're dressy shorts, plus I'm wearing heels. What is this? The fifties?"

"Something like that but there are bank guidelines—for everything—including employee attire. Follow them, like it or not." Alex swiveled in her chair, lowering her voice. "Between you and me, I think the antiquated rules are ridiculous too." She motioned with her head toward a husky male employee taking the stairs two at a time. "See that real estate officer? He wears dirty cowboy boots and faded jeans every single casual Friday. In my opinion, you look much dressier, but hey, your daddy is the president. Take it up with him." *Boom.*

Hannah sank into a chair, obviously defeated. "I don't think daddy will send me home, but I guess I won't wear these again. What's on the agenda today?"

"The bank anniversary," Alex said.

"Again?"

"Yes, again. It has to be right." Alex powered up her computer while Hannah retrieved her iPad.

As the screen came into focus, Alex clicked on a file. "Let's go down the checklist. Did you send out the direct mail pieces?"

Hannah hesitated a bit too long. "Uh, sure."

Alex turned to face her intern, voice rising. "Convince me."

Stiffening, Hannah said, "Trust me, okay?"

"O-kay." Alex didn't like Hannah's nondescript answer but continued checking off her to-do list. "How about press releases. Were those emailed to the media?"

Again Hannah hesitated. "I've been really busy."

Fuming, Alex narrowed her eyes and attempted to contain herself from hissing. "I'm going upstairs for coffee. The anniversary celebration is our *top* priority. I've told you that a hundred times. What in the hell have you been busy doing besides those stupid radio spots?" As she got to the door of her office, she turned. "Be right back."

Typing madly on her iPad, Hannah didn't bother looking up. "Will you bring me a cup of coffee too?"

Only if I can spill it down your shirt. Once again, her maddening intern had somehow managed to get her to fetch coffee. *I don't work for you, bitch. It's the other way around.*

In the employee lounge, the bank president hovered near the coffee pot. "Everything ready for the bank's party, Alex? I know I don't have to tell you how important this event is."

Her heart skipped a beat. "We're on it. In fact, Hannah and I were just going over the final checklist."

"I knew I could count on you two." Jim refilled his SMB mug and left.

Alex's pulse quickened. *Nothing can go wrong. Absolutely nothing.* She got halfway down the stairs before she remembered she forgot Hannah's coffee. *Dammit.*

Reluctantly, she returned to the lounge and reappeared with two cups of coffee. She plunked Hannah's down so hard it splashed over the side. "Here."

"Thanks." Hannah stared at her iPad as she reached for the coffee. "The cup's sticky."

Alex didn't respond. She knew her intern enjoyed this power play and told herself this was the last time she'd get Hannah's coffee. "Back to the press release, let's—"

"Done," Hannah said.

"Done? You hadn't sent it five minutes ago."

"Well, I have now." Hannah beamed. "What's next?"

Glancing at her computer, Alex frowned as she scrolled through her emails. "Did you send me a copy?"

Hannah typed a few keystrokes. "You have it now."

Alex scanned the one-page news release. "Dammit, Hannah. You didn't include the date of the event."

"Oh."

"Not 'oh.' Holy shit. How do you think the media would cover this without a damn date?" Alex shook her head. "Always, always play back in your mind who, what, when, where, and why before you send a press release. Don't they teach that in your fancy marketing classes?" She couldn't resist the jab.

"They teach way more complicated things than that."

Alex scowled. "You need to learn the basics. Honestly, Hannah, why do you always have to argue with me?" She scanned the announcement. "My God there's a typo in the last paragraph. Didn't you proofread this?"

Hannah shrugged. "I rushed to try and please you before you got back." She squinted at her iPad. "It's a minor typo. Not that big a deal."

"Not that big a deal?" Alex felt her face get hot. "Always proofread anything you send out multiple times. Your dad would be furious if I did this and it'll reflect on me, regardless. Dammit."

"Daddy never gets angry with me. *Never*." Hannah gave her a pretend hurt look, undercut by a smug smile.

A vein throbbed in Alex's forehead. "Resend the damn press release. Change the subject line to read: FINAL PRESS RELEASE— PLEASE DISREGARD EARLIER ANNOUNCEMENT. Got it?"

"Got. It. Jesus." Hannah typed a few words and hit *send*.

"Did you add the date of the event *and* correct the typo?"

"Oops." Hannah leaned forward showing her massive cleavage as she clicked a few more keys. "Anything else?"

Alex reread the press release from top to bottom and bottom to top. "Let me clue you in on a great way to proofread. If you start at the bottom and read backward, you're more likely to catch errors."

Stony faced, Hannah narrowed her eyes. "Do you want to be my English teacher or my boss?"

"I know I'm tense about this event, but I'm trying to help you. Teach you. That's what internships are all about, right?" Alex stared at the screen, refusing to make eye contact for fear of saying something she shouldn't.

Hannah held her hands up in surrender mode. "Okay, okay. You've made your point. Let me read this forward *and* backward." She made the corrections. Anything else before I hit send?"

"Did you change the subject line?" Alex asked.

Head down, she typed some more. "All done."

Feeling victorious, Alex said, "Send the edited press

release to the media, every board member, employee, to Jim, and a copy to me."

"You already have a copy."

"Humor me." Alex shifted in her chair. "I'd like the final, corrected copy for the file."

Sighing, Hannah emailed the news and stretched. "I think I'll get more coffee."

Alex slid her cup across her desk and forced a smile. "I'd like some too."

After Hannah left, Alex wondered if she had made a mistake. *She'll probably spit in it.*

While Alex waited for her coffee, she stared out the window wishing she could fly away with two redbirds perched on a branch.

Hearing her intern return, she asked, "Where were we, Hannah?" Before she answered, Alex turned to stare at her growing email messages. "Why don't you work in the employee lounge? I need to return a hundred emails."

"Whatever." Hannah grabbed her bag, shoved her iPad under her arm, and thrust her chest out in defiance. Holding her coffee in the air, she said, "Relax, boss. Everything will be fine."

I wish I could believe her. The pit in Alex's stomach said otherwise. She stared out the window as two of the male loan officers drove out of the bank lot. *Good idea, guys. I'm leaving early to shop or get a pedicure. I've got to get out of this bank.*

Chapter 69

"I can't believe it's finally moving day." Jon poured coffee into a disposable cup and handed one to Fernando. "Are you ready for our life change?"

"Absolutely. I'm already thinking about barbecuing on that shady deck."

"I can't wait to sit on the porch swing in the morning." Jon nudged his husband. "And having Vanessa and Violet around all of the time will be—"

"Fabulous."

Jon drained his coffee. "You've been incredible about this."

"I asked you to stop bringing this up." Fernando glanced around their apartment. "Just think. We won't have to listen to neighbors stomp overhead or play music too loudly."

"Or smell weird food," Jon said.

"I can't wait to live in a real home."

"Me neither." Jon tossed his coffee cup into the last trash bag, threw away their breakfast paper plates, and tucked a roll of paper towels under his arm. "Ready?"

"I was born ready." Fernando stepped toward the hall. "I'll take one last look around and make sure we didn't forget something small like a charger." He returned within minutes. "All good. Let's go."

~ ~ ~

After backing into their new driveway, Jon hopped out and lifted the heavy door of the U-Haul. Fernando unlocked the front door and propped it open.

As they began unloading, Jon said, "I'm glad I thought of labeling the boxes." He winked as he took three to the kitchen.

"I thought I was the one who mentioned how helpful labels would be. You laughed if I recall." Fernando winked as he stacked three boxes and placed them in the bedroom. "I'm glad we told Vanessa to wait and let Violet nap first."

Straining with more heavy boxes, Jon said, "Yup. Me too."

After two hours of unloading and sorting, Vanessa drove up. As she bent over to get the baby out of the car seat, the men spotted her from the living room and rushed outside.

Fernando dangled a blindfold.

Vanessa's forehead creased. "Um, what's that for?"

"You'll see." Jon reached for the baby. "Trust us."

Fernando steered Vanessa between rows of boxes and toward the nursery. Jon followed with the baby.

Once she stepped inside the bedroom, Vanessa wrinkled her nose. "What's that smell?"

Jon and Fernando exchanged worried glances, even though she couldn't see them.

"Maybe Violet should sleep in a different room for a few days," Jon said.

"Until it airs out. It won't take long." Fernando crossed the room and opened two windows. A soft breeze blew the white, lacy curtains.

"When can I look?" Vanessa asked.

"Oh, I forgot." Fernando untied her blindfold.

Vanessa placed both hands on her cheeks and gasped. "It's lilac. The entire room is lilac."

"Actually, it's violet." Jon teased. "What do you think?"

Mouth agape she stared at a white rocking chair, white crib, and a changing table above a white dresser. On one wall a koala bear climbed up a lifelike tree with sprawling branches covered in green leaves, purple, and lavender flowers. An oversized 'V' adorned one wall, and a white wicker toy chest filled a corner. A tiny bookshelf lined another wall awaiting books for Miss Violet's library. A toddler-sized ballerina wearing a violet tutu was poised above the bookshelf.

Vanessa finally found words. "I. Can't. Believe. This." Eyes glistening, she turned toward both men. "Violet's nursery is gorgeous. It couldn't be more perfect. I may sleep in here with her. I love it." She shook her head. "When did you find the time?"

Grinning from ear to ear, Jon said, "We made the time."

Fernando extended his arms wide.

Beaming, Vanessa embraced them.

"Welcome home," both Jon and Fernando chimed. Baby Violet kicked her legs and vomited on Jon's shirt.

Vanessa's face turned pink and Fernando roared. "I see she isn't quite housebroken."

Chapter 70

After several restless days of worrying about the bank party and unable to see Tony who said he was unavailable due to top-secret undercover police work, Alex ate little and slept even less.

Glad to get to work without an 8 o'clock meeting for once, she stared at her piled-high desk while reaching for her trilling desk phone. "Alexandra Mitchell, Market—"

A deep voice didn't bother with a greeting. "I can't be at your bank thing."

Leaning back in her chair, Alex stared out the window as employees parked. She took a few calming breaths that didn't calm her whatsoever. Tony knew how important this event was. Bristling, she inwardly counted to ten before responding.

"Did you hear me?" he asked.

"Why the hell not? You know how important this is to me." She scooted a pile of folders so fast across her desk the documents fell onto the floor. "Dammit."

"Nikki's in the hospital. She needs help with Joey." He paused. "Sorry, babe. You know I'd be there if I could."

"Because you love these types of things." Alex rolled her eyes. "Nikki's in the hospital? What's your ex in for? Mental health or substance abuse?"

"Very funny. You should have been a comedienne." Tony lowered his voice as if someone might overhear. "Apparently, it's some kind of female stuff."

"Yeah, right." Alex's mind raced. "She probably wanted

to keep you away from me. Did you tell her about the bank celebration?"

"Yeah I told her. What does that have to do with anything?"

"Everything." Switching ears, Alex said, "I'm not buying it."

Sounding worried, Tony said, "It could be serious. I've got to help out."

"Whatever. I've got a million things to do." Alex hung up without saying goodbye. Tears stung her eyes. She wondered if she'd ever come first with Tony. Her thoughts immediately went to Cheri's limo driver. *I wish Gage weren't in New York. I bet he'd be there for me in a heartbeat.*

As per her usual bad timing, Hannah appeared and propped her feet on the edge of Alex's desk. She chirped, "The bank anniversary will be lit tonight. I think we've done everything possible."

"We forgot flowers," Alex said dryly. "Why don't you go find a couple of nice centerpieces? Try to get colors in our bank logo."

"Burgundy carnations. Easy." Hannah grabbed her massive yellow and navy striped Tommy Hilfiger bag and left.

I hope to God we remembered everything. If not, Jim will have my head. Thanks a lot for your support, Tony.

Chapter 71

While Fernando barbecued burgers and grilled corn on the cob, Vanessa made brownies. Jon stirred a pitcher of lemonade and kept a watchful eye on a sleeping Violet.

The doorbell rang three times.

"That's going to wake the baby." Jon sprinted through the living room.

Vanessa followed him and peered around the front door. "Suzy, what a nice surprise."

Suzy winced. "Sorry about the doorbell. It got stuck."

"No problem. She's still asleep." Vanessa opened the door wider. "Come in."

I can't stay. Ken and I are going to a movie, but I have a special delivery arriving any minute. I wanted to be here to see your reaction."

Jon stepped onto the porch and hugged his mom. "Is it that gorgeous silver mirror I've been coveting?"

"Even better." Suzy glanced around the room. "Where's Fernando?"

"He's grilling on the deck. I'll go get him." Vanessa returned with an apron-wearing Fernando.

Brightening when he spotted his mother-in-law, Fernando asked, "Mama Suzy, can you stay for burgers? I made chili burgers with green peppers and onions." He formed his fingers together and placed them on his lips, making the familiar Italian gesture as if he were kissing the air. "They're the best."

"That sounds delicious. I wish I could but I'm meeting

Ken." She wiggled her eyebrows. "We're having a date. Izzy is spending the night with a friend."

The loud beep-beep of a delivery truck got everyone's attention. They stepped into the yard and watched as the driver backed into their driveway. Four men hopped out, put a gigantic ramp down, and steadied the massive, covered contents on rollers. One shouted, "Where do you want this?"

"Is that your piano?" Jon's eyes bulged. "You're giving us your piano?"

Suzy nodded. "I never play it anymore, plus the music soothes Violet. I want you guys to have it. Think of it as our housewarming gift."

"That's a helluva housewarming gift, Mom."

"Mama Suzy, thank you isn't nearly enough. You're beyond generous." Fernando wrapped his arms around his mother-in-law and dipped her so far over her head nearly touched the ground.

Clinging to Fernando, she said, "Don't drop me. And you're welcome." Once she was upright, she added, "Besides, as much as I love my granddaughter, those middle-of-the-night piano serenades might get a little old. Ken and I enjoy our sleep. I've gotta run. Tell the delivery guys where you want it. I'm off to meet my husband."

Chapter 72

Alex's heart raced as she glanced toward the clock and lobby every few seconds, wondering why more people weren't at the anniversary party. *First Tony cancels and now no one shows.*

The minute Hannah strutted in the front door wearing a low-cut silky black blouse, ivory pants, and stilettoes, Alex swarmed her. Hissing under her breath, she asked, "Where the hell is everyone?"

"Hello to you too." Ignoring the question, Hannah waved to her father and practically skated across the room to shake the hands of a few board members.

Fuming, Alex plastered a fake smile across her face, stepped across the lobby, and reached for Hannah's elbow. "We need to talk."

Hannah didn't miss a beat. "Go ahead. I'm sure Mrs. Timmons would love to hear anything you have to say."

The elderly silver-haired board chairwoman brightened. "Yes, I would. I love marketing. You know when I was a young woman, we—"

"Sorry to interrupt, Mrs. Timmons, but this is urgent. Hold that thought." Alex narrowed her eyes. "Hannah, I need to speak to you in the employee lounge." When Hannah stood in place, Alex said, "Now."

Begrudgingly the intern followed Alex into a back room. In spite of all attempts to remain calm, sweat formed on Alex's upper lip. "Where is everyone? Did you send out the five thousand direct mail pieces targeting neighborhood residents and businesses? I had hoped ten percent of them would show up. That's five hundred people."

"I can do the math," Hannah said.

"Glad to hear it. So, where are our guests?" Poking her head back out the door, Alex surveyed the miniscule crowd mainly made up of bank employees. Her pulse raced. "We should have five times this many people here." She eyed Hannah's blank face as a sickening thought crossed her mind. "You did send the invitations out, right?"

"Of course." Suddenly fixated on her shiny shoes, Hannah said, "At the last minute, I decided to send evites instead of printed invitations."

Alex's stomach lurched. "Evites? Oh, my God. Why didn't you use printed invitations like I specifically told you to do?"

Shrugging, Hannah said, "It's the modern era, Alex. Everyone has a computer. It's more efficient, no postage costs, and—"

"The evites are probably in everyone's damn spam folder." Feeling a headache bearing down, Alex rubbed her temples. "Everyone has computers *except* for many of our best, longtime, elderly customers and older board members. I spelled everything out for you, Hannah. A million zillion times. Evites are fine *if* accompanied by a printed invitation as well. I don't know why I can't get this through your head." She pounded her fist on the counter. "Dammit."

Seemingly nonplussed, Hannah shrugged. "Think of it as a nice, intimate bank party."

Alex wanted to slap her. "Nice and intimate won't cut it. Your dad wanted a grand event. We're going to have to think fast."

Flipping her hair over her shoulder, Hannah said, "Daddy won't be mad at me. He never gets mad at me."

I hate this bitch. Why did I get stuck with her? Alex

knew she'd get all of the blame and stormed off before she said something that would get her fired.

~ ~ ~

Feeling her phone vibrate, Alex glanced at the screen. Cheri had texted that she was at the back door. Rushing back toward the break area, she said, "The food's here. Why don't you mingle and hope to God more people show up. I'm going to let the caterer in."

"Fine. I'll go keep Daddy company."

Alex wanted to puke. She headed toward the back door and forced a smile when she saw Cheri. "I'm glad you're here."

"Thanks for the business." Cheri handed Alex two bags of containers and brought in three more herself. As they set the bags on the counter, Alex peeked inside. "What did you bring?"

Cheri beamed. "Only the best. Let's see. We have duck breasts and calves cheeks with a blood orange and balsamic reduction. Oh, and I even threw in some caviar at my expense. Nothing's too good for my friends."

Alex's mouth went dry as she wondered how the elaborate hors d'oeuvres would go over. It wasn't exactly Midwestern fare. "Uh, thanks. Anything else?"

Cheri stared at her appetizers. "Goat cheese tarts, bacon-wrapped scallops, liver pate, Caprese skewers, and salmon tartare." Staring at her beautiful creations, Cheri's brow furrowed. "Did I go overboard?"

Alex's tone was wooden. "I don't know what I expected—not a green bean casserole nor mac and cheese—but not this upscale spread either." Sighing, she said, "I suppose I should have been more involved but there's no time to change it now. Let me help you put the food on platters."

"Hopefully, they'll like it." Cheri's upbeat attitude faded. "All of my elite clients in New York City love this food. In fact, these are some of the most requested items on Fifth Avenue Catering's menu. I thought—"

"It's an adventuresome menu." Alex knew she had hurt Cheri's feelings. "It's definitely eclectic and a step up from our usual fare. It'll be, uh, fine. Let's get it on the table."

As they carried platters out of the bank lounge that boasted a small kitchen, Alex noticed Hannah had strategically placed floral centerpieces on the tabletop. *At least she's on top of the flowers.* Cheri arranged the food on the white linen tablecloth, some containers level with the table, with other platters on risers.

Alex stacked white and gold-rimmed Fifth Avenue Catering plates bearing Cheri's logo on one end of the table. The gold silverware was so shiny you could use it to apply lipstick. The aroma soon filled the lobby and a modest group gathered around the food.

Jim gave Alex a nod as he ushered Show-Me Bank's best customers and board members toward the food. Reaching for a plate, he stood stock still and stared at the heaping platters, his fork in mid-air.

Alex stared horrified as her boss wrinkled his nose and took miniature portions. The second Jim got through the buffet line, he made a beeline toward her.

He doesn't look happy.

Holding a half-filled square plate, Jim motioned with his fork. "What am I eating, Alex? Who made this stuff?"

Alex turned toward Cheri whose face had flushed beet red. She watched her friend's eyes well with tears and immediately wanted to protect her. Motioning toward the caterer, she said, "This is Cheri Van Buren. She's a New York caterer and often cooks for celebrities. She even catered a party for Elton John recently." Alex swallowed. "We're lucky to have her."

Jim studied the socialite as he chewed on a bite of duck breast dripping with glaze. Holding his sticky hand in the air, he frowned. "I don't know what you eat in New York, but in the Midwest, we like steak and potatoes. I don't recognize any of this food." He glared at Alex. "And where is everyone?"

Alex wanted to scream that his daughter dropped the ball and screwed up the invitations but knew it was her responsibility as vice president of marketing to oversee the details. "Maybe everyone's running late." She managed a chuckle. "Like me."

Jim didn't laugh.

Alex tried another approach to lighten the mood. "We'll take care of the food situation, boss. Right, Cheri?"

The New Yorker bobbed her head and disappeared in the bank's small kitchen.

"Maybe by the time the guests arrive—if they arrive—we'll have recognizable food." In a huff, Jim turned on his heel.

Alex noticed Hannah chatting up the cute lender. She crossed the lobby and tugged on her blouse. "Follow me."

"What's up?" Hannah asked.

"The food. Your dad hates it. Come with me." They retreated to the kitchen. "Ladies, we have to fix this—and fast."

Cheri had already scraped her expensive appetizers in a trash bin. "What's wrong with me? I should have donated this. Your boss threw me. Sorry, Alex. I'll fix this. Do you have a Sam's or Costco nearby?"

"Just around the corner," Hannah said. "Want me to go with you. This party is a drag."

Alex wanted to punch her. "You're staying here, Hannah. Get on your blinged-out phone and start calling Chamber members."

Hannah's brows knitted. "I don't have their phone numbers."

"Why not?" Alex stood with her hands on her hips. "Didn't they teach you the importance of corporate contacts in business school? Oh, never mind." She fished her phone out of her bag and thrust it in Hannah's face. "Look under 'Crystal City Chamber' and call as many members as you can. Do whatever it takes to get them here within the hour. Tell them you're Daddy's Little Girl who will get fired if they don't show up. Tell them whatever. Just get them here."

The intern's eyes bulged. "You really want me to say that?"

"Of course not." Alex blew out her breath. "Tell them their invitation must have gotten lost in the mail and we'd be honored with their presence since there will be awards later on tonight."

"Awards?" Hannah asked. "I didn't know we were giving away awards."

"We weren't but we've got to entice them somehow. You can mention food too—and the anniversary itself, of course." Alex reached for her purse. "I'm off to a trophy shop. The owner went to my high school. I'm going to see if he'll do me a huge favor in exchange for something."

Hannah snickered. "You think he'll remember you from high school?"

"Shut up and start dialing."

Chapter 73

Alex returned from the trophy shop after ordering engraved plaques featuring a photo of Show-Me Bank with the anniversary dates listed. The owner said it would be impossible to deliver them that evening but he'd get them to her soon.

Driving back to the bank like an Indy 500 racer, Alex rushed inside the lobby, waved to a few more—but still sparse number of guests—and made her way to the kitchen area. She heard a knock on the back door and found a smiling Cheri with more food.

Alex reached for the bags. "Need some help?"

Cheri bobbed as she struggled with the weight. Once inside the employee lounge, she plunked them on the counter.

"What's in there?" Alex asked. "A bear cub?"

"I bought a little of everything as fast as I could."

"Impressive shopping skills."

Cheri plucked out bags of cheddar and pepper jack cubed cheese, four containers of pulled pork brisket, barbecue sauce, potato salad, and coleslaw. Working quickly, she sliced a fresh pineapple and mixed chunks with the coleslaw and Greek yogurt. Winking, she said, "I hope this isn't too fancy for your boss."

Alex snorted. "It looks delicious."

After she rinsed strawberries and blueberries, Cheri expertly cut a watermelon into a basket shape, complete with a handle. She placed the round chunks of watermelon she had scooped out inside along with the other fruit.

Alex peered over her shoulder as she worked. "How did you do that so fast?"

"Practice." Cheri dumped the contents from salsa, guacamole and spinach dip into shell-shaped bowls and surrounded the condiments with chips. "I feel like I'm getting ready for a Fourth of July celebration."

Alex relaxed. "Jim will love it. Honestly, it looks great. Thank you, Cheri. Sorry my boss dissed your expensive food. I'm sure you slaved over it."

Brushing hair out of her face, Cheri kept working. "No worries. I want my clients to be happy. I guess I went overboard trying to impress you."

"Impress me?" Alex's mouth fell open.

Beads of sweat formed on Cheri's forehead. "This is the first time I've had real friends, so yes, I wanted to impress *you*."

Alex hugged her. "You're a sweetheart." While Cheri finished arranging the food, she peeked out the door as Mrs. Timmons welcomed a few more board members who had finally ambled inside.

Jim crossed the room in two steps to greet them. Alex chuckled when he nearly shook their hands off. *This night is so important to him. I've got to pull it out of the toilet.*

Cheri straightened her white and gold apron. "Here goes nothing. Wish me luck." Expertly balancing two heavy trays on each hand, she approached the linen-covered table. Thankfully, Hannah had already placed clean dishes, utensils, and napkins on the table. Moving quickly, Cheri set the hot appetizers on one end and cold on the other.

The smell of the barbecue apparently enticed the bank president who crossed the lobby and inspected the new food. After Jim noticed the redone spread, he reached for the pulled pork and plopped barbecue sauce on top.

Alex stood near Cheri, finding it hard to breathe as she waited for her boss's reaction.

Barely catching a dark red blob before it landed on his crisp, white shirt, the bank president said, "This is more like it, Miss- Van Buren, is it?"

Cheri winked at Alex who blew out her breath, finally able to relax.

Shaking Cheri's hand with his free one, Jim continued. "This is delicious." He took another bite and asked, "By the way, are you related to Thomas Van Buren?"

Cheri's eyebrows shot up. "He's my dad. My mom is Victoria. Do you know them?"

Jim heaped his plate with brisket, pulled pork, potato salad, and coleslaw. "I'm sure everyone in the finance world knows the Van Burens." He crammed cubed cheese in the middle of his overflowing plate.

"I suppose so. Enjoy." She retreated to the kitchen, unhappy her cover was busted.

Alex studied the interaction between her friend and boss while never taking her eyes off the front door. Ten of the fifteen board members had arrived, which given the short amount of time, she'd take. The Chamber president and several Chamber Ambassadors had also arrived. Breathing a sigh of relief, Alex thanked them for coming and pointed toward the food table.

She began to relax as she kept her eyes on Jim who finally appeared to be enjoying himself. Between greeting current and potential customers, he worked the room and seemingly shook hands with everyone. Employees chatted, two lines formed on either side of the buffet table, and realizing she hadn't eaten since breakfast, Alex forced herself to eat a few cheese cubes.

Doing her best to enjoy the event between bites, Alex focused on the dignitaries and board members who chatted. Wishing her boss allowed alcohol at the anniversary event, she could hardly wait to have a glass of wine. After all the mishaps, she sorely needed a drink—or two.

Hannah glided through the lobby as if she were on ice. Alex couldn't hate her more. Normally she was calm and totally in charge, but after the hiccup over the too-fancy food and the evites disaster, she was off her game.

Doing her best to remain attentive and gracious, Alex kept one eye on the door and the other on her boss. *Where are the media? I thought at least one radio or television station would show up.*

Chapter 74

Alex spotted Hannah sucking up to a new executive vice president and smiling like a beauty pageant queen. Crossing the now-almost-crowded lobby, Alex acknowledged the bank officer, asked if she were enjoying herself, and tugged on Hannah's sleeve. "When you're finished, I need to have a word with you."

Hannah said, "Word." She and the EVP laughed as though it were the best joke they'd ever heard.

Alex ignored their ridiculous banter and stepped back into the kitchen where a sweaty Cheri stood over a sink filled with dishes. "Don't you have people to do this?"

"Normally, yes, but this has been one of those days. It's fine. I'll be done soon." Hands sudsy, Cheri glanced over her shoulder. "I'm thrilled they like the new food."

"We do enjoy our barbecue. I should have mentioned that. It's not your fault, plus you made it right. I can't thank you enough."

Waving a plastic-gloved hand, Cheri said, "Any time."

Alex checked her watch again. "I can't believe not one reporter has shown up." She stepped back into the lobby. As if on cue, bright camera lights shone on the crowd. A young, handsome reporter held a microphone that read Ozarks5. A camerawoman was close behind him. Both searched the room, obviously waiting for direction.

Crossing the lobby in three steps, Alex extended her hand, but Hannah beat her to the action.

Shaking the reporter's hand much too vigorously, Hannah

told him she was in charge of marketing, and naturally, she mentioned she was the daughter of the bank president.

Alex stood a foot away, deciding to watch this play out. The reporter's eyebrows shot up. "You're the bank president's daughter?"

Hannah rushed to defend her position. "I'm not a paid employee. That would be nepotism. I'm actually an intern working on my master's degree."

Covering her mouth to keep from laughing, Alex was amazed at how quickly Hannah had worked that nugget into the conversation. *Master's degree. If I never hear that phrase again, I'll die happy.*

The reporter continued. "If you're an intern, who's your boss?"

Clearly taken aback, Hannah did her best to hide a grimace behind a forced smile. Ignoring the direct question, she asked, "Would you like to speak to the bank president?"

"Sure."

Alex swiveled her head and scanned the room but didn't see Jim. Earlier, he had been embroiled in a deep conversation with three Chamber members. She stepped toward the reporter who had begun shifting from foot to foot.

"Hi." Alex extended her hand. "Thanks for coming by Show-Me Bank's anniversary extravaganza. I'm Alexandra Mitchell, Vice President of Marketing."

She heard Hannah mumble, "If she had a master's, she'd be *Senior* Vice President." Alex bristled but let the comment go.

"Good," the reporter said. "Mind if I interview you?"

"Um, okay. Sure." Alex scanned the room again. Her boss was nowhere to be found. She knew Jim loved the camera, so where was he?

With ease, the reporter straightened his tie, nodded to the camerawoman, and spoke into the black box pointed toward his head. "This is Joe Tucker reporting from Show-Me Bank. I'm here with . . ."

He thrust the microphone in Alex's face as the camerawoman turned on a blinding light and pointed the camera inches away from her nose.

At that moment, Alex realized she had never been on live television. Even though she had written scads of television commercials and had coached her boss and several loan officers through rehearsals numerous times, being on live television with a microphone thrust in her face was alarmingly scary.

She froze, staring blankly into the camera. After one or two long seconds, the reporter tried again. "Your name is?"

Swallowing, she said, "My name's Alex. People call me Alex." She noticed the reporter and camerawoman exchange glances.

"Okay, Alex. What's the purpose of the bank's celebration?"

"It's uh, uh, a—" Obviously drawing a blank, she motioned for Hannah to step forward.

Hannah smiled, thrust out her massive chest, and finished the interview as if she were Hoda freaking Kotb. The reporter asked several questions about the bank's history, number of employees, branch locations, and services. Toward the end of the discussion, Hannah had both Ozarks5 reps in stitches. Afterward, she suggested they scan the crowd, the bank lobby, and asked them to be sure the bank logo was prominent on-air. When the reporter finished, Hannah invited them to eat.

She turned toward Alex. "That's okay, right, *boss*?" She drew out the last word for emphasis.

Alex couldn't be more miserable. Fighting back tears from her flop of a non-interview, she couldn't believe Hannah had been completely comfortable in front of the camera and even, gasp, charming. Managing a nod, Alex motioned toward the food. "Sure, sure. Help yourselves."

Embarrassed and ashamed, Alex nearly galloped to the kitchen. Cheri had finished cleaning up and left a note: *Thanks for the opportunity. I hope the anniversary celebration is a huge hit. ~Cheri*

Alex wished she could disappear. *I'll never hear the end of this.*

Chapter 75

After almost zero sleep, Alex drove to Show-Me Bank filled with dread. She had watched Hannah's amazing interview on the ten o'clock news. Hannah was perfect. Freaking perfect. *And I froze.*

Even though there was a cloudless, cornflower blue sky and bright sunshine, Alex's mood felt like the darkest, soggiest, rainy day. Punching in the back door code, Hannah rushed up the sidewalk before Alex had a chance to get inside.

"Did you see my interview on the news? I did pretty well, don't you think?"

"I missed it," Alex lied. She knew it was childish but couldn't stand Hannah's gloating after her own epic failure.

The intern's shoulders slumped. "That's too bad." Then she brightened. "I bet it's on the Ozarks5 website. I'll find it for you." As they strolled through the lobby, Alex darted into her office as she heard high-fives and applause for Hannah. She couldn't face the employees, let alone her boss.

Alex turned on her computer, leaned forward, and pretended to be involved in an intricate budgetary document.

Shouting bubbly thank-yous and blowing kisses to the employees, Hannah eventually entered Alex's office and threw her purse onto a chair. She retrieved her iPad, propped up her feet, and began scrolling. In a singsong voice, she said, "I'll find the video from last night's news. You've *got* to see it. I was really good if I say so myself."

Alex rolled her chair back. "I need coffee first." *Actually,*

I need a barf bag. I'll never be able to face anyone at Ozarks5 again.

Before she made it out of her office, a beaming Jim Hooban blocked her door. When he spotted his daughter, he clapped. Loudly. "Bravo, Hannah. You made me and everyone at Show-Me Bank proud." He glanced at Alex, "Nice of you to let Hannah handle the on-air interview. This'll be great for her portfolio."

Alex studied her glossy red heels, wondering if she should admit she froze on camera and get it over with.

Before she could speak, Hannah said, "Thanks, Daddy. Alex, er, well, she—"

Alex held her intern's gaze, wondering if she'd out her.

Cocking her head, Hannah said, "Alex insisted I do the interview since I did all of the work." She paused. "Except for the weird food at the beginning. She handled that."

Knowing she had to tread lightly, Alex simply said, "I understand Hannah did a great job with the interview. I'll pull it up on the Ozarks5 website soon."

Jim turned toward his daughter. "You were marvelous, honey. Couldn't have been better." He grinned. "In fact, you could be a television anchor but don't get any ideas. We don't want to lose you, do we, Alex?"

Alex gave a half nod and half shake, hoping her boss didn't pick up on her disdain for his precious daughter.

Jim sat in the chair beside Hannah, obviously to gush further. "Mrs. Timmons and two other board members have already called to compliment us on the event. They mentioned you in particular, Hannah. I'm so proud of my little girl."

Alex felt nauseous. She couldn't wait until her boss left her office and knew she'd have to hide out all day or hear how amazing Hannah was from every single Show-Me Bank employee.

Checking his watch, Jim said, "I have a customer. Talk to you two later." He turned to Alex. "Too bad the plaques didn't show up in time. I guess we can hand them out at the next board meeting."

"Oh, Alex handled that too. I forgot." Hannah dared Alex with her eyes. "Better luck next time, boss."

Fuming, Alex couldn't wait to get some black coffee and wished she had some Bailey's to pour inside. *This is going to be another hellish day.* The minute she was upstairs she texted her friends and asked them to meet her after work at Coconuts.

To her surprise, Tony was in her office when she came downstairs. Naturally, Hannah flirted with him—or maybe it was the other way around. "Well, well. Look who is at the bank a day late."

"Hello to you too," Tony said.

Hannah leaned over giving him full view. "I'll leave you alone."

After she left, Tony turned to Alex. "She seems nice. How was the bank party?"

Alex glared at him. "It was a total fucking disaster. I don't want to talk about it."

"I know just the thing to cheer you up."

Alex closed the door and crossed her arms. "Don't you dare mention the Tony and Alex show. I'm not in the mood for that one."

Tony reached for her arm. "We haven't seen it in quite a while. I miss that show. Are you sure?"

Pulling away, Alex said, "Don't test me. Last night went horribly wrong. It couldn't have been worse. I repeat. I'm not in the mood."

Tony shrugged. "Have it your way. How about a nice dinner then? Let me make it up to you."

Alex tilted her head. "That's a start. A tiny start but I have plans tonight."

"Oh, really?" His voice changed. "Is asshole limo driver back in town?"

I wish. Alex paused long enough to make Tony sweat. "No, Gage is apparently still in New York."

"Too bad. I really miss that guy." Tony's sarcasm made Alex roll her eyes.

Me too.

Alex brushed lint off her sleeve. "I wish you had been there last night. Is Nikki still in the hospital?"

"They're discharging her today. It was a UTI."

Alex rolled her eyes. "Big fucking deal. I've had a UTI before. Antibiotics will take care of it. Sheesh. What a drama queen your ex is."

Tony cocked his head. "She said it was painful."

Huffing, Alex said, "Yeah, they burn like hell, but shit. I don't think you had to miss my bank event for that." She shook her head. "Whatever. I'm always last on your list."

"Come on, Alex. You're acting childish. So . . . you're having dinner with?"

She sat behind her desk. "Who else? My girlfriends."

His phone vibrated. "I've got to take this." Tony listened and said, "I'm on my way."

"Gotta run, babe. Dispatch said there's a man on a roof downtown. Apparently, he's threatening to jump." He tapped her desk. "Let's go to dinner soon. I miss you."

"Yeah, whatever. Maybe I should join that guy on the roof."

Tony raised his eyebrows. "The party couldn't have been that bad."

"It was worse. Go. I'm in a bad mood."

"I can see that." Turning on his heel, Tony did a double-take when he spotted Hannah from the side, which only darkened Alex's mood.

Dodging her intern who stood in the lobby regaling the

tellers about her television appearance, Alex gave her a wide swath and went upstairs for more coffee.

All freaking morning, employees popped their heads inside Alex's office to congratulate Hannah on how incredible she was on camera. It was torture. Alex buried her nose in her computer and wished she had ear plugs as Hannah reveled in the spotlight. Unable to take her triumphing one more second, Alex shut off her computer and left the bank. She decided to treat herself to a shopping spree at T.J. Maxx before going to Coconuts.

Chapter 76

After a quick shopping spree where she spent too much on clothes, shoes, and jewelry she didn't need—but didn't care—Alex drove to Coconuts on autopilot.

Arriving first for once, she waved Gus over and ordered their usual drinks—a chardonnay, a merlot, and a margarita. "Put a rush on those drinks, Gus. And don't ask."

"O-kay."

Hope and Suzy arrived together, all smiles, and scooted bar stools up to their familiar table.

Once she sat down, Suzy turned toward Alex. "Wasn't last night your big bank event? How was it?"

Gus delivered their drinks. "Menus, ladies?"

"Just booze for now," Alex said. "Thanks, Gus."

Once the server left, Alex said, "Yes, it was last night. And . . . don't ask." She took a big gulp of chardonnay.

"Uh-oh." Hope studied her friend as she dropped a lime into her margarita. "Anything you want to tell us?"

Alex shook her head. "No. I don't want to talk about it. *Ever.* It was a disaster. A royal freaking disaster. And . . . if that weren't bad enough, Hannah was a star. My intern stole the show when I froze."

Hope's mouth fell open. "Is that why she was on television last night instead of you?"

Suzy's eyes widened. "I wondered that too."

Alex stared at the table, unable to face her best friends. "I said I don't want to talk about it and I meant it."

Patting Alex on the arm, Suzy said, "Enough said, hon."

Hope scrunched her nose. "We get the picture. Ouch."

"Exactly." Alex turned away before her friends could detect tears in her eyes. She was the strong one. She didn't cry. "Let's talk about something else. Anything else."

Suzy leaned forward. "Remember, the Bridal Bonanza is this weekend. I've packed every bridal photo, gizmo, and giveaway known to tulle."

Hope stirred her margarita. "And your booth will be beautiful for it."

Alex brightened. "Thank goodness for a change of pace from banking and far away from Hannah. I'm excited about the cake competition. I can't imagine baking a cake, let alone decorating one in a short amount of time."

"Agreed. Didn't Cheri cater your event?" Hope asked.

Alex shot Hope a look.

"Right. We aren't discussing it. Tell us more about your booth, Suzy."

"I've invited former and prospective brides and—" Suzy grabbed the table's edge and swayed.

"What's wrong?" Alex asked.

"I wish I knew. I've been a little queasy lately."

Hope frowned. "You're pale. Maybe you should go to the doctor."

Alex waved Gus over. "Will you bring our girl some Alka-Seltzer?"

The server grinned. "Hung over?"

Suzy managed a smile. "If so, it's the longest hangover in history. I'd prefer Seven-Up if you have it."

"Coming right up." Gus disappeared behind a group of raucous businesspeople wearing ugly conference lanyards.

After Gus placed the bubbly, icy soda in front of her, she took a big sip. "Thanks. This hits the spot."

Hope licked salt off the rim of her margarita and motioned toward the noisy group. "Teachers are never that loud at conferences." She muffled giggles. "Okay, maybe on occasion."

Alex shrugged. "Any time people are away from home, they overdo the alcohol." Groaning, she said, "I've been so consumed with my not-to-be-discussed event that I forgot to ask Cheri about the cake competition when she catered last night. I feel like a jerk."

Suzy reached for her phone. "Cheri texted a few photos of her trial cakes. They're pretty. Want to see?"

Both Alex and Hope shook their heads.

"I'd rather be surprised," Hope said.

"Same here. I'm in dire need of fun." Alex polished off her chardonnay and motioned to Gus for another. "I'll stop the *poor-me* crap soon, ladies."

"Don't worry about it." Suzy put her phone away. "From what I understand, Cheri has worked really hard on her timing and decorating skills. She'd love to claim the championship for Fifth Avenue Catering."

Hope rubbed her hands together. "Won't it be cool if she wins?"

"I wonder who the other chefs will be. Have they posted their names on the Bridal Bonanza website?" Alex asked as Gus refilled her glass. "I haven't had time to look."

Suzy finished her 7-Up and requested another. "This soda is settling my stomach. I almost feel normal now."

Alex studied Suzy. "You've been queasy more than once lately. I'm beginning to think you're pregnant."

Suzy laughed for far too long. "No way. Nope. Nada."

Hope grinned. "That would be something."

Shaking her head vehemently, Suzy repeated, "I still think it's food poisoning from the sushi I had last week."

Alex cocked her head. "Food poisoning doesn't last a week."

"Do not, I repeat, do not go down that ridiculous path. I'm a grandma now. My son is grown." Gathering her purse, Suzy said, "I've got to go, ladies. I really need to follow up with potential brides to make sure they attend the bridal show. I want to get a lot of traction at my booth. I haven't planned a wedding since Jon and Fernando's. See you soon."

Hope yawned. "I'm exhausted from school. I've got to run too."

Alex had hoped for a longer girls' evening after almost singlehandedly destroying the bank party but let it go. Forcing a smile, she said, "See you at Bridal Bonanza. Let's ride together, Hope."

Chapter 77

On Saturday, Alex and Hope parked in an overflow lot, hustled inside, and picked up an exhibitor map. The tiny print on the Bridal Bonanza chart indicated the booth number for wedding planners, bridal shops, jewelry makers, makeup artists, DJ's, photography vendors, and caterers.

As they perused the huge diagram dotted with pink and red hearts, Alex said, "Wow. This is a huge trade show. I didn't expect it to be this massive."

Hope scanned the burgeoning crowd. "It looks as though everyone wants to get married."

"Sheesh." Alex rolled her eyes. "Not me. Let's find Suzy's booth." Throngs of women filled the vast halls—brides-to-be, mothers of brides, and a sprinkling of grooms-to-be whose glazed-over eyes indicated they'd likely rather be anywhere else.

Alex spotted the Weddings by Suzanne booth and led Hope toward a pink tulle-covered table. Several women were lined up and either poring through Suzy's wedding photo albums or filling out forms for her door prize, a romantic honeymoon to Jamaica.

"Nice touch on that prize." Alex grinned. "I think my marketing genes are rubbing off on Suzy."

Hope nodded. "From those long lines, it's obviously a great draw. I remember Suzy said she worked out a deal with a travel agent for the Jamaican trip in exchange for providing wedding planning assistance."

"Yeah, wasn't the travel agent newly engaged?" Alex asked.

"Yep. Perfect timing all around."

Suzy's booth was draped in pink and black, the colors of her logo. Her brochures stood upright in a clear container on a black tablecloth. A pink backdrop showcased enlarged photos of a variety of weddings she had planned. Weddings by Suzanne pens were fanned out by the dozens near her business cards.

Alex elbowed Hope. "Jon and Fernando are here. Looks like they tore themselves away from baby Violet to help Suzy." She chuckled. "Look at the women unknowingly hitting on them. They don't know they're out of luck."

Hope winked in the guys' direction. "Way out of luck."

When they neared the front of Suzy's booth, Alex whistled at the wedding planner. "You look fabulous."

Winking and mouthing thanks, Suzy put her hands on both hips in a perfect model pose. She wore a silky pink blouse, black heels, and black slacks, her company colors, and held up a finger indicating they should wait while she focused on another client.

Hope turned toward Alex. "I'm excited about the cake competition."

"Me too. I'm a little nervous for Cheri." Alex checked her watch. "It won't be long now."

As brides bustled around her booth, Suzy pulled her long, red hair into a high ponytail, fanned herself with one of her brochures, and broke away to approach her friends.

"Hot?" Hope asked.

"Yes, I scurried around all morning carrying boxes and setting up." Suzy hugged her friends. "Ken had a business conflict. Thankfully Jon and Fernando arrived earlier or I'd still be hanging photos."

"Did I hear my name?" Jon hugged Alex and Hope. "Good to see you both."

Fernando gallantly kissed the tops of their hands.

"Nice touch." Alex winked at Fernando. "Want to train some straight guys for me?"

Hope kicked her foot.

"Ow. What's wrong with that?"

Fernando chuckled. "Not a thing. We're very happy."

Jon put his arm around his husband. "Got that right. Happy but sleepy." He yawned. "Who knew babies never slept at night? I'm beginning to think Violet is either a vampire or an owl."

Everyone laughed as they viewed the newest photos of baby Violet while Suzy returned to her booth to chat with a potential bride and groom.

Alex spotted the stage and pointed. "Shall we head over and find Cheri? Maybe we can give her a pep talk before the competition."

Suzy obviously overheard their conversation and glanced at her watch. "You're right. It's almost time." She waved Jon and Fernando over. "Guys, will you watch the booth for thirty minutes, give or take, so I can cheer Cheri on?"

"Sure, Mom. We'll line up fifty weddings for you. You can handle that many in a year, right?"

"Ha. Very funny. How about keeping it to two or three? I need grandma time too, you know. See you in a few."

The three friends made their way through throngs of women toward the stage. Observing the packed crowd, Alex said, "I wonder where Cheri is."

Hope glanced from side to side. "She's probably backstage."

The women stepped toward the raised platform. On display were three bare cakes atop three tables draped in black. At least one hundred white chairs were arranged theatre style in front of the stage.

Alex rushed to the front row and grabbed three chairs. She stood in front of two folding chairs, put her purse in a third, and motioned to her friends to hurry since the seats were filling in quickly.

Grabbing the back of a chair, Suzy swayed.

"Again?" Alex asked.

Hope reached for Suzy's arm to steady her. "You've got to go to the doctor. I'm worried about you. Maybe you should get an MRI." She shot Alex a worried glance.

Suzy took a seat. "If it lasts much longer, I will. Maybe I have the flu. It could be from all of the Bridal Bonanza prep, helping Jon and Fernando move, the baby, you know, lots going on. I'm probably dehydrated."

"Want me to get you some water?" Hope asked.

"No, we'll miss the show. I'll be fine."

"You probably caught something dreadful after shaking everyone's hand at your booth." Alex dug in the center section of her red purse and retrieved a tiny green bottle. "Want some antibacterial gel?"

Suzy laughed. "I couldn't catch anything within hours. I'm sure it's nothing. I've been crazy busy for weeks, that's all. I'm probably not eating enough."

Alex and Hope exchanged glances as they took seats on either side of Suzy in front of the stage. "Stop worrying. Let's watch."

The three friends sat down as an emcee asked everyone to take a seat and turn their attention to the stage.

Alex rubbed her hands together. "This is going to be fun."

Hope scanned the crowd. "I wish we could have seen Cheri beforehand, so she knows we're here."

"Me too." Suzy shrugged. "I was too busy with my booth."

The greasy-haired announcer with a megaphone voice lifted his arms in a V-shape as if he were about to dance to the "YMCA" song. "Hello, everyone! Are you ready for our exciting wedding cake competition?"

The crowd yelled an enthusiastic, "Yes."

Voice booming, the tall, tux-wearing emcee continued. "We have three amazing chefs who will enthrall you today. I'm sure our prospective brides will be in awe and want to hire all of them. Never fear. I'll bring our celebrity chefs out momentarily. First, a few instructions." The host waited until the crowd grew silent. "Remember, this is a timed competition. The bakers will need to concentrate."

The announcer dramatically pulled out a stopwatch and dangled it back and forth in the air. "When our contestants begin, I'll time them as they decorate their respective cakes." He waved his hand with a flourish. "Each chef baked the naked cakes you see here." Chuckling at his lame joke, he pointed a finger toward the audience.

"*You'll* be the judge of the most beautifully decorated cake in the least amount of time." The host gestured toward three glass bowls underneath each cake pedestal and made another sweeping motion with his hand. "When the contest is over, vote for the most beautiful wedding cake by dropping a pink square of paper into the appropriate bowl." He wagged his finger. "And no cheating."

The audience roared.

The cheesy man surveyed the room, clearly enjoying his moment. He tweaked his handlebar moustache for added effect.

Alex groaned. "Where did they find this joker?"

Hope giggled. "I like him. He's weird but fun."

Alex wrinkled her nose. "You must be kidding."

Spreading his arms wide, the host said, "Without further ado, let's bring out our celebrity chefs."

Chapter 78

"Applause, please, as we welcome Beth Wade from Beth's Bakery."

A short, plump brunette appeared on stage, waved shyly, and stood behind her bare cakes. Taking a little bow, she immediately stared at her white sneakers, avoiding all eye contact.

Reading from an index card, the host continued. "Next, we have Cheri Van Buren from Fifth Avenue Catering in New York City—and it says Branson too. That's quite a combination. Welcome."

Suzy, Hope, and Alex stood, whistled, and cheered as Cheri made her way to the far right of the stage. Clacking across the stage in black stilettos and wearing a white and gold Fifth Avenue Catering apron over silky black palazzo pants and a red blouse, a flushed, wide-eyed Cheri waved to her friends.

The emcee stepped toward the center of the stage. "Our third contestant is *very* special." He paused as several audience members edged forward in their seats. "In fact, this particular chef flew over all the way from Europe."

Several gasped as the host dragged out the suspense. Pausing, he said, "I wish we had a drumroll." Everyone grew quiet and stared at both sides of the curtain awaiting the third chef.

"Seriously?" Alex stared at the ceiling. "Come on."

"Shhh." Suzy clasped her hands in her waist and leaned forward.

Hope swiveled her head toward both sides of the stage. "Who could it be?"

Finally the announcer said, "I can't keep you waiting any longer. Please welcome Julio."

A very handsome chef entered from the left side of the curtains.

Alex noticed Cheri's mouth flew open as the European chef sauntered across the stage taking his place between the two females. He nodded to the baker from Beth's Bakery and gave a slow wink to Cheri whose mouth stayed agape.

Alex knitted her brows as she studied the interaction. "Julio. Julio. I've heard that name before."

"So have I." Suzy scratched her head. "Wait a minute. Is that Cheri's family chef? The one they had when she was a child? The one she had a crush on?"

Alex and Hope sucked in their breath at the same time. "I bet that's him. Oh, my God." Alex scooted forward in her chair. "This is going to be good."

"Look at poor Cheri," Hope said. "She's a nervous wreck. Her cheeks are bright pink and she keeps wiping her hands on her apron."

Suzy glanced from Julio to Cheri. "Being caught off guard like this may destroy her chances."

The announcer shushed the crowd. "Folks, we're almost ready to begin. Please remain quiet while our chefs work." He blew a whistle. "It's go time, bakers. Good luck."

Heads down, each chef spun their cakes as they worked, reaching for multi-colored frosting, piping coming-into-focus creations, and concentrating on decorating their individual masterpieces. As the three worked, the audience sat transfixed in hushed silence.

Cheri's cake consisted of four large, round tiers. She quickly decorated it with edible daisies, roses, pears, and leaves. Using sage green icing for the leaves, she piped peach, yellow, and pink flowers and added hanging dark chocolate tube branches. Working quickly, she encrusted the branches with tiny white flowers resembling dogwood blossoms. Taking a moment to check all sides, she topped her cake with two kissing lovebirds.

While she frosted her cake, Alex noticed Cheri constantly stole glances toward Julio.

"Cheri's cake is perfection," Suzy said. "It looks like spring. My brides will love it."

"It reminds me of romance." Alex flipped her hair over her shoulder. "Or how romance should be."

"It's stunning." Hope turned and gawked at handsome Julio whose cake towered with five square tiers.

The audience ogled the European newcomer as he added various shades of gray. Using a tiny spreader, Julio created lines resembling stones of an historic castle, masterfully swirling green vines along the base and up the sides. He hastily added pale yellow and blue flowers trailing upward like clematis. Finally, he added windows, a brown, oval-shaped wooden door, and at the last minute, piped a tiny knight to guard the entrance.

Alex studied the European chef. "His cake is gorgeous and so is he." Unable to take her eyes off him, she said, "I can see why Cheri had a crush on him as a teen."

All three swiveled to watch the pastry chef from Beth's Bakery. Her cake consisted of three large tiers. She rapidly adorned the first tier with white and gold starbursts and added edible pearls on the other two layers. The baker piped three huge white lilies stacked on top with petals draping over the cake's edges. For the final touch, she added a majestic, deep purple lily to the middle layer. It was offset on the side like a brooch.

Suzy clasped her hands together. "Bravo. That's breathtaking and elegant too. I'll have to use all three of these in my weddings." She reached into her purse for her camera, zoomed in, and took several photos. "I'll share these on my Weddings by Suzanne Facebook page."

"Don't forget Instagram," Alex said.

Hope sat riveted. At the fifteen-minute mark, the emcee blew a whistle. "Time's up, chefs."

The three chefs froze. Cheri poised her knife spreader in mid-air.

Alex noticed peach and yellow frosting clung to Cheri's fingertips. The chef from Beth's Bakery held an edible flower while a smiling Julio had his arms crossed, without so much as a hair out of place, appearing perfectly relaxed, if not ornery.

Twirling the whistle as if he were a lifeguard, the announcer sashayed across the stage. Standing before each cake, saying, "Beautiful. Beautiful. Beautiful. It appears everyone practiced."

He turned toward each chef. "Did you ever think you could decorate an entire wedding cake in fifteen minutes?" Clucking his tongue, he didn't wait for an answer to his hypothetical question and faced the crowd. "It's time to vote."

A bubbly, ponytailed assistant ran down the riser stairs toward the audience and handed out scraps of pink paper.

Everyone was told to place their votes in the strategically placed glass bowls. Alex, Suzy, and Hope cast the first three votes in Cheri's dish.

A flustered-looking Cheri mouthed, "Thank you."

The women sat down to watch other guests vote. Several women stepped toward Julio's bowl, giggled, and even waved to him as they placed pink slips in his container.

"Figures." Alex scrunched her nose. "Just because he's a man—a very handsome man with an accent—he gets their vote."

"His castle cake is unique." Suzy gave Alex a knowing

glance. "Plus, you know you'd do the same thing if you weren't friends with Cheri."

Crossing her arms and hiding a smile, Alex said, "Yeah, so?"

Several women vacillated between voting for Beth's Bakery, Fifth Avenue Catering, and Julio. A few hovered between Julio and Cheri's bowls before casting a vote. Eventually, all three bowls were nearly half filled with pink scraps of paper.

Hope whispered, "What if it's a tie?"

A few more tentative patrons lingered in front of the stage, but the emcee broke the silence. "Chop. Chop. We don't have all day. Brides are backstage and ready to model wedding gowns soon."

A few stragglers cast their votes as the announcer eyed the room. Twirling his moustache again, he asked, "Anyone else?"

Alex leaned over and lowered her voice. "That guy is full of himself. I'll be glad when this is over. I think I'll vomit if I have to take much more of him."

Both Suzy and Hope shushed her.

When no one else came forward, the host dramatically shook each bowl. "Hmm. This is going to be close." After dumping the votes on top of three small tables, the assistant helped him count and tally the ballots.

Chapter 79

Everyone shifted in their seats as the chef from Beth's Bakery chewed on a nail, Julio winked at the crowd, and Cheri stared at her cake, likely avoiding eye contact with her former chef.

Strutting across the stage, the emcee said, "And the winner is . . . *recount*."

Everyone groaned as the host and his assistant quickly shuffled the pink cards like they were Vegas dealers. After they recounted the votes from all three bowls, the ponytailed assistant whispered in his ear.

Alex studied Cheri who was nonchalantly wiping sweat from her upper lip. "I wish he'd hurry up. Cheri looks like she's about to pass out from the stress. I'm sure she doesn't want her childhood crush to see her with a sweat moustache."

Suzy and Hope nodded as the announcer clapped his hands.

"We have a winner but first I want to thank our extraordinary culinary contestants—Beth, Julio, and Cheri. You're all supremely talented and your cakes are nothing short of stupendous." He turned toward the bakers. "I hope you brought business cards because I'm sure every bride will want to hire you."

The crowd had obviously had enough and began chanting "Winner, winner," while clapping in unison and stomping their feet.

"Ah, I see you're getting restless." The host made a fake drumroll sound. "The winner is . . . and by an ounce of frosting, I might add . . . Cheri Van Buren."

Alex, Suzy, and Hope jumped out of their chairs and cheered like high school kids winning a tournament.

Julio didn't appear to be the least bit fazed. Instead, he rushed to Cheri's side and embraced her.

Alex clapped a hand over her mouth. "Cheri's as pink as your blouse, Suzy."

The unknowing audience cheered.

"Looks like Julio doesn't mind losing." The emcee hooted as he once again thanked everyone and announced a short break. "Return in ten minutes to see our wedding gown models. You'll want to put these dresses on your wish list, brides. Tally ho."

"That emcee is a goofball." Alex frowned as the tall, thin man disappeared behind the curtain. Climbing the riser steps, she rushed toward Cheri. Suzy and Hope practically galloped alongside her as they gave their winning friend a group hug.

Suzy squeezed Cheri's hand. "Congratulations. Your cake's gorgeous. I'm sure several of my brides will request your spring love bird cake." She held her cell in the air and pointed toward the screen. "I hope you don't mind but I posted photos online. Your cake is already getting likes and shares on my Facebook page."

"Thank you, Suzy. That's wonderful." Cheri's eyes glistened. "It means the world that you ladies are here."

"We wouldn't have missed it." Hope pointed toward Cheri's cake. "It's stunning. I don't know how you decorated it so fast."

Alex cleared her throat. "Yes, yes, your cake is a work of art, but I want to know about Ju—"

"Well done, Cheri. Bravo." Julio picked the New Yorker up and kissed both of her cheeks. After setting her back on the ground, he placed his hands on her shoulders, giving the socialite a onceover. "Look who's all grown up," he said in a thick Italian accent.

Cheri stammered. "Julio, how . . . how did you know about this competition? About me? About Crystal City?"

He cocked his head. "Your mom, of course. I saw her sitting at a sidewalk café in Paris. We had espressos together while she told me about your catering business." Grinning, he added, "Your mom mentioned the cake competition, so I went to the Google." He waved his hand with a flourish. "The rest, as they say, is history. Besides, I thought it would be great fun to surprise you."

"Or give me a heart attack." Cheri placed her hand over her chest. Once again, she attempted to nonchalantly wipe the sweat conspicuously reforming on her upper lip.

Hope studied both chefs who never took their eyes off one another. Turning to Alex and Suzy, she said, "Maybe we should leave."

"Not a chance." Alex planted herself on stage as she blatantly gawked from Cheri to Julio and back again.

The staggeringly handsome chef draped his arm across Cheri's shoulders. "You surely can't expect me to come all this way and not have dinner with me. How about it, my Cheri?"

Cheri's eyebrows shot up, clearly unable to speak.

Mouths agape, Alex, Suzy, and Hope stared agog at the couple.

Julio nudged her. "I'm thrilled you're a chef now. I can't wait to hear all about your life, my Cheri."

"I love how you pronounce her name. Just like the song, 'My Cheri Amour'." Alex extended her hand. "I'm Alex." She motioned toward her friends. "This is Suzy and Hope. We're friends of Cheri's except we pronounce her name *Sherry*. I like the way you say it better."

"Where are my manners?" Cheri reached for the threesome. "These are my new, wonderful friends."

"They're enchanting—and beautiful." Julio kissed the

top of each woman's hand. "I love American women. Any friend of Cheri's is a friend of mine."

"I may never wash my hand." Hope half-curtsied as if she were meeting royalty. Continuing to ogle Julio, she said, "Nothing like this happens in my life. Not even close."

Chapter 80

Cheri's mind reeled as she studied her childhood chef. Julio looked more handsome than ever. Still tall and lanky with flawless olive skin, jet-black hair that had a slight curl, piercing, dark eyes, and a disarming smile. Almost fifteen years her senior, he now had a slight tinge of gray around his temples but was still as sexy as hell. He smelled just like she remembered as a teen—clean and spicy, with a hint of garlic.

Obviously sensing her hesitation, Julio asked, "Cheri, when was the last time we saw each other?"

She shrugged. "Well over a decade ago."

"Exactly." His dark eyes pierced hers. "What are you waiting for? Say you'll have dinner with me."

Cheri's heart hammered. She stared downward as if for an answer. It took all of her strength to ignore the pink blob of icing on her right shoe. After a deep breath, she said, "I don't have anything to change into. I've got icing all over me."

Julio waved his hand dismissively. "You're gorgeous the way you are. No more arguments."

Her mind swirled. *Why not? It's just dinner.* She waited about ten seconds before answering. "I'll go."

Alex threw her head back and laughed. "I guess we know what your prize is, Julio."

The European reached for Cheri and dipped her head nearly to the floor, as if they were doing a ballroom dance. "My little Van Buren is all grown up." He eyed her from her head to her toes. "Very nicely, I might add. Ready? Tell your friends good-bye."

Cheri hugged her girlfriends. Leaning in, she whispered, "Can you believe this? Thanks again for your support today."

Still holding her hand, Julio led Cheri toward the back door. Struggling to keep pace with the tall chef, she glanced over her shoulder and blew a kiss. "Hold down the fort at Coconuts."

As they approached the back of the massive room still crawling with energetic brides, Cheri's heart pounded. She wasn't sure why but her former childhood chef made her nervous. Wrestling with her apron, she eventually got it untied, and shoved it inside her black Prada purse.

Julio's eyes danced as he motioned toward a back stairwell. "We need to go upstairs."

"Why? I'm parked out front."

With a mischievous grin, he said, "You'll see."

After they walked what seemed like fifty steps, Julio opened an outer door to the roof.

Cheri's eyes widened when she heard the chop-chop of helicopter blades. Shouting over the noise, she asked, "What's this?"

"It's called a helicopter." Julio chuckled as he cupped his mouth with his hand and yelled, "After you."

The wind from the chopper blew Cheri's hair into her eyes. She held her blouse with her free hand as she clumsily climbed inside.

The pilot said, "Welcome aboard," and handed them headsets.

Cheri buckled her seatbelt. "I thought you said we were going to dinner. Where are we going?"

Julio's eyes twinkled. "Dinner, like I said."

"And we need a helicopter?"

He clicked his seatbelt and turned to Cheri. "We're having dinner in Paris."

"Paris?" Her stomach lurched. "I don't have a change of clothes. I can't just go to France. I have a business to run."

Clucking his tongue, Julio said, "You Americans need to learn how to relax. We can buy whatever you want, and if we're lucky, we'll see your parents. I'm sure your mom will loan you some clothes. You look about the same size."

Cheri rubbed her tense shoulders. "I need toiletries, my computer so I can stay in touch with my employees, and—"

"My Cheri. Settle down. We'll only be gone a few days. We can buy whatever you need." Julio's face fell. "If you don't want to go, no pressure. We'll stay here and have dinner. It's up to you." He paused. "But I thought you'd like the chance to see your parents again."

"Of course I want to see my parents. It's been far too long." Cheri leaned against the seat, trying to force herself to relax, but it was pointless. "I don't even have my phone charger with me."

"Tsk. Tsk. Technology will be the end of all of us." Julio glanced out the window. "Where do you want to eat?"

"Three days," Cheri said.

"What?"

"I can only afford to be gone three or four days—counting today. I really do have a company to run." Cheri wasn't sure she liked having her former chef make all of the decisions. Paparazzi jumping out of bushes in New York had ruined her appreciation of surprises. Plus, she was a career woman, not the young teen Julio had danced with in the kitchen. *Maybe this isn't such a great idea.* She groaned inwardly. *But I would love to see my parents.*

"Whatever you want, My Cheri. The jetlag is catching up with me. I'm going to snooze for a bit." Julio closed his eyes but just as quickly reopened them. "How about dinner in Miami tonight at Danny Devito's restaurant? He has amazing Kobe beef. I've got a private plane lined up for midnight to take us to France."

"I like that idea. Maybe I can find a twenty-four-hour Walgreens and buy some toiletries and a charger."

"That phone thing again." Julio shook his head, clucked his tongue, and fell asleep.

Her mind raced. Cheri slept fitfully as lightning strikes slashed through the air. Rain streaked the tiny windows of the chopper. The sky had turned an inky black and the helicopter dipped. Saying silent prayers that they would make it to land, Cheri hoped she hadn't made a horrible decision. Glancing over at Julio who seemingly didn't have a care in the world according to his slight snores, Cheri vowed to kiss the ground if and when they landed.

What seemed like hours later, Cheri relaxed when she spotted a lit runway. Finally, the white-knuckle turbulent flight was almost over. As the chopper clumsily landed, the pilot said, "Sorry about that. Damn storm came out of nowhere."

Oblivious, Julio stretched and yawned. "Are we here?"

~ ~ ~

Devito's was packed, but after Julio asked to speak with the head chef, they were seated in an intimate corner where servers brought out seemingly every item on the menu.

Nervous, Cheri picked at her food and drank too much wine. Julio insisted on paying the five-hundred-dollar bill for the two of them. Cheri wasn't sure how much her former private chef had socked away, but he was apparently doing well.

"Thank you, Julio. That was delicious."

"Nothing's too good for My Cheri, but you barely ate." Julio addressed the hostess. "Will you call a cab for us? We need a ride to the airport."

The hostess muttered something about Uber but relented and called a taxi.

Excusing herself, Cheri went to the restroom, splashed water on her face and glanced at her phone. It showed a seventy-five-percent charge. Julio told her they didn't have time to find a charger and suggested maybe Europe would have one that was compatible. Staring at the screen, she winced. *I want to let my staff know where I am but I had better not waste my battery. They'll immediately send me a hundred texts.*

After the taxi driver pulled up to a private airport, Cheri and Julio climbed inside a nine-passenger Cessna Citation X. A uniformed pilot informed them champagne was chilling. A cheese and fruit tray had been placed on an empty passenger seat and fine china was on a silver tray in another seat.

Cheri climbed across from Julio and buckled her seatbelt. She accepted a glass of bubbly and willed herself to relax.

Luckily the storm had passed and the pilot assured them it would be a smooth flight. He got coffee for himself from a container behind the cockpit, invited them to help themselves, and drew the curtain closed.

After two glasses of champagne, both Cheri and Julio slept for hours.

Awakened by the landing, Cheri yawned as the pilot slid the curtain back and said, "Welcome to Paris."

Chapter 81

After meeting with a new student whose outlandish hair looked as though he had stuck his finger in an outdoor light socket during the rain, Hope gave him his class schedule and an inch-high stack of forms to fill out. After he left her office, she craved an apple and retreated to the teachers' lounge.

After walking up the shiny, poster-filled hallway, she sat at a rectangular table across from Willow who sipped coffee. As always, the art teacher greeted her warmly, barely glanced up, and continued reading the local newspaper.

As Hope bit into the juicy, red fruit, her eyes widened. Leaning forward, she squinted to read the feature article on the front page. After several seconds, she gasped. "Oh, my God." Reaching across the table, she said, "Can I see that?"

Willow lowered the paper, finally making eye contact. "See what?"

"The-The paper." Hope snatched it out of Willow's hands, studied the photo of the woman, and held her breath while she read the article. Her hands shook so much the paper rattled.

The woman in the photo was pictured in what looked like a hospital bed propped up by several pillows. Mounds of braided cotton cord and wooden beads surrounded her on the white sheet. Hope considered every detail of the room and noticed three macramé plant holders—one purple, another blue, and one green—hung from the bed posts. Her mouth opened but she couldn't speak. She had no words.

"What's wrong?" Willow asked. "The color has

completely drained from your face." The art teacher studied her friend. "Your hands are shaking."

Hope stabbed the photo. "I know this woman."

"What woman?" Willow didn't wait for an answer, got up, and read over Hope's shoulder. After a few seconds, she said, "This looks like a nice feature article about someone who makes macramé plant holders." Pointing toward the text, she read aloud. "It says she makes the plant holders for fellow nursing home residents. That's lovely, don't you think? Very sweet."

Hope's mouth went dry.

Willow studied her friend. "Hope, you're very pale. Would you like some water?"

"No." Still pointing toward the photo, she said, "This-This—" Hope's voice wobbled as tears streamed down her face. Putting her head on the table, she sobbed.

Willow wrapped her arms around her colleague. "You're scaring the crap out of me. Who the hell is this?"

After wiping her runny nose with the back of her hand, Hope said, "I think it's Montana."

"Montana?"

"Yes, she looks exactly like the woman who raised me. The woman I knew as *Mom*. The one I presumed had died in the train accident."

Willow sucked in her breath. "That's unbelievable—and wonderful, right?"

Hope sniffled and swiped at tears as she rescanned the article. "It says she's in a nursing home in Nashville." Plucking several tissues out of a box, Hope blew her nose, and continued tapping the photo. "Montana always made those silly macramé plant hangers. In fact, I have one hanging in my office. It's one of the few things I have of hers."

Inhaling and exhaling in an attempt to calm herself, a range of emotions including relief, sadness, shock, and anger overcame her. Narrowing her eyes, she said, "Surely Larry—Mac has mentioned her to you."

Willow's face was a complete blank. It was clear she had zero recognition. Voice flat, she said, "No, Mac never mentioned a Montana. Why would he?"

Hope's thoughts jumbled. *Exactly. Why would Larry mention his thought-dead wife to his girlfriend? He doesn't even remember me.*

Willow glanced from the article to Hope. "I'm at a loss for words. You know I'm here for you, friend. I can't imagine what you're going through. Whatever I can do to—" She stopped mid-sentence as the history teacher and basketball coach walked inside the lounge area. The men said hello and stood by the coffee pot discussing last night's game, oblivious to this extraordinarily awkward, momentous occasion.

After several strained minutes where Hope and Willow stared at one another, then at the newspaper, and finally at the squeaky, polished floor, the coaches left.

When the door opened to the hallway, the light reflected off Willow's left hand.

Hope sucked in her breath. A modest silver band with a tiny, barely identifiable diamond adorned Willow's ring finger. "What the hell is on your hand?"

Willow tucked her left hand between her legs. "We were going to tell you. We've been so excited with our planning that I guess we forgot to mention . . ."

"When were you going to tell me? My God. I can't take any more surprises. I thought you were my friend."

"I *am* your friend. But I'm in love with Mac."

"This is rich." Hope shook her head. "Not to mention uncanny timing." Snatching the newspaper, she stormed toward the door and yelled over her shoulder, "Mac's name is Larry, by the way. I'm sure of it."

Chapter 82

Cheri spread her arms, peered at the blue sky, and twirled in place like a young girl. "I can't believe I'm actually here. In Paris. I haven't been back in years." She scanned the piazza brimming with Europeans and tourists. "I forgot how gorgeous it is." Giggling, she said, "Europeans have much more interesting architecture—and shoes."

Julio glanced down at his brown, sleek Italian leather shoes. "That we do. What would you like to do first? Grab a bite? See the sights?"

"I can't wait another second to see my parents. They've been traveling abroad for a few years."

"I had a feeling you'd say that, My Cheri. I already texted your mom. She's waiting for us."

~ ~ ~

"Darling, it's so good to see you." Dressed in white leggings, an off-the-shoulder white cashmere sweater, and dripping with enormous diamonds, Victoria Van Buren kissed both of Cheri's cheeks and hugged her daughter as if she hadn't seen her in a decade. Placing her hands on Cheri's shoulders, she said, "Look at you. My beautiful daughter."

"Good to see you as well, Mom. Don't get too close. I've had the same clothes on for two days and sweated like a horse at the cake competition." She glanced at Julio. "Seeing this guy was quite a surprise to say the least." Shaking her head, she said, "You two sure shocked me."

Victoria reached for a half-empty martini. "No worries, darling. We can fix the clothes issue. My closet is your closet."

"Thank goodness. You look great, Mom, but a little thin." Cheri eyed her mother. "Are you eating enough?"

Laughing for far too long, Victoria held her drink in the air. "I get plenty of calories—and a lot more fun—from this."

Cheri's mind raced. With the time change she wasn't sure what time it was but knew it was very early in Paris, much too early to be drinking hard liquor. Deciding to change the subject, she said, "I need to charge my phone. I hope you have a universal charger."

"Let's worry about that later." Victoria turned to Julio and embraced him. "Thank you for bringing my daughter here. I've missed her beyond words."

Cheri noticed her mother almost teared up. Normally, Victoria Van Buren didn't show emotions. Studying her still-glamorous mother for the first time in nearly two years, she wondered if she enjoyed living in another country and away from her New York friends. If Julio weren't there, she would simply ask her mom outright if she were happy but felt uncomfortable broaching the subject in front of him.

"How long will you be here?" Victoria brightened. "We can go shopping in Milan, take a gondola ride in Venice, go to Florence, and—"

"Sorry, Mom, just three days and that's pushing it."

"What?" Victoria pouted. "You just got here."

"We'll make the most of our time. I own a business, remember? I have employees, clients, and several upcoming events in New York and Crystal City. Had I known about this, maybe I could have stayed a week or two but it's not possible without prior planning."

Victoria's frozen face almost fell.

Cheri hugged her mother. "I'm sorry I can't stay long but you can always come and see me. We'd have fun in Branson and Crystal City."

Taking another sip of martini, Victoria said, "Maybe I'll

come to New York when you're there, but I don't have any interest in some rural town in Missouri."

"It's lovely and peaceful but whatever." Glancing around the plush, all-white living room, Cheri said, "Where's Daddy?"

Victoria rolled her eyes. "Either at a meeting, the gym, or his office. You know your workaholic father. Hopefully, he'll come by tonight. He wasn't here last—"

Cheri's voice rose a notch. "Didn't he know I was coming?" She watched as something crossed over her mother's eyes and felt a lump swell in her throat.

"I'm sure he'll make time for you if he possibly can." Forcing a likely fake facade, Victoria asked, "Who wants some hot tea?" Before they answered, she led the way through her gleaming home filled with modern art and original Picassos.

Julio salivated over the art pieces as Cheri worried about her mother's too-thin backside. "Let me help, Mom."

After they drank several cups of hot tea, Cheri and Victoria disappeared into her bedroom. Before the door was closed, she asked, "What's going on, Mom?"

Stiffening, her mother said, "Nothing's going on. What are you talking about?" She avoided eye contact with her daughter and led her to a massive mirrored closet. "What would you like to wear? I have a new Coco Chanel dress and a gorgeous red Stella McCartney jumpsuit that would look smashing on you. Oh, and some new gold Louboutin heels. Want to try them on?"

"I'd rather chat or shower." Cheri sat on a plush stool in front of a makeup mirror. Bottles of expensive perfume lined a shelf in the closet. Cheri also noticed a wine bottle chilling but decided to let it go.

"Why don't you shower first?" Victoria plucked a thick white robe out of her closet, gold house slippers with her monogram, VVB, and handed Cheri two luxurious, white towels. "Scoot, darling. We'll chat later." Chuckling, she said, "And use some of my perfume while you're at it."

After showering and washing her hair, Cheri padded into the posh magazine-like living room where Victoria and Julio visited.

Obviously hearing her footsteps, Julio said, "Your mother is catching me up on the latest gossip in New York City."

"You're in Europe, Mom. How do you know what's going on in Manhattan?"

Raising a perfectly arched, dark eyebrow, Victoria said, "Nothing gets by me, darling. Nothing." She dusted fake crumbs off her hands. "Plus, I still have many friends in the city. They all love to talk."

"Have you heard from Daddy?"

Victoria stared at the carpet. "I'm sorry, honey. Daddy texted. He has business in Rome. Some big board meeting. He said he simply can't break away."

Cheri's forehead creased. "Not even to see his daughter?" Her emotions switched from sadness to anger. "How much more money does he need to make?"

"*Darling.* He provides a wonderful life for us. We can't be too hard on him. He's a workaholic, that's all."

Clapping his hands together, Julio stood. "I know just the place that will improve everyone's mood."

Both Victoria and Cheri said, "Where?"

Julio held both hands in the air. "The Moulan Rouge, of course. We can eat, drink, and be merry. We'll have food, drinks, and entertainment at the same time."

"By topless women," Cheri said.

"Exactly." Julio grinned.

Chapter 83

After hours of watching topless showgirls wearing towering Vegas-like headdresses while dancing across the stage, Cheri drank too-strong wine in small bottles, yawned, and couldn't remember the drive back to her parents' home. Crawling underneath a silver cashmere comforter in the guest room, her mind raced. All she wanted was to have a serious conversation with her mother but Julio never seemed to take a hint. Sure, he was fabulous when she was a young girl and was still as handsome and charming as ever, but the sparks and fantasies she once had weren't there. Now she wished he weren't underfoot.

After sleeping fitfully, she awakened to a heavenly aroma and wondered if her mother had learned to cook. She always chuckled at the fact that she became a chef and her mother barely knew how to toast an English muffin. Easing into a pair of skinny white designer jeans—her mother's favorite color—and a long denim shirt, she brushed her teeth and headed toward the kitchen.

Julio danced in front of an expensive Wolf range while making orange and champagne crepes. Victoria stood amused as she watched their former chef while drinking espresso. Plump raspberries were in a strainer and freshly squeezed orange juice filled a pitcher. The smell of robust coffee filled the room.

When Victoria noticed Cheri, she said, "Morning, darling. Why on earth did we ever let Julio go?"

Shrugging, Cheri said, "Because you and daddy traveled

extensively and I grew up." Winking at Julio, she added, "Besides, I'm a chef now too, remember."

"Ah, my Cheri is all grown up and following in my footsteps." Flashing a dimpled smile, Julio said, "In that case, grab a skillet and make some bacon or sausage."

Cheri fished around in the cupboards until she found a skillet and began cooking bacon.

"I'll just have a salad with my crepe." Victoria patted her flat belly. "I need to keep my weight in check, darling."

"Mom, actually, you could use a few pounds. Quite a few. I'm worried about you."

Victoria waved the comment away and refilled her coffee cup. "Anyone else want coffee or juice? I can handle beverages at least."

As they settled around a gigantic dining table underneath an ornate light fixture fit for a theater, Cheri ate like she hadn't eaten in days. "This is delicious, Julio. Maybe I should add champagne crepes to my Fifth Avenue Catering menu."

Julio beamed. "I'd be honored."

After she chewed her last bite, Cheri gathered dishes and headed toward the sink. After she rinsed off the plates and loaded the dishwasher, something sparkly caught her eye beneath the two-sided stainless steel refrigerator. She bent down to inspect the shiny object.

"What are you doing on the floor, darling?"

Cheri scooted closer to the baseboard and reached with her left hand. After she grasped the tiny item, she dangled it in the air. "Mom, I found one of your earrings. How long has this been missing?"

Victoria stared at the blue and gold heart-shaped earring. Turning it over in her hand, her mouth set in a grim line. "That isn't mine."

"Are you sure?"

Julio glanced at the earring over their shoulders. "It's pretty. Maybe you forgot."

Victoria set it on the table. "It isn't even a real blue topaz. I can spot those lab-generated gemstones a mile away." Crossing her arms, she avoided eye contact with her daughter.

Dread filled Cheri. "Whose could it be? Do you have a maid?"

"Of course we have a maid, silly."

Cheri relaxed. "Then it's probably hers."

Shaking her head, Victoria said, "I don't think her ears are pierced. I've never seen her wear earrings."

Cheri's stomach summersaulted. "I'm sure there's a good excuse for it."

Julio stood. "It probably belongs to the previous owner. Who cares? Let's get some fresh air. Anyone up for a walk? We can pretend we're tourists and go to the Eiffel Tower."

Chapter 84

After the stunning news, Hope canceled her afternoon student appointments and walked the halls in search of Hilltop's janitor, the man she was positive had raised her. On the third floor, she spotted his thin frame near his cart filled with mops, brooms, and a trash bin.

As she approached Larry-Mac, she wondered how she'd broach the subject of his thought-dead wife, especially with the new discovery of his engagement to Willow. For months, she had treated him gingerly, hoping against hope his memory would return naturally. Organically. Sadly, it hadn't. He occasionally called her "ma'am" which was like a knife through her heart every damn time. When she heard the phrase she wanted to shout: *I'm your daughter. You adopted me but never bothered to tell me. You raised me—or I basically raised you but still.* She couldn't. Even if the man didn't know her, she took comfort in having Larry around. Besides, she now had two dads—Larry and Paul, her biological father. She had come to peace that Montana was dead but now . . . astonishingly, they both somehow managed to survive the train accident. *I feel like I'm in a soap opera.*

Hope's heart thrashed as she approached him. *Could this earthshattering news jar his memory? Could it work in reverse and cause him some sort of brain damage? Should I consult a psychiatrist or neurologist before telling Larry?* Even with a counseling degree, Hope didn't know the answers but decided to forge ahead. She had waited long enough, plus he needed to know.

Working up new-found courage, Hope placed both hands on Larry's bony shoulders and got almost nose to nose with her dad. She wanted his full attention and spoke gently but firmly, "Stop mopping. Look at me. How could you do this? How could you get engaged to my good friend?"

Surprise lit up Larry's lined, weathered face. "I thought you'd be happy for us. Willow's a free spirit like me. We like the same things. She's easy to be around. She's my old lady." He stared at his worn shoes. "I love her."

Hope wanted to cover her ears. He had always referred to Montana as his "old lady." She had hated the term. Plucking the folded newspaper out of her back pocket, she smoothed it out and held it in mid-air for him to read.

Waiting as patiently as she could while he stared at the article for several seconds, Hope eventually asked, "Recognize the woman in the bed?"

He shrugged and shook his head.

Wanting to slap his memory into him, which was totally unlike her, Hope used every restraint she could muster to keep from screaming. "Listen to me. Think hard. Look at the macramé plant hangers. Remember those?"

Stroking his chin, the janitor said, "I think you have one in your office."

Exasperated, Hope said, "Yes, I do. But do you know where it came from? Do you know who made it?"

He shrugged. "Probably China and sold at some Dollar Store." Glancing at his Timex watch, he furrowed his brows. "Sorry, but I've got to get back to work. I've got one more hall to polish and don't want to get into trouble, Miss Truman."

"My name's Hope, dammit." She refolded the newspaper and stormed off.

Chapter 85

After they ate breakfast, Cheri, Julio, and Victoria strolled the bustling, charming streets of Paris filled with florists, bakeries, cafés, and art galleries. The streets seemed alive with Parisians and tourists.

Stopping at a shop, Cheri admired nearly every bottle of French wine and sampled various cheeses. Next door, she and Victoria window shopped at a chocolatier while Julio spoke with a butcher across the street. Speaking with the chocolatier, Cheri gave her a business card and assured her she'd be ordering the chocolate delicacies for future clients.

Cheri reached for her mom's hand. "Parisians are so fashionable and fun. I love it here. I can see why you and Daddy have stayed so long."

"Darling, nothing compares. It's no wonder Paris is the world's top travel destination. Don't get me wrong. I still love New York City but Paris is next to perfect."

Cheri noticed a faraway look in her mother's eyes. "Something tells me you miss Manhattan."

Victoria shrugged. "I suppose. I miss my friends."

"Invite them here."

"I have. Some have flown over. They always enjoy seeing the sculptures at the Rodin or going to the Louvre. Personally, I'd rather shop, have lunch, and sip wine at a sidewalk bistro."

"Then let's do that right after we go to the Eiffel Tower."

Victoria rolled her eyes. "The tourists."

"It'll be fun. I haven't seen the Eiffel Tower in ages." Cheri motioned for Julio. The threesome eventually made their way past throngs of people who had gathered around the historic monument, taking photo after photo, mostly selfies.

Julio scanned the crowd and ridiculous lines. "Bad idea. Want to go to the Moulin Rouge again?"

"No," Cheri and Victoria both said.

Victoria winked. "One risqué show per week is my limit."

Julio shrugged. "How about a beach? There's a beautiful topless beach in Nice. Let's go there tomorrow."

Cheri knew that was her opening. "Why don't you go to the topless beach? I've been there, done that. Mom and I can shop and chat since we haven't seen one another in forever. I hope you understand."

"Certainly." Julio grinned. "Besides, I'm not into shopping."

"And I've seen enough topless women to last a lifetime." Cheri giggled. "Thanks for understanding."

Victoria brightened. "I know just the place. There's a lovely new boutique by an up-and-coming French fashion designer named Gigi. Her shop is called Gigi's Couture. I'm trying to help her make a name for herself. She's charming and extremely talented. I've introduced all of my society friends to her. Everyone loves her style. I know you will too."

"Sounds perfect, Mom." Cheri yawned. "Can we go back to the house? I'm suddenly exhausted." The earring discovery still nagged at her but she wasn't about to bring it up after her mother's reaction. She decided to file it away. *Maybe the earring is perfectly innocent. Maybe not.*

~ ~ ~

The next morning, Cheri's mother gave the chauffeur the address to the boutique. Julio had taken a train to Nice where he said he'd spend the day at the beach. Glad to finally be alone with her mother, Cheri wondered how much she should pry.

After the driver pulled up in front of Gigi's Couture, Cheri remarked about the gorgeous stain-glass doorway.

"Gigi has remarkable taste. You'll love her." Victoria leaned back inside the limo and instructed the driver to pick them up in three hours. Obviously already feeling like herself again, She placed her hand on Cheri's back and ushered her inside.

As a bell jangled, the stylish designer, Gigi, met them with a big smile and two glasses of Bordeaux. "*Bonjour*." Gigi air kissed Victoria's cheek.

Simultaneously reaching for the red French wine and returning the air kiss, Victoria said, "Thank you, darling. This is just what I needed. I'll have another in ten minutes."

"*Oui*. Of course." The petite brunette practically curtsied. "I always keep your favorite wine stocked." She glanced at Cheri. "This must be your daughter. I see the resemblance. Such beautiful women. You almost look like sisters."

Knowing that was the quickest way to get on her mom's good side—or inside her wallet—Cheri studied the designer. With a dark chin-length bob and short bangs, the clothier appeared youthful. Cheri couldn't decide if Gigi was her age or younger. Admiring anyone who worked hard to make a name for herself, she extended her hand. "Mom has gushed about your designs. I can't wait to see your collection."

Gigi gave a nod. "*Merci*, Mrs. Van Buren."

Putting a hand on her hip, Cheri's mother said, "I've told you a hundred times to call me Victoria. That moniker makes me feel old."

"*Oui*, of course." Gigi motioned toward an aqua sofa. "Please sit. Tell me all about yourself, though I know some since your mother brags about you, as any mother would."

"Thanks, Mom." Cheri discussed Fifth Avenue Catering, living in New York, and her home overlooking Crystal Lake in Branson. She mentioned her friends and their hangout, Coconuts.

Gigi sat riveted. "Co-co-nuts. How fun. It sounds lovely." She giggled. "And sort of *Sex & the City*-ish."

"You might say that but on a slower Midwestern note." Cheri glanced at the fashions featured on mannequins in a variety of poses. "Tell me about your designs." Staring at the artful displays, Cheri said, "From what I see, they're stunning."

Victoria set her almost-empty wineglass down. "I predict Gigi will be a huge success."

"*Merci.* You're too kind, Mrs.—Victoria."

"How did you get started?" Cheri asked.

Gigi regaled them with a story about finding her mother's old sewing machine in their basement at age thirteen. Unlike other girls, all she wanted to do was take apart clothes and design her own creations. Explaining she practiced early designs by cutting up old draperies and sheets. When her mother noticed, she was banned from the sewing machine until her math grades improved. Laughing, she waved her hand.

Cheri liked her hutzpah. "That's a great story."

"*Merci.* It feels long ago. Enough about me. Let's get started." Plucking several black, white, gray, and bold graphic pieces off the rack, Gigi draped them across her arm. The designer added pops of color with scarves, sweaters, and jackets, insisting Cheri try everything on.

While Cheri struggled to find room for all of the clothes in the tiny dressing room, Gigi slid several pairs of shoes underneath the curtain and shoved handfuls of necklaces into her hands. "You must try my designs on with the proper accessories to complete the look, *oui*?"

Over an hour and two glasses of wine later, Cheri chose three outrageously expensive outfits. She noticed her mother was unusually quiet, especially since shopping was her favorite pastime. As she draped her new wares across the counter, she turned toward Victoria. "Mom, aren't you going to try anything on?"

"I shop almost daily. I'd rather watch you."

"That's a first." Cheri sat beside her and studied the racks for something her fashion-conscious mom couldn't resist. "Try this red, silky dress. It'll look great on you and would be perfect for a date night with Daddy."

Cheri noticed Gigi peered over a rack but pretended to busy herself with straightening clothes.

"Date night?" Victoria laughed a little too loudly.

Deploring eavesdroppers even if they were adorable fashion designers, Cheri lowered her voice. "Remember I suggested you plan a trip for the two of you."

Victoria waved her hand in the air. "I gave up on that idea. Daddy's far too busy to be gone for an extended time." She paused. "But the dress would look great on you, honey."

Chapter 86

The next morning, Julio made warm, flaky croissants and strong espressos for breakfast. Cheri cleaned up the kitchen and slid her finally charged phone inside her purse. The driver had already placed her new designer clothes into the limo. Giving her mother an extended hug and smelling a whiff of cigarette smoke, she wrinkled her nose but decided not to mention her mother's smoking—this time. Whispering, she said, "I guess this is good-bye. For now."

Victoria Van Buren rarely showed emotions but Cheri could have sworn she heard a sniffle.

Reaching for her purse, her mother said, "I'm going with you to the airport."

"Good. I'll get to see you that much longer." Cheri glanced around her parents' modern home to remember every detail. It was magazine perfect. But . . . it was lonely, almost sterile. Tears threatened her eyes. "I wish I could have seen Daddy."

Victoria's face hardened. "Me too, darling. Me too."

Before they climbed into the limo, she and Victoria made promises to visit more often—in both directions—across the pond. Wiping a single tearstain off her mother's perfectly made-up face, Cheri's stomach sank. She couldn't remember ever seeing her mom cry.

The drive to the airport was a blur of mixed emotions. Cheri was excited to get back to her routine and see her friends but sad to leave her mother.

After Cheri and Julio boarded the chartered Cessna back to the States, she peered out the window, waved, and blew kisses. Staring at her petite mom, she decided she wasn't ever going to mention the fact that Victoria's newest nose job rivaled that of the late Michael Jackson.

Buckling her seatbelt, Cheri forced a smile as she stared at her wealthy, lonely mother. *I want mom to be happy, but I'm not sure she is. Daddy has always been a workhorse but something feels off.* She swiped at a tear trailing down her cheek.

Still standing in the small plane's aisle, Julio broke the silence. "My Cheri, you're in deep thought. Would you like champagne or coffee?"

Cheri turned toward him. "Nothing. I'm going to sleep." She paused. "I'm glad you brought me here. Thank you. It was great seeing Mom."

"She's a wonderful woman. Too bad your dad couldn't make it. *C'est la vie*." Kissing Cheri's cheek, he lingered a little too long before taking three steps toward the coffee maker.

Cheri's thoughts jumbled. As a teen, she fantasized about this moment but never in a million years thought it would actually happen. But something was missing. Maybe it was his age. Maybe it was her. Julio was charming, gorgeous, and gallant. But he wasn't the one.

After settling in his seat, Cheri said, "Nite, morning, or whatever it is. I'm not sure what time zone I'm in."

"It's morning. We'll be back in the States before you know it. We'll make up six hours you know."

"That's right. Good. I could use some extra time for . . . everything." Covering her legs with a navy blanket, she adjusted a pillow and leaned against the cool window.

After she awakened four hours later, Julio still sipped coffee. "Did you sleep?" she asked.

"No. Can I ask you something?"

Cheri yawned. "Sure."

"I'll be blunt." Julio leaned across the narrow aisle. "Will you hire me?"

She couldn't have been more surprised. "Hire you? As a chef?"

"Of course. As a chef at Fifth Avenue Catering. I need a job, my Cheri. As embarrassing as it is, I must tell you I'm behind on my rent."

Her mouth flew open. "But this-this plane, the helicopter, and expensive meal in Miami . . . How did you pay for it?"

"Your mother paid. She desperately wanted to see you and so did I." He pulled the lining out of his pockets for obvious emphasis. "I'm flat broke."

Cheri stared at the back of the seat in front of her, stunned.

Fidgeting, Julio said, "Just think about it. No worries if you can't. I'll get by. I always do."

Cheri couldn't bear to disappoint him. Her mind flitted to her current chef who she knew would be furious. *What should I do?* Her pulse quickened. After promising Julio a job that wasn't exactly available at Fifth Avenue Catering, Cheri cursed herself for mixing business with pleasure. She was uneasy about this arrangement since Julio was a long-time friend of the family. It was bound to get out at her company that he was her childhood chef. She didn't play favorites at work, never had, and didn't plan to start now. Her stomach sank. *I dread telling my head chef. The last thing I need is fireworks at Fifth Avenue Catering. The food business is volatile enough.*

When the plane landed late that afternoon, Cheri gathered her few belongings and hugged Julio goodbye, with the promise of details and employment paperwork within the week. For now, all she wanted was to see her house, her girlfriends, and drink cocktails. She texted Alex, Suzy, and Hope to request a meeting at Coconuts and smiled when she noticed a text from Suzy asking the same.

Cheri called a cab to take her to the parking lot of Bridal Bonanza. Breathing a huge sigh of relief that her car hadn't been towed, the socialite gave the cabbie such a huge tip that he asked her if she was sure.

"Let's just say I'm glad to be back in Crystal City and happy my car is here."

On autopilot, Cheri started her Mercedes and wondered how much she should tell her friends about her parents, Julio, and the mystery earring. *Maybe I'll keep that to myself until I know more.*

Chapter 87

Still slightly woozy, which could no longer be attributed to food poisoning, nor the flu, Alex's recent pregnancy comment gnawed on Suzy like a toothache. Chewing on her lip, she turned into her driveway, but instead of parking in the garage, did a U-turn and drove in the opposite direction. *It's not possible. Ken and I rarely have sex these days. We're either too busy or too tired. But I've got to know.*

Suzy drove through every yellow light and pulled into the nearest Walgreens. Feeling conspicuous, she strolled the makeup aisle, examined twenty tubes of nail polish, bought two greeting cards, a bag of Hershey's chocolates, and eventually worked up the nerve to purchase a pregnancy test. Fumbling with the items in her cart, she muttered to the bored cashier that the kit was for her daughter.

Once she arrived home with the scary Walgreens bag, Suzy thanked the empty house that no one was there. She plunked her makeup and other items on the kitchen counter and opened the bag of chocolates. Her plan on the drive home was to take the test immediately. Instead, after eating five chocolates, she threw in a load of whites. Cursing herself, she unloaded the dishwasher. *Why am I stalling?* Eventually she reached for the pregnancy kit, got a glass of water, and worked up the nerve to enter the bathroom.

Once she got up her courage, she locked the door. Her heart hammered as she peed on the stick. Seconds seemed like hours. Suzy set the stick on the vanity and washed her hands but couldn't bear to view the results. She combed her hair, decided to cross the hall toward the kitchen, but turned on her heel, and returned to the bathroom.

In a cold sweat, she focused on the applicator that indicated a big, bold + sign.

Oh. My. God. She wrapped the telltale device in toilet paper not once but three times before placing it in the trash. *This isn't possible. Well, it's possible but no. Hell no.*

Suzy glanced at the clock, grabbed her purse, and drove to the nearest CVS, determined to try a different brand. A better brand. A more accurate brand. She bought three more pregnancy tests—all different varieties, some generic and some name brand, to be sure of an accurate reading.

Racing home while she still had the house to herself, she locked the bathroom door again. Tearing open all three boxes at warp speed, she lined them up on the bathroom counter like marching band members, two inches apart. Acting as though she were a research scientist who didn't want to risk tainting the test results, Suzy downed a big bottle of Smart water for good measure and to ensure she'd have plenty of urine and get some added electrolytes in the process.

Peeing on three tests, one by one, Suzy bit her lip and waited—in the bathroom. She paced in the small room, reapplied pink lipstick for no good reason, redid her ponytail, and stared in the mirror. *You can't be pregnant.*

Her stomach did flip-flops. *I'm nearly 40, have a grown son, a feisty teen stepdaughter, and now a granddaughter. I don't want to start over with a second family.* Her heart thrashed. *What will Ken say? What will Jon think? Izzy will assume I'm nuts, and Alex and Hope will be in utter shock.*

Suzy snorted at the thought of Alex's reaction. She knew she would tease her mercilessly. Hope might think it was cool—or not. It didn't matter since, one by one, every single test came back positive. Her mouth went dry as she wondered whether to laugh or cry. She loved children but thought she was finished raising them.

Oh, my God. I'm pregnant.

Once again destroying the evidence with wads of tissue paper, Suzy dumped the used wands into the kitchen trash bag, buried the boxes of kits, and topped the trash with overly ripe tomatoes and moldy strawberries. Then she took the bag outside.

As a dog barked in the distance, Suzy stared ahead in a daze. *I can't wrap my head around this. I guess I should call my gynecologist but I'm not anywhere near ready for that discussion.*

After securing the lid on the trash, she strode back inside and busied herself by placing a roast and carrots in the crock pot. It was Ken's favorite meal. Maybe a nice dinner before the disconcerting discussion would help.

Choosing soothing, ambient music to calm herself, Suzy tried to relax, but the spa-like, swooshing water sounds had an adverse effect. It reminded her of a baby in the womb. She shut the music off and turned on the television. A medical talk show featured an infertility doctor as a guest. Suzy had always felt sorry for women who were unable to conceive. *I can't get away from this.*

Pouring herself a cup of coffee, she added more water to the roast and the remaining coffee on top. That had been her former mother-in-law's secret to browning and tenderizing the meat. Sprinkling salt and pepper on top, she added cream of mushroom soup and dry onion soup, then set the crock pot to low.

Staring out the kitchen window at nothing, her pulse raced. She placed two fingers on her wrists, taking deep breaths. *I should remain calm for the baby.* Suzy rubbed her arms. *A baby.* The mere shock of the news gave her a chill. *I've got to tell someone. I owe it to Ken to tell him first but maybe the conversation will go over better if I bounce this off my girlfriends first.*

Before she could overthink it, she texted Alex, Hope, and Cheri. *Can you meet me at Coconuts in an hour? It's urgent.*

The minute she sent the text, guilt overcame her. Feeling as if she were betraying Ken by not telling him initially, she tried to assuage herself that her girlfriends had been in her life longer. After all, she and Ken had led separate lives with other spouses for nearly twenty years. She wondered how excited her high school sweetheart would be about a new, second child at their age. They had never discussed having children together since they each had one of their own.

A new thought made Suzy's mouth go dry. *What if Ken is miserable about the news and leaves me? I can't handle being a single mom again.* Grabbing her car keys, she headed to Coconuts.

Chapter 88

Suzy got to Coconuts first in an attempt to calm herself before her friends arrived. Choosing their familiar table, an almost-smile crossed her face. *I wonder how long I'll be able to climb atop this high bar stool.*

Gus sauntered over, exchanged greetings, and asked if she wanted her usual merlot. Obviously completely puzzled when she ordered green tea, he shrugged. "Interesting. Be right back."

She glanced around the darkened bar. *I love this place.* Usually, the overhead, lazy palm frond ceiling fans, tranquil beach scene, and fake palm trees calmed her, but not tonight. In fact, her heart sank as she wondered if and when she and Ken would ever be able to go on a tropical vacation.

The unknowing, early Happy Hour crowd chattered, likely excited to be off work for cocktail therapy. As the front door opened and bright sunlight streamed inside, Suzy squinted.

A smiling Hope strode toward her as Gus set a cup of steaming green tea in front of Suzy. Eyebrows raised, she asked, "Detoxing?"

"Something like that."

Hope ordered a margarita and regaled Suzy with the art student van painting story since Alex was late.

Within minutes and in her usual flurry, Alex rushed inside and waved Gus over.

"The—"

"—usual." He finished her sentence and winked.

"You're so good, Gus." Alex adjusted her black pencil skirt.

"Chard coming right up." Gus wove through the crowd, tray high in the air, as he placed the order at the end of the bar. The bartender nodded while simultaneously pouring foamy beers on tap.

After she hung her purse on the hook screwed to the bottom of the table, Alex wrinkled her nose when she noticed Suzy's tea. "What is *that*?"

"I just felt like having green tea. No big deal."

"That's different." Alex reached for the chilled chardonnay Gus handed her.

"Care for any food, ladies?"

"Are you guys hungry? Food is on me tonight," Suzy said.

"In that case, I'm starving." Hope laughed. "How about some crab cakes. I'll share."

"Ooh, and maybe some of those bacon-wrapped dates," Alex said.

"No bacon for me," Suzy said.

Both Alex and Hope turned toward her and stared as if she'd grown horns.

"No bacon?" Hope asked. "That's insanity. Bacon is a food group."

Alex studied Suzy over her wine. "Since when don't you like bacon?"

"Your detox diet must be intense." Hope licked some salt off her glass. "I couldn't live without bacon."

Gus cleared his throat. "So . . . bacon-wrapped dates or not?"

Chuckling, Hope said, "Yes. I'll eat Suzy's."

Alex patted her purse. "I'll spring for coffee and dessert later. It's payday."

"Thanks. I've got a roast cooking for dinner, so I'll munch, but you girls go ahead."

Gus removed their zebra print menus. "Be right back with your food."

Hope tapped the server on the arm. "Cheri texted that she's joining us, Gus. Please bring an extra plate for her."

Alex chuckled. "And she'd probably like an Angry Balls cocktail."

The server gave a thumbs-up as he headed toward the bar.

As if on cue, Cheri rushed inside with her arms open wide. "Ladies, I've missed you."

All eyes were on the cake-winning, European-traveling, New Yorker. Alex, Hope, and Suzy peppered her with questions: "I saw your photos on Facebook." "I can't believe he took you to Paris." "How was it?" and "How are your parents?"

"One at a time." Cheri placed her leopard print Chanel purse on the back of her chair.

Alex scooted over to make room. "Hi, stranger. I ordered an Angry Balls for you. Hope that's okay."

"It's perfect." Cheri glanced from friend to friend. "It's good to be back."

Hope rolled up her white sleeves. "I'm living vicariously through you. Tell us everything about Paris."

Alex clanked her glass against Cheri's. "Forget that. Tell us about the sexy chef."

Holding her hands in the air, Cheri began ticking events off on her fingers. "Let's see. We strolled the streets of Paris, went to the Moulin Rouge, I shopped with Mom and met a cool, up-and-coming French designer, and Julio went to a topless beach in Nice. I've been there half a dozen times so I skipped it."

Hope nearly choked on a crab cake. "Wait. What? You mention going to a topless beach as if you were describing peeling a banana."

Alex elbowed Hope. "Interesting reference given the topic."

"Oh, my goodness. Is your mind always in the gutter?" Hope took another bite. "Back to the topless beach. Tell us about it."

Cheri waved her hand dismissively. "Everyone does it. It's no big deal."

"It would be a huge deal if *I* did it." Hope doubled over laughing.

"It's second nature for Europeans. Usually, the ones who shouldn't go topless, if you know what I mean, are the most carefree." She shrugged. "To his or her own, right? Who cares? It's freeing, actually. Sometimes entire families are on the beach—"

"Really?" Hope's mouth flew open. "Families with little kids?"

Laughing, Cheri said, "Julio is right. Americans are too uptight." Staring at her friends, she continued. "It was great seeing my mom. She's as youthful as ever but is getting a heavy hand with plastic surgery. She's also way too thin."

Suzy went into protective mom mode. "Are you concerned about her?"

"Very, but she gets defensive."

Alex studied Cheri. "Did you see your dad?"

Pausing before answering, Cheri said, "Nope."

All three women swiveled toward her.

Frowning, Suzy sipped her tea. "You flew all the way to Europe and your dad didn't make time for you?"

"Afraid so. I have a feeling that's why mom has lost so much weight, but she never talks badly about him. She loves the lifestyle of the rich and famous."

Alex crossed her arms. "Didn't your mom say he's working out a lot?"

Cheri nodded. Her mind flitted to the mystery earring but she decided against mentioning it. "Yes. Seems he's a fitness buff now."

Alex, Hope, and Suzy exchanged glances.

Ignoring them, Cheri waved to Gus. "Another round, please. On me. It's wonderful being back. I missed you and my work. I mean I loved seeing Mom but—"

"You've barely discussed the sexy chef," Alex leaned back as Gus placed another round of cocktails on the table, including tea for Suzy.

Stirring her drink, Cheri said, "It was almost weird since I had such a crush on him as a kid, you know? I don't feel the same now. I don't know what I expected, whether he wanted friendship or something more, but actually, he had an ulterior motive."

Alex's brows knitted. "Oh?"

Cheri played with the maraschino cherries in her cocktail. "Julio said he's broke and asked for a job."

Alex winced. "That might be tricky."

"Tell me about it."

Suzy blew on her hot tea. "What did you say?"

"What could I say? I said yes." Cheri exhaled. "My head chef will have a fit. The Fifth Avenue kitchen is his domain. I give him full rein to call the shots when I'm away—and usually even when I'm there. I concentrate on building my business, our clients, and employees. He focuses on creating delicious food. He's going to kill me."

Hope shrugged. "Maybe it'll go over better than you think. Can we get back to Europe? Did you see the Eiffel Tower?" She sighed. "That's on my bucket list."

Fishing out her cell phone, Cheri said, "Yes, we went. It's an Instagram selfie heaven." Handing her phone to Hope, she pointed. "There we are. We didn't stay long. There were mobs of tourists, insanely long lines to the lift, plus I've seen it several times."

"It sounds dreamy. What else did you do?" Alex bit into a bacon-wrapped date.

"As I mentioned, we went to The Moulin Rouge where they have topless showgirls and a meal. And lots of alcohol."

"I see there was a topless theme." Alex grinned. "Maybe I should add Paris to my bucket list too. Tony would love it."

Winking, Cheri said, "Gage loves it too."

"I miss that guy."

Cheri grinned at Alex. "I think he misses you too. He keeps asking about you."

Alex felt her neck flush. "Oh, really? When will he be back?"

"Not for a while, I'm afraid. After I told him to lie low in New York City, he went on a month-long vacation with some college buddies. They're backpacking the Grand Canyon and going to Aruba after that."

Alex rested her chin on her hand. "Man, I want to work for you. Think I can send Hannah their way? Maybe they can accidentally knock her into the Grand Canyon."

"*Alex*," everyone said.

Rolling her eyes, she groaned. "You know I'm kidding. Mostly."

Cheri splayed her beautifully manicured, navy nails on the table. "Enough about me. What's new with you ladies since I've been gone?"

Suzy and Hope glanced at one another. Both said, "You go first."

Hope chewed on her bottom lip. "My hands are sweaty thinking about what I'm about to tell you." Fidgeting in her chair, she avoided her friends' now-worried glances. "I have big news. Really big news."

Alex fished inside her purse, eventually retrieving red lip gloss. "What gives, Hope?"

"Get ready. It's a shocker." Hope rubbed her temples and swallowed.

Sliding the gloss over her lips, Alex said, "I feel like we're always in a competition to see who has the most ridiculous life."

Hope didn't miss a beat. "You may find this hard to believe but—" Reaching inside her school tote bag, she retrieved the folded newspaper article and slid it across the table. "I think it'll be easier if I show you."

Chapter 89

Alex and Suzy leaned forward and squinted at the article in the darkened bar. After scanning the photo, Alex's eyes bulged. "Wait a minute." She turned toward Hope. "That woman looks like Montana. But it can't be."

Suzy nodded in slow motion. Finally, she found words. "What Alex said."

Cheri threw her hands in the air. "What's going on?"

Alex glanced back at the article. "It's more like 'who' than 'what'." She turned toward Hope. "Please fill us in while I attempt to absorb this-this miracle."

Plunking the lime slice into her margarita, Hope took a healthy gulp. "Now you know why I wanted to tell you in person." Turning toward Cheri, she said, "Remember the story about my hippie parents?"

Cheri nodded. "Yes, and you think the school janitor is the hippie dad who raised you but he doesn't remember you."

"Right. There's more." Hope bit into a date stuffed with cheese. "I need more sustenance. I only ate chips for lunch." She waved Gus over. "Roasted veggies and Tuscan salads, please."

"Come on." Alex scrunched her nose. "Finish your story first."

Suzy elbowed Alex. "Excuse our little drama queen, Cheri. Alex isn't known for her patience."

Gus took their new orders. "Keeping it healthy, I see. Coming right up."

Hope waited until the server was out of earshot. Picking up the newspaper, she slid it in front of Cheri, pointing toward the photo. "I'm ninety-nine percent positive this is Montana. She and Larry were, *are* married."

Cheri stared at the picture. "So, this woman, Montana, is alive?"

"Apparently." Hope chewed on her thumbnail. "Although, it's unbelievable they both survived." Tapping the paper, she said, "Notice the macramé plant hangers in her room and the braided cotton ropes on her bed? She made those all of the time. In fact, I have one in my office." Eyes rimmed with tears, Hope continued. "I thought it was the last thing of hers I owned." Her voice caught. "And there's more."

As Gus appeared with platters of food, Alex searched in her bag for antibacterial gel and offered it to the others. She shook her head as everyone refused and dove into the food, germs be damned. As their forks clanged against the plates, Alex said, "Take a few bites and then tell us the rest, Hope. I can't take the suspense."

The women reached for the veggies, remaining dates, and nibbled on salads as all eyes fixated on Hope.

After wiping her mouth, Hope said, "The rest of the story is about Larry." She glanced at her friends and over her shoulder. No other patrons were listening. The Happy Hour crowd was absorbed in their own lively discussions while several rowdy college kids wearing wrinkled Greek attire and ripped jeans made their way to the bar. Still, she lowered her voice. "Larry and Willow just got engaged."

Suzy and Alex gasped. Cheri cocked her head. "Who's Willow again?"

Alex interjected. "Does it matter? Larry's still married to Montana, but to answer your question, Willow is an art teacher at Hope's school."

Wincing, Cheri said, "That's a problem."

"What will you do, Hope?" Suzy chased an olive around her salad plate.

"Damn." Alex gawked at Hope. "This is astounding. One for the record books."

"Tell me about it," Hope said.

Fork halfway to her mouth, Cheri asked, "What will you do?"

Hope rubbed her forehead. "The way I see it Larry must get his memory back before anything can move forward with Willow."

"No kidding." Alex patted Hope's arm. "It would be nice if he remembered you too."

"Yeah, I know, but I'll settle for one memory breakthrough at a time. Right now, his remembering his wife, Montana, got pushed to priority number one. I don't want to rush Larry's recall process, but he can't marry Willow. Plain and simple. He's already married. I'm considering asking Larry if he'll go on a road trip with me to see Montana."

Alex popped another date in her mouth. "How will you handle that?"

"I wish I knew. I'm still mulling over the possibility. The shock of seeing Montana might be too much for him—or Willow might throw a fit and not allow him to go. I'm at a loss." She placed both hands around her face. "On the one hand, I'm their daughter and should be involved. On the other, Larry and Willow are happy. Who knows if Montana would remember either of us? Who knows what kind of mental and physical state she's in? Maybe I should leave it alone and let Larry and Willow be happy."

Suzy's brows knitted. "It's hard to conceive all of the extreme highs and lows you've gone through. This accident just keeps on giving. I'm sorry you're dealing with this, hon."

"But your parents are alive," Cheri said.

Hope nodded. "Yes, somehow, someway they both miraculously survived, which is wonderful—except now there's a third person in the mix and Larry's in love with her."

"This is a freaking soap opera storyline," Alex said. "I can see it playing in my head."

Hope's voice rose. "I know. But it's my *life*."

"Sorry. I'm not making light of the situation. I didn't mean it that way." Alex studied her friend. "You have to admit it's surreal."

"Tell me about it. I wish I had a crystal ball."

Cheri brightened. "I know a psychic."

Hope shook her head. "No way."

Alex continued, "Hope, you've got to figure this out on your own. I can see several scenarios, but it's your family and your decision."

Suzy nodded. "It's definitely your call. You know we'll support you no matter what."

"I know." Hope held up her hands in obvious exasperation. "I guess there isn't a huge rush, well, except for the engagement." She groaned. "I'm afraid of damaging Larry's non-existent memory, worried about what it'll do to Willow's happiness, plagued by what I owe to Montana—and to Larry." Hope buried her face in her hands. "Even as a counselor, I don't think I'm equipped for this." She put her sweater on. "I'm not ready to deal with it. Let's don't talk about this again unless I bring it up. I feel like I'm balancing a delicate china doll on one finger. Be right back."

When Hope went to the restroom, her friends studied one another in a state of open-mouthed shock. Alex turned to Suzy. "What would you do? I might leave well enough alone but I'd probably feel guilty for eternity."

Suzy stared at her tea. "This is a tough one. I wouldn't feel right if I didn't at least try to contact Montana, but it's up to Hope. Besides, I have enough family issues."

"And I have boyfriend issues. Hope's on her own with this one."

After Hope returned, Cheri grinned. "It's a good thing I didn't stay in Paris one second longer. Look what I almost missed. I never knew having girlfriends would be so fascinating."

"Oh, there are more revelations to discuss." Suzy cleared her throat for obvious emphasis and ran her fingers through her hair. "Get ready for another shock."

The three women swiveled toward Suzy.

Chapter 90

"Hope isn't the only one with crazy news." Suzy slid her tea cup aside and leaned forward.

"What?" all three asked in unison.

Suzy glanced over her shoulder and toward the empty tables on either side of them.

Frowning, Alex said, "Don't keep us in suspense, Suzy Q. Is it about Izzy? What has she done this time?"

Suzy again peered from side to side.

"What the hell? Did you just rob a store?" Alex asked.

Suzy raised her eyebrows. "That might be easier to explain."

"Oh?" Hope scooted her bar stool forward. "You've got my attention. I'm more than ready to hear about someone else's drama."

"You've got my attention too. Spill," Alex said.

"Mine three." Cheri stared at Suzy who absentmindedly wrung her hands together. "You aren't going to believe this. You really aren't." She searched her friends' faces.

"We can't believe anything until you tell us." Alex tied her paper straw wrapper into a knot. Even though this was an almost daily ritual, anxiety worsened her OCD. "You're making me nervous, Suzy. After all we've been through over the years, I don't think you can surprise us."

"Oh, I think I can." Suzy twisted her ponytail with her index finger.

Hope reached for Suzy's hand. "You can tell us anything. What haven't we encountered together?"

"This." Suzy's eyes reddened. "We haven't encountered *this*."

Clearly alarmed, a worry line deepened between Alex's brows. Reaching over, she put her hand atop Hope's and Suzy's. "Now you're scaring me. Tell us."

Suzy rubbed her still-flat belly. "I'm pregnant." Deciding to blurt out the big announcement before she lost her nerve, she braced herself for her friends' likely astonished reactions. "There. I said it."

"Holy shit. Holy hell. You didn't want to open with that?" Alex's mouth fell wide open. "Even though I joked about it when you weren't feeling well, I honestly didn't expect that newsflash." She jumped up and hugged her friend so hard she almost toppled Suzy off her bar stool.

Hope joined in the group hug. "Suzy, that's-that's- What? It's-" She threw her hands in the air. "It's unbelievable. It's wonderful."

"Crazy wonderful," Alex placed her arms around both women. Cheri hopped off her stool and joined in the hug.

Gus arrived and asked about refills. Grinning, he said, "Looks like we're celebrating."

Suzy said, "Uh, that's debatable. We're still deciding."

He shrugged as he carried several black, rolled-up napkins to a boisterous table of suit-wearing corporate types.

Alex peered over her chardonnay and studied her best friend as the impact of this startling news began to sink in. "What does Ken think?"

Suzy rubbed her forehead. "I haven't told him."

Hope gasped, her brown doe eyes practically popping out of her head. "You haven't told Ken? Are you kidding?"

Suzy picked at her salad. "I just found out. I'm still getting used to the news. I didn't believe the initial pregnancy test, went back to the store, and bought more kits—all different brands."

"This is surreal. How many tests did you take?" Cheri asked.

"Four." Suzy's eyes crinkled. "I peed on four freaking pregnancy wands."

Alex covered her mouth with her hand but was unable to stifle her giggles. "Four tests, huh? It sounds like you're officially knocked up, Suzy Q."

"Oh, God, I hate that term. I'm too old to be knocked up." Suzy nibbled on a roasted carrot.

"Apparently not." Hope held the last bacon-wrapped date in the air. "Not that I know anything about this stuff."

"And . . ." Suzy polished off her tea. "I know it seems like I'm betraying Ken by telling you first, but I suppose I wanted to test your reaction. A baby was not in our game plan. Not even on the playing field. In fact, Ken recently mentioned we'd be empty-nesters in a few years in a swoony, happy kind of way." She grimaced. "He may be disappointed."

"I bet Icky won't like this at all," Alex said.

"Izzy will likely see the baby as a threat." Hope scanned Suzy's now-worried face. "She may become jealous. Be prepared for that."

"See how complicated this is? It spans different generations. What will my grown son, Jon, think? And my ex? My parents and sister?" Suzy's face fell. "I can only imagine the jokes and discussions behind my back."

Alex dipped an asparagus spear in dill aioli sauce and chewed thoughtfully. "You're wrong. No one will joke behind your back. Actually, I'm guessing everyone will love the idea. Give them time." She clapped her hands. "I'll be Auntie Alex."

"And I'll be Auntie Hope. We can throw you a baby shower."

"Ooh. I'll be Auntie Cheri. I've never been an aunt. What fun it will be to buy baby designer clothes." She giggled. "I'll get the baby's first animal print outfit."

"Slow down." Suzy held up her hands. "Thanks for your support. It means the world." She turned to her friends with tears in her eyes. "I love you and am glad you're excited." Pausing, she said, "I hope Ken is."

"Want my advice?" Hope asked.

Suzy nodded.

"Tell Ken about the baby tonight. Who knows? Maybe this little bundle will continue your coupledom magic." Hope smiled at her friend. "I marvel at your happy relationship. It's what I want. Maybe. Someday. Oh, never mind. I'm not even dating."

"Do you always have to be so rationale and make me look bad?" Alex threw a balled-up napkin at Hope, then turned to Suzy. "She's right. Tell him tonight."

"Ditto," Cheri said. "But thanks for telling us first. I'm honored. This meal is on me, ladies."

"Thanks, Cheri. That's sweet. In that case, I'm off to see my husband and tell him the surprise. Wish me luck." Suzy took a cleansing breath, gathered her purse, and stepped between Happy Hour patrons as she crossed the darkened room.

As the front door closed behind her, Alex shouted, "When will you know if it's a boy or a girl?"

Chapter 91

Suzy raced home after meeting her friends at Coconuts. *I've got to tell Ken and Izzy immediately.* She broke out in a sweat wondering about their reactions. *Who am I kidding? I only care what Ken thinks. Like it or not, Izzy will have to deal with it.* Turning on a hard rock station to drown out her nagging doubts, she drove home on autopilot.

Stepping inside the kitchen, Suzy placed her purse on the floor and keys on the counter. Stalling by getting a glass of water, she noticed Ken was in his favorite recliner watching a game. Izzy sat cross-legged on the floor with her face glued to her phone. Suzy could only imagine how a crying baby would turn the teen's life upside down—kind of how Izzy had turned Suzy's life upside down. Karma really was a bitch.

Suzy forced a bright, cheery tone. "Hey, guys. Roast is in the crock pot, but before we eat, can we talk?"

Ken made a noise that sounded like "Mmmm" while Izzy ignored her.

"Okay, then." Suzy clapped her hands. "Can I have everyone's attention? Family meeting time."

Izzy groaned. "What is this? The Army?" She continued staring at her phone, avoiding eye contact. "You're always so formal."

"How would you like for me to say it, Izzy?" Realizing her sharp tone, Suzy dialed it down since she wanted her stepdaughter to get aboard the baby train. "How's this? I want to tell you both something really important. Please hear me out."

Ken's eyebrows shot up. "Important? Why didn't you say so?" He muted the television. "What's up, babe?"

Suzy moved to the couch and patted the seat beside her. Ken got up from his chair and placed his warm arm around her shoulders. Izzy stood, half glancing at her parents and half scrolling through her Facebook feed.

Ken studied his wife. "Well . . . Don't keep us in suspense. What is it?"

Suzy held her husband's face in her hands. Almost in a whisper, she said, "I wanted to tell you this in private. That would have been ideal but—" She glanced at the mostly bored teen. "Maybe this is better since we're all a family now."

Izzy threw her free hand in the air. "Stop with the drama. Geeze."

Suzy's eyes brimmed with tears.

Ken took his wife's hands in his. His focus turned to palpable concern. "You're shaking. Are you okay, honey? Is this about your health?"

Suzy shook her head. "No. Well. Sort of."

Izzy grumbled. "Will you get to the point?" She turned back to her cell. "I have homework."

Suzy glanced from Ken to Izzy. Swallowing past a colossal lump in her throat, she said, "Bottom line: I'm pregnant."

Ken sat eerily silent for far too long. Izzy stormed from the room, yelling, "*I'm* the baby in this house." She slammed her bedroom door.

That's for sure. Suzy rolled her eyes.

Ken shouted, "You'll always be my baby."

Suzy wanted to gag. "This went over well."

Ken turned to his wife. "Are you sure?"

"I took four pregnancy tests from two different stores. They all came back positive. Besides, my period is late. I thought it was due to the stress of Jon and Fernando's wedding, baby Violet, and the funeral." Suzy met her husband's confounded eyes. "I'm sure, Ken. I'm going to have a baby."

He stared at the muted television so hard he didn't blink. After seconds that seemed like hours, he said, "I need to process this."

A tear snaked down her cheek, even though Suzy had tried to suppress her emotions, she expected more positive responses from her husband and stepdaughter. Jutting her chin out defiantly, she said, "I'm keeping the baby."

Ken put his hand on her leg. "Don't get upset. I'm shell shocked, that's all. I need a little time to adjust." He kissed her cheek, her mouth, and then her belly. "You're not keeping the baby. *We're* keeping the baby."

Full-on tears streamed down her cheeks. Suzy kissed her husband through salty tears. She mumbled, "We're going to have a baby."

Afterward, she frowned. "What about Izzy?"

Ken squeezed her closer. "Let me handle her. Izzy will come around. Give her time." He kissed her belly again. "I love you, both of you."

Epilogue

THREE MONTHS LATER

I get to find out the sex of my baby today. Suzy's heart raced with excitement. Palms sweaty, she studied her husband as a cheesy grin seemed plastered on his face. Ken strode toward her in the kitchen and placed both arms around her neck. "Today's the big day. Are you ready for the big reveal?"

"I can't believe you already know the baby's sex. Maybe I shouldn't have agreed to a gender reveal party in front of everyone." Suzy wiped her hands on her clothes. I can hardly take the anticipation."

Ken kissed his wife. "Trust me, it'll be worth the wait."

Suzy turned her head sideways. "Hmm. 'Worth the wait.' Does that mean it's a girl or a boy?"

"Nice try." He poured himself some coffee and offered her a cup. Shaking her head, she pointed toward her hot green tea. "I'm antsy enough without caffeine."

After a few sips, Ken continued. "I'm glad you agreed to wait. I wanted you to enjoy the moment with your girlfriends. I know how much they mean to you."

Suzy's eyes blurred with tears. "I do want them there." She sniffled and dabbed her eyes with a tissue. "Thank you for understanding how special our friendship is." Placing her head on Ken's shoulder, she added, "You're pretty special too. You know that? What time is the party?"

Glancing at the clock, Ken winked. "Two more hours. We arranged it at lunchtime so Alex and Hope could be there.

I didn't want to make you wait until after they got off work."

"Small favors. Will there be food? I'm sure the girls will be hungry if they're coming on their lunch hour."

Ken heated his coffee in the microwave. "You're always thinking of others. You're going to be a great mom."

"I'm already a mom." Suzy grinned. "And a grandma. This is so weird."

"It's not weird. It's wonderful. Now that I've gotten used to the idea, I'm surprisingly excited about a baby at my old age." Sipping coffee, Ken said, "I'm glad the party's today too. I can't tell you the number of times your doctor, nurses, and I have nearly slipped with the pronoun."

"Everyone has been mum. I still don't have a clue."

"You'll know soon." Saying he had to shower, Ken left the room.

Suzy ate a chocolate chip cookie, paced, and alternately checked her watch every ten minutes. She turned her laptop on, pulled up the Facebook page for Weddings by Suzanne, but couldn't concentrate on work, other than noticing several more brides had recommended her services with five-star ratings. A few made inquiries as to her wedding planning pricing.

Making a mental note to make the baby announcement on her page—or not—she absentmindedly rubbed her belly. *Would brides hire me if they knew I was pregnant? Maybe I shouldn't announce it until I can't see my toes.* Still barely showing, she giggled. *I've forgotten how much my body changes while pregnant.*

Closing the laptop, her thoughts seesawed from one sex to the other. *Do I want a boy or a girl? I already have a grown boy and a beautiful granddaughter. Oh, I don't care. I just want a healthy baby.*

Still, she couldn't keep from weighing the options. On one hand, a baby boy would be familiar territory. But a little girl would be new and different and she could be best buds with Violet Grace.

How is it I'm going to be a new mom and a grandmother at the same time? Suzy took deep yoga breaths in an attempt to calm herself before stepping into the master bath.

Kissing Ken's wet back, she said, "What color should I wear to our baby reveal?"

"Whatever you want." He hung his wet towel on the rack and strode through the room naked.

"I thought you might slip and say pink or blue." She studied his firm body and ran her hand along his toned arm. "Too bad we're on a schedule."

"I like the way you think." He buttoned a yellow shirt and pulled on dark jeans. Patting her behind and pointing toward his shirt, he said, "I'm not giving you any clues."

"Can't get anything past you." Scanning her closet, Suzy chose a silky, lavender full-length dress and matching heels. I might as well attempt glamour before I'm as big as a bus. Besides, pink and blue combined would create violet. It's perfect for both sexes—and it's our granddaughter's name. Feeling satisfied with her choice, she added a new silver elephant necklace for good luck and brushed her hair.

Whistling, Ken said, "You look stunning, honey." Kissing her cheek, he said, "Ready to go?"

She glanced one more time in the mirror, frowned, and leaned forward. "I think I'm getting a new forehead wrinkle. New moms aren't supposed to have wrinkles."

"Stop it. Come on, beautiful."

As they drove, Suzy said, "Where's the reveal party?"

Ken cocked his head, wearing a silly grin. "Coconuts. Where else?"

Suzy leaned against the headrest. "Perfect."

After parking, Ken extended his arm as they stepped across the crunchy gravel. "Don't fall in those heels, whatever you do."

Suzy shuddered. "I'll be careful. Don't worry, dad-to-be. I'm hungry all of a sudden."

"Good. Your New York friend insisted on catering the party." He grinned. "At no charge."

"Really? She's the best."

As they stepped inside Coconuts, Hope, Alex, and Cheri raced toward the door and greeted the couple. Giddy, nervous excitement filled the air.

Hope clasped her hands. "I can't wait to hear the baby's sex."

"Me neither." Alex winked at Suzy. "I'm about to bust a gut."

Suzy embraced her friends. "You think *you* can't wait." She glanced toward Ken. "He knows, but I can't get it out of him."

Alex grinned. "All the more reason to get this party started."

"Okay, okay. Let me take it all in first." Suzy noted a table laden with miniature sandwiches, pita bread, veggies, hummus, avocado fries, sweet potato fries, various soups and dips. "This is quite a spread." She hugged Cheri. "I understand you're behind this. Thank you."

After the women embraced, Alex said, "Okay, okay. Let's eat. Some of us are on a schedule." She elbowed Suzy. "Just kidding. I'm taking the rest of the day off. I'm sure most of the loan officers are golfing and won't even notice I'm gone."

Hope chimed in. "I canceled my student appointments. I wouldn't have missed the baby reveal for anything."

As they made their way to the food table, Suzy noticed the usual beachy scene at Coconuts had been transformed into a festive baby affair complete with pink and blue streamers and balloons. Teddy bears were perched on bar stools, and plush, yellow ducks were atop several tables. Eyes brimming with tears, she said, "I can't believe you guys did all of this.

I'm really touched. It's absolutely beautiful."

Holding a glass of wine in one hand and a Diet Coke in the other, Alex said, "It's not every day that one of us has a baby. We need to celebrate in a big way."

"Yes we do. Let's eat," Suzy said.

After they devoured the food, Gus and Cheri rolled out a smaller table covered with a white linen tablecloth, alternating pink and blue napkins, and a three-tiered white cake. A pink and blue balloon bouquet adorned the table, as well as two bottles of chilled champagne and flutes.

Cheri handed Suzy a flute filled with a pink concoction. "A Shirley Temple for you, future mom."

Taking a sip, Suzy said, "Nice touch."

Ken slung his arm around Suzy's waist and nuzzled her neck as he reached for a glass of champagne.

Alex, Hope, and Cheri held their flutes in the air, obviously waiting for a proper toast.

After watching Ken cuddle with Suzy, Alex groaned. "Enough, lovebirds. Ken, are you going to tell us the baby's sex or not?"

"Actually, no, I'm not going to tell you." He motioned with both hands toward his wife, game-show-host-style. "Suzy gets to do the reveal."

"Huh? I can't tell them, honey. I don't know the sex of the baby. You know that." Suzy playfully elbowed her husband. "Come on, Ken. We've had enough suspense."

Poker-faced, he handed Suzy a silver, filigreed knife. "Cut the cake, babe."

Legs shaky, Suzy set her non-alcoholic drink beside the tiered cake and poised the knife above the white dessert. Her voice barely a whisper, she turned to her husband. "Let's do it together."

Ken placed his hand over Suzy's and they jointly cut the cake. Once she removed a slice, the icing inside revealed one blue layer and one pink layer.

"Really, Ken? Stop dragging this out." Alex put her hands on her hips. "That's not funny. This has gone on long enough. Which is it?"

Hope's eyebrows shot up and stayed mid-forehead as she glanced from Ken to Suzy. "Maybe it's not a joke."

As the baby reveal sank in, Alex gasped. "No. No way."

Suzy's face turned ashen. Grabbing the cake table with both hands, she nearly toppled it over.

Cheri steadied the table while Ken caught his wife before she fainted.

As he led Suzy toward a chair and stroked her sweaty red hair off her cheek, his face turned grim. "Maybe this wasn't the best idea."

Wild-eyed, Suzy studied her husband's face as if it were the first time she had seen him. Turning toward her best friends, she pleaded, "Someone please tell me I'm dreaming."

Alex covered her mouth with one hand in an obvious attempt to keep from laughing, but a rogue chuckle broke through. "Sorry, Suzy Q. You're apparently a fertile, almost-forty mama. If my deductive skills are working, it appears you're having twins."

Still pale, Suzy stared at her husband for confirmation. "Ken?"

"Yes, sweetie, you're—we're—having twins. One boy and one girl." Ken kissed both of his wife's hands and then her mouth. "Amazing, isn't it?"

Suzy ran her fingers through her hair. "I can't-I can't . . . We may need to renovate the house. Does this mean we need two nurseries or will they be in the same room? What about—? Wow. Oh, my goodness. This is the last thing I expected."

Winking, Ken said, "I didn't expect twins either but I've had a week to get used to the idea. Like Alex said, you must be fertile." Ken winked. "Maybe I had something to do with it. I wish Izzy were here. She insisted on staying home since she has finals tomorrow."

"I'm going to need her help more than ever." Suzy bit her nail. "And yours, honey. This will take a team effort. Actually, a group effort." Laughing, she said, "Maybe even the Army."

Alex held her flute in the air. "It's wonderful, Suzy Q. But better you than me."

"Haha. Thanks, friend."

Hope clasped her hands together. "I'm really, *really* excited. I've never known anyone who has had twins." She eyed the cake. "What flavors are those?"

Cheri beamed. "I decided on a vanilla bean cake with cream cheese icing. One filling is cherry and the other layer is blueberry." She added, "Ken swore me to secrecy since I made the cake. Congratulations, you two."

Hope brightened. "I'll help babysit."

"I'm afraid of babies." Alex shivered. "I'd probably be of better help with your bridal business. Or not. I wouldn't have the patience for some of your neurotic brides, but hey, I'd give it a shot." She glanced at the cake table. "Are we going to stare at that luscious dessert all afternoon or eat it?"

Suzy seemed to find her composure. "I'll serve. It's the least I can do since I'll never have time to do anything again in the future." A nervous laugh escaped as Jon and Fernando bounded inside.

"Mom, are you having a boy or a girl?" Jon asked.

"Yes and yes." Suzy beamed. "Want some cake?"

"Whoa." Jon froze in place. "What?"

Fernando elbowed him. "You're obviously not in the medical field. I think she means she's having twins."

Jon gulped. "That's cra—" He stood silent for several seconds. "You're taking this well, Mom."

Ken patted Jon on the back. "This has been the season of

babies. Congratulations, big brother."

"That's so weird." Jon scratched his head. "But a good weird, Mom. A really good one."

Suzy's eyes widened. "At my age, how will I handle twins?"

Alex cocked her head. "You can do anything, Suzy Q. Anything. Although . . . this is a lot, even for you."

Beaming, Ken held a piece of white cake in the air. "Who wants a slice?"

Suzy held out her hand. "Pass me some since I'm eating for two. I mean three." She placed her hand on her chest. "Oh, geeze."

Hope reached for a plate. "You know I won't turn it down. Sit down, Daddy. I've got this." After she doled out the cake, everyone was unusually quiet, likely from shock.

Holding her last bite in the air, Alex's face turned solemn. "I just realized something. I guess this is the end of our Coconuts tradition."

"Oh, no." Hope frowned.

"I hadn't thought about that," Cheri said.

"Never." Suzy glanced at her friends. "I'm sure Gus will make me a Shirley Temple, soda, or hot tea. We're still going to Coconuts for our girl time."

"Thank goodness." Alex swallowed her last bite. "Not to be selfish or anything but I couldn't get through life without seeing you three at Coconuts."

"Ditto," Hope said.

"But after the twins are—" Suzy shrugged.

"We'll cross that when we get to it," Alex said. "For now, it's about you and the health of your babies, sweet mama."

Ken polished off his cake and sliced another piece. "This is delicious, Cheri. I'll take a piece to Izzy. Wait until she finds out."

Peering at her husband sideways, Suzy said, "That

should be interesting."

Alex stared at Suzy's belly. "I wonder how much weight you'll gain with twins."

"Really?" Suzy narrowed her eyes. "You're going there?"

"What did you expect? You know me." Alex fished inside her plaid purse for her phone. "Hope and Cheri, let's go buy some baby clothes. Stand sideways, Suzy. I want a before and after photo."

"*Alex.*" Hope reached for Suzy's hand. "You know we'll be there every step of the way." Cleaning up the plates, she said, "The reveal cake was delicious, Cheri. Thanks. And, Ken, yowza on the surprise."

Eyes glistening, Suzy hugged her friends, then rubbed her barely-there baby bump. Whispering, she said, "I'd never get through this next phase of my life without you three." Reaching for a paper napkin, she unfolded it. "Wait a second before you go." Smoothing the white napkin out on the table, she asked, "Does anyone have a pen?"

Ken plucked a ball-point from his shirt pocket. "Here, but Cheri already covered the food and I paid for the drinks."

"This isn't a ticket, honey." Glancing at her girlfriends, Suzy winked as she patted the napkin and made three columns. "This is a babysitting sign-up sheet."

Also from **Soul Mate Publishing** and **Beth Carter**:

THURSDAYS AT COCONUTS
(Coconuts Series Book 1)

As the go-to wedding planner, Suzy can't find her own wedded bliss and has one shocker of a wedding day. It doesn't help that she's still pining for her high school sweetheart, the one who got away. Handling neurotic brides is the best part of Suzy's day until her son brings home a bombshell from Europe.

Alexandra, a beautiful marketer with a "touch" of OCD, falls for a bad-boy cop who's married and possibly stalking her. But he sure is sexy. Alex tries to stay at arm's length after she puts her job—and life—on the line for the officer who isn't always a gentleman.

Hope hates her name, looks, and frizzy hair. As a high school counselor, she dishes out sage advice to students, yet can't see she's enabling her deadbeat, stuck-in-the-seventies hippie parents. After tragedy strikes, she reexamines their relationship and discovers a secret that almost went to the grave.

Friends since high school, the thirty-something women meet every Thursday at Coconuts for their own form of friendapy.

Available now on Amazon: [THURSDAYS AT COCONUTS](#)

CHAOS AT COCONUTS
(Coconuts Series Book 2)

To most, Coconuts is simply a bar. But for three best friends, it's their oasis. That is, until everything comes crashing down.

Socialite Cheri Van Buren makes a splashy, paparazzi-filled visit to Coconuts. Secretly dabbling in disastrous online dating, the wealthy caterer desires normalcy away from the society pages. A few girlfriends would be nice too.

Hope's life is routine, if not dull. The most exciting part of her day is counseling students until a monster tornado heads toward Hilltop High. Now she's in shock—and not just from the devastating twister.

Alex oversees a marketing intern from hell who appears intent on stealing her job. Her relationship with her sexy cop boyfriend isn't so sexy, especially after his ex-wife stalks her.

Suzy's new marriage is challenged by her surly teen stepdaughter, a unique Halloween wedding, and her son's ever-changing nuptials. If that isn't enough, the family discovers an astonishing revelation requiring a giant leap of faith.

Will the women overcome the chaos or will it tear them apart?

Available now on Amazon: <u>**CHAOS AT COCONUTS**</u>

SLEEPING WITH ELVIS

Pepper Langley, an unemployed preschool teacher with a fear of flying and boating, hopes a vacation to remote Key Lime Island will bolster her confidence and salvage her relationship with her rogue boyfriend. From tiny Nowhere, Arkansas, she scrimped all year to afford the lavish trip, but a deadly storm changes everything.

Gorgeous Elvis impersonator Ty Townsend flees to Key Lime Island between gigs. During this hiatus, he reevaluates his profession after twice forgetting the King's lyrics. He craves the isle's solitude—far away from social media haters—where he shares beach life with a cursing parrot. The last thing on his mind is a woman, especially one who isn't supposed to be there.

Will their secrets tear them apart or will they find happiness on the sand and stage?

Available now on Amazon: SLEEPING WITH ELVIS

SANTA BABY
(Part of the *Sizzle in the Snow* Anthology)

Unlucky-in-love Brooke Woods finds herself with a Christmas delivery and it isn't from Santa. When her boyfriend leaves her for their neighbor, she heads to the nearest bar, meeting hunky, nice guy Anderson Bradley. The two only exchange first names, and their hot fling leaves them both wanting more but their anonymity makes that impossible.

Brooke never thought she'd end up in a hospital pregnant at Christmastime. Will a Santa Baby bring the new mother and father together or tear them apart?

Available now on Amazon: SANTA BABY

Beth Carter

After being a bank vice president and a hospital public relations director, Beth Carter shed her suits and heels to reinvent herself at a certain mid-life age. While drinking copious amounts of coffee, she wrote five novels: THURSDAYS AT COCONUTS, CHAOS AT COCONUTS, BABIES AT COCONUTS, SLEEPING WITH ELVIS, MIRACLE ON AISLE TWO, and SANTA BABY, a novelette.

Carter is a multi-award winning author of a 2015 RONE Award, named Best Debut Author in 2015, and a 2017 & 2018 RAVEN Award runner-up for Favorite Contemporary.

The author also pens children's picture books including WHAT DO YOU WANT TO BE?, SOUR POWER, THE MISSING KEY, and SANTA'S SECRET. Additionally, her work appears in four six-word memoir collections and numerous anthologies.

Splitting her time between Missouri and Florida, Beth Carter is often found writing at Starbucks—if she isn't shopping at T.J. Maxx or boating.

~ ~ ~

Connect with Beth Carter here:

Website:
http://bethcarter.com

Facebook:
https://www.facebook.com/authorbethcarter

Twitter:
https://twitter.com/bethcarter007

Amazon Author Page:
http://amazon.com/author/bethcarter

BookBub:
https://www.bookbub.com/authors/beth-carter

Beth's Book Babes – Request an invitation to this online private reader group through the author's website, www.bethcarter.com

CPSIA information can be obtained
at www.ICGtesting.com
Printed in the USA
BVHW040145260420
578531BV00014B/855